WHERE THE CHILDREN CRY

Also by Jenny Jones:

THE BLUE MANOR

WHERE THE CHILDREN CRY

Jenny Jones

VICTOR GOLLANCZ

LONDON

First published in Great Britain 1998
by Victor Gollancz
An imprint of the Cassell Group
Wellington House, 125 Strand, London WC2R 0BB

© Jenny Jones 1998

The right of Jenny Jones to be identified as author
of this work has been asserted by her in accordance with
the Copyright, Designs and Patents Act, 1988.

A catalogue record for this book is
available from the British Library.

ISBN 0 575 06157 X

Typeset by Rowland Phototypesetting Ltd,
Bury St Edmunds, Suffolk
Printed in Great Britain by
St Edmundsbury Press Ltd, Bury St Edmunds, Suffolk

98 99   5 4 3 2 1

For all my York friends, especially Jef, Tim and Victoria, Susanne, Juliet, Anne and John, with love and thanks

Chapter One

He supposed he would have to buy champagne. Lily would expect it. She'd been thrilled by the news, excited, pleased for him, proud. Champagne, and possibly cashew nuts for Leo.

He wrote *champagne* on the back of his hand and drew a half-moon shape for the nuts.

It was good news of course, a promotion, an opportunity really to make something of all he'd been working towards, all he'd wanted.

That morning, Peter Dennison had told him that he would be managing one of the company's regional bases. It would mean a large hike in salary, a team of experts to utilize, up-to-date equipment, a venue, in other words for Joss to fulfil every dream he had ever had within the sphere of computer archeology.

'This is wonderful news,' he had said to Dennison, meaning it.

At the time he felt only joy. Happiness. He saw stimulating vistas of fame and fortune, of travel and exotic locations.

It was only at the end of the interview that Dennison dropped the bombshell. 'And the best thing about this is the site,' he'd said. 'It'll mean moving to York. You'll like that, it's a great city. Wonderful shops for the girls, although one shouldn't say things like that these days . . . Lily will love it. And so will you, of course.' It was a statement, not a question.

As he drove home that night, Joss gripped the steering wheel with unusual force.

York.

You'll like that, won't you?

No. The thought emerged strongly, a hard block in his mind, an undeniable obstacle. No, he wouldn't like it at all. To return there.

Somewhere between the Wake Arms roundabout and Bell Common he decided to make the best of it and buy vintage champagne. He knew his Lily: tough, competent, complicated Lily. He was not so cynical as to imagine that the extra money would influence her much, but she'd enjoy the prestige. A new car, sofas . . . what was it she wanted, a conservatory? He pulled into Tesco's.

It had to be celebrated, this promotion. What else could he do?

Leo wasn't even in bed. He was sitting on the stairs in his dressing gown, smelling of soap and talcum powder. He jumped at Joss, hanging round his neck.

'Mummy says it's good news, something special—'

'Oh Leo, lad, such an adventure! We're going to move house, pack up everything, even *all* the Lego, and get a brand new house—'

'Mummy said, new friends, new people . . .' All at once his voice hesitated.

'It'll be great,' said Joss, meeting Lily's eyes over the dark head of his son.

She came forward immediately, kissing him while Leo remained sandwiched between them.

A light, elegant embrace. She smelled of gardenia. She said, 'There's champagne in the fridge. Shall we have that one as a follow-on?' She gestured to the bottle on the hall table.

'Lil—' He wanted to hold them there together, still and close, dollies in a bunch, as the children said, hold them safe and fast and move nowhere, go nowhere. Stay where they were, safe and sound.

'This is brilliant Joss, I'm so excited!'

'Really? You don't mind? Uprooting, packing up, leaving everything behind?'

'It's such a chance, an opportunity. How could we not take it?' She was always impulsive, always energetic.

Joss sat Leo down, ruffling his hair.

'Aw, Dad!' He didn't like that.

'Bedtime, babe,' he said. 'Fireman's lift or sack of potatoes?'

'No, not bedtime yet.' Firmly. 'I want some of that fizzy stuff, and what's that little packet?' Unerringly, he'd found the cashews in Joss's jacket pocket.

'Eight years, and the man's on the booze already.' Lily shook her head. 'What do you think, Doctor Fletcher? A spell in the cooler?'

'I think a little stimulation might be in order, Doctor Gehrman,' said Joss from the kitchen.

He watched Lily's eyes glint as she made for Leo's feet.

'No, gerroff, don't!' Leo shrieked.

A sudden pop, a frivolous and delightful sound. Joss stood in the door with two glasses and a thimbleful of golden bubbles, watching them laugh.

In bed that night. They'd made love happily, and Lily lay in the crook of his arm, turned towards him so that her breath was warm against his chest.

'What's wrong, Joss?' she said sleepily. 'It's not the job, is it? You've always said how much you wanted your own department. Is it York? Something about the place?'

'It's so long ago it seems stupid.' He sighed. 'I lived there once, just for a couple of years after I was ten. I don't think I ever told you about it. I went to a school in the city. It wasn't a good place.'

'Poor baby. Was the little Jossy bullied in the playground?'

'Something like that.' But it wasn't me who was bullied in

the playground, he thought. It was David who got the worst of it.

David Seifert.

That name. He hadn't thought of David for years, even after Dennison's bombshell that morning. He'd known that he didn't want to go to York, that the place held unhappy memories, but he hadn't remembered David.

He'd spent years, all his adult life, without remembering.

Gently he disengaged himself from Lily and turned over. 'Night, love,' he said and she folded round him, sliding against his back. He heard her sigh once, the deep sigh of total relaxation. Her breathing became slow and heavy.

David. Why did we fail you?

I'm sorry.

His ankle was hurting again.

Chapter Two

They drove to York that weekend. Lily had been reading guide books in preparation and told Leo, as they entered the city through Micklegate Bar, how the heads of wrong-doers were once displayed on spikes there.

'Honestly, Lil, what a thing to tell him!' Joss was trying to work out how the one-way system went. Twenty years ago it had all been quite different; you could drive straight through the centre and there was none of this pedestrian nonsense. Although he had to admit that there were certain improvements. The place seemed scrubbed, much cleaner than he remembered, the streets free of litter, the walls almost gleaming in the feeble November sun.

It was smaller than he remembered too, more crowded with people, more cramped. They found a car park outside the walls down Gillygate and began their tour of estate agents. They discussed their particular requirements with helpful girls behind desks and found it all a little depressing. Very few gardens in the city, hardly any of any size, they all said. Not until you get outside the walls and then you need to move to Clifton or Fulford.

Over a pizza lunch they discussed it. Leo was swinging his legs, making small cones with Amoretti papers. He didn't seem to be listening.

'Three choices,' said Joss. 'One. We live in the city and do without a garden. Two, suburbia. Nice, unremarkable houses with okay gardens and lots of neighbours. Other kids around for Leo—'

'Tupperware parties and babysitting circles for me.'

'You're a snob, Lil my love. And dated. Tupperware parties went out years ago.'

'You're an expert?'

'And neighbours can be fun.'

'In Australia they're a pain,' said Leo distinctly.

'Or we can go further out,' said Joss, ignoring the interruption. 'The Howardian Hills or the Wolds. Lots of space for Leo there, trees, open fields—'

'I want to live *here*!' said Leo emphatically. 'In the city. Did you see that man on the unicycle? He got someone from the audience—'

'You'll get tired of street theatre soon enough. And all those tourists.'

'Only in summer,' said Lily. 'It's not so bad now.'

Winter. A cold wind had blown round their ankles all the way from Gillygate to Walmgate. At the Minster it had nearly knocked Leo off his feet. The sun had given up the struggle and heavy clouds scudded overhead. There was a promise of rain or sleet in the raw air.

'Tourist summers last from April to October,' said Joss. 'The Christmas rush starts about now.'

'Let's see what turns up,' said Lily. 'We'll know the right place when we see it.'

'I want to live here,' repeated Leo. 'In the city. I like it here. There are all these paintings where you walk, I think it's brilliant!'

And although they went round detached houses in Fulford and Clifton and Stockton Lane, although they made tentative suggestions about farms in Elvington and Sheriff Hutton, both Lily and Leo knew, as soon as they saw the photograph in the window, that the town house in Aldwark, with its beautifully proportioned windows and elegant railings, was exactly what they wanted.

Joss disagreed. They'd been tramping round houses all day

long and he was tired and hungry. His right ankle was beginning to ache in a way he thought he'd forgotten, nagging and depressing. He very much didn't want to go round this last house.

'But it's got a conservatory *and* a garden,' Lily said, looking up from the agent's details. 'And it's really close to the Archeological Centre—'

'What's the address?' He peered over her shoulder. St Anthony's Lane. 'No. It's a dreary area round there, a dumping ground. I never liked it—' It was where he went to school, he thought with a shock. St Anthony's School, in St Anthony's Lane.

'They've done it all up. The whole area has been renovated, lots of new housing.'

'This is an old house. It'll need everything doing to it. Do you want to live in a building site for months?'

'Just this last house. Please, Joss, it's not far from here.'

He stared at her helplessly. How could he say it? I don't want to live there, it's too close to my old school. It's where it all happened.

But he wanted Lily to be happy. She was backing him up all the way about this move, undaunted by the huge chore of buying and selling houses, of packing and rearranging everything. She was being wonderful and he desperately wanted her to find a house she liked. This one probably wouldn't be any better than all the others, anyway. This was only their first house-hunting trip, and he knew that moving always took ages. To please Lily, he agreed to look round the house in St Anthony's Lane.

There was a red front door with a lion's head knocker. It caught Leo's attention immediately. It had been the first thing he had noticed about the house, it was the first thing anyone noticed. Bright and shiny, the lion's teeth were bared round the ring, but its eyes were friendly, gleaming at him. Leo had a lion's name himself, he knew that lions were special to him, although this was a secret he kept to himself. He would be embarrassed to tell anyone, even Mummy. He just liked lions, he wanted to live in a house with a lion on the door.

Inside, his mother exclaimed about how well maintained the house was, how little redecorating they would have to do. To Leo, the house was merely a collection of light, airy rooms, full of stairs, but it had one other great charm. There was a fire-escape leading down the back of the house, right from the top attic bedroom. The house had been divided into flats at one stage, the agent said. That was why there were so many bathrooms.

'Can I have *this* room?' said Leo, in the back attic bedroom, one eye on the painted iron railings outside the window. Before answering, his father went to the window and tested the catch. The sash slid up with only a little difficulty.

'This is really dangerous,' he said. 'It should have a lock on it.'

'Easily done,' said his mother. 'And bars, perhaps. Can't have Leo tumbling into the conservatory, can we?'

Below them, the glass roof rose to a point over a seething mass of leaves and branches. The conservatory was overgrown by a vine and Leo knew that his mother was itching to pull it down and let the light in. No one had said anything about buying the house yet. Nothing was settled.

'Look,' he said, pointing out over the rooftops. 'What's that?'

His mother craned round to see. 'It's a tower of some sort,' she said. 'Perhaps it's part of the walls . . . Do you know, Joss?'

But Joss was looking at a building just at the end of the road. 'That's where I went to school,' he said reluctantly. 'St Anthony's.'

Leo was fascinated. 'Can I go to school there too?' he asked. 'Please, can I?' To go to school at the end of his own road seemed wonderful. 'It would be really useful. I could go on my own,' he said, 'I could walk there, and bring friends home and—'

'Put that out of your mind right away, Leo,' said his father. He sounded unusually tired. Leo wondered if his ankle was hurting him again. He'd stumbled on the kerb as they turned into the lane. It wasn't like Daddy to be clumsy. It had taken him ages to get up the stairs. He was still talking. 'I don't even know if it still is a school.'

'There's a playground,' said Leo, unerringly identifying the high netting. 'And someone's made cut-out people on that window there.' He pointed at the string of paper figures clinging to the glass of one of the lower windows.

'Well, it would certainly be convenient,' said his mother. 'What about it, Joss?'

'It'll be expensive. And I didn't like it then, it was a horrible place. Anyway, we haven't decided about this house yet. There's no point in thinking like this.'

Leo saw his mother lay her hand on his father's arm. 'It was a long time ago,' she said softly. 'People are much more aware of bullying these days.'

'Yes, I know. But there must be dozens of good schools in York, there's no need to go private—'

'Let's wait to see if we get the house, shall we?' she suggested calmly. 'And we'll do some research on schools, see what's on offer.'

Leo crossed his fingers, hoping.

Everything fell into place without difficulty. They moved into The Lion House in early January and the cold wind was still blowing round their ankles as Joss, Lily and Leo walked the hundred yards that separated their house from St Anthony's School.

Joss was limping again. 'It's the damp,' he said crossly when

Lily expressed concern. 'This damn city has the highest incidence of bronchitis in Yorkshire. It's low lying, and the river floods every winter. It's the damp that's set it off.'

This was one of a series of interviews. They had visited three other prep schools and two local junior schools. Any of them would have done, although they both liked the quieter, more ordered atmosphere of the private schools, the higher staff/pupil ratios.

The playground at St Anthony's was silent, although they could hear shouts from the gym. Inside the tall double doors the hallway was warm and dark, scented by the pot-pourri on the carved oak chest. It hit Joss as soon as they opened the door.

It was all he could do to keep moving. It felt as if his feet were embedded in clay. The smell of the place, the same flowery stink undercut with boiled vegetables and disinfectant. The ranks of names printed on the panelling in gold, the scratched, polished surface of the parquet flooring, slippery and insecure. The embossed pig on the ceiling, its fat cheeks full of acorns. He'd always hated it, the vicious, greedy expression in its eyes.

There was a rush of water in his mouth and he was horribly afraid that he was going to be sick. And then the staff-room door opened and it was as if he'd never been away, as if he was ten again and his friend was coming to rescue him—

'Christ, *Ben!*'

'Joss, how very good to see you again!'

And as Ben seized his hand, drawing him into a great bear hug, he felt the world resettle itself in patterns of order.

'Christ, Ben,' he said again, no longer on the edge and desperate, 'I just can't believe this. Is it really you? What on earth are you still doing here?'

'Earning an honest crust,' his old friend replied placidly. 'It's really me. I came back. I teach music, believe it or not.'

16

For a moment they surveyed each other. Ben Bowen had always been big, but looking at him now Joss was rather shocked. Eighteen stone, at least, a florid complexion beneath sandy, wispy hair. His eyes were sunk in flabby folds under the thick wire-rimmed glasses, but still as bright, as observant as ever. He wore an ancient suit of an exceptionally fine herringbone tweed and a flamboyant tie with parrots on it.

Joss suddenly remembered Lily and Leo, waiting patiently by the oak chest.

'Ben, this is Lily. And Leo, of course.'

'This is such a pleasure, Mrs Fletcher,' said Ben, holding out his enormous hand.

'Oh no, you must call me Lily!' Joss saw at once that they liked each other, that it was going to be all right. He felt irrationally reassured. If Ben was here, there would be nothing to worry about, no reason at all to fret about Leo.

'You'll be in good hands here,' he said to his son, as Ben and Lily went through the social hoops. Leo grinned happily. His absurd black hair was standing up like a lavatory brush again.

'I've been detailed to show you round while the headmaster finishes his meeting. He asked me to offer his profound apologies.' There was only the barest hint of irony in Ben's voice. 'Mark Morrell is running late for some no doubt crucial reason and I for one couldn't be happier.'

He waved his hand expansively through the dark air.

'It's much the same, but there's a new science block and the music room has been revamped. I'll show you later. But first, come with me to the end practice room, to my own domain, where there's a real welcome waiting!' He winked and led the way down one of the quiet corridors.

It was quiet until a bell went. And then the corridor was immediately filled with children dressed in navy, walking at a fast rate and only occasionally colliding. Some were as tall as

Lily, but most were very small, too small, Joss thought for the piles of books they carried. Their voices were shrill and excited, but no one shouted, no one ran. They even halted to open the double doors and said, 'Good morning sir,' to Ben and it felt to Joss like a time warp, as if nothing had changed at all.

Except the children were smaller, the corridors more narrow, the hall darker. Ben flung open a door that could have been mistaken for a broom cupboard. There was a battered Bluthner in one corner, with cascading piles of music all over it. A poster advertising a production of *Rigoletto* flared blood-red on one wall. Ben opened a violin case on top of a filing cupboard and drew out a bottle of single malt whisky. Ardbheg, at least twenty years old. Joss and Lily sat together on the piano stool and Ben dragged the chair from behind the desk.

'Here, Leo, bored with these yet?' He handed Leo a Gameboy, taken from a drawer. 'Confiscated from Jerry Fuller two weeks ago,' Ben said to Lily. 'Hope you don't disapprove?'

She shook her head. 'So, you and Joss were in the same class, then?'

He grinned. 'For our sins. The terrible trio ... did you know Owen's still in York?' he said to Joss. 'His daughter's my star pupil.'

'I didn't even know he was married—'

'Divorced, I'm afraid. Marie's touring Europe with The Twenty-three.'

'I just don't really believe this. That we're drinking this divine nectar together and you're sitting there telling me about Owen and his daughter and Leo's here ...'

'Funny the way we lost contact wasn't it?'

'Well, I was only in York for two years.' He paused. 'It seems so vivid that time, so highly coloured compared with the rest of my life—'

'Well, thanks.' Lily scowled at him.

18

'Apart from you and Leo of course, my dearest delight.' She flicked a drop of whisky at him. 'Don't waste it!' Joss cried.

'There's plenty more where that came from,' said Ben. 'A little top-up?'

Joss felt nicely mellow and relaxed by the time they left Ben's cupboard and returned down the long corridor. Even the limp wasn't so noticeable. A shaft of light from the head-master's study shot across the hallway and in its light he saw someone he knew.

The snow-white hair was receding but the tight curls were still in place round his ears. The set of that jutting jaw, the small eyes and chunky build were unmistakable. Kenneth Pyper strode across the hallway in front of them and pushed open the front door. The feeling of sickness and panic returned. The pain in his ankle gripped like a bear trap. Joss stood still in his tracks, unable to move. He felt Ben's hand on his arm.

'Kenneth's got two children at the school,' he said mildly. 'Sam's just a bit older than Leo here. Splendid on the sports field, I understand. Geoffrey's five years older. Musical, like his father.'

Joss stared at him foolishly, unable to say anything.

And then the door to the head's study opened and the headmaster emerged, ready to talk. 'Mr and Mrs Fletcher, come in, do come in . . . I'm so very sorry to have kept you waiting but I trust Ben here has been showing you the ropes?'

Joss took a deep breath. 'Indeed he has—'

'But of course, you won't need much showing, will you, Mr Fletcher? As an old boy?' Morrell's eyes were twinkling at the mild teasing. He was an immensely tall man, his thin shoulders slightly bent in a useless effort to appear shorter.

'There was no science block in my time, and we're extremely

impressed by the music room,' said Joss conscientiously, avoiding Ben's eyes. He thought, with misgivings, Damn, we're *still* lying to the head, does nothing change?

He was aware of Morrell's gaze on him, aware that keen grey eyes had missed none of this.

'And this is Leo,' Lily said, nudging her son forward.

'Well, Leo, how would you like to come to your father's old school?' said Morrell, bending down a little.

'We live just down the road, so it would be sensible,' said Leo with his strange streak of pedantry.

'You could nip back to Mummy whenever you forgot your games kit, is that it?'

'Mummy is busy when I'm at school. She has to practise,' Leo said.

'Indeed? Are you a musician, Mrs Fletcher, or are we talking golf here?'

'I play the flute,' Lily said, 'but I'm strictly amateur.'

'I rather suspect that you're going to enjoy yourself here, Mrs Fletcher. York is full of excellent orchestras. My wife plays the viola in at least two of them. You must come and have a chat with her soon. I know they're always in need of good wind players. She'd be delighted to introduce you . . .'

'And it would be so lovely to play in an orchestra again!' Back home, Lily was making sandwiches for lunch. 'I really liked Mark Morrell, didn't you?'

'He's certainly an improvement on old Redmond.' Joss was looking for the pepper. He hadn't got used to the new system of kitchen cupboards yet. 'I don't know, Lil. It's ridiculously expensive.'

'We can afford it. And besides, doesn't Leo's education come first?'

'Of course. But we have no proof that St Anthony's offers anything particularly special in the way of education.'

'But didn't you notice that art room? I thought the quality of the stuff on the walls was quite stunning.'

'It was good,' conceded Joss. Mark Morrell had taken them round himself.

'Art is rather one of Leo's things—'

'He's not even eight yet, Lily. There are so many aspects to consider . . .'

'And your old friends there! Lovely Ben teaching music and who was it—? Ivan, with his daughter there?'

'Owen. Owen Rattigan.'

'Well, why don't we get in touch with him? Ask him how he finds the school? Wouldn't you like to see him again?'

It was indisputable. Of course he'd love to see Owen again.

Before going to bed later that night, Joss had gone into Leo's room to turn off the bedside light. The curtains were open and there was an orangey glow from the city all around. He went to the window to draw the curtains and stood for a moment looking out at the floodlit Tower. They'd had a man in to put bars over the lower half of the window that day and the cement wasn't quite dry.

He was glad the bars were there, between him and the school. But he knew he was going to have to remember it all over again.

The web of the past was catching round him, holding him fast, and there would be no escape this time.

Leo waited until his father's footsteps had reached right to the bottom of the house. Then he crept out of bed and crossed the room to the window. Carefully and almost silently, he wiggled the three central bars in the cement as he had done on and off all day, making sure that the cement hadn't set around them.

Three was enough. He'd be able to get out any time he wanted to.

Chapter Three

Joss stared at the skull. 'How accurate is it?' he asked.

His assistant, a neat and tidy man called Martin Shaw, said, 'Pretty good, though of course we can't know about all the fleshy bits, the ear lobes, end of nose, complexion, that kind of thing. But deep eyes, jutting noses, strong chins . . . we can reproduce Viking, Norman, Tudor bone structures, whatever you like.'

Joss returned to the skull. He knew about the technique of course, although he'd never seen it in action before. The skull was rotating on its plinth while the fine red line of the laser scanned its contours and fed the information into a computer via a video camera. The computer would then stretch a modern control face on to the skull, and a three-dimensional image would be used to guide the milling machine.

'We use a local sculptor for the final stage,' said Shaw. 'It's how we did the faces for the Yorvik Centre. One of our great success stories.'

'What's this one you're working on?' He gestured to the skull rotating in front of the cameras. Mirrors on either side of it ensured that the computer received a stereo image.

Shaw glanced at it. 'Oh, that's Norman. Twelfth century, we think. Someone found the ruins of an abbey in their back garden years ago, and it's only recently been excavated. Up in the Dales, Coverham, or somewhere. The Trust archeologists had to make sure the skull didn't belong to some local two-timing husband first, before they could determine that it was indeed a twelfth century burial from the pottery shards found in the same context. We thought we'd try it out, to see if the

Norman influence made much of a difference to the Viking remains . . .'

'Much call for mediaeval history, is there?' Joss's mind was working down the possibilities.

'Limited.' Shaw shook his head. 'It's a bit distant.'

Joss thought aloud. 'There's Barley Hall, of course. But earlier than that . . . well, I suppose it's rather murky. There's the building of the Minster, of course. It'd be something, to show what it was like in 1400, painted, gaudy as a fairground, instead of all this tasteful pale stone we're left with now.'

'Virtual reality headsets, you mean?'

Joss grinned. 'Could be.'

Shaw raised an eyebrow. 'Rather brash, don't you think? Don't know what the Minster authorities would make of it.'

'Do them good to be stirred up. But we really need something else. A Robin Hood figure, something like that.'

'Guy Fawkes and Dick Turpin are too late. Unfortunately, there's nothing much earlier. The other great mediaeval story is nowhere near so upbeat. In fact, not something anyone wants to dwell on. The Jewish massacre, of course.'

It was like a jolt to him. A sudden, overwhelming feeling of sickness. He stared at the head turning slowly, bathed in red light, on the plinth in front of them, and hardly heard Shaw's words.

'Hardly likely to bring the crowds in, is it?'

'Doesn't quite fit in with the idea of heritage, does it?' Joss said slowly. 'The cosy, orderly past, where everyone knew their place, and summers were summers and it snowed every winter. Where the deserving poor received alms and the rest died in ditches.'

'Quite poetic, aren't you?' There was dislike in Shaw's voice.

'It's what the public likes. We're not purely in the business of educating here. This is entertainment.' He looked again at the skull: entertainment, riding on the bones of the past. 'If

Barley Hall gets going again, we could put people in it, perhaps.'

'Real people would be better.'

'This was a real person,' Joss reminded him.

'Let's use him. If we're going to bother with accuracy as far as wall coverings and food are concerned, why not go for the right ethnic mix, too? This twelfth century monk is much closer to the people who made Barley Hall than we are.' Martin Shaw clicked the mouse and the image on the screen grew until it filled the space. The eyes were black caverns, the nose angular as a beak.

'Turn that thing off.' Joss returned to his office, disquieted. There was something wrong in this. All very well to teach people about the past, but what about the terrible things? The way humanity betrayed itself?

It was a familiar problem, one he faced daily in his profession. He knew the easy answer: people didn't learn from history, so why dwell on the terrors? He sat at his desk and began to go through his post.

The sun was beaming through the picture windows and he turned on his chair to draw the blind a little. In the next office, he knew that Martin Shaw would be investigating the e-mail, his particular delight.

Jilly had brought him coffee, the local press was coming to interview him that afternoon, and their Viking CD-Rom program had just been chosen by the Schools Council. Lily had joined an orchestra and Leo was looking forward to his new school. He leaned back in his chair, sipping his coffee, and thought that perhaps the move to York had been a good thing for them all.

The past was the bricks on which they built, that was its only value. Raw material, up for grabs. Bring in the crowds, earn a penny or two . . .

In the office across the hall, the laser and camera were

focused on the skull. The computers were switched off, no electrical power enlivened the cameras. But through a crack in the open door the sun caught there too, and the dull, yellowing bone gleamed in the silent room.

It bridged past and present, that potent old symbol of life and death. And it remembered, it remembered so much.

First day of term. Mum had just gone to find a hair brush so I crawled up on to the window seat to have a look at the new boys. Only one I didn't recognize this time. Jenkins was wheeling a trunk across the playground while Mummy and Daddy said goodbye. Fond farewells undoubtedly, but no embarrassing hugs or tears. They were rather elegant, cool people and the Daimler looked new. Stylish, I thought.

Old Redmond swiftly disengaged himself from the boy as soon as the parents had gone and moved on to speak to the Reverend and Mrs Stroud.

The new boy was left standing by the gate. His blazer sleeves were too long and hung over his knuckles, his shorts were baggy and reached below his knees. But his cap was set straight, his tie neatly knotted over a snowy shirt.

I sighed.

He didn't look too bright that day, his mouth slightly open. Adenoids, I confidently diagnosed, cashing in on my superior knowledge. I knew he'd get colds and bronchitis and earache and tonsillitis. He'd be in and out of the san all the time and it was all going to be boring.

He was still by the gate when the last of the trunks had been trundled into the school, when the last of the big cars had pulled away and Mr Redmond had retreated to his study.

He was watching Joss and Owen belting each other with their caps. They were shouting and yelling at each other, although I could hear nothing from my perch on the window-sill. The new boy was frowning, clearly unsure whether the fight was serious or not. I could have told him, but I never went out in the playground on the first day of term.

When I looked back at the gate he wasn't there any more. Instead, there was a crowd of older, taller boys, pushing and shoving, and I suspected that the new boy was in the middle of them. I felt vaguely sorry for him even then. Adenoids or no, first day at school was hard for everyone. Mum called me then and raked my hair into tight plaits and by the time she'd finished, the bell had rung.

I returned to the window and watched all the boys form into lines, the new boy only slightly out of step. There had been other new boys, waiting uncertainly by the gate. Over the years I'd watched them on that first afternoon, nervous and unsure. I didn't know why this one had caught my attention, standing there in clothes that didn't fit.

I didn't even know he was Jewish.

Next day I joined the boys at prayers, standing in line next to Owen and Nigel. I looked along the line but there was no sign of the new boy. Someone pulled my plait and I swung round to find Joss standing behind me, grinning. I stuck out my tongue. Anything more and Tony Turner would see. Mr Turner to you, my girl. But I'd seen him with my mother, and heard her ask him to open the wine. 'Tony,' she said, 'Tony, could you do this for me?'

I told Joss and Owen, and they'd been embarrassed.

'With Turner? Your mother? How could she?'

And it was difficult to understand, him with his scratchy tweeds and yellow stained fingers, Mummy, all neat in her starched aprons. Some men like uniforms, Owen said once. It's a turn-on, perhaps she orders him around, tells him what to do.

It went no further. We found Owen's observation a little puzzling, and pondered it for a while. Owen was often oblique. Another Owen word, one I rather liked. Although Joss was my

26

closest friend, Owen was special. I never took him for granted.

He was clever, for a start. Really clever, taking Greek as well as Latin, star of the chess club. He read science fiction and not just Asimov and Heinlein like the rest of us. Moorcock, Cordwainer Smith and J. G. Ballard. Grim stuff I thought, guiltily hiding away the Georgette Heyers and Mary Stewarts I borrowed from my mother. I liked Owen, well, we all did, but he was never quite comfortable. Not easy. Not like Joss, who was irresistibly giggly, and Big Ben, who beamed shortsightedly through his pebble-thick specs and never said an unkind word about anyone.

Owen was sometimes unkind. Not to me, not usually, but I was aware you couldn't push him too far and get away with it. I'd seen him lacerate Kenneth Pyper once, after rugby when Kenny had knocked him over. I hadn't seen the incident, so I didn't know whether it was a foul or not, but Owen laid into Kenny so that Kenny went red then white and then red again and lashed out.

It was only words. Owen never needed anything else. He said that Kenny was an embarrassment to his mother, that his father had left them because Kenny was so lacking, so stupid, so thick.

'Who could blame Pyper senior for flying the coop?' I can remember the words. They were in the corridor outside Redmond's Room, always a risky position. Their hair was still damp from the showers. 'A feeble mewling runt and a stupid wailing cunt. No wonder he's gone.'

And the head's door opened and Kenneth had run away while Redmond thundered, 'What's all the noise about? What's going on?'

He saw that it was Owen and me, and shrugged. He couldn't have heard what Owen said. 'Rattigan. And Louisa. Come on now, where should you be? Third period, history isn't it?' He always knew. He was never cross with Owen either, and this was one of the considerable benefits of being part of Owen's charmed circle.

We went together down the corridor to the history room and Owen said to me, softly, 'Saving your presence, of course. My regrets.'

I didn't understand him then, and I'm not sure that I do now. But anyway, after prayers, when we were all going to our classrooms, I saw Owen take note of the new boy, who'd emerged from the library, and move over to him.

'Why weren't you at prayers?' he asked directly and the boy said, 'I've been excused. I'm Jewish.'

And for the first time I saw Owen blink, taken aback. Then he smiled. 'Ah, a heathen in our midst. An exotic, a stranger from a far shore, the mystery of the Middle East.'

'And what are you? Welsh?' The new boy spoke calmly. 'Are you sure that your dark hair and hook nose don't originate from some more distant culture?'

And looking at them coolly, standing outside the history room, it would have been difficult to tell which of them was Jewish and which Welsh. David was a name which went either way. Both were fine drawn, slim, with darting, deep eyes. Except David Seifert didn't go to prayers and Owen played rugby as if demented.

The answer seemed to please Owen. Because, from then onwards, he never again used his tongue against David. They became friends. Sometimes, Owen even pretended they were brothers, to the mystification of the teachers.

Joss, Ben and I discussed it, this strange affinity between David Seifert and Owen Rattigan. They were both only children, both bookish and articulate and good at languages.

'It's because they've got no brothers or sisters,' Joss said wisely. Joss was interested in popular psychology that term. 'A book I was reading said that first-born or only children often achieve more than others. That's you too, Louisa, except you're a girl, so I expect it's different. But Ben and I will be held back while our elder siblings take all the glory.'

Both Joss and Ben had older brothers at other schools. Ben mimed playing the violin, singing along in his clear, absurdly beautiful voice.

'Yes, but they're missing out really,' said Ben thoughtfully. 'Owen and David. They don't know what it's like, do they? To be part of a family—'

'To be surrounded by arrogant idiots all through the holidays? Lucky them.' Joss didn't get on with his brothers.

'Anyway, that's one reason why Owen and David are here, isn't it?' I said. 'People send only children to boarding school so they can learn how to get on with their contemporaries.'

'It's better than being a day boy anyway,' Ben said.

And that was true, too. Day boys were second class citizens at St Anthony's. Even I felt it, and I was at least fourth class, being the only girl in the school.

Not the only female. There was a French assistante, Mademoiselle Jurand, and Miss Leigh, who came in on Tuesdays to teach the flute. Mrs Redmond, the head's wife, was always fussing round the school, on the look-out, as she said herself. She told new parents that she regarded all the boarders as her own little brood, but I think she loved having an excuse to pry into our lives. We never believed that she'd had children of her own, although she was always talking about them. 'My own little Johnny would always clean his own shoes,' she'd say and we'd try, with difficulty, to envisage what kind of child could possibly have resulted from a union between Mr and Mrs Redmond.

Mrs Redmond was always there. Every time you ran down a corridor or tried to sneak out to the bakery, she'd be lurking round the corner. She heard our whispers, broke into the boys' tabbies and read their letters home. After Gerald Brooker, she was the most hated figure in the school. But she'd been to school with my mother, and it was due to Mrs Redmond that my mother took up her post as Matron at St Anthony's when I was four years old. And, credit where it's due, it was Mrs Redmond's bright idea that I should be educated alongside the boys.

'It won't do them any harm at all to have a little feminine influence,' I remember her saying. 'And Louisa will know that her mummy is on the premises at all times. She could go to ballet, to Brownies, if you feel she needs to meet other girls.'

My mother had been doubtful, but she was not in a financial position to send me to a private school otherwise. My father had left before I was born and she'd always had to work. Of course, at St Anthony's I was excluded from all sporting activities, nor was I allowed to play for the chess team or take part in any inter-school activities. But I did prep with the boarders and ate with them and slept every night on the premises, in the small flat I shared with Mummy at the top of Alcuin House.

On Wednesday afternoons, under protest, I took ballet classes with Miss Holder. I loathed this. All the other girls seemed to know each other and hung around in little giggly cliques between classes. I found them precious, feeble and uninteresting.

I liked the boys, I liked their sense of humour, the brisk unsentimentality of their company. They sometimes fought, but I thought they were honest with each other. From my infrequent conversations with the girls at the ballet class, I thought honesty came pretty far down the list of priorities.

Of course, none of it would have worked if I hadn't made friends, quickly and lastingly, with three of the boarders, Joss, Ben and Owen.

David came later.

Chapter Four

He was crying. It's funny how it goes like that, I thought later. That moments of weakness should draw people together. It didn't always work, because I went on to remember how tears sometimes only inspired greater depths of cruelty.

It happened two weeks after the start of term. Everything was chugging along nicely. This was only the spring term, and so no one had had to wrestle with new teachers and different class-rooms. We all slotted back into the patterns started last autumn and looked forward to longer days, warmer nights.

Warmth was a big issue. St Anthony's was centrally-heated, but there were no radiators in the dormitories. I was well aware that I had it soft, as Joss put it, sleeping in my own little room with its electric fan-heater.

Getting a sickie was considered fortunate: the san was heated, even if the ailing one did have to endure my mother's bracing ministrations. There was only one other place in the main school building where boys could get warm out of hours.

This was the basement, next to the boiler room. And that's where I found David, late one evening. I'd gone down to get my outdoor shoes because Mum said they needed polishing. All the adults at St Anthony's had this obsession with gleaming shoes. It drove us mad.

It was quite late, almost time for lights out. I clattered down the steep steps, humming under my breath. I didn't see him at first, in the feeble light from the sixty watt bulb. Pegs were nailed to a narrow board which ran round the bare brick walls at eye level. Pale, embroidered bags bulging with indeterminate shapes hung beneath the pegs. Then the pipes, the central heating pipes from the boiler, in imperfectly lagged layers. And another shape, awkward and hunched, crouched against the hot pipes, sobbing.

I stopped at the bottom of the stairs. I couldn't see David's face in the gloom, but I knew who it was. The only new boy that term. They all came, almost every one of them, to cry at some stage. Homesickness, Mummy called it, poor little scraps, they'll soon get used to it. And so they did, although this initial keening was painful for all who witnessed it. I wondered whether to slip away before he saw me, but I knew I'd get into trouble if I went back to the flat without the shoes. He looked round and saw me and screamed. I jumped, and it was as if I had been drenched in icy water. All at once everything ordinary dropped away.

It was his scream that did it, distorting all my senses so that I felt cold and deafened and tasted blood and wanted to block my ears. I smelt evil. We were somewhere else, somewhere out of our own, ordinary time. A dark, dim place where pale shapes bulged at us, where strange murmurs ran round the walls and the icy floor stabbed through my feet.

And all I could understand was David, trying to edge along the bench away from me. I could see the whites of his eyes glinting in terror.

'What's the matter?' I took a step towards him and the look on his face became horribly fixed, the eyes wide, the mouth drawn back so that the teeth were bared.

His words were hissed. 'Oh no, go away, please go away, don't, don't hurt—'

'I won't hurt you.' My voice disappeared into the dim air. I don't think he heard me. 'I came to get my shoes,' I said and it made no difference. I hardly believed it either.

He gibbered at me.

'Come on, don't be silly—' It was then that I realized that he was looking beyond me. He hadn't even noticed me. He was staring at something behind me.

But this was the strange thing, the thing that disturbed my dreams for weeks to come. I could not look round. I was blocked, forbidden to turn. It was as if my head was held in a vice, gripped in iron.

This was impossible. There was no one else there, no one at all. I knew it. I had walked down the stairs from the school corridor and there had been no one there. The stairs down to the basement creaked. I would know if someone had followed me. I shook my head, trying to break free. And again I tasted blood and shivered. David was still staring beyond me, and I needed to know what he could see. I took a step towards him and that was better. The feeling of compulsion eased. I was allowed to move forwards.

So I concentrated on David and crossed the tiled floor away from the stairwell. With every step the terror faded. I kept my eyes on David's face and began to wonder if perhaps he was asleep; perhaps we had both been caught in some kind of waking nightmare. Mummy told me that boys sometimes got night terrors, nightmares when they couldn't wake up, no matter what you did.

She poured cold water over a boy once and it made no difference. She said that it was really frightening to deal with, that you felt as if you were being drawn into the nightmare too.

There was no water in the basement, so instead I went up to David and slapped his face.

He gulped. And then his left shoulder hunched up high and he turned his face away in a great, expressive shudder.

'What's the matter?' I asked sharply. I think it was the memory of terror that made me sound so irritable. 'Crying doesn't help.'

He stared at me with dislike. He seemed calmer. 'What do you know about it?' he said, hiccoughing.

I sat on the bench beneath the pegs, a little way along from him. 'Everyone cries here,' I said. 'There's hardly a boy in the school who hasn't come down here and bawled his eyes out at

33

some time or another.' This was an exaggeration, of course. There were some boys, like Kenneth Pyper and Philip Stroud, who had forgotten how to cry when they left nappies behind. But that wouldn't help David. 'All of them cry,' I said. 'And they've all survived, they've managed to get through the next day and the next week and the next term—'

'Until it's time to go home,' he finished for me.

I nodded. 'It's not so very long. Just twelve weeks or so. Do you live far away?'

He shook his head. 'Terrington. But I wasn't homesick, you know. Not very much. It was the man over there. Didn't you see him?'

He was pointing to the corner of the basement at the bottom of the stairs. I turned round and for a moment, for just a second, I thought that I saw him too.

A suggestion of bleached bones, of whiteness and burning eyes and tempered steel, wrought tight and hard as a wire lash.

I said nothing, my hand reaching towards David. He took it, pulling me over to sit beside him.

'See?' he said. 'You saw him too?'

I nodded, although now I looked again he'd gone.

There was a few moments' silence.

'It's Jenkins' overalls,' I said at last. 'The caretaker hangs his overalls here.'

'You know better than that,' said David. His hands were tight clenched on mine. 'He's called Sheepshanks.' Or at least, I thought David said it but I could never be quite sure. Did he actually say it? Did I imagine it? The name was in the air, almost tangible.

It was some time before either of us could contemplate edging past Jenkins' overalls and leaving the basement. And I sometimes wonder if we'd still be there if it hadn't been for Joss.

I heard him whistling some way off and then footsteps clattered down over the creaky stairs and he stopped at the bottom and grinned at us.

34

'What's this? Secret meetings?'

I stood up. 'Just came to get my outdoors,' I said.

'Fit of the blues,' David said and I stared at him. To admit it, straight out, to Joss!

Joss took it like he took everything, light and easy. 'Come on,' he said. 'There's parkin with cocoa tonight. One of the few things even Mrs Harris can't ruin.'

David followed Joss up the stairs and I trailed behind listening to them argue about the relative benefits of parkin and gingerbread.

I didn't look back.

Chapter Five

Sooner or later you meet everyone in Sainsbury's, Mum had said that morning and Louisa replied that she knew no one in York nowadays. She'd been away for over twenty years. You'd be surprised, said Mum, from her high bed in the District Hospital. All sorts of people stick around in York. It's one of those places. You're almost certain to meet someone who knows you.

Later that day, Louisa stared across the carrots in Sainsbury's at the man choosing avocados and thought, is it? Is that really him? Is it possible to tell someone after twenty years by the back of his head? And then the man's face turned towards her and she recognized the aquiline nose and dark eyes. For a moment she couldn't think, far less move. And then he raised his eyes and looked at her and she dropped her carrots back into the tray.

'Owen?' It came out as only a squeak and he was frowning, uncertain. She started gabbling. 'It's me, Louisa, don't you remember? Although—' She stopped suddenly, thinking, we were children then. And my hair was brown . . .

'You've dyed your hair,' he said. 'Lou, I never thought it of you! Selling out, isn't it?'

A moment's slightly awkward pause as she remembered, yes, this was Owen and nothing had changed. This was always how he made her feel. A small girl stood at his side, her hand resting on the trolley. Owen was speaking again, breaking the pause.

'But what are you doing here? What's brought you to the frozen north? I see your photos every now and then in the *Guardian*, you've done well for yourself . . .'

'Thank you.' She felt absurdly touched that he had noticed, had followed her career.

Owen indicated the little girl. 'Let me introduce my daughter Sophy, Lou, she always helps with the Saturday shopping . . .'

'Hello, I'm so glad to meet you!'

The girl gave a small, self-contained smile. When she spoke, it was calmly. 'How do you do?' she said, holding out her hand.

Louisa blinked. A child, acting like an adult from the fifties? But with barely a pause she took the girl's small hand and gave it a brisk jerk.

'Do you live here?' she said to Owen. 'Is this your local shop?'

He nodded. 'We're just round the corner. How about you? Here for a visit or to stay?'

'Visiting Mum,' she said. 'She's in the District.'

'I'm sorry to hear that. Nothing serious, I hope?'

Louisa concentrated on the avocados. 'It is, rather . . . I'm feeding the cat for her, looking after the house.'

'I didn't even know that Jamie – Matron Jamieson – was still in York.'

'She never left. But she's not been well. You probably wouldn't have seen her around anyway.' Louisa shook her head, trying to remove her mother's drawn face from her mind's eye.

Owen was fishing in his pocket. 'Well, this really is a bonus, Lou. Coming for the weekly chore and running into such a very old friend!'

'No older than you,' she said sharply.

'And still so prickly. What's your address and phone number?' He scribbled it down on the back of an envelope and then raised an eyebrow at her. 'Joss is here too, now. And Ben. He's teaching at the school. Did you know?'

She could hardly believe it. 'Still here? All of us, after all this time?'

'Well, perhaps we weren't as adventurous as you. Actually, Joss plus wife and son have only just moved to York. He's with Past Present—'

'An archeologist?'

'Sort of. With computers, I understand. Big business in York these days. But you can ask him yourself. They're having a house-warming on Saturday. Why don't you come too, give them a surprise? I'm sure Joss would love to see you.'

'It's almost irresistible,' she said. 'And you're married too?'

She could tell nothing from his face. 'No. Not any more. Marie and I divorced a year ago.'

'I'm sorry.' Louisa thought, how can you catch up on twenty years? How to fill in the gaps?

'We'll need about a decade's worth of conversation,' said Owen softly, reading her mind.

'Do you still do that?' she said. 'I'd forgotten how you could always tell what people were thinking . . .'

'Fat lot of good it's done me.' He grinned at her and she wondered if perhaps he had changed after all, softened. Sophy was tugging on his sleeve. He looked round. 'Watch out, Lou, someone's after your trolley.'

A small boy was scooting dangerously on the back of it. Louisa ran to retrieve it.

Owen held her hand and gave her the briefest peck on the cheek when they parted, and Louisa went back to Claremont Terrace carrying her two heavy bags, unable, really, to assimilate what had happened.

Joss here. And Owen and Ben, still. How amazing, what an extraordinary coincidence. But as she put the tins away in the kitchen, she frowned.

She remembered Joss screaming. And Owen and Ben moving like zombies, white-faced and desperate with shock.

She was here in York to witness the end of her mother's life. Did she really want to get caught up with them all again? Wouldn't it have been better to ignore that familiarly shaped hairline and do her shopping and get the hell out?

She'd never liked York.

She poured herself a glass of white wine from the fridge and sat down at the kitchen table.

She wished she'd gone to Tesco's.

Leo saw her arrive. There was a certain fuss about it all that caught his attention. He saw his father open the door and then step backwards, surprised. Then his arms opened and he hugged the tall woman who stood there and Leo heard their voices rise, excitedly chiming together while Sophy's father waited. He was smiling that strange smile of his that Leo didn't understand.

Mr Bowen was there too and he was beaming, excited as Leo had ever seen, chattering like the rest of them. Leo noticed that the tall woman's shoes had golden buckles on them, ornate twists of metal he wanted to touch. He liked her face too, the way her wide mouth grinned so that her eyes crinkled.

'When are you starting then?'

Unwillingly, Leo turned round to the girl sitting back against the wall. He'd met Emma Morrell before, but he still didn't know whether he liked her or not. Her father was headmaster of Leo's new school. He and Emma's pretty mother were in the drawing room, talking to Leo's mother. Emma had come to join him upstairs early in the evening, bringing with her a plate of twiddly bits. She'd finished all the Twiglets already, Leo saw with disapproval.

Downstairs there were avocado and Roquefort puffs but they were for his parents' guests.

Emma said, 'Why does your dad laugh like that?'

'Like what?'

'Like he's frightened.'

'Don't be silly.' Leo stared at her. She'd started on the peanuts now. 'He's never frightened.'

'How do you know?' It wasn't a challenge. 'Have you ever seen him cry?'

'Cry?' Leo's mouth dropped. 'Of course not! He never cries!' A pause. 'Does your dad cry then?'

'Piss off.' Half-chewed peanuts splattered all over him. A glance across the hall from Leo's mother.

She sketched a small thumbs-up sign at him and then moved forward to welcome the stranger with some warmth. Leo saw that she was wearing his favourite creamy dress, the fine-knitted one which flared out at the hem.

Leo said, 'My mum doesn't cry either. Even when she hurts herself.'

Emma said nothing. But later, when all the adults had moved through to the drawing room, she took Leo by the hand. 'I'll show you something, if you like.'

He followed her downstairs and through the kitchen to the back door. 'I live over there.' She pointed over the rooftops towards the Minster. 'Would you like to see my house?'

Leo hesitated. 'I'm not allowed out at night on my own.'

It wasn't quite true. His parents had never said, you must not go out at night. He had never thought of doing such a thing. He knew they would hate it.

Emma was still talking. 'You won't be on your own. You're with me. It's not far anyway, we'll be back in five minutes.'

She opened the door and together they skipped through the garden into the back alley.

Dim shapes of rubble and thistles, behind a chicken wire fence. They dodged round the dustbins, ignoring the empty wasteland through the wire. Everything was indistinct.

Billowing clouds hid the stars and the moon was old, dim, fading, obscured. Beneath its uneven, wavering regard, the city fell silent.

Somewhere between St Anthony's Lane and Ogleforth, Leo got left behind.

Emma hadn't done it deliberately, he knew. But he'd stopped to stare at one of the inn signs in Goodramgate and when he looked round Emma had gone. The street was quite empty, damply glistening in the street lamps.

Mid-evening, the pubs not out yet, the restaurants in mid-sitting. The doorways were clouded by huddled figures and Leo hurried past them nervously. The dogs gazed at him, bright-eyed, observant and eager. Leo didn't like dogs. He'd never lived with one, although his dad had had a Labrador when he was little. Leo really wanted a cat, a lion-cat to live in his new lion-guarded house.

He decided to go home, but where was it? It couldn't be far away, although he wasn't perfectly sure which of the alleys to take. He plunged down one of the dark tunnels between the houses in Goodramgate and found himself standing on grass, staring at a low squat building. A church, hidden away behind the shops.

It was utterly unfamiliar to Leo. He wasn't even really sure it was a church, there was no steeple or vaulted windows, but he could see a gold-embossed notice floodlit to his right.

His breath showed cloudy in the February chill. He dug his hands into his pockets and turned round, wanting to get back to the main street.

There was someone there. A vague, shadowy figure blocking the passageway. Leo could see no features on the man's face but he knew he could not possibly go that way. The path to the church door branched, leading off towards another shadowy tunnel. He ran away from the church, pelting through the tunnel as fast as he could. He burst out into a totally unfamiliar street. Two raggedy men with dogs were coming towards him. He ran forward again, into another dark alleyway.

There were footsteps behind him and he knew they were from the man at the church. He tripped suddenly, falling head first to the ground. It was damp and mucky and, scrambling to his feet, his shoe skidded and he nearly fell to his knees again. Ahead he saw someone in the mouth of the tunnel, a silhouette he recognized with flooding relief.

'Emma!' he shouted, but she made no move towards him. Somehow he scrambled along to the end of the tunnel, careering into her and clutching at her arm.

'Ugh!' Emma pushed his hand away. 'You're filthy. Did you fall into a dustbin?'

He was too shaken to answer her.

'Come on.' She began to walk away from him across the wide square where the fountain played.

'Wait for me!' He rushed after her, knowing only that he didn't want to be alone and lost in the city. 'Where are we going?'

'I want to show you something.' She strode ahead of him, swiftly passing the fountain and conveniences and turning then into a narrower street, curving on a slight rise. He followed her, entirely lost. It was only a small city; he'd probably been here before, it was just that everything looked so different in the dark.

'Please wait!'

She was far ahead and didn't look round, although her step slowed a little. Ahead of them a wide open space led to a steep, grassy hill. It was floodlit, but not brightly. The Tower at the top of it rose into darkness.

'Race you to the top!' said Emma. Leo was already panting from the effort of trying to keep up with her. He sighed and dutifully clambered up the damp grass underneath the shadows cast by the curving walls.

Of course Emma got there first. She stood with her hands on her hips watching Leo's clumsy progress. Then she darted off round the perimeter and Leo trailed miserably after her. He saw that the curve of the walls was interrupted by a jutting wall. A gatehouse stood out from the main building, and Emma was standing by the portcullis gate barring the entrance to the Tower. Beyond it, the walls were sheer around them and Leo wondered if they were really vertical. They seemed to be sloping outwards, as if they might fall apart. Under his feet the ground fell steeply away. There was a flight of steps leading to the gatehouse.

It was very cold. The rain clouds had rolled back, leaving the slither of moon overhead. In its pale light, Leo saw Emma's face gleaming at him.

She said, 'Do you know what this place is?'

He shook his head.

'They died here, years ago. All those people came here and killed each other. And then it caught on fire and they were all burned.'

She took a step closer to him and the shadows of her face became more pronounced, her eyes disappearing into darkness, her teeth glinting as she spoke.

'What?' he said. 'When? Who were they?'

She answered only his last question. 'The Jews. All the Jews in York.' Another step towards him and he saw all the bones in her skull highlighted.

'You're Jewish, aren't you?'

He stared at her, open-mouthed.

'What?'

'Jewish. You. Your name, your mother.' She put her hand on his shoulder and it felt like a claw. 'Inside the Tower the stones are all red. You can see a bit of it up there.'

He followed the line of her pointing finger.

In the dim light it looked like rust.

'That's blood,' she said. 'It's blood stains left by the Jews when they killed each other.'

'I don't like you.' He took a step backwards, nearly overbalanced down the slope. She was laughing at him. He whisked away from her, plunging down the steep steps, raving across the grassy slope.

Her voice sang after him.

'See you on Tuesday. At school.'

Chapter Six

'Did you find us much changed?' Owen said. He was walking Louisa home some time after midnight.

She was silent for a while. 'It's difficult to say. Yes, of course, we've all changed completely, and it's not just a question of scale.'

'Joss seems the most the same to me,' said Owen. 'He's done well. Lily suits him, I'd say.'

'I'm glad he's happy.' At one stage, she'd thought that Joss would never be happy again. 'But Ben . . .'

He sighed. 'Ben's gone to seed, I think. He drinks, of course. And has put on too much weight.' He sounded rather severe.

'He was always plump.'

'It's got worse.'

'Do you see much of him?'

'Not much. He's still involved with the church. And the musical life in York is absorbing. Orchestras and choirs all over the place.'

Louisa glanced at him speculatively. His ex-wife was a musician, she remembered. 'Did you ever get away?' she asked.

'Only to go to Oxford. And a year in Italy, studying architecture. I always knew I'd finish up here.'

'I couldn't wait to leave, I always hated it.'

He didn't immediately comment. 'Ben went to the Royal Northern. And then came back. No one was surprised, people often seem to come back here. You have, too, of course, even if you did hate it.'

She thought, neither Owen nor Ben really managed to leave. A brief flirtation with the fresh air of other places, other lives, but then they'd returned. At least Louisa had made a life, had lived in New York and Rio for a while.

And what was that worth? What remained of that pretty flat in Greenwich Village, or the house in Rio? A few photographs, some letters and the diary . . . She hadn't ever made a real base anywhere. No enduring home, no family. It was rather depressing, when you thought about it. Although she hadn't been unhappy: there had always been friends, some of whom became lovers. Rob had lived with her for two years . . . but that was over five years ago, she realized with a shock. She'd been entirely alone since then.

They were passing through Monk Bar, leaving the city centre.

'Is it difficult, returning? Of course, the circumstances of your mother's illness can't help.'

She sighed. 'Perhaps this isn't quite the ideal time to meet old friends.' Or perhaps it is, she thought. Attending her mother's death, she was also recapturing the events that had formed her. 'Does Sophy really go to St Anthony's?'

'How could we bear to send her there, do you mean?' He looked at her sideways. 'Schools change, you know. Mark Morrell is a good man, someone with an excellent record.' He named an eminent prep school in the south.

'He seemed all right,' Louisa said cautiously. 'And I suppose Ben being there helps.'

'Dear Ben. Yes, of course. Sophy takes after her mother: she's very musical and adores Ben. St Anthony's has the best academic record of the local prep schools—'

'Did you never consider the state sector?'

'Aha. The politics are never far away with you, are they, Lou? Some of those photo-essays . . . Wear your heart on your sleeve, don't you?'

She felt a flash of anger. 'Don't change the subject. It was a serious question. Are the state schools so very bad in York?'

Owen shook his head. 'Not at all. It's just that Sophy is really quite especially talented and may very well get a scholarship one day . . .'

'And so you start her off in the fast lane?'

'You haven't got children, have you?'

'No.' They had reached her front door. She smiled tightly at him and held out her hand. He took it briefly.

'I'll see you soon, no doubt. In Sainsbury's, if nowhere else. Remember me to your mother, will you?'

'Yes. Goodnight, Owen.'

She shut the door and put the chain on it. Her mother's cat Pinkle curled round her ankles and she bent down to stroke her. She felt unreasonably upset. The evening had been by turns delightful and dreadful. She couldn't make sense of it. They had all been so glad to see her, genuinely pleased, she could have sworn to it. But, but . . . Ben, overweight, drinking too much, something unhappy in his eyes. He'd not married either. Perhaps he was gay. She turned it over in her mind as she waited for the kettle to boil. No real sign of it when they were children, no obvious sign now. But still she wondered.

And Joss, lovely Joss, as friendly and warm as ever. Complete with beautiful and charming wife and child, although she hadn't met Leo yet. There was something nagging at her about Joss, although everything seemed perfect on the surface.

She realized what it was as Pinkle curled up on her lap. Louisa put down the rosehip tea, frowning. Joss was limping still. That broken ankle had never healed properly. Poor Joss, she thought, having to take that reminder everywhere.

And Owen. Cool and clever as usual, although the failed marriage must have hurt. How would he manage as a single parent, she wondered? Conscientiously, she imagined, but how patient would he be? Patience had never been a strong point . . . Would he ever use that wicked tongue on his little Sophy? It was not a pleasant picture. She went to bed, uneasy about

47

them all, remembering the other thing that Owen had told her during the course of the evening. Kenneth Pyper was on the Board of Governors.

Lily surveyed the kitchen. A few canapés left on plates, wine glasses, ashtrays. It had probably been a success, she judged. Joss had already turned on the dishwasher. He was stacking the empties in a box in the conservatory. 'I'll take these for recycling tomorrow,' he said over his shoulder.

'Joss, did you go to check on Leo?'

He came back into the kitchen. 'Not yet. He's all right?'

She nodded. 'Fast asleep. But his clothes are filthy. It looks like he's been rolling round in the garden, grass stains and mud everywhere.'

Joss stared at her. 'He was with Emma Morrell, wasn't he?'

'All the time, as far as I can tell.'

'Did they leave the house?'

'Surely not! They wouldn't, would they?' An element of doubt in her voice.

'Leo wouldn't. Not on his own. But she's a minx, that girl. Did you see the way she was emptying every glass she could find?'

'You were young too once, weren't you? I must say, I liked Caroline Morrell. What a gorgeous creature she is!'

'She's too thin; looks neurotic. But yes, I'll agree she's beautiful, although not a patch on you, my love.' He moved towards her and held her.

After a while Lily abstracted herself. 'What about Louisa? What was it like, meeting her again after all these years?'

'God, Louisa! Caught in a time slip. She hasn't changed, not one bit, apart from the hair. She was always over the top.'

'I liked her.'

'So do I. She's a good sort.'

Satisfied, Lily moved back into the circle of his arms. 'Let's leave all this till tomorrow,' she said. 'Bedtime?'

In bed, Leo turned over. His dad always made him leave the window open and although the room was somewhat chilly, he found the duvet intolerable. It clogged round him like cotton wool. The mattress beneath him was lumpy and uneven. He shifted again. And then whimpered as something caught the soft skin of his calf, pinching, a button on the mattress catching the flesh perhaps. But he was not awake. The prick of pain on his skin made him dream of fingers pinching. They pulled and tugged at his clothes, scratching and snagging his skin. His hands fluttered irritably, uselessly. Someone scratched him and he felt a trickle of blood on his leg. He moaned, his head turning restlessly and heard the murmurs, the noise of the mob.

Next morning Louisa went shopping in town first and then along to the District as usual. Her mother was in an uneasy doze, her brown-stained hands twitching on the sheet. Louisa sat there for a while and then went in search of a coffee. When she returned, her mother's eyes were open.

''Lo, darling,' Louisa said softly, bending over and kissing her mother's soft cheek. 'I've brought you some little treats. Look.' She emptied her bag of Crabtree and Evelyn goodies on the blanket. 'What would you like, handcream or cologne? There's room freshener too, and some lemon pastilles. Or three white Belgian chocs, all for you . . .'

'Ridiculous girl. Lovely girl. Cologne, please and half a choc-olate. You can have the other half—'

It took her minutes to say and they were both still giggling when the doctor came on her rounds. Louisa waited outside during the examination.

Afterwards the doctor came to find her. 'You're Mrs Jamieson's daughter, aren't you? I assume you have been informed that there is very little we can do for your mother?' Her tone was not unsympathetic. Louisa could only nod. 'And we feel she may be happier at home, with her own things around her, now that you're here—'

'I don't live in York. My home, my work is in London.'

'Well, there are agencies who could help out. The Social Services . . .'

Care in the community, Louisa thought. 'You have to keep the waiting lists down, of course.' She spoke sharply. The doctor continued as if Louisa hadn't spoken.

'Hospitals are not geared to the extreme sensitivities of someone in Mrs Jamieson's position. Her friends, her belongings – has she a pet? A cat or dog?'

Louisa said, 'A cat. Pinkle.'

The doctor nodded. 'She'd be happier at home, you know. It's not merely a question of clearing the bed. Really.' She started to walk away. 'Think about it.'

Back in the ward, one of the other patients was crying softly. Her mother looked distressed, as if she wanted to help. 'They're so slow coming round with the painkillers,' she whispered. 'Or they don't give her enough. Poor old girl, she's not got long to go.'

'Mum, would you like to come home? The doctor thinks it would be good for you.'

'Too much trouble.' She shook her head minutely. 'You're busy, you have your own life, and I don't want strangers.'

'What about a nursing home then? Would you be happier in a private room?'

Her mother's washed-out eyes twinkled. 'Actually, dear, it's already arranged. The school insisted I took out insurance years ago. It doesn't cover the cost of treatment, but R and R – rest and recuperation – certainly comes under the terms.

I'll be moving into The Elms on Thursday. There, I knew you'd be surprised.'

'The school? The school insisted? How could they?'

'They paid, too. All the premiums. Kenny Pyper's father arranged it.' Her voice was fading. Louisa stared.

'When? When did he arrange it?'

'Oh, you were little. Twelve or so. It was a long time ago—' Her eyelids flickered.

'Was that when David Seifert—' Louisa stopped. Her mother was clearly exhausted. She left the hospital, her thoughts in a turmoil.

Chapter Seven

I lay under the bedclothes, my eyes fastened on the luminous dial of my watch. I'd heard Mum return from her rounds half an hour ago. She sometimes read for hours before going to bed, but luckily, this night it seemed that she was tired. I heard the flush of the loo, the wash-basin filling, the emptying gurgle in the bathroom. A little while later Mum poked her head round my bedroom door and I tried to quieten and regulate my breathing.

She noticed nothing. The door shut softly and then I heard the faint click as her own door closed.

Give it an hour, Owen had said strictly. Make sure she's asleep.

Kenny had grumbled. 'Why's Louisa got to be there? She's bound to wake someone up coming through the house.'

'I've tested the floorboards,' I said hotly. 'I know where the creaks are, I'll be careful!'

'Of course you will.' Joss was encouraging. 'It's Lou's idea, of course she must be there.'

My idea. It was, too.

I avoided the creaking stairs successfully, and arrived in the dorm just after one. Pale faces gleamed expectantly at me.

Joss, Owen, David, Ben, Philip and Kenny, the six boys in Bishop dormitory, the six boys who had been in the library the day I discovered the book. It was just after David's panicky episode in the basement. During English we'd been sent in dormitory groups to the library to choose a reading book for the next week and Mr Williams had sent me with Bishop dormitory, as he always did, because he knew that Joss was my particular friend.

Anyway, Joss, Philip and David were hanging round the fiction shelves, while Owen scanned the history section and Ben and Kenny were mooning over the scores. I'd gone through everything I wanted to in Fiction and was desultorily thumbing through the heaviest of the art books, the volume on Greek and Roman statuary, always a potent source of fascination.

I saw the edge of the other book down the back of the shelf as I was struggling to wedge the huge volume back into place. I used my fingers to scrabble it out of the narrow gap, and a vicious splinter buried itself down the nail of my middle finger. I was still sucking at it as I thumbed through the slim pamphlet with my left hand. Its cover was of a strange, pale leathery material I didn't recognize, halfway between cloth and leather. It was fraying round the edges, yellowing at the seams. The writing inside was a cramped italic, difficult to decipher. There was a spindly drawing of a fat pig decorating the first initial, but this entirely disguised what it was. I understood only enough to guess that it was probably Latin, although it contained none of the structures I recognized and precious little of the vocabulary. 'Look at this.' I took it over to Owen, who was by far the best of us at classics.

He turned it over in his hands, frowning. 'It's very old,' he said. 'I can't really make much sense of this . . .'

'Shall we ask Mr Williams?' I suggested.

'Redmond would be the one. He's a classicist.'

By this time the others were peering over our shoulders, mildly curious.

'Redmond? He'd just take it away.'

We all knew this to be true.

'I'll check it out first,' said Owen. 'See if I can make any sense of it.'

It took him several weeks to get anywhere with the first page. The title alone had been interesting enough to keep him at it. The Enemies of God *it said.* How to defeat the ways of the

Devil. *He'd transcribed it in his elegant scrawl and hidden the original in his tuckbox. Copying it out had absorbed Owen for several nights, and I found him more irritable than usual during the day. There were dark rings around his eyes and I knew that his headaches, never far away, were increasing in severity. But he wouldn't let it go. Neither would he tell anyone else what he was discovering. To begin with, we nagged him to reveal all, but soon we lost interest.*

Life raced on at St Anthony's. Full timetables, prep, choir, and the boys had endless sports. There was chapel on Sundays and chess club on Wednesdays, drama on Thursdays. At night I knew they tumbled into beds with little energy even for pillowfights. I knew this because my mother occasionally worried about it. She once told me that it was all a diversion. I didn't really understand and asked her to explain. 'It's to fill their minds so that they don't miss their homes too much.'

Her mouth tightened as she folded socks into neat bundles. Usually I never heard a word from her in criticism of the school. How could there be? This was our home, our society. It provided our daily bread, our entertainment, our circle of friends and everything I knew. Later I understood enough to recognize all this frantic activity as displacement technique. A way to stop thought, to batten down on speculation and perception and desolation. The aim was to wear out the children so that they had no energy to miss home. At the time, I was simply exhausted.

It was after chess club that I found a note from Owen in my pencil case. After prep, it said. In the basement.

'It's a grimoire,' said Owen softly, holding the thin pamphlet carefully, almost as if afraid that it might burst into flames. 'It gives instructions how to summon forces to help.'

'What kind of forces?' This was nowhere near specific enough for me.

'That depends who's doing the summoning. This seems to have

something in common with The Book of Common Prayer. *You call up the saints, the martyrs, those who have died in good causes...'* He looked at David, who was shifting from foot to foot as if impatient to get on.

'Why did you ask us to meet here?' I asked. I also was looking at David, who appeared nervy and on edge.

Owen shrugged. 'It's quiet. No one comes here much.'

'It stinks.' Philip Stroud was looking through everyone's shoe-bags. He was taller than the rest of us, dark-haired and thuggish. Apart from Kenny, none of us liked him much, but he was part of the dormitory, and it would have been difficult to conceal our midnight escapade from him. He'd already found two packets of cigarettes, a penknife, a tube of Smarties and some putty, all of which he'd appropriated. 'This is going to be a complete waste of time. Who cares about old books in Latin? Who's ever going to summon up a saint these days?' This was typical of Philip, we felt. Bad-tempered and grudging. His father might be a vicar out in the Dales but Philip himself was hardly a pattern for Christian good behaviour.

'Actually,' I said. It was my favourite word that term. I was aware of using it far too often. 'Actually, I think this room might be haunted. We saw something, didn't we?' I said to David.

'It was dark, I don't know—' He hesitated.

'It was dark, but there did seem to be someone there, over by the door.'

We all looked over to the bottom of the stairs. 'There's nothing there now,' said Joss.

'I know. But—' I stopped.

'Do you want us to give it a try?' said Owen.

'I don't think we should even consider it,' said Ben. I noticed that he was sweating, his glasses steaming up. He took them off, rubbing them against his jumper. 'It's nothing to do with us, we don't need it.'

'There would be no harm in it,' I said, wanting to show off, *wanting to impress. The only girl, I had to prove over and over that I was as brave, as strong, as clever as the others. And this was all my doing. I had found the book, I had suggested that we meet in the night. At that moment the bell for cocoa went. We trooped back up the stairs to the main hall and collected our cocoa and biscuits from the trolley. It seemed that we had forgotten Owen's grimoire.*

But it was my fault. I told Owen about the figure in the corner, I gave him the idea. And so, at one o'clock at night, I padded down the long corridors to Bishop dormitory, where they were all waiting for me, Owen's tuck-box open on the table before them.

'Shhh,' said Joss unnecessarily. He drew the book from the box and handed it, with ceremonial grace, to Owen. Ben was holding a candle and some matches. Philip, Kenny and David were waiting by the door. Together we padded down the creaky stairs to the hall and along the west corridor. The door to the lower stairs was closed and we all remembered how it banged. Joss held it open, reaching round to turn on the light switch. He waited while we filed through, shutting it with extreme care after turning on the light.

The room was warm and musty from the presence of the boiler next door. The bags and overalls hung in bulging shapes against the cream-washed wall.

I glanced at David and saw that he was unsmiling, rather pale. He looked uncomfortable. Perhaps he was nervous of getting into trouble, I told myself. Perhaps that was all it was.

Kenny made the most noise, loudly sniffing. He was in the grip of a persistent cold, which he never hesitated to spread all around him. Kenny thought handkerchiefs were for girls. We sat on benches beneath the shoebags and looked expectantly at Owen.

'I wish you wouldn't do this,' said David suddenly. He stood up and stared at us. His eyes were too big for his narrow, thin little face.

'There's no harm in it.' Owen was severe. 'It's an experiment, that's all. A scientific experiment.'

'How can it be scientific?' His voice rose.

'What we're doing is proving that such things don't exist. Don't work. How can they? This is the twentieth century, and this—' he held up the book, 'is the product of primitive superstition.'

'Don't be daft, Owen. This is dangerous. Dangerous mischief.'

'You didn't have to come. You could have stayed behind,' Joss said fairly. David didn't answer. But I knew how he felt. He was new, and needed to show he could be trusted, that he was one of them. I wasn't new, but female, which was worse, because that could never be changed.

'Yellow, are you?' This was Philip, his voice flat with dislike. He held Owen's translation. 'Look what it says here, A Curse For All Men Who Lie and For The Infidel. That's you. You're an infidel.'

'Don't be a prat,' said Owen. 'That's all rubbish.'

'Well, why are we doing this, if it's all rubbish?'

'To prove it's rubbish.' Owen sounded exaggeratedly patient.

'It's a joke,' said Joss lightly. 'A bit of fun. That's all. Let's get on with it.'

No one said anything else. Owen stood up in the centre of the floor and said, 'First I'm going to read the English version, so you know what it says. Then I want us all to hold hands, and I'll turn out the light. Ben has got a candle ready to light. And then I'll repeat the Latin version in the dark.'

'What, all of it?' This was Ben. Although the pamphlet was thin, there must have been twenty pages of closely written text.

'Don't be ridiculous.' Clearly Owen's patience was wearing thin. 'I've learned one bit – it's a couple of lines. It's supposed to call up a man of God. Now are you all ready?'

'Why does it have to be in the dark?' David asked.

'The summoning goes on and on about the angel of God being

robed in light, coming to us out of the darkness. I think we ought to give it a chance, don't you?' He looked round us all. 'Shall I begin?

'In the name of God the Father, God the Son and God the Holy Spirit, we beseech your aid, spirit of shining goodness, spirit of the light, spirit of the righteous.' He walked calmly across the floor and climbed the stairs to the light switch.

'Ready, Ben?' he said.

Ben held up the candle and matches. His eyes were gleaming with excitement. We heard the footsteps returning down the stairs and then Owen's voice continued. 'In nomine Patris, Filii et Spiritu Sancti . . .'

It was Kenny who spoiled it, although he never admitted it. He was sitting on my left, and I heard it all. As Owen's words became more elaborate, losing the reasonably familiar patterns of the Latin Mass, Kenny began to breathe deeply. I knew what was happening to him. I knew what was going to happen.

He was getting ready to sneeze. His breath was mounting in indrawn gasps. And when he did sneeze, just at the high point of Owen's peroration, David laughed.

That so much should hang on such an innocent, involuntary, blameless act! It seemed to me even then that it was grossly unfair. A sneeze, followed by a laugh. Merely that.

Only later did I remember the old superstition about sneezing. That the soul leaves the body momentarily. To forestall the devil entering, the sneezer must be blessed.

Bless you, we say. Gesundheit!

No one blessed Kenny. We all turned instead to David.

'Oh really, it's not funny!' This from Owen, piqued that his impressive showstopping act should be interrupted.

'What the hell are you playing at?' Philip, enraged.

'David!' Ben, sounding worried. 'Are you all right?'

'Idiot!' Joss, unable to resist laughing.

And Kenny flew at David, pushing him back against the bench, his fists pummelling and smashing into David's face before we pulled ourselves together enough to haul him back.

David's face was covered in blood.

'What – why did you do that?' he spluttered through the tears.

Kenny was furious, his own face running with snot. 'I hate you, you spastic, smarmy, Jewish git!'

'What is going on?' A strong, all-too-familiar voice from the top of the stairs. Jamie, Matron, my mother, stood at the top of the stairs in her dressing gown, tight-lipped with fury.

Her face changed as she saw David. 'All of you get to bed immediately. I'll deal with you in the morning. David, Louisa, come with me.' She stood by the door, waiting as we all filed out. She said nothing more, not even to Ben, who was, I knew, one of her favourites.

She shepherded David and me back to the san, where she mopped up David's bloody nose and put lotion around his eye. He was still white and shaky and Mum, who was never unkind, held back her traditional scolding. She put him to bed in the san and then came to see me where I lay shivering in bed.

'What on earth were you doing?' she said. There was no anger, but I'd never seen her look so worried before. 'David's in a terrible state and it's not from the fight. All boys fight, but David's frightened. What's been going on?'

I sat up in bed, hugging my knees. I couldn't look at her. I didn't want to give anyone away. 'It's my fault,' I said. 'I made a bet.'

'A bet? With whom?'

I wasn't going to tell her. Indeed, it suddenly seemed very unwise to tell her any of the truth. 'I said I would make up a ghost story that would frighten them. I said I could stop them sleeping and they said, nothing I could ever do would be frightening.'

'Oh, Lulu, they're such silly boys! You don't have to impress them!'

'They never listen to me,' I said, seeing a diversion here.

'But that doesn't explain why Kenny attacked David, does it?'

'Did David tell you that?'

'No, he hasn't said a word. But I saw Kenny's knuckles were scraped. What happened?'

'Kenny sneezed, and David laughed.' There could be no harm in this.

'You are ridiculous children. How absurd.'

'I think he was jealous. Kenny used to be Ben's best friend before David came.' This was true, although I had only just remembered it. Kenny was musical, like Ben, and they'd attended music theory lessons together. Sometimes they even practised together, Ben on the piano and Kenny on violin.

'I shall have to tell Mr Redmond of this.'

'Must you? We'll all look such fools.'

'It's what you are, isn't it? And you must see that we can't have nonsense like this going on at night. And besides, David's been hurt and everyone who sets eyes on him tomorrow is going to know it.'

'Please, Mum.'

'Louisa, I don't think you understand. You personally have broken not only several school rules, but one of my own. You are not allowed in the Main School after Lights Out. You are never to go there and if I find such a thing ever happening again, I'll send you to Queen Margaret's instead.'

I knew this was an empty threat. Mum didn't have the money to send me anywhere else.

'But Mum, if you tell the head I might get expelled any-way—'

She looked at me thoughtfully. We both knew I was at St Anthony's under sufferance. One step out of order and I'd be out. It might even affect my mother's position. She stood up. She'd made up her mind.

'I'll see all members of Bishop dormitory after breakfast. I'll *deal with this myself. But Louisa, one more little escapade like this and you may find yourself taking your chances at Park Grove Junior like all the other kids who live round here.'*

So it was that Owen, Joss, Ben, Philip, Kenny and David were taught how to iron shirts and sew on buttons and other essential household tasks for an hour, a humiliating, tiresome and boring hour, every day after school for two weeks.

Mr Redmond knew nothing about it. He didn't even comment on David's black eye, although he must have noticed it. He rather prided himself on the way St Anthony's turned out tough, self-reliant children. 'The odd scrap does no harm,' I'd heard him say to my mother. 'They'll get far worse later.' He meant, when they took the Common Entrance and left for other schools, of course. But nothing any of us ever experienced later compared with what happened to David. We had no idea of it. We realized that the enmity between Kenny and David was growing, that they seemed to have taken an unalterable dislike to each other, but this was nothing out of the ordinary.

Feuds were not uncommon in the school. They might flare for a term or two, but rarely did they endure at white hot intensity. Friendships and alliances formed and reformed at much the same rate. There were one or two constants, Ben and Kenny having remained close for their entire school career to date. They were united by their talent for music, both having won scholarships to St Anthony's. They were in the orchestra, Ben on French horn and Kenny on violin, and enjoyed playing piano duets together. Kenny had nearly got into the Minster School, or so he never failed to remind us, but there had been some mix-up over the entrance exam and his place had gone to someone else ...

This was typical Kenny, we felt. Full of grudges and sulks. We could never see why Ben put up with it, but Ben was always genial, always generous in his assessments. Besides, he and Kenny were both in the Confirmation class, and taking it rather more seriously than Owen, who loathed the whole process. Owen was doing it to please his mother, but Kenny and Ben were being Confirmed for real. Philip had been through the process earlier, having been brought up in a professionally religious household.

Joss and I were exempt, being the proud possessors of cheerfully agnostic parents, and so spared all the claptrap. I felt most at home with Joss, of all the boys, but they were all mates. I didn't see much of Philip, who was always mucking around in the gym or out at the nets, and Kenny was no great favourite, but I reasoned that if Ben could find good in him, then surely I could, too.

Of course, when it came to the punishment for our midnight adventure, I was treated the same as the boys. I had to help out with the ironing etc., and I hated it. It felt awkward, partly because I already knew how to iron and darn, and partly because Matron was my mother. I was embarrassed in front of my friends.

My response to embarrassment was never to shrink away. I decided that I needed to amuse them all and dredged through my mother's book shelves and found a volume of ghost stories. This was promising stuff, and my retold version of The Monkey's Paw gratifyingly terrified everyone.

Joss contributed a stylish (we thought) story by Dennis Wheatley he'd read at an uncle's house in the holidays. And Owen brought along the best of all with tales from Bradbury's The Golden Apples of the Sun. We paraphrased half-remembered plots about Satanic Rites, green men and black dogs and the time passed reasonably, although the ironing suffered and buttons were not too securely attached. On the whole, we enjoyed the sessions, although no one admitted it.

Except for Philip and Kenny. They were both in the rugger team and had to miss two practices, like Owen. They kept quiet about it, but sometimes I caught them watching David.

Owen didn't mind. He was growing bored with rugby and he'd never liked Philip or Kenny much anyway.

*   *   *

That wasn't the only trouble within the ranks of Bishop's dormitory.

The next thing was a surprise to us all. We were in the dining room eating Scotch pancakes at teatime, just after half-term. Most of the boys had been away for days and I was glad to see them back.

That first teatime I was sitting next to Kenny, across the table from Ben. Ben had arrived late. He sat down heavily, looking at no one.

'What's up?' I said.

'Nothing.' But then he looked up, glaring at Kenny. 'Why weren't you there?' he said bitterly. 'I waited for ages, and then Mr Brooker had to go, and it was all wasted!'

Kenny shrugged. 'There was an extra rugger practice. I went to that.'

'You could have let me know!' Ben glanced at me. 'I'd composed this trio for horn and violin, and Brooker was going to play the piano, as a favour, so I could hear it properly, how it would sound. We'd been rehearsing it for ages!'

'It was a rubbish piece. Mr Brooker would have hated it. It's girly, anyway, playing the violin. I'm giving up music.' Kenny continued to spread margarine on his pancake.

This was clearly a bombshell to Ben. I saw him blinking behind his thick glasses as he always did when he was perplexed or hurt. 'No one could ever say that people like David Oistrakh and Isaac Stern and Yehudi Menuhin are girly!'

'They're all Jews. Every one of them.' Kenny spoke unconcernedly.

'So what? What does that matter? You told me once that your grandma was Jewish—' Ben stopped suddenly.

I put down my mug and paid attention. This was news to me. Since the beginning of term we'd all heard Kenny tease David because of his Jewishness.

It looked like this was news to Kenny as well. He had gone

63

even whiter than usual with the sheer surprise of it. 'What the hell do you mean by making up lies like that?'

'But you told me.' Ben was puzzled. 'At the audition, years ago, don't you remember? You showed me your violin and said that your gran had given it to you, that she'd escaped from Germany during the war because she was Jewish . . .'

'Fuck you.' His voice was thick with violence. 'That was between you and me. Nothing to do with anyone else—' He stopped, aware that this was an admission of accuracy. He swung round on the bench, glaring at me as if this were all my fault. 'If you ever tell anyone, I'll kill you, Louisa Jamieson. I mean that. I'll put my hands round that scrawny neck of yours and I'll squeeze the life out of it—'

'Don't be absurd.' This from Ben, coldly. 'Whatever does it matter if your granny is Jewish? What on earth does any of that kind of stuff matter?'

'She married an Englishman, so she's English. Not Jewish. I was only talking about when she was little—'

'It's a beautiful violin,' said Ben calmly. 'You're very lucky to have it.'

'Maybe. But I shan't need it now. I said, it's stupid, girly stuff—' He was beginning to regain his confidence, but I could see the sweat running at the back of his neck.

'You've been staying with Philip. This is Philip's idea.' Ben spoke with absolute certainty and clarity. I knew he was right, and that this was dreadful to him. Kenny and Ben had been friends from the start, but now it looked like Kenny had found someone else.

'We went camping,' Kenny said. 'So what?'

'You're different. You've changed. You have no ideas of your own. You only follow others. You're pathetic, Pyper.' Ben was only being horrible because he was so hurt, I knew.

Kenny picked up his plate and mug and ostentatiously moved down the table to where Philip sat on his own, as usual.

Ben never mentioned it to me again, and neither did Kenny. And in fact I believed what he said, that his gran was English because she'd married an Englishman. It made sense. But after that, Kenny had very little to do with Ben and spent most of his time with Philip instead.

The persecution of David continued.

Chapter Eight

'Let's have a party.' Lily leaned her chin on her hands and grinned at Joss across the breakfast table.

'Lily, my dear, are you feeling quite well? Short-term memory loss setting in already? I seem to recall a small gathering in this very house less than a week ago.' Joss put down his paper, trying to respond to Lily's mood. He was dimly aware of a hollowness in the pit of his stomach which had nothing to do with the breakfast he hadn't been able to eat.

It was Leo's first day at St Anthony's. Joss had promised to take him there himself and Joss had spent most of the preceding night considering how much he would rather go to the dentist, present VAT accounts or recycle cat food tins. Leo was in the sitting room, checking through his satchel for the thirtieth time. He hadn't eaten much breakfast, either.

And here was Lily, proposing another party, although the last one had been ridiculously expensive and there was now a wine stain on the new pale green carpet in the drawing room.

'It's not Dotheboys Hall,' she said softly. 'He'll be all right, you know he will.'

She was wearing matching earrings and rings, thought Joss, irritated. Didn't she know how awful that could look?

Her musical, contralto voice continued, 'We're on hand, almost next door. He's not boarding, he'll be home before you are. And Ben's there, and the Morrells are perfectly pleasant people—'

'I know, I know.' He shook his head in self-mockery. 'What's this about another party? Are you bored or something?'

He was making a deliberate effort.

'A lunch party. For Caroline Morrell and Rosie Jenkinson, and I was wondering whether to ask Louisa too?'

'An all-girl affair? Does that mean I have an exeat?'

'Of course. What about Louisa?'

'It would be a kindness. It can't be much fun watching your mother die.' His own mother existed on a steady diet of sherry and peanuts in the Home Counties. She was going to live for ever, he assumed. He glanced at his watch. 'Leo? Ready, lad?'

'I – think so.' The small voice was unsure. For a moment Joss and Lily's eyes met. *It'll be all right*, she mouthed silently to him as Leo came into the kitchen, the silly grey cap balanced on the back of his head.

'Not like that, squirt.' She bent down and straightened it. 'Now, pencil case, gym shoes, ruler, tuck money—?'

He nodded. Joss was standing by the door.

'See you later, hon. I'll be at the gate.' She gave him the lightest of kisses, a quick hug. How can she smile? wondered Joss. Not for the first time the emotional toughness of his wife bemused him. On the short walk to the school, he was aware that Leo was clutching his hand rather fiercely. Just before they came in sight of the gate, Leo let go.

He'll be all right, Joss told himself. He's up to it, he knows what's needed. He handed Leo over to Mark Morrell in the hall of St Anthony's and made his escape as quickly as he could. It'll be better for Leo, he reasoned. Don't hang around, don't draw it out. He walked swiftly across the playground towards the gate.

The smell of the hall hung round his clothes. He was limping again.

'Joss!' He turned to find an ungainly figure springing towards him.

Ben, his magenta tie flapping wildly. 'Good, caught you,'

67

he wheezed. 'How about a drink later? When do you finish work?'

Joss looked at the kind face, so familiar and so changed, beneath the folds of flesh. He didn't want to disappoint, but . . . 'Not tonight, Ben, if you don't mind. Leo's first day, you know. I rather want to be there.'

'Family time, and all that?' Ben's eyes were not unsympathetic. 'It's no big deal, you know. Leo will be finding out where the smokers go even as we stand here now—'

'*What?*'

'Joke, Joss, joke . . . Lighten up, man. Leo's bright, attractive – he'll be fine.'

'So Lily keeps telling me.'

'A woman of style and sense. Tomorrow then? An introduction to some of York's finest hostelries?'

'Yes, I'd like that.'

They arranged to meet and all the time, Joss's eyes were flickering over Ben's wide shoulders towards the school. The front door had slammed shut, but he could hear the bell.

Ben looked at his watch, distracted. 'Must go. I'll keep an eye out, don't you worry.' Joss watched him disappear round the side of the building and felt minutely cheered. For a moment, he felt as fond of Ben as ever. He made an effort to concentrate on something else and by the time he'd crossed the threshold of the old warehouse which contained the spanking new offices of Past Present, his mind was full of advertising campaigns and budget forecasts.

'Now this is Leo Fletcher. I won't tell you all their names, Leo, you'll find them out all too soon. Volunteers to show Leo the ropes? What about you, Rachel?'

'I've got piano next.' Sulkily.

'I'll do it.' Mr Thompson looked faintly surprised as Samuel Pyper put up his hand. 'Thank you, Samuel. Now Leo is doing the same subjects as you are so keep a firm eye on him until he gets the hang of it all. Here's a timetable, Leo. Don't lose it.'

Leo was still holding the piece of paper when Mr Thompson left the room. He could make no sense of the blocks of writing, all with numbers at the side.

'Come on then!' the boy called Samuel shouted at Leo. His almost-white hair was cut brutally short, his rather narrow eyes a startlingly bright blue. He'd waited until Mr Thompson's footsteps faded. Then he disappeared round the door at the double, leaving Leo standing.

All the other children were picking up piles of books, chattering to each other familiarly.

'You'd better hurry up,' said one of the girls. 'Sam won't wait long for you.'

Leo seized a miscellaneous pile of textbooks and rushed to the door in a panic.

Samuel was still there, his snowy hair gleaming. He was kicking the radiator in the hall aimlessly. 'Got a tab?'

'What?'

'Tab. Fag. Cig. Cigarette!'

'No.' It was a whisper.

'Where's your lunch money?'

Leo said nothing but his hand moved to his side pocket.

'We're in 2B next. French. Give me your money and I'll show you where.'

'No!' More strongly.

Samuel came closer. 'Didn't anyone tell you? What was your last school?'

'Daiglen.'

'What? Where's that? Far from here? It's not a York school!' At every word he edged nearer, across the chilly corridor.

Then the classroom door burst open and the rest of the class came tearing out, not running, but doing that fast, straight-legged waddle that all children adopt when forbidden to run. Leo stepped out of Samuel's way and went with the flow.

It was all right until break. Leo was struggling, nose just above water and made it, with the flow, to French, Maths and History. But in break his form dispersed through the playground and Leo couldn't see anyone he recognized. A bell rang and everyone made for the door and Leo went with them and found himself suddenly standing in an empty and deserted hallway. In the distance a fading clatter of feet tramped up stairs. A door slammed somewhere. He heard chairs scrape and a man's voice announce indecipherable words before falling into a mumble. Far away, a piano started. Children's voices chimed in with 'Early one morning'.

The hall stank of disinfectant and flowers. Leo stared at the piece of paper Mr Thompson had given him. He tried to make sense of it. 034, said the block halfway down the Wednesday column.

He wandered up and down the corridor, looking at room numbers. They all began with A, not O, and continued with a number between ten and nineteen. Did O refer to the ground floor? Would the rooms upstairs begin with a 1, like in the hotel they'd stayed in once?

He plodded along the western corridor clutching his pile of books nervously. A door on the right hung open, swaying slightly in the cold wind from the open window. The far-off voices of children singing ceased. There was no other sound.

The silence was overwhelming, crushing down on him like a weight. Cold light slanted in patterns across the dark wood panelling.

The open door waited. He could see the edge of steps leading downwards. O had to mean the basement. Leo stood opposite the open door, his back pressed against the wall, looking at the dark chasm. The stairs were steep, with only a thin wooden handrail as protection on the way down.

He knew, somewhere in his heart, that his form would not be down there. But his reasonable, logical mind rattled through the rationalizations.

There will be a door to the outside down there, he thought. Probably they're doing nature-study or art or something in the grounds. They needed to change into outdoor shoes, or get overalls or something . . . I'll find them, if I go down there.

And yet still he hung back, looking down the corridor to the left and right, hoping for someone, anyone, so he could ask what he should do.

As he paused there, uncertain, at the top of the basement steps, a door opened beyond the main hall. In the dim light of the wintery sun, a figure dressed in white drifted towards him on silent shoes. For a moment he nearly panicked. Nearly threw himself down those steep steps, nearly collapsed into a snivelling heap of misery. As it was, he made a small moan and stayed where he was.

'Now, what have we here?' The figure approaching so silently, so swiftly, revealed itself to be a man dressed in some kind of loose overall. His thin face was smooth, his eyes almost buried in deep violet shadows. His cheeks were hollow, his fingers stained yellow with nicotine. He bent down to Leo from a great height.

'Who are you, little one? Lost your way perhaps? We've not met before, have we?' He held out his hand and Leo took it. A cold, angular bundle of bones imprisoned his small fingers. 'My name is Dominic Allbright,' he said. 'Mr Allbright to you, or Sir. I teach art to all your ungrateful and undeserving classmates.'

'I don't know where they are!' Leo hardly noticed what the man was saying. He was simply relieved that now someone else could take charge.

The man whisked the crumpled timetable out of his hand.
'Ah, one of Thompson's brats, are you? Name?'

'Leo Fletcher,' he said. 'It's my first day.'

'Well, Leo Fletcher, see here. Wednesday, 4th period. After the break.' He squatted on his heels so that Leo was now looking down at him. A faint smell, something spicy and exotic, came from him. His knees jutted out beneath the white smock, angular as a grasshopper. For a moment, Leo's inner eye envisaged him suddenly springing up, higher than his head, and landing on the other side of the hall. The thought amused him and he smiled.

Mr Allbright smiled back and stood up. His bony hand ruffled Leo's hair. 'I think I'd better give you a brief tour of the school, before this gets any worse.' His hand rested on Leo's shoulder, gently propelling him along the corridor. 'Now, all the room numbers beginning with O refer to the main building, where we now stand. Those prefixed A are in Alcuin block, to our right. Those with a W belong in Wheldrake block, over there . . .'

All the way round the school, Dominic Allbright's hand rested on Leo's shoulder. His soft, lilting voice hummed on, listing subjects, names, times, rotas, odd little facts about the school, about his classmates, and Leo took in less than five per cent of it all.

Eventually Allbright delivered Leo to W23 in time for the last period before lunch. Just before he handed Leo over to Miss Chapman, who taught science, he said, 'Listen to me, Leo. If you really want to feel confident here, put some effort into understanding the geography of the place. It's complicated: three houses knocked into one. It will repay close study. Watch the details, the way the cornices fit, the shape of the ceiling roses, the decoration on the door posts. Each of the three houses has a different style, you see. You'll always be able to tell where you are, as long as you observe. Use the old eyes, boy. And you can always come and find me if you're stuck, if you want any help at all. I'm easy to find, on the lower corridor, just off the main hall.' He opened the door into W23. An elderly woman stood there in front of a class of people Leo recognized.

'Miss Chapman, allow me to introduce Leo Fletcher to you, our latest recruit. He's had some trouble finding himself. I'll see you at two, Leo. Don't be late.' His hand briefly squeezed Leo's shoulder.

'At two?' Leo frowned.

'Yes, dear boy. Observe the timetable.'

His yellow finger underlined the place. 'You have Art all afternoon. Till then.'

He drifted off down the corridor, his silky smock billowing round him.

Chapter Nine

'And the Art teacher seems to have rather taken him under his wing. He came home after that first day just full of it, thrilled to bits with all those ideas, all that input—'

'Dominic Allbright is certainly an excellent teacher.' Caroline Morrell took a sip of her Perrier. 'An immensely talented man, although perhaps a little eccentric.'

'Leo says he wears a sheet,' Lily said with a question in her voice.

'It's an artist's smock, slub silk, something of an affectation and Mark did wonder a little about it. But the parents don't seem to mind, they find it rather romantic. A touch of Montmartre, we say when pushed.' She said it absolutely straight, without an iota of irony.

Louisa looked out of the window at the winter garden. For the last half hour Lily and Caroline Morrell had done nothing but discuss St Anthony's. Louisa's glass had been empty for at least two thirds of that time. She found herself wanting to smoke, after ten years' abstention.

Lily was all right. In fact, Louisa rather warmed to Lily: she was confident, amusing and sharp. A good partner for Joss, she thought. Louisa looked forward to getting to know Lily, but Caroline was another matter.

How could someone as beautiful as Caroline Morrell be so colourless, she wondered? Louisa had rarely encountered such classic good looks outside professional media stars. The combination of tiny, straight nose, enormous green eyes under natural (she'd swear to it) dark lashes, fine ash blonde hair caught in an Alice-band, presented a perfect picture. It went further than that. She was unfailingly courteous, sweetly tempered and doubtless an excellent mother, thought Louisa sourly. Never an unkind word about anyone. Everyone on the staff at St Anthony's was talented or brilliant or wonderful with the children. The confection was completed with classic *Telegraph* opinions on everything from law and order to religion.

Well she would, wouldn't she? Louisa reprimanded herself. Being a headmaster's wife required public perfection. It was not unlike the old-fashioned concept of the vicar's wife. Caroline Morrell existed to back up her husband and in addition to show the parents that their precious offspring would receive only the very best influences, examples and table-manners at St Anthony's. Aren't we all lovely? That was her exclusive line and Louisa wondered if Caroline ever thought of anything at all beyond the school and her children.

At that moment she was glancing at her simple, unostentatious watch. 'Lily, I'm afraid I must dash. There are some potential parents coming to tea, and I promised to do the tour with them.' She wrinkled her exquisite nose.

Louisa dragged her attention away from the garden. 'Do you show them all around? Even down to the basement?'

'The basement? No, why should they want to see the basement?' Caroline looked genuinely puzzled. 'Was it one of your favourite hideaways as a child?'

They'd already established Louisa's credentials as an old girl.

'I hated the place. All of it, but especially that nasty little box of a room. That and the evil-eyed pig on the ceiling in the hall.'

'St Anthony's boar, do you mean?' Caroline raised an eyebrow. 'Our patron saint, our very own mascot. I always found the boar rather sweet.'

'It symbolizes greed. The sins of the flesh.' Louisa held out her glass towards Lily. 'May I have some more?'

'I'm so sorry. Of course, here, help yourself.' Lily pushed the bottle across the table. 'I'll just see Caroline to the door.'

'Goodbye.' Louisa stood up.

'Come and have a look round the school, why don't you?'

The devastating eyes considered her and Louisa felt heavy and ungracious and plain. 'It was a long time ago, wasn't it? Twenty – thirty years? It must have changed rather a lot since your day.'

Then she left the dining room, chatting amicably to Lily, leaving Louisa almost open-mouthed with astonishment. Who'd've thought Caroline Morrell had it in her? She sat down again and drained her glass.

When Lily returned, Louisa said, 'Did I imagine that, or did I just hear the perfect Mrs Morrell make a bitchy remark?'

'I'm afraid you may rather have asked for it.' Lily poured herself more wine. 'All that nonsense about private education.'

'A bit OTT was I?'

'You could say that.'

'Sorry.' This was going from bad to worse. Louisa stood up. 'Perhaps I'd better be going too.'

Lily was watching her. 'Is your mother in much pain?' she said unexpectedly. Louisa stopped, a sudden rush of tears to her eyes.

'No, it's not that. She's – frightened.'

'My mother died three years ago,' Lily said quietly. 'I found it very hard.' She paused. 'Did you go to the hospital this morning?'

Louisa nodded, aware that the tears were about to fall. She found that Lily was holding out a clean handkerchief to her. 'I didn't know she was frightened, not until today. I've never seen her frightened before.'

Had they been late round with the drugs? Or had Mum been depressed by that other woman in the ward dying during the night? Whatever it was, Louisa had arrived at eleven to find her mother in a desperate state, her hands shaking, tears rolling ceaselessly down her face.

And the monster stirred. Flexing deep muscles, the memory of pain gave it energy. It lifted its maw and tasted the sweet air of another time.

'I can cope with nothing,' Mavis Jamieson said. 'If it's nothing, that would be manageable. But what if there's judgement?' Her old hand plucked at the sheet. 'What if there's hell, or another life, as a slug or something—?'

'Oh really, Mum, if there's any justice in the world, you'll be sitting in fields of lilies singing your heart out.'

She cradled her mother's head against her chest.

'No I won't, there'll be fires, fires all the way and pain and no healing, no forgiveness—'

A nurse had come then and shooed Louisa away while a doctor administered another dose.

Louisa had arrived at Lily's lunch party strung up with puzzlement and worry. She had not behaved well with Caroline Morrell and she had drunk too much. And now Lily was looking at her with sympathy and Louisa wanted to sink through the floor with embarrassment.

'Come on,' said Lily. 'Come through to the kitchen with me.' Louisa helped her carry out the dishes and then sat at the kitchen table watching miserably while Lily stacked the dishwasher. 'Joss is very fond of your mother,' Lily said. 'I think he'd rather like to visit her. Would she be up to that, do you think?'

Louisa shook her head. 'Not on today's showing. But I know she always liked Joss, and Ben too.'

'Tell me something.' Lily sat down opposite Louisa. 'Did you know Joss well? Were you best friends?'

Louisa nodded. Lily would understand, she thought. 'We even kissed. Twice it was, I think. Didn't he tell you?'

'He never talks about his childhood, that bit of it anyway. His time at St Anthony's.'

'I'm not surprised.' Louisa stared at her hands. She didn't want to talk about it either. Let the past lie, she thought, let the monster rest. 'Joss was my best friend at the time. But it was Owen I had a pash for.'

'Has he changed much? Owen?'

'Difficult to tell. He seems both – more gentle, and more cynical. That's what parenthood does for you, I suppose.'

'That and divorce.'

'There's all that black hair, of course.'

'Makes him look artistic, don't you think? Or like a musician, perhaps? I could just see him with a cello, rather like a young Paul Tortelier.'

Louisa giggled. 'Owen's tone deaf. What on earth possessed him to marry a professional soprano?'

'Perhaps he'll tell you one day.'

'Doubt it.' Louisa sat back. 'Owen was never one for self-revelation. Evidence of weakness, he called it.'

'He may have changed. How long ago was it according to our dear friend Caroline? Twenty years?'

Twenty-three years. A little unsteadily, two hours later, Louisa picked her way through the crowds towards the market. In twenty-three years she'd dyed her hair, grown eight inches and put on at least two stone. Her skin had cleared up, her eye for colour and form sharpened. She'd lost her virginity, the double-headed snake ring her mother had given her, a cat and numerous books. She'd broken probably about eight glasses, five plates or so and one large pottery casserole. She'd planted countless seeds and murdered dozens of houseplants. She'd made a name for herself as a photographer of current social issues, and still had a weakness for Led Zeppelin.

And now, walking through York, it was as if it were all for

nothing. Nothing had changed at all. Here they all were, Owen, Joss and Ben, and still the games of loyalty and friendship preoccupied her, still she knew that she was fond of Ben and Joss, and Owen made her weak at the knees.

Nothing had changed. She was back in York and failing even to walk straight. Too much wine and not enough food. She and Lily had got high on silly speculations about Owen Rattigan and Mark Morrell and it had been fun, for a while, a welcome distraction from the visit she was going to make that evening to the District Hospital.

She plunged down the alley between Swinegate and Parliament, uneasily aware that her feet were not connecting quite solidly with the ground. Ahead of her the pavement was rucked up, the stones unevenly overlapping. She was having to pick her way now over rubble, the sharp-edged stones rigid like the teeth of a comb. There was litter everywhere, bits of torn newspaper which billowed around her, caught in the through-draught. Surely the council should keep things in better repair than this? Abruptly she put her hand out to the wall and something raked at her skin, a nail or jagged shard.

Ahead the alley became impossibly disturbed. Between one step and the next, everything changed. The snag on her hand, the small spilling of blood and the fragments of paper had opened a door, had given permission. Louisa could see no movement, no sign of the stirring of evil, but her senses knew better. She could feel the whole city shifting beneath her shoes, swelling like the movement of lava boiling through the layers of rock.

It moves, she thought, an unarticulated knowledge that flared through her with remembered potency, it moves and it lives.

Far away, sparkling in the winter sun, she saw people walking across the square, continuing their ordinary business with no awareness at all of the emerging horror in the alley, where the paving stones were being shrugged aside, shuffled together like a pack of cards.

She turned and ran back the way she had come, stumbling and tripping, and found herself suddenly amidst crowds once more, pale preoccupied faces who gave her only puzzled glances. She turned again to look down the alley, and its surface was broken only with the unevenness of ancient, worn stone.

'My God, my God,' she murmured under her breath. What had happened? A hallucination? A drunken delirium? But she knew that this had happened before, she remembered almost all of it.

Chapter Ten

Every city has its own character, its own flavour, she thought later that night. She was sitting on the carpet in her mother's back room, leaning against the sofa, watching the predictable flames of the artificial gas fire as a mug of hot chocolate cooled at her side. Rome was a wolf, Venice a lion. But did English cities share a similarly exotic mythology? The information was in no tourist guide, but she thought she knew the truth of it where York was concerned. It needed no myths, no symbols. Its authentic, documented history was enough, more than enough. Its history was written in the stones of the city itself.

Where were its industries now? There were none left, only the chocolate factories, and they were in foreign hands. Even the railworks had closed. Heritage, that was the name of the game now. York's only trump card, something it did supremely well. Museums, exhibitions, festivals, architecture, the incomparable Minster and the dozens of small churches, the Guildhall and other merchant houses. But what did that heritage mean, what was it really about?

What people did, their acts, their thoughts and feelings. What they made was all around, all the buildings and roads and statues, but what they did animated these bare stones, gave life to the city. (And made the stones heave? Made the pavements lift like waves in a threatening storm?)

And now the industries were gone and the city was full of closed shops. The newly built precincts were deserted, and a cold wind made hands and face ache.

There was a knock on the door.

She was startled: it was nearly midnight. She kept the chain on, bearing in mind her mother's instructions, and opened the door a couple of inches. Somehow, she was not surprised to see Owen standing there.

He said nothing, waiting patiently while she closed the door to unloop the chain. For a moment she wondered whether to leave it in place and make some excuse. Some part of her wanted to shut him out, keep him away.

She didn't know him. Her silly conversation with Lily that afternoon made her feel hot with embarrassment.

'Hello, Owen,' she said. 'How are you?'

There are pathways. They run along the arteries of a place, pumping energy like blood, to and fro and if you get caught on them ... Snakes and ladders, mazes and labyrinths, tramlines of colour that you find in hospitals. Follow the green line to find your way home, pick up the pebbles, watch for the clues and you'll be settled and comfortable and safe.

Or you may find yourself at the heart of it, where something now stirs, lifting its great, yawning head. Tendrils creep from its dead black heart, animating the shades of the past, the memories that are the only real heritage. Memories of sin. Of revenge and ancient, deep-seated enmity. The city stirs and the living pathways of its old soul stretch out, luxuriate and rustle with vigour.

There are no barriers, no places of safety. No one moves in the centre at night. Very few even live there. The pavements ripple, the pub signs swing and in the doorways vagrants shift and stir uneasily in their nests of newspapers and old blankets. And then the city rearranges itself once more, presenting its daytime face of tacky tourist shops and buskers and hurrying crowds.

'There's something wrong,' he said. 'I wanted to see that you were all right. I'm sorry it's so late ... look, may I come in?'

She stood aside and he brought into the house the cold breath of night. Even then, on edge, tired and tense as she was, she wondered what he'd make of her mother's flowery wallpaper and patterned carpet. Owen had always inclined towards the austere. She took him through to the back room and tried to get him to sit down on the sofa but he remained standing in the centre of the small room, his fringe of wavy black hair standing out like some mad professor in a cartoon.

'What is it Owen? Of course I'm all right.'

'Things have started happening, things I find worrying. I wonder if it's because you've come back, is it because of you?'

He was probably drunk, she realized, with a brief wave of relief. Owen drunk she could handle, an altogether easier proposition.

'Do sit down, for goodness sake.'

'I saw you this afternoon. In that alley.'

She went cold. 'You weren't there!'

'At the Parliament end. You were – upset. Panicking.'

Her hands clenched. 'I thought I saw something . . .' she whispered.

'No, you didn't. Don't fool yourself. You were imagining something, just like you did before.'

She said nothing. Couldn't speak, really, feeling it all closing in once more.

She knew what he was doing, he was going to make her deny it all.

'Are you referring to that time when David was running away from old Redmond? You were there, weren't you?' She was intense.

'Yes, I am referring to that.' His face was blank, impervious. 'Even though it wasn't that alley anyway, it was just off Stonegate—'

'Yes. But they're all connected, aren't they?'

*   *   *

Yes, all connected. All the snickleways and alleys and paths. I remember thinking that we shouldn't do it. The fact that it was strictly forbidden to leave school premises without permission was the least of it. We all knew the school rotas well enough, we knew what the chances would be. No, the problem with the bet was that too many people knew about it. Not just Bishop dormitory, but Kenny had brought in Nigel Sunman as well.

It was a race. A competition, all on the strength of a dare. Owen had bet Kenny that he could get round the Minster and back to school in less than ten minutes. They'd spent hours discussing the route: clearly, Deangate was too exposed, too full of traffic. Petergate would have to form the central leg of the route, they decided. Eventually the course was agreed. The dare became more elaborate with the decision to provide each runner with three team-mates, look-outs really, who would be stationed at regular intervals on the route. Their job would be to cause a diversion should a member of staff materialize.

Owen chose Joss, David and me. Kenny picked Philip, Nigel and Ben.

Joss and Ben were to wait at the school with stopwatches. We wanted to establish a tradition, the St Anthony's run. If it worked, we could all have a go at it, and then there would be a league-table. These plans of grandeur were all Kenny's idea. He always thrived on competition. Nigel and I were placed at the junction of Goodramgate with Petergate. Philip and David were to wait at the west end of the Minster, by the gate through to the Minster Gardens.

The real danger lay through the Gardens. They were virtually deserted at this time of year and the sight of two boys in Anthony's uniform, running, would be bound to cause comment.

And this was Minster School territory. There had always been rivalry between the two schools. Naturally, the Minster school, known locally as the Song School, was way ahead in the music education stakes, taking scholars who performed in the Minster daily and twice on Sundays. But Anthony's had a reputation for turning out first-rate instrumentalists, boys who often attained excellent scholarships to their next schools. Minster staff were always on the look-out for misbehaving Anthony's boys, and the Minster Gardens were their natural stamping grounds. Any trouble at St Anthony's was good news for the Minster school.

The difficult bit was round the west end of the Minster and through the Gardens. It was a cold, rainy November afternoon, just before the twilight really became established. I didn't see what happened at all clearly.

Nigel and I were stamping from foot to foot in a vain effort to keep warm. He was a pale, thin boy often to be found hanging round with Philip and Kenny. I neither liked nor disliked him: he was just colourless, a follower, whose only distinguishing characteristic was the generous outcrop of acne on his face. He was wearing the shorts which constituted Anthony's uniform and I was in a short-skirted version of the same and both of us were freezing. It was with some relief that we saw Owen and Kenny come tearing up Goodramgate, dodging and weaving through the crowds. Any pedestrian accidents would count as disqualification, we had decided, and I watched with approval Owen's almost balletic grace. And then they were round the corner and haring along Petergate. We followed, of course, eager to see the next stage. There was hardly anyone there. A brief lull in the afternoon's marketing, just a few people staring in windows, a couple putting up an umbrella outside Yates' Tearooms. I saw David at the top of Stonegate, excitedly hopping from foot to foot. He was backing Owen, of course. He was looking towards us, along the curve by the Grape Lane junction, and this next bit I did see.

Owen and Kenny were only yards away. In his excitement, David leaped out of the way and somehow became disentangled with a passer-by. The shopper's parcel went flying and at the same time the man reached out a long hand and caught Owen by the collar. Kenny was already out of sight.

David shot a glance at the passer-by's face and bolted. So would I have done, if I'd been him. The passer-by was only the headmaster, old Redmond, and whatever he'd been carrying now lay smashed in the gutter.

David disappeared into the crowded length of Stonegate. Redmond swung around to face us.

'Get back to school at once,' he said to Owen, Philip, Nigel and me.

We were only too glad to get away. I saw that Owen was white and strained beside me. 'Stupid fool,' I heard him mutter in ragged breaths. He was referring to David. 'Doesn't he know this can only make it worse?'

'He panicked,' I said.

'Cretin,' panted Philip. 'Look, there he goes!'

We saw the small figure dive off to the left just beyond the Red Devil Bakery, into Coffee Yard, the longest covered alley in York.

'Let's leave him to it.' Philip slowed to a walk. He took a packet of cigarettes from his pocket and held them out to Nigel. 'Come on, let's get out of this.'

'Yeah. Waste of time . . .' They lit up, and walked off in the direction of St Helen's Square.

Owen and I went to the end of the alley and looked after David. There was no sign of him. But a ripple ran along the length of the yard, all that we could see of it, and it seemed to us both that the stones were moving, disturbed like cat's fur stroked backwards.

I clutched Owen's arm. Further down the yard, trapped in a doorway, his feet only inches from the moving stone, David's terrified face looked towards us. His mouth was open and although I could hear no words, I knew he was crying out for help.

I took a step nearer. Owen hung back. And then someone pushed me aside, someone tall and bony. Not Mr Redmond, but someone dressed in white.

Whoever it was swept past into the alley and the pathway quietened beneath his feet. He reached the doorway where David stood and that was when Redmond caught up with us and pulled us away from the alley and neither of us saw what happened next.

The head sent us back to school. He took no notice of my stammered description of the alley and besides, there was now no evidence of it. Owen said he'd seen nothing out of the ordinary. And this, taken together with Redmond's refusal to admit that anything had happened, led me to suppress it all.

My mouth was stopped, a block planted in my thoughts. There was a barrier between Owen and me and I never spoke of the heaving pavement in Coffee Yard again.

And when David returned to class the next day, after a night in the san, he too had no satisfactory explanation for the long scratch, raised red and flecked with blood, which ran the length of his left forearm. 'I must have fallen,' was all he'd say, but his eyes glanced away from us and I knew he was not telling the truth.

'Why don't you remember?' Angrily, Louisa turned away from Owen, reaching up to draw the curtains more securely together. She turned on the standard lamp, wanting to make the room brighter, clearer. Wanting to flood away the shadowy corners with merciful light.

'What is there to remember?' He sounded very bleak. 'We were just children, imaginative, excitable and cruel . . . What happened to David was the result of bullying. Simple, sordid, childish cruelty. Nothing else of significance happened.'

'It must be hard, being you. Shutting your mind to everything.'

'Louisa, it was a long time ago. What relevance can it possibly have now? Today, I thought you looked in distress in that alleyway. I called to find out if you were all right—'

'Why didn't you come and help? If you saw me there this afternoon?' She spoke without consideration. With bitterness. These were familiar patterns (as before, she had not helped David . . .).

He flung himself down on the sofa, his fingers drumming on the arm. He would not look directly at her. Her attention was caught by the strands of black hair spiking untidily from the back of his head. Then he looked at her and she saw that his face was quite without colour, stretched taut with something she recognized from long ago.

'I could not,' he said. 'I was not free. Sophy was with me, I couldn't take risks—'

'What did you see? What did you see, exactly?'

'I don't know.'

'Don't know? Come on Owen, what is this?'

'Not – anything concrete. You seemed upset, there was some rubbish in the alley—'

'Upset?' she shouted. 'Christ, Owen, why don't you remember? What about the man in white?'

He stood up again, starting to pace the small room. 'Who? What are you talking about?'

'Sheepshanks.'

As she said the word, its sibilant sound spread through the room and it seemed suddenly that her gallant attempt to light the place only served to emphasize the black corners.

Corners, secrets, veils, lost memories.

Owen's voice was soft. 'That again.' And then his hand lashed out, slamming the door shut. 'Damn it! I resent this! I resent being scared again, we're adults now, not silly kids! What are you stirring up this time, Louisa Jamieson? Why haven't you left all your poltergeist nonsense behind, why couldn't you let it lie?'

She felt like slapping him. Violence is always catching once it's out of the bag, she thought, it sets its own agenda and people begin to operate within that agenda, without options.

'Is that how you explained it away? For all these years, have you been thinking it was all about adolescent hormones? For God's sake! Had you nothing to do with it, then?'

He still said nothing, staring at her with intensity.

'And if it's starting again, it's because you and Joss are sending your children to that horrible place! That's what this is all about, it's the school, that's where Sheepshanks always came from! So why are you picking on me?'

'There is no Sheepshanks! What madness is this? Why can't you forget what happened, it was all dreams, all nightmares, it was nothing – *nothing* – to do with reality!'

'Oh, Owen!' And this was why, why she had never married, why Owen's marriage had failed, why Joss was so strained and Ben drank, why nothing ever worked . . . She believed that he knew it all. He understood it all, just as she did, and still, as ever, refused to accept it. He had never admitted the existence of Sheepshanks, and cruelty, and the death of innocence.

It was desperate. But there was something else, something that she could do. Keep the dialogue open, she told herself. At whatever price, keep him talking.

'Let's have some tea. Let's think about it calmly, rationally. We are, as you say, adults.' Louisa opened the door and went through to the kitchen and Owen followed her, as she knew he would.

Bright flooding light again. ('It's north facing and I can't stand dark kitchens—' her mother's voice, her mother's colouring: sunshine yellow walls, daisies and poppies and cornflowers on the curtains, pretty blue and white striped china on the shelves.)

Her mother. The dialogue was fading there. Ending, with so much unsaid. So many half-lies, so many misunderstandings . . . (Why did the school pay her medical insurance?) She became aware that she was standing blankly by the kettle, one hand on the switch and that she had been standing like that for some time.

Owen hadn't noticed. He was looking closely at the flower painting on the wall by the door. 'This is rather good,' he said. 'Who did it?'

And then she knew that he had noticed her momentary paralysis. For Owen surely knew as well as she did who had painted the flower picture, he'd commented on it before, all those years ago.

'My mother,' she said and felt his hand on her shoulder, turning her around so that she leaned against him and his arms were so warm, so comforting round her.

'You inherited a touch of genius there,' he said against her hair. 'An eye for colour, for balance and shape. I always admired it.'

'Rubbish. You liked black and white and clear lines, you could never stand clutter—' The words were difficult, the dilemma echoing down the years, reverberating over centuries . . . (Centuries? her mind said. What is this?)

'Have you not thought that I might have changed?'

She shook her head. 'No. I'm with the Jesuits there. You're shaped by the time you hit seven. Anything after that, it's just fiddling round the edges, window dressing—'

'And may God help all those forking out small fortunes to get their children educated.' Wryly, as if it was a joke.

'More fool them.' She pulled away from him, putting mugs out on the side.

'Just because you didn't like Anthony's, doesn't mean that all independent schools are a waste of money.'

'Yes it does.' She knew it sounded unreasonable but she

was tired and worried (and frightened?). This was a welcome distraction. 'And why call them independent? They're public schools, home of the old school tie, the establishment, all our grotty, rotten, two-tier class system—'

'Lou, half the parents who send their children to Anthony's are hardworking middle management, by no stretch of the imagination upper class or establishment or any of those daft *Guardian* simplicities—'

'They're social-climbing then. They're trying to give their little darlings a foot in the door.'

'And why not? What's so wrong with trying to do your best for your children?'

'Nothing. Of course, nothing. But who's to say that schools like Anthony's are the best?'

'Their results—'

'Of course, their results are better, smaller class sizes, better equipment—'

'So why should my Sophy have less than the best?'

'Because it's not fair!'

'Don't be childish, Louisa.'

'Do you want this tea or not? Hadn't you better be getting back? Won't the babysitter be waiting?'

'Sophy's staying the night with a friend.' They stared at each other for the briefest moment, each appalled at this sudden plunge into enmity. 'I suppose it is rather late. I'll give the tea a miss, if you don't mind.'

She saw him down the long hallway, wanting all the time to make some friendly comment, some *rapprochement* to heal and keep him there. They had said nothing of use. They had touched nothing important.

At the door, he said, 'I'm sorry Lou, this is not a good time for you.'

She felt tears again, for the second time that day.

'I'm sorry, too.'

He touched her hand briefly. 'I'll be in touch. Goodnight, Louisa. Sweet dreams.' And then he was off, striding down the street, and the street lighting gave him deep moving shadows.

She shut the door and leaned against it and the pretty wallpaper crowded round her.

'Oh shit,' she said quietly, but it came out differently and the soft sibilants blended themselves into the sound of Sheepshanks' name.

He was there. Another presence in the house, something that belonged to the corners and cupboards and cracks.

All at once, her knees gave way. She sagged against the door.

He was standing at the bottom of the stairs only a few feet away from her. His face was almost entirely covered by the white cowl, but she could still see the bony jutting of the nose and jawline.

'Louisa Jamieson,' he said. 'I know you. But it's not you I want.'

Chapter Eleven

Earlier that evening, Lily said to her son, 'What are you doing, honeybun?'

Leo looked up from his drawing. 'Making a map. A plan of the school. Mr Allbright said it would be a useful thing to do.'

Lily leaned over his shoulder to look. 'Come and see this, Joss,' she said.

He put down his newspaper with reluctance. He'd come in late and it had been a difficult day. The funding for the Roman Festival wasn't working out and he could see it all slipping away. He'd rather staked his reputation on this one, his opening shot across the bows of the archeological establishment. And now it looked as though they were right.

York had more than enough festivals already, from the musical to the historical to a hundred different cranks, from model railways to pyschic fairs. It was virtually impossible to find a free weekend. There was even talk of a royal visit later that spring, a civic jamboree on a grand scale, celebrating the glorious heritage of York. Martin Shaw was wildly enthusiastic about that one. No one wanted to know about Joss's Roman project.

He glanced at his son's drawing and then paused, putting down the newspaper.

Leo had drawn each room on the ground floor in three dimensions, viewed from the door. It was an unwieldy design, but he'd managed to give each room elements of its essential character, almost its own smell.

Joss picked it up, fascinated. The clearest part of it was the entrance hall with its bowls of bright flowers and lists of names on the panelling. Leo had drawn a silver rose bowl set against dark brown and gold, indecipherable lettering. A right-angled, moulded design suggested the edge of a door: through it, with the paper tilted, there was an impression of the next room, as if it was the view from the hall.

Allbright's room. An easel, splashes of poster paint colour mixed on a tray, a wisp of the muslin curtain which hung at Allbright's window. The next opening in the colourful impression led to Redmond's – no, Morrell's study, with its leather-bound books and fossil paperweights.

'There's no room to do W or A block,' said Leo. 'I really need bigger paper. And then there's the other floors . . .'

All at once he sounded very tired.

'It's going to be wonderful, honey, a real work of art!' Lily took the piece of paper from Joss and held it up to the light.

'It's brilliant, Leo. But there's another way to do plans of houses, did you know that?'

'When you look down from the top?' Leo nodded wisely. 'But you can't show so much that way. And Mr Allbright says that it's all in the detail.'

'That's one way of looking at it. But you could get the whole school in that way, and even the grounds.'

Leo was silent for a few seconds, his eyes curiously blank, as they often were when he was planning some mischief. 'Are there plans of York like that? Of the whole city?'

'Scores of them. Tourists use them all the time to find their way round.'

'Do they cost much to buy?'

'Hardly anything,' said Joss, amused. 'In fact I'll get you one, if you like . . .'

Leo nodded slowly. 'But it wouldn't show the detail, would it?'

'Perhaps you could make one yourself,' suggested Lily. 'Start

94

with St Anthony's gate and then work outwards, putting in all the things you find interesting.'

'Like the lion on our door,' Leo said. 'I'd like to do that.'

He began with the lion. He took his pad of paper outside after dinner and used his gold pen to give the lion a mane that reached out well beyond the confines of the door. The door didn't matter, but the lion did.

Across the street a small tabby cat watched him curiously. Its belly was distended with pregnancy and when Leo at last noticed it, it slunk off into the shadows. Leo followed it. He'd always liked cats, he'd asked and asked his parents to let him have one, but his mother had put her foot down.

'They scratch the furniture, they moult, they get sick, they torture and murder birds and besides, they make me sneeze.'

'But I'd look after it, I'd keep it away—' Leo always said and she always laughed.

'For ten days, perhaps. And then what?'

'No, really, Mummy, I'd always feed it.'

'No. Just accept it, Leo. No cats in this family.'

And then she turned back to her gardening or her practising or reading and missed the half-sympathetic glance from his father. He always agreed with Mummy, it wasn't fair!

So he followed the pregnant tabby into the maze of newish flats and maisonettes off Bedern and very nearly got lost. But then he heard his mother calling his name and went home. In his notebook, there was a rainbow and a red bicycle. He'd copied the dolphin knocker on one of the doors and a sunburst window over an upstairs window. Some of the chimney pots had interesting shapes so he put those in too.

By the time he'd reached home once more his neck was aching from looking upwards. His mother gave him a brief scold and packed him off to bed.

He kept the lion drawing on his bedside table and his dreams were full of cats that sang and chimneys overflowing with goldfish.

Joss sighed with contentment as Lily rested her head on his chest. Her hair was soft and scented and one hand was lazily stroking the length of his leg. Their love-making had been energetic and inspired with laughter, but now he felt the depression that occasionally accompanied the resurgence of the pain in his ankle.

'Do you think Leo's settling in all right?' he said. 'He's such a strange, lonely little chap.'

'Perhaps we should have had more children.' Lily's hand had stopped moving.

'Not at that risk,' he said. She'd nearly died giving birth to Leo. In the end it had been an emergency Caesarian and it had been touch and go for both of them. 'We can't go through all that again.'

'But it's not good for children to be brought up on their own.'

'Come on Lily, we don't need this now. It's why we're sending him to a school just down the road. Kids on hand all the time.'

Actually, it wasn't so. Most of the pupils at Anthony's lived in the country, some in the big houses down Clifton. Very few came from within the city walls and virtually none from the area between Goodramgate and Peasholme Green. Their neighbours were all wealthy elderly people or young professionals who were not yet in the family way.

'I thought you were happy about Leo at the school,' Lily said. 'His art is coming on splendidly, you saw it for yourself this evening.'

'But he never brings anyone home, he's never invited to anyone's house—'

'It's very early days yet. He's not had six weeks there yet.'

'Long enough.'

Lily rolled over and sat up, snapping on the bedside light. 'Give him a chance,' she said. 'He seems happy enough to me, he chatters on all the time.'

'I know . . .'

'Don't worry about our Leo, he's a winner if ever I saw one. Do you mind if I read for a bit?' She picked up the latest Fay Weldon. The subject was dismissed.

'Of course not. 'Night, love.' He turned away from the light and tried to sleep.

Lily stared at the clever, ironic prose and took none of it in. Leo had wet his bed for the last three nights. It was not unknown: he'd wet his bed before leaving Epping, he sometimes had accidents when very excited . . . He'd made her promise to tell no one, especially his daddy, but she worried all the same. How might she find out what the trouble was? Some subversive instinct, one she had no desire to question, told her that the school would reveal nothing. To Caroline Morrell, to other parents she had met, everything was always fine. It had to be, they'd all invested so much money in the place. On the other side of the fence, the teachers, people like Ben Bowen, had too much invested in the school, too.

Status, career, livelihood. Owen Rattigan, she thought. His daughter Sophy was at the school, and he'd been there himself. Sophy might know if Leo was being upset or anything . . . She resolved to meet Owen, to find out what she could.

She did not for one moment contemplate bothering Joss. He had too much on his mind, she decided. He didn't need this, too.

Outside the bedroom door, Leo froze. He saw the light beneath his parents' door, heard the murmur of their conversation, although not the words. He couldn't risk going that way. He returned up the narrow stairs to his attic bedroom and went to the window. It was open a couple of inches at the top and Leo carefully pushed the sash up so that there was room. Then, as quietly as he could, he turned one of the bars round and round in its socket and lifted it out of place. Its neighbour yielded to the same treatment. Leo sighed with relief. It worked.

He was wearing jeans, T-shirt and jumper and his trainers. In his back pocket he'd stuck the small sketchpad and a torch borrowed from the drawer in the kitchen. That was all he would need for his midnight expedition.

He'd not used the fire-escape before. He hadn't even given a thought to what it would feel like to be out there, suspended high over the garden.

He felt powerful. He could see the floodlit central tower of the Minster through a gap in the roofscape behind him. To his right, Clifford's Tower shone gleaming white. Church spires broke up the steep lines of the roofs. Beneath him the garden was full of hidden shadowy places and strange-textured plants. In the starlight, what leaves remained were shining waxy silver. He felt he owned it all, that the darkened shadows and silvery fronds were his own country, his own world and no one else would ever know it. It was a cold night but mercifully dry and windless. He was in luck.

This was an expedition that had awaited him ever since moving to York. He had not, of course, crystallized the ambition to make his own pathways round the city, but he had known that one day he would explore at night-time. He liked the night, he always had. When he was very little, his parents had sometimes found him wandering round the house in the dark trying to find his way by touch and memory alone. 'It's a game,' he said in answer to their puzzled questions. 'Things are different in the dark.'

And now he thought again, yes, the city is different in

the dark. In daytime it's noisy and crowded and busy, but now—

Now it was held in stillness. He could hear no traffic. It was after midnight and nothing moved.

Not quite nothing. Far beneath him a cat trod silently along the garden path towards the back gate.

'Wait for me,' he breathed and found his way down the stairs, running his hand over the rough, rusty railing. His trainers made no noise, which was just as well because the fire-escape descended right outside his parents' window, where the light still shone.

The cat had reached the back gate. It stood there, its tail twitching with impatience, waiting for Leo to open the door. The alley used to hold dustbins, but the council now collected from wheelie-bins at the end. The alley was empty, a border separating the row of houses from the wasteground.

Leo had never been much interested in the wasteland, which was an empty stretch of scrub and rubble awaiting development.

He liked artifice, the things people made. He was enchanted by the carvings in the stone, in the colours of the stained glass windows, in the curlicues and flowery wands which decorated so much of York's architecture. He liked the pub signs, even the mysterious ones like the Burton Stone, he liked the pavement paintings. He had no sense of danger. He came out of the alley at the side of Newitts and crossed King's Square to Petergate quite happily, making small notes and sketches in his book as he went. So absorbed was he in this that he hardly noticed the ragged heaps in the doorways, the stench of urine, the rustle of scavengers round the litterbins. He rather preferred the city as it was now. In the daytime the details were blurred, lost in the kaleidoscope of colour and movement.

He carried on his way towards the Minster and didn't notice that he was no longer alone.

*   *   *

The figure at the bottom of the stairs tilted its head as if listening. Louisa's hand covered her mouth. The sense of chill in the hall was absolute and she was paralysed within it, all her muscles and bones frozen. Movement and reaction were both impossible.

The figure in white said nothing more directly to her.

The remaining words were in the nature of musing. 'He comes,' it said, not to her. 'Ah yes, he comes again . . .'

Its attention was now somewhere beyond where Louisa cowered on the floor. It moved towards her, not treading, not walking, but at speed, as if it was falling from a great height. White robes fluttered behind it, trailing like a jet stream.

In utter terror she saw it coming at her. She threw herself to one side and a shock of intense cold slammed through her. When she looked again it was gone.

It had passed through her, as it had passed through every memory in her life. Events of crucial significance lay in that tall, bony figure, its eternal quest, its hunt for revenge.

It was gone, but it left no peace in its wake.

Chapter Twelve

Sheepshanks, she thought in panic. Back again, on his mission to bully and torment and destroy. A child, too. It's always a child at risk, but why should it be so? What had children to do with that tall figure in his shabby white, pointing his bony finger with such accusation? What harm could children ever have done to him to prompt such a response?

And yet she knew from her own experience that the cruelty of children was exactly comparable to the cruelty of adults. The only difference was that children rarely enjoyed the power and strength to exercise their cruelty. She had never fallen into the trap of thinking them innocent, unspoiled. They had imagination, and terrible curiosity, and waged their power battles much the same as anyone else. But they were not cynical, that at least could be said. And one of the worst things an adult could do to a child was to destroy his or her hope, leaving only cynicism, the everyday face of despair.

But the cruelty was always there. From the torture of helpless animals, to pretty little girls teasing their contemporaries. Children had been barred from the Garden of Eden too. But what could David ever have done to deserve such punishment? He had never been cruel, he had never tormented anyone . . . And who was at risk now, who had caught the attention of old Sheepshanks?

It was something to do with the school. This thought came without logic, with no reason behind it. But Sheepshanks had first appeared at the school, had exerted his revenge through the children there more than twenty years ago, and she knew, she absolutely knew that it was to do with the school again.

Owen's little Sophy? Or Joss's Leo? And would the revenge be wrecked on the children unto the fourth generation?

Sheepshanks was busy once more because they were all in York, for the first time for more than twenty years. It was aimed at them, at Louisa, Owen, Ben and Joss. It would work through them, as it did last time.

Shakily, she hauled herself to her feet. She found herself looking at the phone. She would have to find out, of course she would. Without hesitation, she rang Owen's number. He'd had time to get home.

He picked up the phone almost immediately. 'Sheepshanks?'

His voice was uneven. A pause then, and Louisa felt like babbling, like shrieking at him. 'In your house? Lou – have you been dreaming? Drinking? Do you want me to come over?'

'No!' She took a deep breath. This was a mistake. He was no use to her. 'Don't waste time coming here. He's gone, not here any more. Go to Joss's, you're nearer than I . . . It's Leo. He's after Leo—'

'How do you know?'

'It's not Sophy. Sheepshanks said, *he comes*, "he" don't you see? And I know this is to do with us, this is because of what happened when we were children.'

There was a pause, a silence at the end of the phone. Believe me, Owen, she silently shrieked. Believe this!

'And you think Leo is in danger? If I accept your thesis – and I'm not for one moment suggesting that I do, why not us? You, or Joss at the least?'

'I don't know. But Joss isn't Jewish, it's not that old thing again.'

Another pause. Then he said, 'Lily is. Didn't you know? It's inherited through the female line.'

She couldn't afford to absorb this now. 'Will you ring Joss or shall I?'

'Forget it, Lou. You're dreaming. It's not true, none of it.'

She slammed the receiver down and then spent a nerve-wracking five minutes trying to find Joss's number. In the end she had to resort to Directory Enquiries.

No one answered. At one in the morning, they were all asleep and no one could hear the phone. She envisaged it at the bottom of the stairs in Joss's tall thin house, ringing over and over. She paced the hall for a moment and then grabbed her coat.

She half ran to the end of the terrace. No traffic, none of the usual queue at the junction. She crossed the yellow grid to Lord Mayor's Walk and suddenly stopped.

Undoubtedly, Lord Mayor's Walk was the quickest way to Joss's house. But something held her, indecisive, hesitating. The danger was elsewhere, it was in the city, inside the walls. It called to her, it was part of its power to drag her in too. This was her danger, her responsibility . . . She turned on her heel and made her way swiftly up Gillygate towards Bootham Bar.

No hesitation now. There were lights on inside some of the shops, but not many. In one doorway a pair of lovers were twined together. She stepped over a patch of vomit outside the Bay Horse and started running again. It was urgent that she get inside the city walls quickly.

The shop signs were swinging wildly about her head. As she turned into Bootham Bar, she felt the world tilt. She was unstable, out of kilter, tumbling as she moved. Walls of stone revolved around her, as if she'd walked into a gigantic swing door. She experienced dizziness and dislocation and a rush of wind from the Minster suddenly gripped her and hurled her back out into the street.

It's always windy round the Minster, she thought crazily, as she scrambled to her feet. But I've never felt it like that before—

There were bars blocking the gate. A portcullis of iron clamped it shut. The two side entrances were filled with repellent blackness, dense and thick as obsidian. There was no way through for Louisa, nothing she could do.

She flung herself against the grid and tried to make out in the darkness, what was happening.

Leo reached the Minster. The biting wind which so often swirled there, to the peril of frail old ladies and girls with full skirts and mothers with pushchairs and men with umbrellas, ruffled through the pages of his notebook and tugged it out of his hand.

He leaped up, reaching for it and found himself confronting a tall figure dressed in white. It was too dark to see much more than the shadows beneath his over-hanging hood.

Was there a hood to Mr Allbright's smock? He couldn't remember. But the thin hands with their bony fingers were entirely familiar.

'Mr Allbright!' he stammered, and then to his right a cat screamed, and he jerked round just in time to see the pregnant tabby leap for cover into the doorway of St Michael's. He forgot all about Mr Allbright. He rushed across the paved forecourt and bent down where the cat cowered. At once it jumped into his arms, a great rumbling purr filling his senses. With one hand he supported her considerable weight, with the other he stroked the top of her head. Her fur was damp, but he could feel her warmth, the pattering of her heart. Murmuring meaningless soothing sounds, he carried her along Deangate, close by the Minster and past St William's College.

He was home in less than ten minutes, making the cat a nice little nest in the sheltered area beneath the fire-escape with sacking. He considered taking her up to his room, but knew it would be chancing his luck. They might even find out about his nocturnal ramblings. He settled the cat and then climbed the stairs and wriggled in through the window. He could barely bother to take his clothes off. In two more minutes he was asleep in bed.

He'd not looked back once.

Louisa wrenched herself away from the bars. Two options: back the way she'd come or on, past the theatre and into Deangate. It would be far quicker to go on . . .

She put to the back of her mind the problem of the revolving gate and the anachronistic portcullis. She ran along under the arches to Duncombe Place.

She was just in time to see a small figure, carrying something heavy, unhurriedly making his way beneath the great walls of the Minster, safely returning home.

She felt suddenly deflated. What had that all been about? What was going on? The sense of panic had disappeared, she knew that the child was all right, that the threat was over, for a time at least. To make sure, she followed Leo, at some distance, to see him safely home and then returned to her mother's house.

She rang Owen, although she didn't know why.

'Louisa? What now?' He sounded faintly irritated.

'Leo was out,' she said. 'Walking the streets, on his own. He was at risk, Owen, wandering the streets, a very little boy . . . And I saw him through Bootham Bar, but I couldn't get through, the portcullis was down—'

'Don't be absurd. How could it be down? Are you sure this happened? Did you fall asleep? Was it a dream?'

'Of course not!' She felt like crying. 'I saw him there, but he's all right. Leo came to no harm. I saw him walking home, carrying a cat . . .'

'You sound dreadful.' There was some kindness in his voice at last, and it nearly defeated her.

'It's okay. I'm all right.'

'Shall I come round?'

'No.' Aware that this sounded worse than ungracious, she tried to soften it. 'No, I'm tired, it's late.'

'Lou, we need to talk. We have to try and work out where you get these ideas from. Let's meet tomorrow.'

He thinks I'm mad, she realized. But this offer to talk was a start, something she could work with. 'Come for lunch,' she said.

'Yes, fine—'

'About one?'

'Yes, see you then.'

He didn't come. She'd made soup and bought olive bread and smelly cheese and put wine in the fridge but he didn't come.

At half past two she gave up and went out. She needed to get money, and then she'd go and see her mother.

Her bank overlooked Betty's tearooms in St Helen's Square. Coming out, checking her statement, she looked up and her eyes rested for a long time on Owen's face through the plate glass windows. He was talking with animation, his face slanted away from her.

Opposite him, carefully manipulating a forkful of cream cake into her exquisitely painted mouth, Lily looked stimulated, happy and amused.

Louisa flushed. Turned on her heel and flounced back towards her house.

Did Joss know? she wondered on the way back from her afternoon visit to the hospital. Her mother had been sleepy and disinclined to talk. It was a relief, in a way. Louisa found Owen's strange behaviour dominating all her thoughts. She had not stayed long.

Now, at the late end of the afternoon, pulling the curtains against the fading light, she found her hands wreathing together. Twining and folding, rubbing, restless, uneasy. What was happening?

It wasn't Sheepshanks. That encounter was locked away somewhere in her unconscious, waiting, she was aware, to trip her up, to pounce, to drag her under.

But not now. Think about the broken lunch date, she told herself, staring into the fire. Think about the soup left cold, the wine unopened in the fridge.

Owen had met Lily, instead of coming to lunch as arranged.

Was it so significant? A moment of carelessness, simple forgetting? What was so odd about two friends meeting for lunch at a famous and very public tearoom?

Why hadn't Owen rung? She sat on the floor of her mother's sitting room, leaning back against the chintz-covered sofa, and knew the answer. He was hiding. He'd been in hiding for years. Owen Rattigan was one of her oldest friends, but what did she know of him? What did she know of him *now*? Virtually nothing. Her only useful knowledge of Owen lay in what had happened when they were children. Since then, they'd met as polite, remotely affectionate strangers. Who was he? All his adult life was a mystery to her. There were the bones of it, of course, the failed marriage, the gifted, pretty little daughter, the successful career . . . (Were his walls still painted white, she thought? Did he still have that etching of St Theophilus over his bed?)

She rather hoped not. It had always seemed a little pretentious (*poseur*, she thought to herself). People had to change, of course they did. They were the result of their experiences, their responses to their experiences. You accumulated guilt and cynicism and regrets as you grew older, as life threw its unfairly weighted bag of troubles at you.

Things rarely got better as you got older. She paused there. Her own life had not been particularly hard, she had been more than successful at her chosen career, she had never been short of money or friends. And yet her work had taken her to Africa, to the Far East, all over the world and she realized that she was privileged beyond the dreams of most. The fact that she had never married ('There's plenty of time,' she had told her mother just the day before), or even lived with anyone for any appreciable length of time, was something she chose not to consider deeply.

Children were not on her programme either. In her work, she'd seen too many children suffering to want that obligation. Owen had done better there. He'd made commitments, that ultimate proof of faith in the future: he'd fathered a child.

Okay, so the marriage had broken up, but it was beyond Louisa how people managed to stay together for any length of time under the best of circumstances. She'd never known her father, for example. He'd disappeared in a cloud of dust to New Zealand as soon as Mavis had revealed the existence of the unborn Louisa. He'd left behind him two hundred pounds (not an inconsiderable sum then), a stack of 78 rpm records of Erroll Garner and a hand-carved scale model of the Cutty Sark. There was no pattern in Louisa's life for a successful partnership. She had literally no idea how they worked.

Owen's broken marriage seemed more comprehensible to her than Joss's stable relationship. For a while, she pondered that strange fact, wondering at herself. A child of the sixties, a teenager in the seventies. A potent combination of confidence and idealism and cynicism, she thought. They were all of them caught in it.

And yet Owen had always appeared hidden, a bit of a puzzle, even when they were children. His father was never there (in the Navy, was it? Louisa couldn't remember). And his mother was a vague, wafty woman whose rather striking beauty (huge sunken eyes that glittered like jet and the kind of figure and posture that made clothes look twice their value), concealed a will of iron. She was also highly neurotic, prone to debilitating headaches and depressions, happy to play devious emotional blackmail games on Owen.

Louisa had realized it even then. Her mother had always discussed people with her, had speculated with her about the backgrounds of the boys. It helped her to deal with them, she explained. It was private between the two of them, and Mavis Jamieson never used her privileged knowledge. She was gentle with Owen, bracing with David, jolly to Kenny, comfortable with Ben.

'Everyone deserves special treatment,' she explained.

When Louisa first met Owen, at the age of eight, he'd been nervy and anxious, writing home with unnecessary frequency, fighting like a fiend with anyone who criticized the French . . . Of course, Owen's mother was French! And Owen had acquired his love for, his ease with languages, from having been bilingual since birth. (And also his sense of separation, she wondered? Of not quite belonging here, in this most English, most provincial of schools?) Was that why he had hit it off so immediately, so irrevocably, with David?

Owen had been strangely guarded. Not quite at ease, not at home. His clever verbal games were a disguise and a barrier. She had only seen the guard down twice. She never wanted to see it again.

It was Owen's eleventh birthday party. Not everyone was there: his birthday fell over the Autumn half-term, and many of our friends were no longer in York.

About a third of Anthony's pupils came from abroad. Another third were from other parts of the UK. That left a third from York and its surrounds: ten boys from Transition, and me.

This was long before David arrived. A couple of mothers had offered to share the transportation out to Leppington. We gathered at the school gates one afternoon in late October, shivering slightly at the wind whipping at our coats. There were ten of us to be driven to Owen's home, a Georgian rectory in the rolling countryside between Stamford Bridge and Malton. It seemed a long way and when we got there we were dismayed to find that there were balloons on the gate, bright and garish against the heavy laurels that lined the drive. We didn't look at Owen. This was all a little embarrassing.

And when his mother met us at the front door, flinging it theatrically wide, we hung back in a huddle, ill at ease. She was dressed all in grey, in layers of fine fabric that shifted as she moved, draped round her wrists, falling in handkerchief points round her knees. A rope of pearls hung round her neck.

'My dears!' She drifted towards us, hands outstretched. Beside me, Ben took a step back. Joss shot a furious glance at him.

'Hello, Mrs Rattigan,' he said bravely, coming forward to take one of the thin hands.

'Joss, my old friend!' To my certain knowledge, she'd met him only once before, at Speechday. Her accent struck me as ludicrously pronounced. She honoured the rest of us with a beaming smile. We were not introduced. 'And all our other friends! Come in, come in, there's fun and games and cakes and – well, you'll all see, won't you? This way.'

We trooped after her into the Rectory and stood there, gaping.

There was a table stretched the length of the hall. It was laid as if for a banquet. Cut glass, silver cutlery, an enormous epergne cascading with fruit. Candles blazed. A fire burned in the huge fireplace beneath a great, gilded mirror. There were decanters along the sideboard, decanters filled with ruby wine (Ribena, we discovered later, with mixed relief and disappointment), with lemonade and a frothy, yellowy substance known as Snowball, which we all adored. Against the odds, it worked. There was no seating plan: we sat where we liked, and I found myself between Joss and Kenny. After we had demolished most of the food and drink, Mrs Rattigan handed out envelopes containing the names of characters for an elaborate murder game. This was a great success. We pounded through the Rectory, from the attics to the basement, searching for the body and then the clues and then the murderer. Owen's dark eyes were gleaming with satisfaction as we roamed the house, with its art deco figurines, its elaborate Tiffany lamps and Morris fabrics. Rather hideous, we thought it. Current fashions included psychedelic colours and plastic. This was all romantic, rather soppy, we thought.

It didn't take us long to discover the body. It was languishing in the bath. A fully dressed tailor's dummy with a cabbage for a head and wearing a long white dressing gown lay with a dagger jutting from its breast and a sign round the neck.

My name is Anthony, it said. Avenge my death!

With delighted shouts, we called to each other. Soon we were all crammed into the bathroom, looking for clues.

They were not hard to find. A pair of secateurs lay in the wash-basin, a trowel on the laundry basket. A small trail of seeds led across the floor and out on to the landing and downstairs . . . The conservatory! Where else?

'But what's the motive?' Joss said to me as we trooped down-stairs. 'Why should anyone kill Anthony, the noble namesake of our school?'

I shrugged. 'Perhaps cabbage heads are aliens from outer space. Perhaps he was sent to take over the world—'

'To see if he had any allies here—?'

'Cabbages of the world unite! You have nothing to lose but your caterpillars!' We clattered down the remaining stairs, giggling foolishly. It was then that I saw an alternative trail of seeds leading back up the stairs, across the landing and into one of the bedrooms.

'Come on,' I said, tugging at Joss's hand. 'Let's not follow the crowd.'

Together we pushed open the door to the room. White walls, polished floorboards with a small dark blue rug by the bed. And

111

over the bed, that sketch of a man in a funny hat standing on a dolphin.

On the bedside table was one of Owen's favourite books, Walter Miller's A Canticle for Leibowitz. He was always going on about it, and I really meant to read it one day . . . 'This is Owen's room,' I breathed, feeling suddenly guilty. 'Perhaps we should go—'

I stopped. Joss was peering at the bookcase opposite the bed. 'No,' he said. 'Look at this. This is a clue if ever I saw one.' The book he held fell open at a page where cabbages illustrated the text, savoys, spring, Dutch, all the brassicas, and pressed between the leaves of the book was a letter, written from 'Anthony' to Sir Richard Rosetree, the character allotted to Philip Stroud.

The letter explained how Anthony had discovered the secret of the missing Cherryham diamonds. Buried beneath the compost in the tubs of bulbs outside the kitchen, the diamonds lay waiting discovery.

We caught Philip dashing through the kitchen. Everyone else was still searching the conservatory.

Mrs Rattigan sat at the kitchen table, smoking, and watched with approval as we tackled Philip and heard his confession.

At the end of the party, after several games of sardines, we prepared to go back to York. Joss had got some plan on: he asked if he could borrow the telephone, and after a brief conversation with his mother, he and Owen went to find Mrs Rattigan.

'Can I go home with Joss?' Owen asked. 'To stay the night?'

'It's your birthday, Owen!' Her enormous eyes were wide. 'It's a special day for me, too, special to both of us . . . And you spend so much time away—'

'I'm sorry, I'm sorry!' I'd never heard Owen sound like that before. He was ashen.

She went on as if he hadn't spoken. 'And I thought you'd enjoyed the party, all the little treats, everything I'd done, I thought you might be grateful—'

'I am, of course I am, it's been marvellous, Mummy, I didn't think—' He burst into tears, buried his head in her dress, flung his arms round her waist.

Joss and I stood there in shocked silence.

We never referred to it again.

Owen didn't go through with being Confirmed. I ran into him one day on my way to meet Joss. He was standing outside the head's study, his back to the wall beside the door. He was actually shaking: I saw his hands tremble as he pushed back the wild black hair from his face. It was always falling forward, no matter what he did.

'Are you all right?' A stupid question, because he clearly wasn't.

'I don't want to go in.'

'Can't blame you there. Whoever wants to see old Redmond?' I kept my voice down. There was a delicious thrill in saying this right outside the beast's den.

He shook his head. 'Confirmation class,' he said. 'And I can't – I'm not going through with it, Lou. I can't.' He sounded desperate.

'Come on.' I pulled him across the hall to the history room which was invariably deserted at this time of the day.

He sat on one of the desks, his feet on a chair, and dropped his head between his hands. I waited.

'It's all lies and I can't take any more of it. I can't fake it—'

'I always wondered how you could swallow it.'

'Imbibed with mother's milk. But, but. I have a brain, why shouldn't I use it?'

'Faith isn't to do with intellect,' I said, mimicking the Canon's unmistakably wheezy voice.

He almost smiled. 'But what about when faith is utterly opposed to intellect? What if it makes me feel as if I'm wilfully embracing idiocy?'

'You don't have to do it. I wouldn't dream of it.'

'You're lucky.' Nothing more. But then I realized what the distress was about, why Owen found it so difficult to drop out of the Confirmation class. 'What will your mother say?' I said and he groaned. And then winced, and I saw the colour drain from his face. But he said nothing, and I felt a sudden urge to take hold of his hand.

He reached out for me. His hand, with its fine, long, sensitive fingers rested on my forearm and it felt strange, warm and strong.

But then he said, 'Christ, my head . . . I feel awful.' He paused. 'Funny how the tongue still believes it, even if the mind doesn't . . . I think I'm going to be sick, Lou—'

'Something you ate?' Facetious, that was what I was. Fatally facetious. I caught it from Joss, and it wasn't at all appropriate here. Owen didn't seem to notice. So I went with him to the san, where my mother provided a bowl, and the moment passed.

That night, I remembered his touch on my arm, and knew I wanted it again. I wanted to be Owen's friend, his best friend. I wanted to be trusted by him, I wanted to hear his secrets, I wanted to be on his side, his intimate.

But we were young, and people change.

Chapter Thirteen

Leo stared in disbelief. His pencil case was missing. He was sure he'd put it in that morning, in fact, he knew he had. Again he rifled through the tightly wedged exercise books and textbooks. He pulled out his gym shoes and shorts and then with a sudden fury, emptied the whole bag out on the locker-room floor. It wasn't there.

It was only the second period and he hadn't used the pencil case at all during the first, which was singing. A rehearsal for the half-term concert. Like the rest of the choir, he'd left his bag hanging on his peg here in the locker room and now his tin pencil case, coloured to look like a Crunchie bar, was gone.

He pushed the mess of books aside and bent down to look under the racks of shoes. Balls of dust and old sweet and cigarette wrappers met his gaze, but no reassuring glint of orange and gold.

This was not the first time he had lost something. Two days ago his cap had disappeared, only to be discovered lying in a stinking puddle of urine in the latrines.

He'd fished it out with his ruler and washed it under the tap, holding it under the running water for ages. What else could he do?

He'd worn it home, as the rules demanded, and never had those two hundred yards seemed further. It was cold and wet on his head and he wondered if the dye was running down the back of his neck. He was in dread of meeting someone who might notice the water running or worse, the vile stink which Leo knew hung all around him.

He hadn't told his mother. He'd washed the cap again in

the bathroom, using shampoo, and then rung it out before leaving it in the airing cupboard to dry. It still smelled, but now of coconut oil.

He couldn't bear it if they'd done the same to his pencil case. It would rust, he thought. And his birthday fountain pen, clogged with urine, would be ruined.

There was no one he could tell. The other boys of his age tended to snigger whenever he approached them and the girls always kept to themselves. He'd spoken once or twice to Sophy Rattigan, but she wasn't in his class and they didn't often meet.

Mr Allbright was his only real ally, although Mr Bowen was a possibility. But you couldn't go crawling to teachers.

He cadged a Biro off Stephen, one of the youngest boys, and found a pencil under a desk in the Geography room. The spine of his maths book was marked off in inches and centimetres, but the fabric of the binding was too soft to be much use. He hacked his way through the morning until lunchtime.

There was a gathering in one corner of the playground. Samuel Pyper was in a huddle with Emma Morrell and some of the older children. They looked up as Leo entered the playground and he knew that they had been talking about him.

'Phew!' said Sam melodramatically. 'What's that stink? Smells like someone's wet himself, someone should be wearing nappies—' He caught sight of Leo with elaborate surprise. 'And who's this? Little Leokins, teacher's pet, baby boo-boos.'

'Wet your pants Leo? You don't half stink!' Emma was never subtle.

Leo flushed. Could they still smell it on his hair, even now? Or was his pencil case somewhere about? Why else should they bring this up now?

'Look at our blushing baby. Going to do a poo-poo now,

116

are you? Shall I help?' Samuel came right up close to him and yanked at Leo's trousers.

The belt buckle gave way. Leo pushed at Samuel, and started to run.

But his trousers were sliding down, and he tried to haul them up and it slowed him so much that Samuel was on top of him before he knew it. He fell on to the gravel yard, rolling over and over, while Samuel's hot breath reeked in his face.

'Jewboy, Jewboy, Jewboy,' he said. 'Let's see it, let's see where they cut it off—'

'Stop it! Stop it at once!' It was Mr Allbright who hauled Samuel off Leo. 'What on earth do you think you're doing?'

Leo said nothing. He was struggling with the buckle to his belt, but his fingers were shaking so much that he could hardly manage it.

Samuel said nothing. He stared sullenly at his shoes.

'Let me,' said Allbright, crouching down by Leo, his hands searching for the button. 'Leo, you've lost the button, you'd better go to Matron and get a safety pin,' he said, 'before you disgrace us all with a display of your nether regions. Go on, scram!'

Leo nodded wordlessly.

He was puzzled by the way Mr Allbright's hand had moved over the seam in his trousers. He didn't like the way Mr Allbright was talking to Samuel Pyper either, because it looked like they were best friends, and he thought Mr Allbright was *his* friend, his particular ally.

He didn't hear what they were saying and missed the perfunctory scolding Allbright gave Sam.

He was also oblivious of Allbright's eyes following him across the playground. He wouldn't have understood, even if he had seen the expression in those dark eyes. He still thought that adults could be trusted.

*   *   *

Joss went straight from work to meet Ben at the Royal Oak. They found a table in the front bar and sat down with their beer. In less than a minute, Ben's glass was empty and he was standing at the bar again for a second round.

Joss was faintly surprised. 'Thirsty work, is it? Teaching music?'

Ben raised his eyebrows. 'You don't know the half of it. It's been a bloody hell of a day. Bloody Associated Board exams. Examiners needing nursing like babies, coffee and lunchbreaks and tea-and-biscuits all the time, children panicking, broken strings, cracked reeds, parents twitching, almost wetting themselves with anxiety, forgotten music, sprained wrists, slow watches ... you name it, it's high stress all the way.' He watched carefully as Joss brought over the next round. 'Over the last two weeks I've arranged six extra lessons for Geoffrey Pyper, who's hoping ... But it's still touch and go and God help us all if he fails—'

'What do you mean?'

'Pyper major is due to do Grade Five theory tomorrow. He has to pass before he can take Grade Six Clarinet, on which the fortunes of the Pyper family depend.'

'Sorry, Ben. Not with this at all. What fortunes?'

'With Grade Six, young Geoffrey is likely to get a good scholarship. A certain proportion off the school fees. Forget culture, Joss, we're talking serious money here. Thousands of pounds.'

Joss stared. 'I'd never realized. At least we're spared that with Leo, he's got no particular skills in that area—'

'Dom Allbright tells me your Leo's a whizzo with the old lead pencil. And paints. Says he's got an eye, and the patience to see it through. You might make something of that.'

'A scholarship, do you mean?'

'I'm not sure of the details. Allbright would be your man for that. But some schools – Stowe might be one – recognize

Art as a marketable commodity. Fifty per cent off the fees would come in handy, wouldn't it?' His grey eyes considered Joss.

'I suppose so . . .' Joss frowned. Leo seemed much too young to be thinking in terms of future schools.

'It's worth investigating, you know.' Ben leaned forward across the small table, gazing at Joss with intensity. 'Shall I find out for you?'

'Thanks.' Joss sat back. 'So, is this your local?'

'It's convenient. You know I've a place out on the Wolds? Thixendale?'

'I thought you lived on the premises?'

'In term time. The old house-master's flat in A Block. We can go there later, if you like.'

There was an edge to his words, investing the invitation with more than a little pressure. He's lonely, thought Joss. He'd like someone to talk to. 'I'll ring Lily,' he said.

'No, don't. I shouldn't take the time.' Ben visibly pulled himself together. 'I've got a whole pile of marking to get through.'

'For music?' Joss was surprised.

'Oh yes. We're engendering a race of budding composers, didn't you know? Using Sparky's Magic Piano, otherwise known as the Atari SX7.'

'Well, I'd never thought before of Anthony's being at the thrusting end of educational technology.'

'It's not. A job lot from one of the parents, in part payment for fees. Daddy is a dealer who overstretched himself: but little Jamie's superior education is safe for a year or so yet.'

'It's a bit hand-to-mouth, all this,' said Joss. He was rather appalled by Ben's financial obsessions.

'You have it in one.' Ben sighed. 'Not doing too well, Anthony's. Shouldn't be telling you of course, punter that you are—'

'Punter?'

'Parent. Dictionary definition: someone prepared to part with money for something other people get for free.'

'Good Lord, Ben, do you always talk like this?'

· 'Only to confidants. Publicly loyal and privately seditious, that's me. I shouldn't mock. Why, one of our mothers even works on the tills at Tesco's so that little lambkin can get his nose in the trough. There's heroism for you, self-sacrifice and devotion. Although school rolls are falling . . . Don't tell anyone. It's the feel-bad factor.'

'Is your job secure?' Joss watched Ben's hands. Always eloquent, always a reliable indication of emotion.

The elegant fingers shivered. And then Ben was patting his pockets and finding a box of More's and lighting one with fingers which still expressed doubt and anxiety and paranoia.

(Even paranoics have enemies, thought Joss.)

'Perfectly safe. I genuinely and honestly believe so. I've been there for donkey's years, it's the newer staff who will cop it. Them and the part-timers.'

'Sure.' Joss drained his pint. 'Do you want another?'

'A Scotch, if you please. Large as they come.'

Joss stayed on halves and Ben drank large Scotches and pretty soon, his fingers had stopped shaking. He leaned back against the wooden bench and visibly relaxed.

'So, how's family life progressing? Settled in all right?'

'Past Present is a bit fraught. Funding difficulties. You'll understand that . . . Lots of bright ideas and no resources.'

'So what's new? Hard times all round, eh?' A flicker of amusement behind the wire-rimmed glasses. 'Didn't think it would come to this, did we? I was going to become a professional pianist or possibly a composer of genius. And you – what was your ambition? Tutankhamun's tomb?'

'Carnarvon got there first. But yes. The secrets of the universe, caught in strange runes on a tablet of stone, all a bit 2001-ish. I knew it was daft, even then.'

'Has it been good, Joss? Has it worked out?' The twinkle had vanished. Ben was entirely serious.

'Leo's at the centre,' Joss said plainly. 'Leo and Lily. They're what matters, I don't think, really that there's anything else. The career is icing on the cake.'

'What about professional pride? The admiring glances of beautiful women?' Back to teasing again.

'It gets boring after a while.' Joss grinned at him. 'What about you, Ben? No inamorati?'

'You behold before you the dedicated pedagog, private life entirely subsumed by the demands and niceties of educating the next generation not to be the crass yobs we were—'

'Not you, Ben. You were never crass, or even remotely yobbish.'

'Kind of you. Wrong, too. Although perhaps "yob" doesn't do it justice.'

'What do you mean?'

'Worse than yobs.' The noise in the pub had receded. There was a brief pause and when Ben looked up at Joss again, there were tears in his eyes. 'Weren't we?'

Joss rang Lily and went back to Ben's rooms and there was whisky there too, so Joss joined in. They spoke of everything except their shared past. Politics, sport, food, holidays. At one stage, Ben threw together sardines and red peppers and pinenuts and spaghetti, a strangely successful combination, and they wolfed it down with a bottle of Rioja. Then they hit the brandy. At two in the morning, Ben started playing late Liszt on the piano, those creepy gondolier songs, and Joss took his leave.

His head was swimming. He didn't want to go home right away, although it was so late. He needed to clear his thoughts, get things straight once more. And work out what this bitter, vulnerable man had to do with the loving and gentle boy he'd once known. He found himself wandering down St Mary's towards the river.

It wasn't raining. And he'd be out of the infernal wind that blasted round the Minster on the riverside. There were a few boats moored, but no lights were on. He walked along a little way towards Lendal Bridge, shivering slightly. His head was beginning to ache. There was more than a touch of frost in the air, he reckoned. Wouldn't do the daffodils any good, and then the tourists would complain and go somewhere else and then Past Present's business would decline and Martin Shaw would gleefully point out that he'd always said so, and then where would *he* be? Bitter and cynical like Ben?

He sat on one of the benches and thought about Ben. He was depressed by what had become of his old friend. It wasn't just the loneliness: Ben was desperate. He had sounded quite confident about his job, he'd spoken with genuine enthusiasm about the whole subject of schools and education and scholarships. It was the past, still. Guilt about David. And then Joss realized something that had always been lurking at the back of his mind. David had been Owen's special friend, but it had been Ben who had loved him. After Kenny, David had come to mean everything to Ben.

Joss had loved David too. Lightly, not possessively. It was different with Ben. He remembered Ben's house at Appleton Roeback, a village lying close to the confluence of two rivers between York and Tadcaster.

They'd gone badger-watching one night with Ben's parents' blessing. Midsummer, a clear night, but not warm. They were out in the park of Nun Appleton, a small and elegant manor house. Huge, ancient trees stood on the short-cropped grass. There were thistles and brambles and treacherous cow-pats; the dew was already beginning to fall. Owen had complained about the dark and discomfort of their hide and had eventually fallen asleep, his head resting on one arm. But Joss, Ben and David had stayed watchfully awake and just as the first light of the day tinged the horizon, David reached out and touched Ben's hand. Joss noticed it, but then he saw the badgers too.

They were coming from the spinney, creeping through the rough grasses, scenting the air with sensitive noses. Ben had insisted that their hide should be downwind from the sett and it seemed to have paid off. There were four of them, a mother and three cubs. The thick, heavy body of the mother trotted purposefully towards the sett, but her offspring darted and jumped at each other, tumbling, playfully nipping each other, making tiny growling noises. The mother suddenly tensed.

Joss swore afterwards that he, Ben and David had neither moved nor made a sound. Perhaps the wind had changed, perhaps it had carried to the creatures the rank smell of boy at night. Whatever it was, the cubs and their mother vanished into the sett in a couple of seconds.

The clearing was calm again, empty and quiet under the early morning haziness. Joss's head drooped. David leaned against Ben. They fell asleep together, and when they awoke Joss saw that they were both still holding hands.

There was no danger of sleep now. Joss's fingers were numb and his breath rasped in his throat. He should be getting back, Lily would be worrying.

Ahead of him were the steps up to the bridge, to his left the cobbled slope which led up to the gates to the Museum Gardens. A group of youths had gathered there. They were bent over something, murmuring to each other. As Joss approached, one of them swung round to face him. He was holding a broken bottle in his hand and the glass glinted with red liquid. His mouth was drawn back in a rictus of savagery.

Joss took an involuntary step back and his foot slipped on the damp stones.

He fell backwards on to the river walk, his ankle catching and twisting and with a nauseous flare of agony, he knew it had broken. For a moment or two, no longer, he was so gripped by the overwhelming pain that his mind retreated. When he looked back at the slope, the youths had gone.

On the steps in front of him, its limbs splayed out as if crucified, lay a cat. Its throat had been cut.

Cursing, Joss pulled himself upright against the river railings.

His foot was a ball of indescribable fire. Knowing the futility of it, leaning all his weight on the rail, he tentatively touched the sole of his shoe against the step and the wild flaring knives made him gasp.

He could not move. It was the darkest part of the night now: there was no traffic, no pedestrians. Even the late-night dog walkers were tucked up at home. He sagged against the rail and gently, carefully, lowered himself back to the steps. In front of him the York shield with its five lions failed to hide the cavernous iron struts of the bridge. Shadows multiplied around him. It was going to be a long night.

He must have fallen asleep: it must have been that, although later he thought he'd been much too uncomfortable for sleep. He saw a scattering of paper fall through the air, white fragments drifting down like snow from the bridge above him. He heard the tread of people passing by. He raised himself painfully on one elbow, ready to shout out.

The words froze in his mouth. There were people crossing the river, making for the Minster. They were processing silently over the water, hooded and robed like monks. For a moment, Joss wondered if this was a part of one of the usual York mediaeval pageants, and then, in the light of the street lamp, he recognized two faces from the mob who'd killed the cat. But worse than that, worse than anything he'd ever imagined in his entire adult life, he saw that the procession was headed by a figure dressed in white.

The hood was pulled forward so that the eyes were mercifully hidden. But there was no disguising the jutting chin and bony nose. A whimper; Joss could not prevent it. And although the sound was puny and insignificant, the hooded figure turned its head and looked down over the bridge railing to where Joss lay sprawled on the steps.

It was bizarre and grotesque, what happened next. The hooded figure stretched out an arm towards him, two fingers pointing directly at his eyes. Then it lifted up one knee, curling its elongated body down, the other knee bent so that everything, all power, all force, was focused through that extended hand to Joss.

It said nothing. There was no need. A concentrated beam of malevolence struck his heart with hammer blows. Despair set its claws in his mind, dragged his spirits into a black hole. He was cursed: he knew it without doubt. Everything in that figure's hunched, horrible stance emphasized it. There would be no more peace, no more love, no more happiness. He was almost fainting, almost paralysed by dread. But somehow he managed to say one thing, one tiny word. '*Why?*'

Then it spoke, and its voice stripped the world of hope. 'You know,' it said, uncurling until it stood, tall and lanky, over the continuing procession. 'You know it all.' It laughed once, and moved on.

He saw the procession continue, streams of people. The silent, hooded figures were followed by a jostling, shouting mob. They were furious and dangerous, hundreds of them passing over the river, hundreds, a never-ending stream, and every now and then one of them would look down at him and laugh. Sometimes they spat, sometimes they threw stones at him. And then they were gone and Joss was left alone with the discarded body of a cat.

Somewhere near dawn, Joss stirred from an uneasy doze to find a policeman shining a torch directly into his face.

'I fell,' he said. 'My ankle's broken, I think. Can you give me a hand?'

In less than an hour he was sitting in casualty, waiting to be X-rayed, holding Lily's hand and doing his best to appear calm. But all the time, he felt the black creature in his soul flexing its muscles, pushing outwards, spreading through every fibre.

No peace, no hope, no love, no safety.

For ever more.

Chapter Fourteen

The examination, the X-rays, the plaster setting all took ages. It was nearly lunchtime before Joss and Lily were free to leave the hospital, and both of them were exhausted.

By the lift shafts, they ran into Louisa.

'Joss, good heavens, whatever's happened?' She looked both shocked and concerned.

'Slipped on some slimy steps down by the river,' he said shortly. Louisa was almost the last person he wanted to see right then. But the down lift arrived and of course they all entered it and there was no avoiding her.

'Have you been visiting your mother?' Lily asked. 'How is she today?'

'Not well.' Louisa spoke quietly. 'She keeps talking about transferring to a convalescent home, but the doctors say she's not up to it. There's something worrying her, something nagging. She's not been sleeping and won't tell me what it is.'

'How very difficult,' said Lily sympathetically.

'Have you any idea what's worrying her?' said Joss reluctantly. It was becoming horribly familiar, this expression of anxiety and incomprehension on the faces of people he knew. Even Leo was beginning to look tired and strained. Ben, Louisa, himself and Leo.

Louisa had not answered him.

'Have you seen much of Owen lately?' he found himself asking her as they negotiated the glass corridor towards the exit.

She looked guarded. 'Not much.'

'I had lunch with him yesterday,' contributed Lily.

Joss stopped abruptly and stared at her. 'Why didn't you tell me?' he asked, his voice unusually harsh.

She coloured, but her words were unstressed. 'You didn't come home last night, if you remember. When was I supposed to tell you?'

'Sorry.' Joss shook his head. 'Not thinking straight . . .' But still his eyes considered her, his elegant and beautiful wife, her cheeks faintly flushed. He suddenly realized that he'd seen very little of her since the move to York two months ago. Even before that, they'd been so busy house-hunting and packing up, that it seemed ages since they'd been out to dinner or spent an evening at the theatre. He was so tired after a day at Past Present and by the time Leo was in bed, felt capable only of watching the box for a bit, dozing away. And Lily was often out, at orchestral rehearsals and concerts.

He had to be glad. She'd quickly made use of the school's networks and joined both an orchestra and choir. It was one of the myriad things he loved about her, that she was so friendly, so confident and good at making friends. She had such relish for life.

They'd reached the automatic doors by this time. 'Look, you wait here while I go and get the car,' said Lily. She walked swiftly towards the car park, leaving Joss with Louisa.

'It'll be a nuisance, won't it?' She gestured to his ankle.

'Hmm?' His eyes still followed his wife's progress. 'Oh, the ankle. Yes, a damn nuisance. We live in a house of stairs too.' He wasn't really paying attention. His mind was full of speculation about his wife.

'Joss, is Leo doing all right at Anthony's?'

'Fine, fine—'

'It would terrify me, you know. Having children.'

He glanced at her curiously. 'Is that why you didn't?'

She frowned. 'Years ago, when CND started up again – late

seventies, I think it was, a friend of mine told me that she had fantasies about killing her children—'

'Before they died agonizingly from radiation, is that it?'

She nodded. 'It struck me as so terrible, so unmitigatedly awful, to find oneself thinking of that, of killing the person you love best . . .' She paused, and then shrugged. 'Of course, I never met the right man, so it didn't arise. You've been lucky.'

'Mmm.' But he wasn't really thinking of Lily, he was remembering dreadful, similar fantasies of his own, when Leo was a baby. Anything to save him pain, to leave him without a protector and an agonizing death. He'd have done anything, anything at all.

Lily drove up. With an effort Joss jolted himself back to the present.

'Can we give you a lift?' he asked Louisa.

She looked as if she might be about to say something, but then she shook her head. 'I need to go to the post office. Hope the ankle mends soon.'

He smiled vaguely at her, and then had an uncomfortable minute or two trying to fit himself and crutches into the car. They'd driven off before he looked back. Louisa was already walking away.

He turned to Lily. 'How come you had lunch with Owen?'

'It wasn't arranged. We ran into each other in Banks and got talking.' She shrugged, keeping her eyes on the road. 'That was all.'

'How do you get on?' He hoped he didn't sound jealous, he hoped it wasn't that.

'Well,' she said. 'He can be amusing, can't he? And he's intelligent, too. Quite a wide-ranging mind.'

Joss felt depressed. 'He was rather charismatic at school. He dominated us all.'

'We talked about Mozart. And Mahler and minimalism.'

'Did you indeed? Owen's come on. He used to hate music.'

'Perhaps it was Marie's influence.'

'Perhaps.' Joss shifted uncomfortably. The codeine he'd been given earlier was already wearing off.

She was lying to him. He knew he should tackle it then and there, work out what was really going on, but he was simply too tired. Too exhausted and depressed and frightened. He couldn't face adding to it.

Louisa worriedly watched the car drive away. Joss's appearance had shocked her. His face was haggard, taut with anxiety and fear. As well it might be, she thought. His ankle broken again, his wife making impromptu dates with Owen, his son at that bloody awful school.

She would have to tell him. Warn him about Sheepshanks. Yet as soon as she made that decision, the impossibility of it loomed. Owen hadn't believed her, why should Joss? She would have to try, she thought. Risk their mockery and disbelief. A child's life was at stake, just as it had been twenty years ago.

She'd give Joss a day or two to get over the trauma of his broken ankle. Then she would tell him everything she knew.

Ben Bowen gave in the exam papers with a sigh of relief. No one had seen him do it, he'd swear, no one had commented. It had worked like a dream.

The theory papers had arrived two days before the examination, as usual. Ben took the sealed envelope from his pigeon-hole with hands that shook only slightly. He'd planned this already. He took the envelope up to his flat and turned on the kettle. Carefully, slowly, he waited until the glue had dissolved and then slid the papers out on to his desk. He took up one of them, read it through, and then quickly and without

130

hesitation filled in every one of the answers. The only space left blank was that of the name.

Then he placed it at the bottom of the pile and put the entire stack of papers back in the envelope. A small dappling of glue sealed it once more.

The glue didn't matter. No adult would watch him unsealing the envelope. The only chance of failure lay in the unpredictability of Geoffrey Pyper. Would he raise the alarm, would he be too slow-witted to realize what Ben was risking for him?

He considered Geoffrey Pyper. Tall for his age, fair-haired like his father, he was reserved to the point of self-obsession. He never looked anyone in the eye, never made friends, kept himself very much to himself. Once, Ben had caught him going through the pockets of coats hanging in the basement.

'Lost something?' he enquired.

'No. Samuel wanted me to get his penknife—'

'That is not Samuel's blazer.'

The boy had stared at the name tape. He let it drop on the floor and a shudder ran through his body, almost as if he was on the verge of making a run for it.

'Pick it up at once.' Ben kept his voice deliberately cool. Geoffrey was unpredictable in the extreme. But this time he was going to play ball. He picked up the blazer and replaced it on the peg. Then he pushed past Ben, jostling him in the doorway, his shoulders hunched, his head averted. Ben had said nothing. He felt sorry for the boy, although he could not like him.

He felt sorry for him because Kenneth Pyper cared only for Geoffrey's younger brother, Samuel. It was clear to everyone who had seen the family together: Pyper's eyes glanced over Geoffrey and lingered on Samuel. His hand rested on Sam's shoulder, his eyes searched him out whenever they were separated. He never attended parents' evenings for Geoffrey, but always came to Sam's.

But Geoffrey was the golden goose. It was Geoffrey who had inherited his father's talent for music. He was going to have to pass Grade 5 Theory. He was probably up to Grade 7 standard on the clarinet, but would not be allowed to take even Grade 6 until he had Grade 5 Theory securely under his belt. It shouldn't have been impossible: Geoffrey was musically gifted and highly motivated. Ben had had several stressful interviews with the Pypers and was fully aware of the pressures on Geoffrey. They insisted he practise at school for an hour a day: in the holidays, they claimed that he practised two hours daily.

The pressure came from both Pypers. Janice was an ambitious, dedicated social climber, and saw clouds of potential glory trailing her talented elder son.

Kenneth was not given to investigating his reasons. The memory of his early love of music was forgotten and he obviously thought only in terms of pounds and pence now. The keen sportsman had grown fat and indolent over the years. His shockingly white hair was greying, swept casually and artfully to one side over his smooth, bronzed face. He wore couturier suits and Italian shoes. His wife was sour-faced, fashionably thin. She painted her long nails sugary-pink and her hair was streaked blonde. She too was expensively dressed and her fingers sparkled with diamonds.

Ben was wiser. He knew exactly why they were so keen to push Geoffrey. He understood the difference that a few thousand off the fees could make to them. The punters, the fee-paying parents, had brought that one home forcibly all his adult life and he knew that the Pypers' contract laundry business was in questionable shape. But he also remembered the look on Kenny's face when he heard the Bach *Chaconne* for solo violin for the first time, and wondered what that denial had done to him. What was he trying to relive in his son's life?

As the examination approached, the pressure from the Pypers worsened. And strangely, for all his undoubted musical talent, Geoffrey could not do theory.

It was inexplicable. The conventional wisdom held that if you could do maths, you could do theory, and Geoffrey was in the top division for maths. Ben pointed out to him again and again the mathematical relationship between sounds, the subdivisions for rhythm, the rules and regulations, the sense of proportion which lay at the centre of music theory.

Geoffrey was unable to make sense of any of it. His mind slid off the problems. Over and again Ben caught him staring blankly out of the window, dreaming, while he made his careful explanations. Geoffrey would not fasten his mind to it. Occasionally he turned in a good homework, and Ben's hopes rose. But he suspected that Johnny Crawford had probably been involved and the result was not Geoffrey's sole effort.

He gave the boy extra lessons, cramming sessions which drove his patience to breaking point. The boy was wilfully obtuse. Gradually Ben began to suspect that this was a test of power. Geoffrey had decided not to work: it was up to Ben and his parents to do all they could to make him. So far, Geoffrey was winning.

And the Pypers blamed Ben. They'd come into the school a week before the exam and had taken Ben aside.

Janice Pyper had said little, although her sharp little eyes darted everywhere in his room, scanning, noting, silently criticizing his pictures, his books, the clothes he wore, his life. Kenneth Pyper had done most of the talking.

It wasn't subtle. 'I understand you have failed to inspire Geoffrey with any enthusiasm for musical theory. Tell me truthfully: is he going to pass the damn thing?'

Ben shook his head. 'There are two alternatives, Kenneth. He could be deliberately setting his will against us—'

'Not Geoffrey.' There was no arguing with this degree of certainty.

'Or,' continued Ben, 'it may be a form of dyslexia.'

'Dyslexia? Middle class excuses for their brats' innate stupidity? Bowen, you're out of your mind.'

'It's a recognized medical condition and surprisingly common.' All the time, Janice Pyper's eyes flitted over the room, seemingly paying no attention at all to this discussion of her son's abilities.

'Listen to me, Ben Bowen. You and I have known each other for a long time. A very long time indeed. And you can believe me when I tell you that my son is *not* handicapped in any way. He's neither dyslexic, nor stupid, nor trying to "set his will against us". We're talking here about *your* failure—' his thick index finger jabbed the air, '—your failure as a teacher. And let me also inform you, Bowen, that there are staff cuts on the way here at Anthony's. Rolls have been falling for some time, and it's because our results are not quite good enough. Not quite so many parents are willing to honour us with the education of their brilliant offspring. Not so many pupils means not so much money. It's simple enough. Not so much to spread around, employing expensive staff who cannot get their charges through even the most elementary of examinations—'

'Grade 5 Theory is extremely difficult. There's nothing elementary about it at all—'

Pyper's fist crashed down on the desk. 'I know what Grade 5 Theory is about. And don't you dare argue with me!'

'And anyway, cutting staff is a false economy. How are you going to attract more pupils if the staff/pupil ratio worsens?' Ben wondered at himself. And then it came to him that he was fighting for his livelihood here. Kenneth Pyper was a powerful force on the Board of Governors.

'Ratios won't change,' said Pyper, more softly. 'We'll take

on bright, eager little college leavers who can fill the post at half your salary, old thing.' The cold fishy eyes looked almost amused. And then Pyper's expression altered once more. 'He has to pass, Bowen. See to it.'

They'd left Ben alone then. He stared blankly at the shut door and without even thinking his left hand moved to the lower drawer of his desk.

Just one, he thought as he drew out the bottle. Just one before the bell goes, before I start trying to din some sense into Geoffrey Pyper's devious little skull. It was only later that night that the plan to fill in Geoffrey Pyper's paper came to him.

He'd carried it through and posted the papers back.

He didn't know that one of the other children had seen the answers already filled in. Puzzled, and entirely without malice, the boy had asked his mother about it. She telephoned a friend.

By the end of the week, Mark Morrell had called Ben Bowen to his office.

Chapter Fifteen

Owen Rattigan slammed his door. His head was aching again and it was late, almost too late to do everything he'd planned that evening. It was his own fault. The meeting had gone on far too long and he hadn't held it together. They'd waffled and squabbled and nothing had been decided and his mind felt like cotton wool. His concentration was all to pieces and he didn't even want to consider why.

At least Sophy was staying with her friend Rebecca again. She was always there these days, and Owen couldn't blame her. He wasn't much company. And Rebecca's mother was good at all the home baking bits, the cosy, frilly things he despised so much and were so necessary to a child . . . although, to be fair, Sophy wasn't one to pine for such frivolities. She was a serious girl, too solemn, he sometimes thought.

He dumped his briefcase in the hall and went upstairs to change into tracksuit and trainers. He ran along Lord Mayor's Walk and through the hospital grounds to the river and down to Clifton and back again. He ran smoothly, not too fast, but not jogging, and finished up with forty pull-ups on the bar in the kitchen doorway.

It barely made him tired these days. He opened the wine then, on his way to the shower. The wine was French, a Fronsac left over from his last holiday with Marie. There were still a couple of cases in the cupboard under the stairs. She hadn't really liked red wine, and had been happy enough to leave them behind.

He dressed in jeans and open-necked shirt and guernsey

sweater and made ready to settle into a quiet evening writing letters and preparing a report for the meeting the next day. He drank a glass of wine while he fried chicken breast and fennel and mangetout peas in sesame oil. And then he sat at the table and looked at the meal and the wine bottle and his glass and knew he didn't want any of it.

He wanted, purely and simply, to pick up the phone and get Ben and Joss and Louisa to come round. He wanted to say to them, have you seen it, is it happening to you too? Is the past reaching out with its dead claws to clutch you too? A dread replay, an echo of a nightmare that was real.

Instead he phoned Jill and Patrick's and had a few words with Sophy before her bedtime. She was happy and giggly and asked him what was brown and sticky and he said, warily, that he didn't know.

'A stick!' she said, exploding once more and he found himself almost grinning.

Almost. He ate some of the food and drank a little more wine and wondered whether to read or write letters or watch TV or pick up the phone.

He sat in the living room and stared at the dark windows. After a while his attention switched to the phone on the table at his side.

As he looked at it, it rang.

'Hello, Owen.' Marie's voice was cool and balanced. 'Is Sophy there?'

'She's at the Pattisons'. Do you want their number?'

'I've got it, thanks.' A pause. 'So, everything going all right then?'

'Fine, just fine. And you? I saw a review of the Byrd masses the other day. Sounded good.'

'You wouldn't like it. But I'll send a CD for Sophy, shall I?'

'She'd love that.'

'Yes. Okay, then. I'd better ring her now before she goes to bed. 'Bye, Owen.'

' 'Bye.'

He put the phone down. A wasteland. His life was a desert, abandoned by nourishment and water and life. No wife, no child either, most of the time. And the worst of it was that it was his own fault. A mistake he'd made. Thinking that someone kind, someone who valued family, would be enough. Marie was kind: she'd adored her elderly parents, idealized them even.

On the run, he thought. They'd had her on the run. She'd tried to achieve excellence all her life, academically, musically, whatever, anything to impress her parents. That came first, always. Children, partners, whatever, had always come second best. Nothing matched up to the ideal of a perfect family life, something remembered only in fantasy. A perfect family, a perfect phrase of music.

Was it what happened to all musicians? He remembered Ben saying once that most instrumentalists were flawed like that: 'learning an instrument requires hours – months, *years* of solitary practice. Players don't like people. They prefer to lose themselves in their music, their instrument. It's easier. It gives an illusion of humanity, a taste of emotion and warmth. But it's only second-hand. It's not the real thing.'

That was Marie. Obsessive, depressive, self-centred. Marriage was difficult for her, parenthood impossible. So, while one part of him rejoiced in her success and undoubted talent, the rest of him experienced immense sorrow, that someone so gifted should be so flawed and that he hadn't seen it earlier. He'd been so impressed by her fame, by her elegance and sensitivity. But even in the good times, she was never here when he came home. She spent hours each day practising, when she wasn't on tour. He and Sophy took up the merest fraction of her attention and it wasn't right.

He wondered about Lily. She was musical, but Leo and Joss clearly came first for her. She was content to remain amateur. There was no comparison really: Marie was a professional, a dedicated, hard-working career musician. This was the late twentieth century and most women of any intelligence had professional careers, and would he seriously want a dilettante as a wife?

Not Lily, at any rate. Not only was she happily married to an old friend, but she was content to be the middle-class housewife. She'd spoken of bridge playing, tennis clubs, charity lunches . . . He wanted someone of passion and commitment, but also someone who would match him intellectually, emotionally. He was lonely, but he was beginning to think it was an impossible requirement.

He went back to the kitchen and put the cork back in the bottle and scraped the food away. Then, for the twentieth time, he put on Marie's recording of Purcell anthems.

Her favourite.

He tried. He really tried. But still it meant nothing to him.

Joss stared at the screen with frustration. He'd written the damn program himself, he knew it worked. And he knew all the slips, all the highways and byways where the uninitiated might come to grief and this was nothing to do with any of them. It *worked*. But there had been five complaints since Monday and you couldn't always blame the public, not these days, when everyone had computers.

The program wasn't even a particularly new idea. A standard educational presentation in an accessible, child-friendly form. You asked questions and the Roundhead soldier told you about the siege of York, the Roman centurion told you about the garrison, the Viking trader about his encampment, the burgher about the wool trade. They each gave the enquirer a guided tour of the city as it stood in their own time.

It had run perfectly for over a month, one of their more popular attractions at the Resources Centre. But there was a glitch now in the mediaeval section of the program and Joss couldn't discover why.

He ran it again. There stood the burgher in his tunic and flat cap and again the colour drained from the screen. The man's features became blurred and indistinct. His cloak *ran*, there was no other word for it. It became like a tail trailing behind him, dangling on the ground like a great fat worm. He no longer gave answers, he no longer gave the guided tour through the mediaeval streets of York. Instead the face turned towards him and the colours slotted into place, fell into recognizable shapes. His face seemed changed, the teeth were blackened, the eyes sharp with malice as he gazed directly into Joss's eyes.

No wonder the children had complained. This was the stuff of nightmares, of disease and despair and hatred. The malice reached out like a hand, to clutch at his throat.

Who was it? Who could be inspired by such hatred? The computer representation seemed almost photographically detailed, as if this were indeed the likeness of a real man.

Perhaps the .AVI files had got corrupted, maybe a virus. But this was curiously specific, and besides, they frequently checked *all* programs for viruses. He'd run the original copy from the tape backup too and the same thing happened there as well. But only the mediaeval man. It didn't make sense, unless he or someone else had mistakenly over-written the backup with corrupted files.

His ankle ached continuously, distractingly. They had told him that it would take a while to settle down, but no one had warned him that it would be this bad. He'd forgotten what it was like. He was younger last time, of course, and everyone knew that the young healed quickly . . .

It had taken months, even then. A miserable time he didn't want to remember.

He dragged his mind back to the present. There were other unexpected problems here too. The Resources Centre, the office and his home were all less than three hundred yards apart and it certainly wasn't worth getting anyone to drive him. His day was split between the three locations and he didn't want favours. So he stumped the distance three or four times daily and now his left hand, the hand he wrote with, was numb between thumb and forefinger with the constant repetitive strain of the jolting crutches.

Other things were going wrong, too. Martin Shaw, his second in command at the Centre, had ambition gleaming from the toes of his shoes to his glossy, wavy hair, and was only just co-operative. Joss discovered early on that Shaw had expected to be promoted to Joss's position: he'd been passed over and although he'd joked with Joss about it, and they'd been out for a drink together, Joss wasn't entirely sure that he was trustworthy.

He also had a hair-brained idea of involving the royal family in some kind of historical jamboree.

'The Duke of York!' he'd said, persistently. 'Get him to back the project; now Fergie's out of it, he'll want to do something about his image. Get him involved, bring him up here: concerts in the Minster, fireworks at Clifford's Tower. We could use it to revitalize the York Festival, get the media involved, it could mean mega-bucks—'

Joss hated the idea. But Shaw had friends, he was personable and fluent and persuasive. It would be difficult to talk down this one. Joss had no intention of letting it go ahead.

Predictably, Shaw chose that moment to turn up. He put his head round the door to Joss's office. 'Your wife just rang,' he said without preamble. 'She won't be home till late. Something about a school trip to Bradford.'

'Oh yes. Right. Thanks, Martin.'

Joss knew all about this. Lily had wanted to accompany the outing from Anthony's to see the RSC's *Tempest*, but there'd been no places left. For her sake, he was glad that someone had dropped out. And he was also glad that she'd been there for Leo, in case anything went wrong. He could not rid himself of the unease about Leo. He couldn't like the school, for all the friendliness of the staff. Leo still had not brought anyone home and there was a set look about him in the mornings. Joss sighed. Nothing was going right. The evening stretched before him, lonely and boring. He looked at his desk, at the cascading piles of papers surrounding the computer, and decided that he might as well work late. If he could clear some of the mess he might feel a bit more positive about the job.

Between five and five-thirty the office magically emptied. Joss barely noticed. He was fighting his way down the in-tray, wishing all the time that a secretary would stay, some nice reliable person to disentangle the urgent from the necessary from the irrelevant.

Soon his desk and the surrounding floor were covered with piles of paper, although the in-tray didn't seem to have noticeably diminished. He glanced at his watch; half past seven. It was completely dark outside and rain splattered against the windows.

The fax machine was clattering in the corner. He let it run, staring at a memo from the Health and Safety people about fire escapes at the Centre. Urgent or necessary? Something to delegate to Shaw, perhaps?

He experienced a certain unwillingness to allow Shaw much responsibility. It was one reason why he was so snowed under. He'd once found his deputy altering the wording of one of his memos: nothing drastic, just a phrase here and there which changed the emphasis from polite to peremptory. Since then he'd avoided sending anything through Shaw.

He put the memo down and wondered whether to go and get a sandwich. Or a pizza. But he'd have to get downstairs, crutch his way towards Goodramgate and back again in the wet, and anyway, how could he carry anything? He might as well go to a restaurant. All at once, his mouth watered at the thought of a crisp pizza with garlic and tomatoes and bacon and dripping mozzarella.

He crossed the office to the door, stopping casually on the way to look at the fax, still clattering away, the same monotonous irritable patterns. He propped his crutches against the desk.

The fax had jammed. One sentence, repeating over and over again.

Forgetting is evil, remembering is worse.

There was no address, no number to say where it came from. He slammed his hand down on the switch and the noise ceased. He tore the paper away, crumpling it up in both hands, throwing it towards a wastepaper bin. Then he reached for the crutches.

They were gone.

For almost a minute he stood there, blankly. Not against the desk, not on the floor. Not across the fax machine or on the carpet behind him. Not anywhere within sight.

No sound, no movement. But still he said, 'Who's there?' loudly, twice, because someone must have taken them. 'It's not funny,' he said and his words echoed back at him and he knew, immediately, that there was no one there.

He slumped against the desk. He couldn't get his mind round it. He couldn't begin to think what to do next. And he remembered, he remembered the words on the paper.

Remembering is worse.

Louisa sat on her mother's sofa, her head in her hands, and regarded the carpet. Scarlet flowers and green leaves on a honey-coloured background, worn thin in places. She knew every repeating pattern of it. It had lain in the sitting room of the flat in Alcuin and she had sat and stared at it a thousand times before.

Her mother was dying. The doctors no longer talked of freeing the bed. They no longer even said how much happier she'd be at home. Everyone knew there was no possibility of happiness now for Mavis Jamieson.

She had stopped sleeping. Pills propelled her into artificial oblivion for odd hours, but nothing resembling ordinary, restorative sleep was now an option. Louisa sat with her, hour after hour, trying to work out what was wrong, why her mother was so frightened. Mavis Jamieson's eyes searched the ward, never resting, never drooping, always avoiding Louisa's anxious gaze. Sometimes she cried. And all Louisa's other worries fell away under the force of her urgent preoccupation.

To bring peace to her mother.

Sometimes Mavis Jamieson spoke. She gave Louisa vivid and horrible descriptions of hellish landscapes culled from Bosch and Bacon and Foxe's *Book of Martyrs*. But as soon as Louisa asked *why?* the tears would start again and this was even worse. The wasted body would heave and writhe and the nurses would come running and give her yet more morphine.

She drifted in and out of desperate hag-ridden dreams, all the time slipping further away from real life, further into the kind of death everyone fears.

Louisa had wondered whether a priest might help, but her mother's extreme reaction to the suggestion made it impossible. Louisa had seen death before, violent, untimely death. She'd not sought out the dramatic trouble spots, making her career more in the area of social issues. But following the life of a sixteen-year-old mother of four in a Rio slum, working in a hospital for the elderly insane in Romania, investigating

144

a rehab centre of druggies in Aberdeen had all opened her eyes in more ways than one.

She could shock *Guardian* readers, had once even made a slot on Channel 4, but the power of her pictures lay in the detail. The wisp of hair over the sweating brow, the discarded magazine in a corner. Arty, posed, somehow artificial, although she had also seen the suffering and the tears. But she wasn't ready for this, the onslaught of her mother's distress. As she hadn't been ready to have children, to make the great commitment.

It was getting late. She should get back to the hospital for an hour or so before they came round with the night sleepers. She shuddered. And stood up, and went to the mirror in the hall and made a half-hearted attempt to straighten her hair, rub some blusher into her cheeks, look bright and cheery and on top of it.

The phone rang. The voice on the end was vaguely familiar. And then Louisa remembered the nurse who was often on duty in the afternoon shift, the large woman with greying hair and a kind face, the nurse who sometimes took time to stop and chat.

'Miss Jamieson? I don't know if you were planning to come in tonight, but I thought I'd just let you know that your mother is sleeping—'

'Is she all right?' Leaping anxiety.

'She – was in rather a state earlier. So the doctor gave her something and she's fast asleep now. Really. There's no need for you to come in, she won't wake again for hours.'

Louisa could hardly bear it. 'Are you lying?' Her voice came out too loud. 'Really asleep? Or drugged dreams? I'll be right over—'

'No.' Patiently. 'There's no need, Miss Jamieson. Have some rest, let it go for a bit.'

Louisa put the phone down feeling like a traitor. She should be there, she knew it. There was no real sleep for her mother, no real rest, and she should be there, to help, to do what she could.

Nothing. There was nothing she could do. This was the worst kind of waiting game. She sat down on the sofa again and looked at the carpet. The flowers and leaves writhed together like snakes.

Ben Bowen had heard them whispering. His acute hearing informed him that he was talked about. It was out. People knew. The cheat was exposed, the lie made plain. That morning Mark Morrell had asked for his resignation. The exam was going to be declared null. Geoffrey Pyper was not going to get his Grade 5 Theory or any other grade, at least under Benedict Bowen's tuition. Ben could barely approach it, the shame of it, the looks, the whispers, the hidden malice. He didn't dare show his face in church. He had rivals in the school, he knew. People who resented his status as an old boy, or were suspicious of his single state. He knew that some parents thought he was gay, and worried, but he'd always been careful, there was never any reason for anyone to suppose . . .

Anyway, it had never been children he wanted. He wanted only friends: men or women, he didn't mind. He was lonely, that was all. At heart, there was no one, not since childhood. Talking to Joss a few days ago had been the closest he'd been to anyone for years. He was occasionally invited to acquaintances' houses, but he knew he was never central to their lives. He had no talent for intimacy, he didn't know how you did it. Did you listen? Or tell jokes? Or give presents, buy rounds? He'd tried them all, but still people went home early and didn't ask him back.

He had no future now. There was nowhere else to go. He knew only York, he'd always lived there, and now it would be jammed with people who would know what he'd done. He couldn't face it, and he was too old to move anywhere else . . .

He had a headache. He'd drunk almost a bottle of whisky and now he was cold, cold and lonely. He walked into his bathroom and started to fill the bath. He looked in the mirror over the sink and then looked away again. On the shelf under the mirror were a number of bottles, including a new bottle of paracetamol.

Was this the worst thing that had ever happened to him? Was there any way of surmounting this one?

Through the open bathroom door, he could see his bedroom, where the crucifix on the wall shone in the light.

Miserere nobis.

Chapter Sixteen

It started after the race. Kenny and Philip withdrew from the activities of Bishop dormitory. This happened naturally enough: both of them were involved in all the school's sporting activities and at half-term Philip applied to move into one of the sporting dorms, accompanied by Kenny. Mr Redmond agreed: he liked to make concessions for boys who did well on the field. It was the sporting connection, a link which often endured into adulthood.

The four remaining boys in Bishop were disdainful. Trivia. That's what Owen called it. 'Anyone can have muscles and run if they're prepared to put in hours of training,' *he said.*

'You've done the odd bit of circuit training yourself,' *said David.* 'You like playing rugger, you're good at it, getting filthy and falling over all the time—'

'That was when I was younger.'

'Two months ago. If that.'

'Beside the point. Anyone could do what I did, if they really wanted to. But you can't train to be clever.'

'You can read,' *objected Joss.*

'Kenny's clever,' *said Ben.* 'He's really good at music too. But look at him now, bashing his brains out to be a he-man. Just shows you that cleverness is nothing like wisdom,' *he concluded solemnly.*

We all stared at him.

'Wisdom? What do you mean?' *I said.* 'Little old ladies in forests being all mysterious? Monks on mountains?'

'I don't know.' *Ben shifted defensively. We were on the roof of the old bomb shelter in the wasteland behind the school. A strictly forbidden, highly prestigious venue.*

He struggled with the thought for a while. 'Clever is – super-ficial. Smart, flashy. It doesn't mean much.'

'Sour grapes,' said Joss, throwing a handful of gravel at him. 'Just 'cos you can't add four and four without mistakes—'

Ben leaped at him and the two of them rolled over and down the side of the roof and into the soft sand beneath. Owen, lying on his back, sucking a straw, said, 'It's a good point though. You can't decide to be clever, but you can become well-informed and you can achieve wisdom. So which is the most valuable? What do you think, Davey-boy?'

David was watching a cat stalk a magpie over the rubble towards the school. 'What? Cleverness or wisdom? Who cares? What does it matter?' The cat pounced and the bird lazily evaded it, swooping to settle a little further away. He glanced down to the seething mass of limbs, now half buried in sand, which was Joss and Ben. 'The level of intellectual debate seems to be thriving here, at any rate.'

Ben's leg was hooked round Joss's neck and both were grunting like pigs.

'That it should come to this.' David was dry. 'The graceful athleticism of youth should be admired on the field—'

'I expected more of you,' said Owen, sitting up. 'What's this, enthusiasm for sporting activity?'

'You're a fine one to talk. And anyway, Kenny's all right,' said David, a connection which made perfect sense to us both.

'No he's not,' I said. It seemed important to me that David's naïve trust should not be misplaced. 'He doesn't like you, he never did.'

'He doesn't know me. Doesn't appreciate my many and various excellent qualities.'

'He's a poisonous little jerk,' said Owen. 'Just like his sancti-monious, Bible-thumping mate Philip.'

'No, you've got it wrong,' David said seriously.

'David. Listen to me, child.' Owen lightly touched his hand

to the scar over David's eye. 'They're no friends of yours.'

'Kenny was scared.'

'That's no excuse,' said Owen.

'Yes it is,' said David, and I knew he was right.

I knew Owen was right too.

I saw it the next day. I was late for third period maths and found myself caught in a crowd moving down the main corridor towards A3. David was a little way ahead of me. To one side I heard someone say, 'Seifert!'

He looked round. Saw me and raised an eyebrow. I shook my head. The crowd pressed us onwards.

Again, David's name, this time merely whispered so that the sibilant hiss spread. I couldn't tell who it was. It was repeated by someone to my left and then again behind me. I saw David turn once more, his face pale and strained. He looked about to speak, but didn't. He avoided my eyes and hurried on.

It wasn't the only time. During the next few weeks I saw it spread. Wherever David went a chorus of whispers followed. What must it be like to loathe the sound of your own name, I wondered? I saw him turn and face only the impassive, innocent gazes of his classmates.

I saw him walk through the playground and suddenly swing round. It made him look nutty, mad. Only two inches away from full-blown, eye-rolling, certified lunacy.

I said to him, 'Why do you keep turning round? They're just teasing you.'

He was searching his satchel for something. 'I know,' he muttered.

'Ignore them,' I persisted.

'Yeah.'

It didn't grind him down, not at first. We were still there, the boys of Bishop and me, we were his friends, we gave him somewhere to go.

Towards Christmas, it began to fall apart.

Ben was out of it most of the time. His voice hadn't broken and he was the star of the Christmas spectacular, a musical nativity presentation put together by Mr Brooker, head of Music and Mr Williams, who took English and Drama and rather fancied himself as a poet. Ben was the Archangel Gabriel, a central, starring role, and his high, clear voice floated effortlessly down the corridors at odd times throughout the day.

Owen was involved too. He had been detailed to recite Williams' sub-Eliot epic while a series of tableaux were presented by the less talented members of the school.

I too had a starring role, essential even. I was Mary, naturally. Even then, I knew it was a bit part. It was of course non-speaking and I was required to attend the dress rehearsal only.

But my time was taken up with all the other girlie jobs, largely dished out by my own mother. Sewing costumes, baking mince pies, making Christmas decorations. I resented it furiously. I hated sewing and was useless at it and I deliberately spoiled one batch of mince pies by using salt instead of sugar.

Mum regarded me with resignation. She knew perfectly well what I'd done.

'Very well,' she said, acidly. 'Go and present yourself at the art room. Mrs Redmond can find you something to do.'

Mrs Redmond had dreams of grandeur. All the windows of the school were to be decorated, those on the ground floor as if they were stained glass, those on the other floors with cut-out snowflakes.

This was drudgery, pure and simple. But at least Joss was involved too. We sat together companionably in the art room, cutting out coloured Cellophane and sticking it into place with black tape. This happened during the late afternoons as the sky darkened and Ben's voice soared, cold and eerie, in the far distance.

Kenny and Philip were on the rugger field. David was lost

somewhere on the sidelines, wandering between playing field and chapel, art room and library, hall and study. He had a heavy cold and was excused both sports and a role in the entertainment. He was notoriously clumsy with craftwork and no one had a place for him.

Nonetheless, he seemed preoccupied and I wondered if the constant teasing was beginning to get to him. But we were all so busy, so caught up with the hectic preparations that I did nothing. What could I have done? I didn't see much of him, to be honest, during those last few weeks of the Christmas term.

Outside the school, the city was at its Dickensian best, the shop windows pretty with tinsel and holly, chains of lights bright as jewels everywhere. Groups of carol singers did their best against the ceaseless wind and drifts of melody wove in and out of the constant traffic.

Joss said, 'Do you often have nightmares?'

We were perched on stools in the art room, working together on a stained glass representation of the Annunciation.

'Sometimes. Quite a lot recently.'

'The worst I ever had was about Philip.' Joss was fingering the small white dove shape, turning it over between his fingers. Then he put it down, and started laying tape down the columns which surrounded the Mary figure. He went on, laying the tape down, smoothing it out while he spoke, 'I dreamed that I had his face in my pocket. Just the front of it. It was all bloody at the back, but the eyes, the nose and mouth were all still in place. Like a Hallowe'en mask, only real.' His hand went to the pocket on his hip, patted it as if he might still feel the presence of the face in his pocket. 'It's bloody, and soft, and pliable like Plasticine, like real flesh, but it keeps its shape . . .'

I wrinkled my nose. 'Why Philip, do you think?'

Joss looked at me, his round face worried and perplexed. 'I don't understand him,' he said. 'Who he is, what he's doing here.'

152

'Being brung up, edicated, like the rest of us.'

'But he's different. Strange. A bit creepy. I know he likes sport but that's all he likes. He's not brainy like Owen, not a muso like Ben and Kenny, he's no fun, he doesn't even collect stamps. He doesn't belong.'

'Neither do I.'

'True.' Joss grinned at me. 'It's the horrible way you eat your toast, all nibbly round the edges.'

I ignored this. 'My worst nightmare is about this man. He's called Sheepshanks. He's tall and thin and he wears this hooded robe thing, like a dressing gown and he stands on one leg—'

'Like a stork?'

'No. It's – different. Like, he's about to fly, to take off. To pounce.'

'Doesn't sound all that frightening to me.'

Mrs Redmond came in then to see how we were getting on and so I never finished telling Joss about Sheepshanks. Anyway, I was lying.

It wasn't a dream at all: I'd seen him in the basement that day with David. It was David who'd given him his name.

Ben sang. Standing on a step-ladder, his arms held out like wings, he negotiated the strange arabesques in Gerald Brooker's music with ease. The rest of the hall was in darkness, but Ben knew that David was somewhere at the back, watching and listening.

He was singing for David. With hopeless, hidden yearning, he sang to David and everyone who heard him stopped talking, stopped working and fidgeting and dreaming and thinking.

There was only love.

It was all Ben cared about, that and music. They were difficult to separate. For if he could no longer reach Kenny, there was still music, and it seemed at last that David was listening to him.

His voice soared, clear enough to break hearts. From his high perch, Ben saw the back door to the hall open. A halo of white hair, caught in the backlight, showed the late-comer to be Kenneth Pyper. And although his voice did not falter, it lost some of its quality of sweetness. Ben saw Kenny move away from the door, passing David without a word. He became lost in the shadowy hall. And as Ben's voice floated through the chromatic phrases of music, he found himself wondering what Kenny was doing there, now that he had given up all interest in music, and all interest in Ben himself.

The passage he was singing became more elaborate, and Ben had to concentrate hard. When he looked again, David had disappeared too.

The scene came to an end. Ben climbed down off the stepladder and crossed the stage to the wings.

Kenny was there, his halo of white hair ruffled and damp. Against all the rules, he was still wearing his rugger boots. He gave a slow handclap as Ben poured a drink from a jug of water.

'Very nice, dear. Mummy will be well pleased. Feel good, did it? The Archangel Benedict, lording it . . .' he said.

Ben frowned. There was a nasty edge to Kenny's words. 'It's pretty ghastly music, don't you think?' he said. 'Like Puccini, only worse. Makes me feel like I ought to go and wash my hands after singing it.'

'I always feel like that after listening to your caterwauling.'

Ben tried to ignore this. He carried on as if Kenny had not spoken. 'All those smarmy harmonies, thick chords . . . funny how old Brooker fancies himself as a real composer.'

He was conscious of the dislike in Kenny's eyes. He wants to hurt me, Ben thought despondently, because I'm involved in this, and he's not. He's missing music, perhaps even missing me. And his heart began to race, his thoughts filled with hope. 'Have you still got your violin?' he asked gently. 'I'm sure they could find a place for you in the orchestra, if you wanted to have a go at all this syrupy junk.'

'I'd rather shovel shit.'

'It's not just for girls, you know.'

'No, all the pretty, pink little pansies in the world like to have a go at it too.'

'What are you suggesting?' But Ben knew exactly what Kenny was suggesting and that it was well out of bounds. No one talked like this, made suggestions of that kind: these were unmentionable matters. If boys were sometimes close friends, if sometimes they liked the warmth of human contact, what was the harm in that? There was never any indication or thought of anything else.

'I've seen you, making eyes at that Jewish git.'

Ben flushed. 'Don't be absurd.'

'You can't hide it,' said Kenny, making the words sound like obscenities. 'I know you inside out, Ben Bowen, after all those bloody music lessons. I know what moves you, I've seen you cry. Soft, sentimental, hopeless. I know just what you're like . . . You're one of them.'

'If I am, then so are you,' Ben said crudely. He was not without defences, although this made him feel sick and ill. It was hard, after the recent moment of hope, to be on such bad terms.

Kenny's eyes were like daggers. 'Fuck you, Bowen. Except I wouldn't, not for a million pounds. I'd rather fuck St Anthony's pig.'

And Ben had a sudden picture of it in his mind, its evil little eyes and heavy shoulders, squatting on the ceiling over the hall, watching them all.

'The feeling's mutual,' he found himself saying.

They stared at each other in absolute animosity and Ben was appalled to discover the extent of the reversal in his feelings. Where there had been love, there was now only loathing for the white-haired, pale-skinned boy in front of him.

Kenny smiled, and it was horrible. Then he spat, and a gobbet of slime hit Ben's glasses and slid down on to his cheek. He clattered off then, his boots leaving muddy marks on the boards.

Ben took out his handkerchief, and mopped his face and glasses. His heart was racing, he felt as if he'd just been hit. When he replaced the glasses, he saw David standing by the curtain pull.

'Did you hear that?' Ben asked.

'Some of it. What's got into our mutual friend?'

'He's jealous, I suppose.'

'Daft bugger.' David smiled slightly.

'We don't need him, do we?' Ben tucked his hand under David's arm.

Gently, without fuss, David withdrew. 'Let's not add fuel to the fire of gossip,' he said softly.

Ben wanted the ground to open up. 'Sorry,' he mumbled. 'I didn't mean—'

'I know.' David was still smiling.

But the distance between them increased and Ben began to know loneliness.

Kenny stormed along the lower corridor, meaning to find Philip. The door to the basement was open and the light was on. It shone across the corridor, a vivid rectangle of yellow. He suddenly, sharply, desired a cigarette. Kenny had smoked his last in break and was fresh out. But he usually managed to find the odd fag in someone's pocket.

He decided to give it a go.

The familiar smell of gym shoes and damp coats and dust and also something animal, musky, decaying. He wondered what it was. Perhaps a rat or something had got itself trapped. He crept quietly down the stairs, clinging close to the wall, as was his way.

He was tall for his age, broadly built, with tight curly hair, almost white. His watery, bluish eyes had a pinkish touch, although he was not a true albino. He knew his appearance attracted attention, that his name would be among the first a new teacher learned. So he determined to be immaculate, to succeed at work, to appear polite and obliging and always on time. He found these things difficult, and the inevitable frustrations and failures drove him to develop strategies. They generally took the form of minor acts of cruelty. (There was always someone else smaller, more vulnerable who could complete his homework, give him money, provide excuses.) He used extortion, blackmail and simple brute strength and usually managed to get his way. He also managed to find himself, rather to his own surprise, playing in the school rugger team. No ingenuity was needed for this: his only innate talent, now that he had given up music, lay in physical dexterity and force.

Like Philip. It was strange how like Philip he was growing, how Philip's attitudes now seemed to him attractive and meaningful. The half-term they had spent together at Philip's home in the Dales had – what was the word? Converted him, that was it. Shown him another way.

The basement was deserted as usual. He went systematically to the furthest rack, where the oldest children hung their coats. He found little in the first few: a sixpence, some Rolos and a rubber-band full of sweet cigarette American Civil War cards. He sat on the bench and thumbed through the cards, lingering over the graphic, detailed representations of terrible wounds. The amputation scenes were particularly interesting. It might be worth starting a collection himself. He could use these to start it off, and had no doubt that he would very soon find himself in possession of the whole set.

He became aware that the smell was increasing. It itched in his nose, which he rubbed. It didn't help: with sudden force, he sneezed, loudly and explosively. The cigarette cards scattered everywhere like confetti.

There was no one there to bless him.

The door opened and a shaft of light briefly illuminated the stairs. Philip was standing there, dressed in his costume, the silly white tunic which barely reached his knees. He was holding some *papers in his hand, but as soon as he saw Kenny he clattered down the stairs towards him.*

'Got a letter this morning,' he said. 'Father says they've discovered ruins in the garden. Some old abbey or something. You remember, where we went camping that night.'

Kenny did remember. He still had nightmares about it. It had been one of the worst nights of his life. It happened that half-term and Kenny was staying at the Strouds' house at Coverham. It was an unusually warm and late Indian summer, hot and sultry by day, beginning to be chilly at night. The idea to camp out had been Philip's. He had stolen some Scotch from the local store and wanted to drink it outside, well beyond his parents' control. A tent down the bottom of the garden had seemed like a good idea at the time.

Kenny drank some of the whisky, but not much. He didn't feel all that well: Mrs Stroud's cooking was rich and creamy and he'd had far too many profiteroles at dinner. Philip had swigged almost half the bottle before falling into a predictable stupor soon after midnight, clutching the bottle to his chest. Kenny had smoked several cigarettes before trying to sleep. Then he'd tossed and turned for hours, distracted by Philip's snoring, wondering whether it was worth getting up to empty his bowels. There was an owl calling somewhere nearby, and trees rustled overhead, their low branches scraping against the roof of the tent. For a while he wondered if they might tear its fabric or even bring it down.

He crawled out of the tent and relieved himself in the long grass under the apple tree. On the way back to his sleeping bag, he knocked over the jar he'd been using as an ashtray and white dog ends and a film of ash fell all over the bag, so that he coughed and choked and swore as he tried to settle himself down. But eventually he fell into an uneasy sleep and that was when the dream took place.

There were knives in the dream, knives and flames which

made him stir and flinch, because the fire was burning at the back of his neck and the knife in his hand glinted. He didn't know where he was but there were dim and indistinct shapes all around him, people he didn't recognize, people who did not care what was happening to him. There was no story, no narrative to the dream. All he knew was that death was present there, death caught on the edge of the knife, in the flicker of the flames. Fear ran through him as if the knife was already buried in his heart, a deep, paralysing dread. His stomach clenched, his hands were cold and sweaty. And there was a rumbling sound, a distant, massy, shifting of earth and stone and that brought death too, that was no better—

And it went on, for hours and hours, the same thing. The night endured, that night in Philip's garden, with dreams that ran monotonously on one theme only, death caught in flames, death caught in steel and rock. He was caught on a death-drawn rack and he whimpered and turned on the hard earth and it seemed to him that there were hands reaching out of the earth to hold him there, to keep him imprisoned on this rack. Hands reached down from above, and poked out his eyes, but he could still see and what he could see was the knife, glinting and the fire, burning and the sound of tumbling rocks filled his ears.

Exhaustedly, in the morning, he saw that the branch overhead had indeed torn through the tent's fabric. Twigs like fingers beckoned over his head. He shuddered. But they went to Church that morning and Kenny found himself soothed by the peace, the sanctity and beauty of the ceremony. And later, when they dismantled the tent and packed it away, Kenny found stones jutting from the grass where he had been lying. They were smooth and curved, as if part of some ancient building.

'There were those funny stones there,' he said to Philip in the basement at Anthony's. 'I couldn't sleep at all that night with them jabbing into my backside.'

Philip nodded. 'That's it. An abbey. Father says here that it was run by—' he paused, scanning the letter, '—white canons from the Premon – Premonstrat – atensian Order.' He stumbled over the word several times. 'They'll probably excavate it one day. There might even be treasure there, you know, crosses and things like that. Abbeys used to be really rich in those days.'

'Let's get a metal detector,' suggested Kenny. Something for nothing, he thought. Finders keepers was a central point in his philosophy.

Philip's also. 'And look what else I've found,' he said, holding a book out to Kenny. It wasn't really a book, he saw, but a pamphlet, a familiar, dirty pamphlet covered in incomprehensible words. 'It was hidden in the Frog's tabby.'

'So what? It's that old rubbish Owen tried to read us that night.' Kenny didn't even bother to take it.

'I know,' said Philip briefly. Let's give it another go. I can't read it, the writing's weird. But Rattigan's left his translation stuck in the back. Listen.'

He began to recite the summoning, mimicking the French accent Owen didn't have to an absurd degree and as he did so, Kenny felt the world change. The yellowy single light bulb became tinged with red, so it glowed feverishly into the dark corners. Philip was in the far corner by the stairs. He'd dropped the pamphlet or something, and was now kneeling on the stone floor. It looked like he was praying, thought Kenny incredulously.

Kenny watched him for a while in silence. He couldn't see Philip's face, which was hidden by the hood of his shepherd's robe. But his fingers were clasped together so intensely that the knuckles shone in the difficult light. He was praying and his white robe was stained red by the strange light.

'What are you doing?' Kenny asked after a while, puzzled and uneasy.

Philip was muttering to himself, and then, to Kenny's complete astonishment, made an elaborate sign of the cross. He stood up then, and Kenny saw that it wasn't Philip after all, but someone else. How could he have mistaken him? And where was Philip? This man was immensely tall, with bony legs jutting beneath his plain, woven tunic. He turned towards Kenny, and his hands, which had been clasped together, opened.

A cloud of whiteness billowed out into the orangy air. It fluttered and dispersed and filled every corner of the basement. Moths, pale as bone. Some of them settled on Kenny's clothes and he brushed them off, his mouth open with amazement.

The man in the corner said something, words Kenny didn't understand, and the white moths began to settle in groups, in strange humanoid clumps, and forms emerged beneath their fragile wings, forms with arms and fingers and blunt, weaving heads.

Kenny took a step backwards, but the moths were behind him too, their fluttering wings stilling as people began to struggle free of their imperfect camouflage.

The people, the crowd, the mob were talking together, grabbing hold of each other's arms, noisily exclaiming at Kenny's presence. He couldn't understand what they were saying either, but they were pointing at him, circling round him, clearly agitated. Like the first man, they wore plain tunics, but most of them were ragged and filthy. There was a dog slinking around their feet, a moth-eaten mongrel with a torn ear. One of them, better dressed than the others, trailed a long cloak behind him like a tail. He seemed to be some kind of a leader, and the dog with the torn ear belonged to him.

Kenny glanced at the man who had been praying. But everything changed again. This was Philip, after all, his old friend Philip. Why hadn't he seen it before, what was wrong with him? He was disturbed by these people, by the strange moths, but at some very deep level, he wasn't panicking. He knew he was one of them. They were his people, his and Philip's kind.

And they felt it too. The man with the long cloak held out his hand to him, and others with straggly hair and dark stumps for *teeth came up and embraced him. He could feel their bones through the flesh, as if the skin and muscle were not entirely substantial, not truly composed of blood and tissue and fat and muscle. He didn't mind. He enjoyed their companionship, their winking eyes, the sense of complicity. They were playing a fine game here, and Philip himself was having a go at taking off his dad, the Vic, again.*

Philip approached Kenny and solemnly took Kenny's head between bony hands and kissed the top of Kenny's head. It felt like a baptism, a serious and significant embrace of welcome into a new order.

Kenny had found his home. The conversion which had started at Coverham became fact. And this was where he belonged.

Chapter Seventeen

Her mother said, 'David. Because of David—' and then her head tossed on the pillow once more and her hands started to flutter in that appalled, uncontrolled way.

Louisa caught the wild hands and clasped them together. '*Mum!* What about David?'

The turning head, inspired by desperate energy, paid no attention.

She tried again, leaning forward so that there were only inches between them. She could smell a sweetly sick scent on her mother's breath, so unfamiliar that for a moment she almost wondered if this was indeed the woman she'd always known.

'Mum, listen to me! Mum, look at me! What about David?' For a second or two her mother's eyes fastened on her. There was a dreadful clarity in them.

'David's dead,' she said, precisely.

'Yes, I know,' said Louisa, willing her to keep concentrating. 'But tell me. Please. Tell me what happened.'

The restless head-tossing had resumed. Louisa released her mother's hands and stood up. She pulled aside the curtain and went to find the nurse. The plump nurse who had rung her was on duty. She had a shy face and short, beautifully cut greying hair. She was sitting at the nurses' station, filling in forms. She looked up, her face changing, saddened. 'Mrs Jamieson? Poor soul, you can sometimes calm her a little with cool water. I haven't had much time today, I'm afraid.' She gestured at the sheaf of papers on the desk.

'Thanks.' Louisa was about to walk away, but she hesitated.

Perhaps the nurse could help ... 'I really need to talk to my mother. I wondered if you'd any idea what's bothering her. She won't tell me and there's something wrong.'

'There certainly is. She keeps on and on about this David. Do you know who he is?'

'Yes. Long ago ... Cold water, you say?'

The nurse nodded briefly before returning to the paperwork with a sigh.

Louisa dipped her handkerchief into the flask of drinking water by her mother's bed. Gently she stroked the damp cloth over her mother's forehead.

There was no immediate change. Louisa moved the cloth down her mother's face, along the jawline, over the neck.

Gradually, almost imperceptibly, her mother quietened and Louisa leaned over again and said, 'Mum, what happened to David?'

'You know.'

'Not all of it.'

'I can't!' It looked as if the threshing was about to start again. Louisa resumed the cool stroking.

'Mum, please tell me. There's no point in keeping secrets now.'

'Now that I'm dying?' A sudden sharpness in her voice, an acute reminder of intelligence. 'Lulu, there's people who would be upset, even now. There's no point in bringing it all up again, I mustn't talk about it, I mustn't, but David, oh, poor David—' She was slipping away again.

'You must tell me!'

'No.'

'Mum, it's going to happen again, I can feel it growing again, I know it will.'

Her mother said nothing. But her eyes were now fixed on her daughter's face with intensity.

'Mum, there's a little boy. Joss's son. You remember Joss?'

The smallest of nods.

'He's called Leo. I think he's being bullied, there's something at the school—'

'Louisa!' Her mother clutched the sheet. 'Don't, don't – You should go back to London, don't stay here, I don't need you—'

'Mum!'

'Don't get mixed up in it! It comes to no good, to evil, to horrible – There's nothing you can do and it comes to no good—' Tears then, overbrimming and running, and Louisa hadn't the heart for more. She stood up and found the plump nurse standing there, understanding on her face. Louisa said, 'If she says anything more concrete about David, will you tell me? Please? It's very urgent.'

'I'm off duty in five minutes. Perhaps, if you told me a bit more about all this, I could be of some use.'

Louisa glanced at her watch. She hesitated. 'That's very kind of you. My name's Louisa,' she said. 'And you are?'

'Tish. Letitia Farmer.'

Tish lived down by the river near Clifton Bridge so they went to one of the pubs in Marygate. It was early, and there were only one or two regulars in the lounge bar. Louisa brought their drinks over to a table in the window and sat down opposite the nurse.

'It's a long story,' she said but did her best to keep it short. Tish sat completely unmoving, staring at her gin and tonic while Louisa explained what had happened to David and her mother's part in it.

'What was David's surname?' Tish asked at the end of it.

'Seifert,' said Louisa. 'Why?'

She sighed. 'I thought so. I asked because I nursed a Mrs Seifert in intensive care. Five or six years ago, it was. She had cancer.' There was a pause while she downed the gin in one.

'She told me that her son David had died when he was a boy. She didn't recover: it was a bad death. I wouldn't want to see your mother suffer like that.' Piercing grey eyes regarded Louisa with equanimity. 'These things have a way of reverberating down the years, don't they?'

'You can say that again. I always wondered what happened to David's parents.'

'I remember Mr Seifert. He seemed – upset, of course. But not, I would say, devastated.'

'Unlike my mother.'

'I'll have a think about this. Perhaps there may be something I can do.'

There was something so competent about Letitia Farmer, thought Louisa. They spoke further, but more general topics seemed false and inappropriate. Tish was a career nurse, someone who had refused promotions to management, preferring to devote her life to patient care.

'And to my dog Gerda,' she said finishing her drink. 'Which reminds me, I'll have to be getting back. Gerda will be desperate for her walk by now.'

They went together to the door and there Tish shook Louisa's hand, a sharp, downward jerk. 'I've got your telephone number,' she said. 'I'll ring you if there's anything.'

'Thank you.'

Louisa put on her coat and left the pub.

She went straight to the Fletchers' house, walking past the end of Owen's road quickly. She was tired of rowing with Owen, tired of the misunderstandings. Joss had always been easier, more approachable. She used the lion knocker and rang the bell and waited and tried again, but there was no answer.

She'd had enough of vague memories, strange hints, horrible apparitions. She wanted it plain and clear now, and it seemed unlikely that her mother was going to provide the answers.

They had to pool their knowledge, their memories, their experiences. And if Joss wasn't there, she'd have to tackle Owen, like it or not. So from Joss's house she went back to Owen's and knocked on the door before she had time for second thoughts. It opened almost immediately.

'Owen, may I come in?' She was beyond social niceties.

He looked amused. 'Of course.' He stood aside and she swept past him into the hall.

She'd not been there before, but she would have recognized it as a place inhabited by Owen anywhere in the world. A dark blue carpet and plain white walls, decorated only by monochrome photographs of architectural details, cornices, columns, doorways. The only incongruous touch was a collage of bright felt shapes hung on the wall as a calendar, immediately identified by Louisa as Sophy's work.

'Can I get you a drink? Coffee? Wine?'

'I – This is not a social call. Owen, we need to talk.'

He led her through to the living room, and somehow she found herself sitting on the plain midnight sofa with a glass of red wine in her hand and Owen was sitting opposite her, regarding her with the same faint amusement.

'My mother cannot rest. She won't let go. She's in agony and it's all to do with David. I need to talk to you, and Joss and Ben, about what happened.'

'You were there. You know as much as any of us.'

'No, I don't.' She put down the wine. 'I was in the yard outside the main hall, don't you remember?'

The amusement had faded from Owen's expression. He even looked at his watch, a deliberately offensive gesture she chose to ignore.

'It was so long ago. Is it all this Sheepshanks nonsense again? Honestly Louisa, have you seriously thought about getting some counselling? Therapy of some kind?'

'Damn it, Owen, I'm not mad!'

'Not mad, no. But under stress, certainly. It can't be pleasant, watching your mother in that place.'

She took a deep breath. Denial. That was the fashionable word for it these days. Owen was every bit as terrified as she was, but he had no reason to examine the cause. He'd rather be offensive and call her mad to her face than risk stirring it up again.

'Humour me. Please, Owen. We were friends once, weren't we?'

His expression flickered for the briefest of moments, but he wouldn't look straight at her. 'Dear Louisa, I hope we still are. But this was a long time ago, as I keep repeating. Let sleeping dogs lie, don't you think?'

'But they're not sleeping, are they? It's not just my mother, or even me. It's Leo, don't you see? Sheepshanks is after him. Can you really bear to risk Joss's son? Take that kind of chance?' She stood up, looking round for her coat. 'Joss isn't at home, there's no one in. Do you know where he might be?'

'At work, perhaps. His office is in St Saviourgate.'

'And Ben? He has a flat in the school, doesn't he?'

Owen nodded. He accompanied her to the door and held it open.

She had one last resort, risky and unfair. She said, 'What if it were Sophy? And people were too frightened to do anything? What would you feel then, Owen?'

He looked furious. But when he spoke, it was lightly, without stress.

'Damn you, Louisa,' he remarked pleasantly. 'You always did fight dirty, didn't you?'

He was reaching for a coat.

'Lily's worried too,' he said as they approached Monkbar. 'That day when I had to stand you up for lunch, she told me that Leo's having a hard time at school. Wetting his bed and so on. Bullying is serious, of course, and why she doesn't tell Joss I can't fathom – something about not worrying him, I think. She certainly has no idea that there's anything else involved.'

'Why didn't you ring to explain? About the lunch?' She stopped walking and faced him.

'But I did,' he said. 'Rang your house and someone took the message. I assumed it was a friend of your mother's . . . Don't tell me you never got it?'

She shook her head. 'We've had no visitors for weeks. There was no one there to take a message that morning except me and the phone never rang.'

Owen frowned. 'A wrong number? But I'm sure the man said it was your house.'

'It can't have been. You must have misheard him.'

'I suppose so . . . But, Lou, have you been thinking all this time I stood you up without a word? What must you think of me!'

'It's a mystery, but I'm very glad you did at least try to explain . . .' It felt as if she could breathe again, as if they could start being friends again. She put to the back of her mind the mystery man who had failed to pass on the message.

'Shall we call for Ben, too?' Owen said.

The school was on the way to Joss's office, Louisa realized. She felt a huge reluctance to enter the premises. Owen must have picked it up. He glanced at her in the hectic street lighting.

'You did say that Ben was part of it, too,' he pointed out.

'He's got troubles enough of his own at the moment, don't you think?' She'd heard all the rumours about the theory exam. But it wasn't the only reason she didn't want to go into the school, not by a long way.

It would smell of flowers, she thought. Daffodils or roses or chrysanthemums, depending on the season, and underneath the flowery scent would be polish, and under that again disinfectant. There would be new names written in gold on the panelling, different examples of children's work on the walls. But the smell would be the same, the smell and the desperation. The pig embossed on the ceiling would still look down with its greedy eyes on everyone below.

They tried Joss's house again on the way, but there was still no answer. Only a few steps further on and they were at the gates of St Anthony's. Owen said, 'Ben *was* in the basement at the time, and Joss was outside in the yard, remember? If you really want to find out what happened, I think we should make an effort at least to get Ben involved. I'll go and get him. You wait here.'

'Thank you.'

She stood there by the street lamp, her back to the school, and looked at the curtained windows of the houses opposite. Smarter than she remembered: the paintwork fresh and in good condition, the doors with their shiny knockers and bootscrapers. Most of them were divided into flats, she realized. From one of the doorways a figure stepped into the light.

A ragged man, in holey jeans and corduroy jacket, a cloth bound round his forehead, lank, greasy locks falling over his shoulder. He came towards her and she gasped.

He trailed behind him a tail, a thick, twining snake. It fell behind him over the damp pavement, bulbous and unwieldy. She was on the verge of running after Owen when the man smiled at her and bent down, turning to one side. He picked up part of the tail and began rolling it up.

A sleeping bag: that was all it was.

The relief made her smile. He looked up and caught her expression. He apparently took it for friendliness because he came across the road towards her.

'Got any change? It's cold out.'

She fumbled in her bag and took out a pound coin. 'Here

you are,' she said. He took it, turning it over in his fingers as if it were unfamiliar.

His eyes considered her dispassionately. Uneasily she smiled once more, wondering if perhaps she should have given him a fiver.

'It's not much, is it?' he said. 'What do you spend on food, on booze? What would a pound buy you?'

He didn't wait for a reply but wandered off down the street and Louisa watched him go, wondering whether perhaps to make her next photo-essay a study of the homeless. But this man repelled her, contributed to her sense of unease, her sense that things were going wrong all around her. And of course, photojournals of the homeless had been done a thousand times before, although not in York, she thought. The contrast between architectural, touristy attractions and the increasing numbers of hopeless, abandoned tramps might catch some editor's eye.

'He's not in.' Owen's voice at her shoulder made her jump.

'Come on then. Joss's office?'

'This is probably a wild goose chase, you know. He'll be out with Lily, they'll be at dinner or the theatre or some-thing.'

'Perhaps.' She was walking swiftly, impelled by an urgency she didn't understand. They came to the offices of Past Present and found the ground floor lights on, the plate glass door wide open.

She knew at once that something was wrong. The rain was blowing in, splattering over the carpet. Owen was ahead of her, running up the stairs, taking them two at a time. She rushed after him as fast as she could. Two flights: and then she nearly careered into Owen's tall figure, standing in an open doorway.

Over his shoulder she saw a scene of devastation. Chairs were upturned, blinds pulled from their rails. And the room was filled with paper. Small, torn pieces of paper fell in drifts over desks and tables and chairs. Just inside the door the fax continued to spew out even more of the stuff.

Owen jammed his hand on the off switch. For a moment there was silence. But then the machine started up again.

'It keeps doing that.' A familiar voice behind them. Joss, leaning tiredly against the hall landing. 'I can't get it to stop,' he said. 'There's something wrong with the controls.' He was very pale. He looked not at all surprised to see them.

'Unplug it?' Owen was keeping his hand on the switch and there was a merciful silence.

Joss gestured to the wall of filing cabinets. 'The socket's behind there. I couldn't move them on my own. I was going to find the mains switch, but then I heard you.'

'Joss, sit down.' Owen pulled over one of the chairs and Joss subsided into it with a sigh. 'Are your crutches under this lot somewhere?'

'I suppose so. I couldn't find them earlier.' He seemed suddenly to take in the fact of their presence. 'What are you two doing here?'

'Looking for you. You'd better ask Louisa to explain.'

She was dimly aware that they had stopped talking. She was staring at one of the pieces of paper. *Forgetting is evil, remembering is worse.* She picked up another. It said the same. And another, and another.

'What is this, Joss?' she flung at him. 'What's been going on, what are you playing at?'

She saw that Owen was examining one of the scraps of paper. He was frowning, increasingly incredulous as he looked at more of them. They covered every surface of the room, drifting like snow into every corner, every doorway.

And to one side there was a small cubicle, where a light from the main room fell on a plinth. Paper was piled into this room, slinging round the base of the column like folds of cloth. On top of the column, she saw a skull, stained and dirty, yellow with age. She shuddered.

And then there was a sudden gust of freezing cold air and the drifts of paper rose into the air like so many white moths, fluttering with swirling vortices all around them.

Louisa shouted, 'Owen?' but her voice was unsteady and the paper wings were rustling together and she could hear nothing from Owen or Joss.

She couldn't see them, either. Her sight was filled entirely by white moths and her mind was filled with their terrible message.

Then she felt warm hands on her shoulders, and Owen said calmly, 'It's only paper, Louisa.'

The paper moths subsided, settling once more in drifts on every surface. She stared at Owen with disbelief. 'Only paper? Did you read what it said?'

Joss had found his crutches. He was at Owen's shoulder. 'Just a glitch,' he said. 'A mechanical fault.'

'What? How can it be that? Listen, we have to talk!' she said angrily to Joss. 'This is important. Urgent, too. Where can we talk?'

'We could go back to my house,' said Joss. 'It's nearest. But I haven't had anything to eat yet tonight, have you?'

Louisa shook her head.

'I was thinking of eating out,' said Joss.

Owen said, 'That sounds like sense. Well, Indian or Italian?'

'Italian's nearest.'

'I don't believe you two. Does this look ordinary to you?' She gestured to the room.

'The cleaners are going to have a fit,' said Joss. 'Come on, Lou, let's have a bite and then you can tell us what's worrying you.'

It took ages to get Joss down the stairs. He seemed completely exhausted, but Owen took much of the weight, asking

Joss all the time about Leo's art, telling him the silly things Sophy had done, keeping the tone light and easy.

And when they were all sitting in the noisy pizza restaurant in Goodramgate, it seemed easier at first to pour wine and examine the menu than to discuss the bizarre behaviour of the fax machine.

But when the order was given, Joss said, 'You see, it's not an isolated occurrence, this thing with the fax. Nothing has gone right at Past Present since I've been there and it's difficult to pin down exactly what's to blame.'

'Things like machines going berserk?' said Louisa incredulously. 'Saying things like *that*?'

Joss shook his head. 'That's at the extreme end of it. More mundane things.'

'Funding difficulties, do you mean?' said Owen.

'Yes, but that's more or less universal, don't you find? No one I know in any line of work has noticed any kind of feel-good factor. No, it's more like sick building syndrome or something. Even the pot-plants keep dying.'

'Isn't there some nice secretary bird to keep them in order?'

'A fine feminist you are, Lou. What on earth would the *Guardian* say to a comment like that? As it happens, we can't keep a secretary for more than a month at a go. The last one burst into tears and said that she didn't like having bits of dead bodies around all over the place.'

'*Do* you have bits of dead bodies decorating the office?' Louisa asked.

'One skull. That's all. It's well cleaned, neat and dust-free and why an otherwise sensible girl with a fair number of GCSEs and all the right, relevant experience in archeology should take against it, I can't imagine. She says that it was watching her, that it tilted towards her.'

'Inventive. Whose skull was it?' said Owen.

'It was discovered in the potato patch in someone's back

garden up in the Dales. Coverham, apparently. It's been dated as twelfth or thirteenth century, and we know that there was once a religious settlement in the region, an abbey. We're trying to get permission to excavate more, but as usual the money's short. Anyway, it doesn't matter, the thing couldn't have moved on its own. The girl was over-imaginative, too sensitive.' He stopped, picking up his wine glass. He stared into the golden liquid. 'Although . . .'

'Although what?' said Louisa. She remembered the skull sitting in the drifts of paper only too well.

'Bloody Martin Shaw, my second-in-command, seems to be doing his best to fuck things up. Not only does he mislay or misinterpret instructions from me, but he teases the girls: in fact one of them took offence and said it was harassment, although she went no further with it. I wouldn't put it past him to fiddle with the skull, alter its position, things like that. He may even have played the odd practical joke with the fax machine, too, come to that. He's a whizz at electronics.'

'Some second-in-command. Why don't you get rid of him?' said Owen.

'I've no evidence!' Joss put his glass down heavily, spilling some of the wine. 'He's overtly friendly and efficient and charming. No one else seems to notice anything else. But I know he applied for my job, I know he was disappointed not to get it. He's not likely to make anything easier for me. And I suspect that he's been meddling, at the very least. Messages never get through. I bet the fax machine is down to him.'

Owen was nodding. 'Seems all too likely,' he said.

'It's easier, don't you mean?' Louisa said hotly. 'You can blame Martin Shaw, the techno-whiz-kid or sick buildings, or silly secretaries and you don't have to face what this is about—'

She stopped. She could tell that they were withdrawing from her and felt the familiar frustration. They weren't taking her seriously, even though it was staring them in the face. If she wasn't careful, it would happen again. And she couldn't bear that on her conscience.

She suddenly realized what her mother was worrying about. Mavis Jamieson felt responsible for what happened to David. She thought it was her fault. Louisa put her knife and fork down and wiped her face. Then she stood up, fishing in her bag for some money. 'Look, I'm sorry. I've just remembered something. I have to go to the hospital to see my mother. I'll find you later. Sorry.'

She pushed her way through the restaurant, aware that they were staring after her, and not caring at all. She knew what to do. She knew how to give her mother peace.

She was too late. She knew it as soon as she turned into the corridor. There was a curtain drawn round her mother's bed, and as she approached one of the nurses came bustling up to her, someone she didn't recognize.

'Miss Jamieson? We've been trying to reach you. Please come with me—'

'My mother—?'

The nurse shook her head. 'I'm so sorry. Just after you left, she had an aneurysm. Something quite out of the blue, we hadn't expected anything like that. It happened very quickly, she didn't suffer at all. Would you like to sit here?' She'd taken Louisa into an office, steering her carefully by the elbow to a low armchair. 'I'll get you a cup of tea.'

Tea. How many cups had she made? Sleep had been far away. She'd returned to the house and sat in the living room making lists, mug of tea at her side.

Undertaker. Friends: address book? Probably next to the telephone. She wandered through to the hall and stood there for an unmeasurable time staring at the telephone. She'd known it was coming, she'd returned to York knowing that she was coming to attend her mother's death. So why this *fury*? Her hands were clenched, the nails biting into the palms.

It was unfair. There might have been something she could have done, she and Letitia Farmer, some comfort which would have eased those last few agonized hours. She remembered, unwillingly, something she'd once read in a book about Buddhism. The dying should be eased in their passing; this was crucially important. The mind is a continuum: something consisting of habit. It retains, from life to life, its habitual responses. Not events, not people, nothing concrete. But if you die screaming, then your next life is coloured by screaming. Screaming is its tenor, its atmosphere, the terrible legacy of the manner of death.

The image of the wheel grinds on: what escape, what hope? She hated this. If religion, that terribly flawed product of humanity's imagination, was to be of any use at all, it should at least be a consolation. It should be something to make tolerable these hours, days, weeks, when someone dies. But this was stark and inescapable and she could not forget it. She tried to put it aside, for the moment. Picked up the address book and returned to the living room. She began to make lists.

Chapter Eighteen

Leo stared at Samuel Pyper with delight. 'Really?' he said. 'Tomorrow, for tea?'

Samuel smiled. 'Emma's coming. Her mother and mine play bridge together, they're friends. Your mother's coming on later, she's going to play with them.'

Leo nodded. This made sense, although Emma's presence was quite a drawback.

But that day, Samuel had been almost friendly. At least, he hadn't bullied Leo into parting with his lunch money. And Emma had walked the length of the long corridor with him and hadn't tried to push him over at all. He was cautiously optimistic. Mummy had told him that it took a while to settle in, for people to get used to you. 'Hang in there, lad,' she'd said. 'It'll come right, you wait and see.' Yet more evidence of his mother's good sense.

Samuel's mother collected them that afternoon and drove them to one of the large houses leading down to the river off Bootham. Geoffrey Pyper sat in front with her. They didn't talk. No one in the car talked apart from Sam and Emma and they were whispering. Leo noticed that Mrs Pyper had painted her fingernails bright red, like Cruella de Vil. She never smiled either.

Leo didn't like the Pypers' house. The huge hallway was carpeted in a sour, murky green and the walls were crowded with hundreds of pictures. But when Leo looked at the pictures, each of them was boring. He'd seen sets of pictures for sale in furniture stores like that. Pictures by the yard, his mother had said. They were pretty, old-fashioned, but somehow not real. Cute little children with cheeks like apples wearing lacy smocks in brownish tints . . .

Mrs Pyper still hadn't said anything much to them. She told them to help themselves to juice and biscuits and then to disappear.

They took chocolate digestives, a jug of apple juice and some glasses on a tray up two flights of stairs to the playroom. This was a huge attic room which ran the width of the house. Late afternoon sunlight filtered through the dormer windows. There was a television and video in one corner, a tape deck and CD player at the other. One wall was taken up with music technology, keyboards, amplifiers, complicated computer things Leo didn't understand. The walls were painted black and covered with posters of monsters.

'Have you seen *Alien*?' said Samuel.

Leo shook his head. He knew all about it, he'd heard people at school talking about it just the other day, but he'd never seen it.

'Would you like to?'

'Yes,' he said without hesitation. He was curious about the film, he felt that watching it would give him a way into a different world – like a password, a key to the bright, friendly, successful world of the others.

'We've seen it before,' said Emma. 'We're going downstairs.'

All at once, Leo realized his mistake. They'd be somewhere else, together, talking, laughing—

'I don't mind not seeing it right away,' he said, shrugging. 'It can wait.'

'You're scared.' There was no contempt in her voice. She handed him a glass of apple juice. 'See you later,' she said. Samuel set the video going. He drew the curtains so the room was in darkness.

'Enjoy yourself,' he said, and went with Emma.

Geoffrey was still in the room, hunched over a tiny laptop.

Leo looked at him doubtfully. 'Won't the noise disturb you?' he asked, as the opening titles came up on the wide screen.

Geoffrey didn't reply. Leo turned back to the screen, and within moments was deeply involved in the dreadful circumstances aboard the spaceship. For comfort, every now and then, he took a sip of the apple juice. Once he jumped so much that he spilt some of it, so he drank it all off quickly.

He lost all sense of time. All sense of place. Nothing existed for him but Lieutenant Ripley's epic battle against the monster.

'Did you drink all the juice?'

The voice emerging out of the dark made him jump again. Geoffrey had stood up, was looking across the room towards him. The reflected, greyish glow from the video threw his features into sharp relief. His hair, pale like Sam's, looked like ash.

'I – yes, I finished it.'

'You realize that Sam and Emma both spat in it?'

Leo's head jerked round. 'What?'

'They spat in it,' repeated Geoffrey, coming nearer. 'They always do, when they've got someone else here. Sometimes Sammy pees in it, too. What did it taste like?'

Leo felt his stomach heave. 'I don't remember,' he said. 'I didn't notice.'

'It was probably just spit, then,' said Geoffrey. He stood right next to Leo. 'Watch this bit, it's really good,' he said, as the monster devoured the penultimate crew member.

Leo's stomach still churned. He wondered whether he was going to be sick. He wondered where the bathroom was, but he'd have to cross the length of the attic and it was all dark and he didn't know where anything was.

And it was necessary, absolutely necessary, that he find out what happened at the end of the film. He sat down again and stared at the screen, while the taste of sickness grew in his mouth.

*   *   *

180

'I'm so sorry to be late!' Caroline Morrell did indeed look unusually flustered. 'Something rather awful has happened.'

'Tell us,' said Lily. She had been drinking tea with Lucy Lindhurst in Janice Pyper's high-tech kitchen. Conversation had not flourished. They were waiting for the fourth to arrive and Lucy kept looking at her watch. She yawned frequently and refused any of the offered refreshments. She was going for dinner with the Archbishop that night, and made sure that Lily and Janice were properly impressed. She was rather up against it: Lily did her best to look interested but Janice seemed hardly to notice, flicking through the pages of a magazine as Lucy talked.

She's playing, thought Lily. Bridge isn't her thing, neither is afternoon tea with other women. So why, why does she do it?

Caroline Morrell was over an hour late. And her hair was very slightly out of order, escaping from the Alice-band to fall over her perfectly-sculptured cheeks.

'What's up?' said Janice languidly.

'Ben Bowen's done a flit. Walked out, which is bad enough in itself, but he's broken all the keyboards and computers in the music block. It must have been him. They're lying in fragments all over the school.'

'Isn't he the chap who fiddled the exam?' Lucy was interested.

Caroline nodded. 'It's all rather dreadful. Hard to see how we can keep the school's name out of the press now. Lily, wasn't Bowen a friend of Joss's?'

'They were at the school together,' said Lily blankly. She very much wanted to go and get Leo and leave. She needed to find Joss. She didn't want anyone else to tell him, because she knew how upset he'd be. And Owen, too. Sophy was doing great things in music with Ben . . .

She stood up. 'I'm sorry ... I think I should leave now. Joss will be upset,' she said.

'Oh, come on, we're all here now,' said Lucy. She was already shuffling cards. 'There's nothing you can do about it—'

'But Joss and Ben were – are – close,' said Lily.

'Were they?' A flicker of interest from Janice Pyper. 'Funny how boys make friends, isn't it? Friends that last so long.'

'Joss won't know yet,' said Caroline, sitting down. 'No one knows, Mark's dealing with it all.'

For a moment Lily was undecided. But then Lucy asked her to cut the pack and so she sat down and tried to concentrate.

The film had ended. Leo took a deep breath. He'd never seen anything quite that strong, quite that gripping before. He wondered whether he'd be able to put it out of his mind at bedtime. Things like that had a way of re-running in the dark.

Somehow he found his way across the attic to the door. Geoffrey was still crouched over the laptop. He didn't look round.

It was a relief to get out into the main part of the house. He went down the narrow steps to the upper landing and as he did so, Emma poked her head round a door.

'Leo, can you come here a moment? Sam's gone to sleep and I can't wake him up.'

Leo went into the bedroom and saw Samuel lying on top of a large double bed. His eyes were closed, barely breathing.

Emma stood at his side and shouted loudly in Samuel's ear, 'Wake up!'

There was no effect.

'Tickle him,' suggested Leo.

'You do it,' said Emma. 'Under the chin's a good place with Samuel.'

Leo knew it was a trick. They'd spat in his drink. He could feel her eyes on him. 'No, you do it,' he said.

'All right. Come here then.' He stood on the opposite side of the bed to Emma. She bent over Samuel's unmoving body, her hand poised like a claw.

'Look here, Leo,' she said suddenly, her voice excited. 'There's a mark on his neck—'

She pointed and Leo bent down to get a closer look.

All at once a leaping monster burst out of Samuel's chest, spraying scarlet all over Leo's face. It grabbed at Leo's nose with its open maw and he fell backwards on to the carpet, screaming wildly.

Emma was convulsed with laughter. And Samuel sat up, readjusting his clothes, putting his red-stained hand back through his sleeve . . .

Leo scrambled to his feet. He was gasping with shock. But somehow, he found words, disjointed, difficult words. 'That's a horrible trick! Horrible, I hate you, Sam and Enema! I hate your horrible games and your stupid films and I don't ever want to come here again—'

He made for the door and their laughter followed him all the way down the next flight of stairs.

He saw a door open to a bathroom and dashed inside it, locking the door after him. For a moment he leant against the door, tears streaking down his face. Then he caught sight of himself in the mirror over the sink. He couldn't let his mother find him with blood – no, it was only paint, all over his face.

He made some attempt to wash it off, but he was not at all successful. It spread alarmingly all over his shirt and tie.

And so when he presented himself at the kitchen door, where the four women were playing bridge, his mother, looking up, screamed.

She saw her only child covered in blood, his face pale and ghastly.

And she still had to tell Joss his friend had gone mad.

Chapter Nineteen

'What did he call you?'

'Emma.'

'No, he didn't, it was something else.' Samuel held open on his lap a dictionary. 'I've heard it somewhere before. Enema, that was what it was.'

His finger slowly ran down the page. 'Ha!' He fell over backwards, whooping. 'Enema!' he shrieked, 'ENEMA!'

Emma's face was tight with fury as she picked up the book and found the entry. 'If you ever ever tell anyone of this, I'll kill you.' She thrust her chin forward, her large blue eyes unblinking. 'Did you hear me?'

Samuel was still rolling round on the floor. 'Don't kill me!' he yelled. 'It wasn't my idea!'

'True.' She sat back, thoughtfully. 'Leo. Little nerd.'

'Turd.'

'*Merde* – French, to you.'

'I know.' Samuel pulled himself together. 'Little Jewboy.'

'Don't you dare tell anyone!'

'Okay,' he said. He was used to lying.

Downstairs, Leo was being cleaned up. 'It was a game, that's all,' he said. 'It was an accident. I got in the way and so I got splashed, it wasn't anyone's fault—'

Children did not split on each other, not if they were at school together, Lily knew. She borrowed a jumper from Janice Pyper and bundled the red-stained clothes into a carrier bag.

'For goodness sake, Leo, what was going on?' she said as

soon as the door shut behind them. 'You can tell me, I won't tell anyone.'

'It was a game,' he persisted. 'Painty balloons. But one burst and I was in the way.'

He could be very stubborn. They hurried towards Bootham Bar and the cold wind cut through the layers of coats and scarves. 'This is an awful spring,' Lily muttered. 'I can't believe summer's ever going to come.'

'It would be warmer in Essex, wouldn't it?' said Leo.

'Too right,' she said feelingly. They were passing in front of the Minster and Lily saw a woman struggle to keep her skirt in place, while wrestling with a double pushchair full of infants. Their wails blended with the wind.

Lily was dreading getting home and telling Joss about Ben. He was so depressed these days, and she knew he was finding the job disappointing. She was beginning to loathe the sound of Martin Shaw's name. Was the job also too much for him? Of course, the broken ankle complicated everything, made everything difficult. She was beginning to wonder if it really had been such a good move, coming to York. She had assumed that she would easily find friends here, but Janice Pyper was impossibly vague and the malice in Caroline Morrell's voice when she spoke of Ben had shocked her. Caroline's preoccupation seemed to be entirely with the adverse publicity for the school. She seemed not to care at all about a man who had devoted his life to the place. Really, Louisa was the only woman Lily liked so far, and she had more than enough troubles of her own.

Lily was miserable about Ben: she had both liked him and had looked forward to getting to know him better. She knew that he'd been keeping an eye out for Leo too. She glanced down at her son as they hurried past the Minster and into Goodramgate. His shoulders were hunched, his head bent. In a way, she was glad he hadn't tried to pass the buck to anyone else. It showed he was growing up, making decisions for himself about loyalty and honour. At last, it seemed to her that he was beginning to make friends.

Joss was standing in the hall when she arrived, reading a note. As soon as she came in, he said, 'Louisa's mother has died. This is from her.' He gave the note to her and then stumped on his crutches through to the kitchen. Lily glanced at the note with its bald message. 'Go and change,' she said to Leo, pushing him gently towards the stairs. 'Run a bath, you could do with it.'

For a moment it looked like he was going to rebel, but then he turned and ran up the stairs two at a time. She took the bundle of dirty clothes through to the kitchen, where she found Joss filling the kettle.

'I'm sorry about Mrs Jamieson,' she said, putting her arm round his shoulders. 'It's a shame there wasn't time for you to go and see her, isn't it?'

He shook his head. 'I was always too busy. Too busy and important. And what use is that, if you can't go and see someone dying in hospital?'

'Louisa said she wasn't up to visitors . . .'

'Louisa's in something of a mess herself.'

'Joss, sit down. I'll do that.' She took the kettle from him and plugged it in. 'I've got some additional bad news, I'm afraid. It's about Ben. He's—' She stopped. How could she say this?

'I know about Ben,' he said quietly. He clasped his hands together on the table in front of him. 'I called in at the school this afternoon to collect Leo. I'd forgotten you were both going to the Pypers'. Everything was in a tizzy, people muttering in corners everywhere.' He paused, looking into space. 'Someone had even gone out to his country cottage to find him, but there's no one there.'

'Poor Ben. Where will he have gone, do you think?'

Joss shook his head. 'I don't know. I wish he'd come here. He never had a chance, really. He never found anyone to love him, no family, nothing to secure him. He put everything into the school, and the school was never, not for one minute, worth it.'

'When you were children, who was his best friend?'

'Strangely enough, it was Kenny at first. Kenneth Pyper. But that all changed when David arrived. Although Owen was also close to David too. And I, and Louisa . . .' He looked up at her and she saw his dear, kind face, set hard. 'We all loved David. But Ben never got over it. Ben always blamed himself.'

'What about you, Joss? Are you "over it"?'

'It was years ago,' he said, standing up. 'It's nothing to do with me now.'

'Really?' She remembered what he had told her about the night when he broke his ankle. About that strange dream of the mob passing him by, the cursing figure.

'Where's Leo?' he said, ignoring her question.

'In the bath. He managed to get himself covered in paint at the Pypers'. He's fine.'

Joss sat down again. 'I'd better write to Louisa. Could you find me some paper?'

'Oh, let's go and see her! She doesn't know anyone much here, she'll be all on her own and there will be all those awful arrangements—'

'You go,' he said tiredly. 'I'll stay here with Leo. Give her my love.'

'What about supper? Shall I bring her back here?'

'No. Don't.'

'Joss, why?'

'She's – too extreme, these days. I can't take it.'

'Her mother's just died!'

His face was still shuttered, unfamiliar. It came to her,

suddenly, that perhaps he was frightened. He sighed, running a hand through his light brown hair. 'Oh, very well,' he said. 'Have it your own way.'

She hesitated by the door, looking back at him. This was deep, unfamiliar water for her. Joss was behaving quite out of character. She didn't know what to do. She put her coat on, hoping that perhaps Louisa wouldn't want to come to supper.

Louisa answered the door, her eyes red, clutching a handkerchief. Without hesitation, Lily put out her arms and hugged her, kicking the door shut behind her. A storm of weeping, then great shuddering sobs. Lily found her own eyes wet with sympathy.

She remembered it well, this abandonment of grief at the death of a parent. Eventually, Louisa calmed down a little. 'What a greeting,' she said indistinctly.

'I was of course expecting you to be perfectly composed, perfectly calm and together, the day you lose your mother,' said Lily gently. They went together through to the back room, where the floor was littered with papers, mugs, wine glasses and screwed-up tissues.

'It's rather a mess,' said Louisa unnecessarily, subsiding on to the sofa. She was still gulping back sobs.

'Doesn't matter,' said Lily. She picked up the half-full bottle of Scotch. 'May I help myself?'

Silently, Louisa handed her a glass from the cabinet by the sofa.

'Joss sends his love,' said Lily. 'I came to see if you needed a hand with all the arrangements.'

'I think I've done it all. I've been up all night.'

She looked it, too. Hair unbrushed, make-up smeared, clothes crumpled and unlovely.

'Don't take this wrong,' said Lily carefully, 'but why don't you go and have a bath and go to bed? You look washed out.'

Louisa sighed. 'I can't sleep. I need to talk. There's something wrong, I really need to talk to Joss and Owen and Ben—'

'Ben's not there. He's left. Packed his bags and gone.'

'What?' Louisa was on her feet again.

'At least, that's what the Morrells think. He's trashed all the computers in the music department, too.'

'Good God.'

Lily took her arm. 'Go and wash your face, at least. Then come back home with me and I'll make some supper and you can tell Joss whatever's worrying you.'

'And Owen,' Louisa said firmly. 'I need to talk to Owen at the same time.'

Lily sighed. She hadn't planned on entertaining that evening and this was getting more complicated by the minute.

'We could get a take-away,' suggested Louisa. 'You go ahead. I think I will have that bath . . .'

At the door, she hugged Lily again. 'You're brilliant,' she said. 'See you later.'

Chapter Twenty

Leo was still up when Louisa arrived. He'd had his bath, was sweet-smelling in pyjamas and dressing gown. 'You have to come up and read me a story,' he was demanding Joss. 'You haven't read me a story for ages—'

'But I can't get upstairs easily, lad. Can't we do it down here, on the sofa?'

Lily was bustling round in the kitchen, opening wine, making phone calls. Louisa had subsided into one of the arm-chairs, wondering if she should offer to help. Leo had greeted her with guarded friendliness, but she knew he was beyond the stage of automatically finding strangers interesting.

Leo said, 'It's not the same, down here. I can't just go to sleep, I have to walk upstairs again—'

He brought out a book from his dressing-gown pocket and pushed it into Joss's hands, who glanced at it and handed it to Louisa. 'Remember this one? Wasn't it one of your favourites?'

She stared at the familiar blue covers. '*Jennie*! Of course, Paul Gallico. Joss, fancy your remembering that!'

'This lady,' said Joss to Leo, 'when we were children at school together, used to read this book all the time. She used to know bits of it by heart.'

Leo glanced at her. 'Can you still remember it?'

She shook her head. 'But I'd really love to read it to you, Leo. I can hardly remember it at all, although I know it's wonderful. Would you allow me to read you your bedtime story?'

'Lou, do you want to bother? Today?'

'I think I'd rather like to, Joss. Something to divert me . . .'

Over Leo's head, Joss smiled at her. Leo said nothing, but nodded, once, and set off out of the room.

It wasn't a take-away in the end. Lily threw together prawns and garlic and parsley and lemon and poured white wine and the conversation limped along, subdued and hesitant.

It was Louisa who broke the mood. As Lily poured coffee, she said, 'I found this in my mother's writing desk today. I had no idea of its existence.'

She spread the piece of paper on the table between Joss and Owen. 'It's an insurance policy,' she said. 'For private health care. And this was the covering letter with it.' The second piece of paper was handwritten, and signed with a flourish. *George Redmond*, it read. It was addressed to *Mavis*.

It spoke of loyalty, of unspecified services rendered and gratitude.

'What's this?' said Owen, picking it up. He scanned it briefly while Louisa watched him with anxiety, willing him to understand. He passed it to Joss without saying anything. He didn't look at Louisa.

'Don't you see?' she said passionately. 'There was a cover-up. My mother was *bribed* to keep quiet. They gave her private health insurance as a bribe!'

'Don't be ridiculous.' For two pins, Louisa thought, Owen would screw up the papers and throw them in the fire.

'Listen to me!' she said passionately. 'David was killed! It wasn't an accident. And the school tried to cover it up, because a public scandal had to be avoided at all costs! It's why my mother – Mum – couldn't—' Her treacherous voice was swamped with tears again.

'You're upset,' said Lily, unnecessarily. She put a box of tissues at Louisa's elbow.

'It's the *school*!' she said when she'd calmed a little. 'Don't you see? The evil of it!'

'Nonsense, Louisa!' Owen drained his glass. 'I think you should go home and get some rest. You're not thinking straight.'

She drew a shuddering breath. 'It's what happens when you confuse money with education. When you think you can pay for the things that matter.'

'There is no confusion. There are solid values at the school that are irrelevant to money and this—' he waved his hand at the two pieces of paper '—means absolutely nothing. It's not a bribe, Louisa, it's just a reward for work well done!'

'Why should my mother then die in such distress?' She sounded ragged, but she was not going to give way to tears again. 'There was some *sin* that would not allow her any peace. And I think it was this: David, and the way he died.'

'This is nonsense, Louisa, as well you know.'

'Well, tell me what happened. What do you remember? How did it go?'

'I see no useful purpose at all in bringing this all up again.' Joss's voice was empty of expression. 'There are enough troubles in the world because people won't let go of the past: Northern Ireland, the Middle East, all the small private feuds which ruin family life. Let it go, let it rest, Louisa. Your mother is beyond worrying now, no useful purpose can be served by dragging it out again.'

'*Forgetting is evil, remembering is worse!*' she shouted. 'Are you so frightened?'

'Damn it! This is not about fear! Just because you've got it in for private education—' Owen was shouting too.

'It's why David died!'

'Rubbish! It was an accident!'

'Describe it then! I wasn't there.'

'And that's what I find so remarkable,' said Owen, his voice now dangerously quiet. 'You weren't even there. You couldn't begin to know what happened, and I assure, *assure* you, that it was an accident!'

'Then why won't he rest?'

'What are you talking about?'

'Why is it still going on?'

'It isn't!' Owen's fist slammed down on the table. 'There's nothing wrong with the school, nothing wrong with the past! There are no secrets! It's all in your over-heated imagination, Louisa. Go home, take a Mogadon, go to bed and get some rest!'

'Because you've chosen to spend money on it, the school can do no wrong.' Louisa's voice was equally heated. 'None of you will look at it coolly, because you've invested money in it. You'd look like fools, wouldn't you, spending all that money on a substandard product. There's something else, too. It made you what you are. Warts and all. And if you're pleased with yourselves, happy and content with your lives, you can't criticize the process which made you what you are.'

'Louisa! Stop it! This does no good.' This was Lily.

Sympathy and understanding were beginning to wear thin. The strain in Joss's face was there for all to see. Owen's anger was flaring dangerously.

Louisa didn't care. She was determined to make them understand this time. Lily was irrelevant. She hadn't been there and because of that Louisa discounted her. Joss's wife liked the school, she was friends with the Morrells. It was easy to see why: it represented a world of old-fashioned, establishment values. Ordered, well-mannered, and rotten to the core, Louisa thought furiously.

'You can't buy morality,' she said.

'You can trust people though.' Lily spoke coldly. 'We're not all paranoid.'

'Let's try again.' Louisa was passionately aware that this could be her last chance. 'Why do you think Ben made such a stupid error of judgement in that theory exam? Was he particularly fond of Geoffrey Pyper? Or scared of Kenneth Pyper's influence?'

'He did say to me once, that music exams represented cash, in hard terms,' Joss said unwillingly.

'There you are!' she turned on him triumphantly.

'Nonsense.' Owen stood up. 'I've had enough of this. It's slander, Louisa. You're in no state to argue anything today, and no one could blame you. You need rest, time to reconsider—'

'But it's Leo who's at stake now!'

'What do you mean?' Joss, sharply.

She took a deep breath. 'Sheepshanks. Remember Sheepshanks? He's after Leo.'

'What on earth are you talking about?' Lily was mystified.

Owen glanced at her. 'When we were children, we played this stupid game. It was a *game*, Louisa! We invented this ghosty figure and gave each other nightmares – and none of it was real.'

'Do you mean that?' Louisa stared at him incredulously. 'Have you really forgotten it all?'

'We were kids, that's all.' He was standing in the doorway, putting on his coat.

'Joss, do you believe this too?'

He looked embarrassed. 'So long ago,' he said, vaguely.

'Well, you listen to me. Just listen to this. Sheepshanks turned up at my mother's house. He said – *said* – to me that it was Leo he wanted.' With bitter satisfaction, she saw Joss's face drain of colour. 'Now do you believe me?'

He said nothing.

And Lily said, 'Joss, that dream . . . when you broke your ankle. On the bridge—'

'I – it was only a dream. Nothing important—' But his eyes said something else, and Lily suddenly pushed past Owen. They heard her footsteps, running upstairs. Two flights: a door opening, the faintest murmur of voices.

Louisa said, 'I'm going home now. You have to take seriously what I say. This time, let's not let him win.'

She'd whisked out of the house before Lily returned.

Lily met Owen and Joss in the hall. She looked furious. She said, 'Leo's perfectly all right. Of course he's all right. She's out of her mind.' She went through to the kitchen and started clearing up. They heard the saucepans clash together.

Owen and Joss stared at each other.

'"Out of her mind"? Do you think so, Joss?'

'I hope it's that. I really hope so.'

By the end of the next day there was not anyone in the school who had not learned Emma's new nickname. She threw her lunchtime yoghurt at Samuel, but she'd known it was hopeless. As soon as she'd read that dictionary definition, she knew it was inescapable. Emma the Enema, enough to make you shit.

The first Leo knew of it was that he enjoyed a sudden, brief, surge of popularity. People smiled at him in corridors. Johnny gave him a thumbs-up sign across the playground. He too heard the nickname and played it cool until he'd had time to dash to the library to look it up.

He went hot and cold at the enormity of it. He had been in the closed circle of the school for long enough to understand the significance of such a thing. And although Emma Morrell was powerful within the school, she was not much liked among the younger children. He flushed with pleasure to think that he – he! – inadvertently or not, had originated something which delighted so many.

And then he saw a fleeting expression on Emma Morrell's face and his heart sank. He could identify hatred when he saw it. Beneath her bravado, the uncaring arrogance she presented to everyone, something else lurked. And Emma had allies, most particularly Samuel Pyper, and he had no one.

He went to bed that night dreaming of monsters bursting from their hiding place and deceiving, devouring, destroying the innocent.

Chapter Twenty-One

It happened at Christmas. At first, it seemed ordinary, just like all the other Christmases at St Anthony's. We all had colds, as usual; I couldn't remember a winter when my mother hadn't spent a considerable portion of her time dishing out cough medicine and throat pastilles, and laundering handkerchiefs.

It wasn't surprising: we lived in close quarters and York itself was notoriously damp, lying low round a sluggish river. Hardly anyone escaped the virulent colds that periodically ran through the school. David, with his slight tendency to adenoids, always came off worse.

In fact that day, the day of the dress rehearsal, my mother had been looking for him. 'He could do with a day in bed,' she told me. 'He's not in the play, is he? A day off and he'll enjoy the end-of-term celebrations so much better.'

She went bustling down into the school, intent on finding him.

I finished my scrambled egg thoughtfully. It wasn't fair. I was one of the honoured few who never seemed to catch cold. I was never ill, never privileged enough to get a day in bed, undivided attention from my mother, hot-water bottles, and honey and lemon drinks . . .

Tough as old boots, Mum said approvingly.

Joss's and Owen's colds were at the streaming stage, while Ben had no more than a tickly throat. But David was feverish, I could tell. Like my mother, I'd noticed his too-bright eyes, his pale, sweating forehead.

He was in English, first period, and also in French, sounding appealingly husky. I was late arriving at Maths, having mislaid my geometry set, and when I finally made my way to the long

196

corridor, Kenny and Philip were in a huddle with David at the top of the stairs to the basement. I didn't see what they were doing, but they broke apart when I approached and Kenny said, 'Here, let's see if Lulu knows the answer.'

'What do you mean?' I couldn't see David's face, he was hanging back in the corner.

'It's a joke,' explained Kenny. 'But David here doesn't seem to understand it. It's easy enough. How do you get fifty Jews into a telephone box?'

'I don't know . . .' I was keeping an eye out for the arrival of Mr Turner.

'Throw in a sixpence,' said Kenny triumphantly.

I said, 'Ha very ha.'

'That's not all,' he said quickly. 'How do you get them out again?'

I shrugged.

'Throw in a pork pie.'

'You're so stupid!' said David, savagely. 'You don't know anything—'

I stared at him, aghast. It must have been the cold: usually he took no notice of such low-level digs. Then Philip said, 'Hitler, Stalin and a Jew fall out of a plane. Which one hits the ground first?' A pause, a silence.

'Who cares?!' shrieked Kenny.

'You're ignorant, crass idiots.'

'You're a smarmy, lying, cheating Yid, and you don't belong here. Why don't you get your filthy people to move somewhere else, this place doesn't like Jews, it never has—'

'Don't be so stupid, look, here comes Turner—' I had never been so glad to see a teacher approach. It was the white-hot fury in David's face which scared me, not the petty malice of Philip and Kenny.

I had never seen David in such a state. Someone normally so gentle, so sweet-natured, was now glaring at two boys who were both bigger than he was, and his fists were clenched tightly.

'David, come on, leave them—'

And then Mr Turner was on us, hurrying us along in his clipped, no-nonsense way, and we settled down to Maths.

I didn't see David after Maths or at break and assumed that Mum had towed him off to the san. I was glad: he'd be out of trouble there.

After break, while we were waiting for Mr Williams to arrive, Kenny found a worm in his pencil case and swore and said, 'I'll kill him.'

I knew immediately that he meant David.

There was some reason for this. David had an eccentric sympathy for worms. He was always picking them up off pavements and paths and putting them back in the earth. He told us at length about the way they conditioned the soil, how they benefited both gardeners and farmers. He always refused to go fishing with the others because of his absolute revulsion at what happened to the worm.

I did not think at the time that David would be the last person ever to put a worm in a pencil case, in amongst the sharp lead points, the compasses and penknives. I just saw the poor creature writhing on the desk and thought of David.

As did Kenny. He jabbed the worm with his compasses and threw the whole ensemble at Joss, David's friend. Joss dodged, and the compasses, with worm still wriggling, landing at the feet of Mr Williams, who had just arrived.

He'd seen Kenny throw it.

'Out,' he said. 'Library. Number 111 of Palgrave, first forty lines by heart by afternoon school.' He bent down and picked up the compasses. 'And dispose of this, in a civilized fashion . . .'

Kenny scowled and took it from him and I felt a pang of regret for the worm. Kenny knew nothing of civilization, in my view.

*   *   *

198

The day wore on. Still no sign of David. There was a dress rehearsal in the afternoon and so I hung round in the entrance hall, helping Joss arrange paper snowflakes on the windows of the porch. I was inconveniently dressed in the long navy robe which constituted my Mary costume. Joss's nose was red and sore and his pockets were swollen with soggy handkerchiefs. But he clowned around, sticking the snowflakes on each window in risky patterns: TIT *read the window over the door,* BUM *to its left. We were still foolishly giggling when Owen came out of the hall, blowing his nose.*

'Got any pastilles?' he asked Joss. 'Willy Williams says he can't understand a word I say.' And it was true that his voice was nowhere near as clear and articulate as usual.

Joss drew an unlovely bundle of rags from his pocket. 'No, but there's a packet in my coat pocket. In the basement.'

'Do you mind if I help myself?' Owen was already making off in that direction.

'Wait for me.' Joss ran after him. 'I could do with some too—'

'Joss!' He'd already gone, leaving me with the incriminating snowflakes still on the windows. Resignedly I climbed up the step-ladder in order to remove the evidence before a member of staff emerged. Joss was taller than me, and so I had to stand on the penultimate step to the ladder, leaning with one hand against the cold glass. Outside the sky was overcast, heavy with rain. The street was deserted except for a man hurrying past, his collar upturned, clutching an open umbrella.

Then Kenny suddenly rushed in from the back entrance, bringing with him a gust of bitterly cold air. He was in filthy rugger kit, his boots clogged and heavy, his shorts streaked with mud and grass stains. He was looking furious.

'David!' he yelled at me. 'Where is he?'

I shrugged. 'I don't know.'

Someone came out of the hall, one of the shepherds. It was

Philip, dressed in a white tunic and hooded cloak, as one of the shepherds in the play.

'He's not in there,' said Philip. 'Bloody little traitor.' He came over to stand with Kenny at the bottom of the step-ladder. Kenny put out his hand and jogged it.

'Careful!' I scowled at them both.

'Tell us where the Jewboy is. He's a friend of yours, a little girly's pet, and we've got things to discuss with him.'

They were on either side of the steps and I couldn't get down. 'I haven't seen him since Maths,' I said truthfully.

'But you know,' said Philip. I saw something glint in his hand. A penknife, open.

Owen, I thought. Joss. Where are you?

'Bog off.' I kicked out with my foot, hoping to dislodge the knife. Instead, the blade caught my calf, a sharp, precise pain. 'Bloody hell, look what you've done!'

'Going to tell Mummy all about it?' said Kenny nastily.

'Look, I don't know where David is and even if I did, I wouldn't tell two thickos like you—'

'I'll get you, Louisa Jamieson. Remember that. But you're small fry, you'll keep,' said Philip.

'Come on, Phil,' said Kenny. He tugged at Philip's sleeve. 'We're wasting time.'

Philip's mouth curled. 'Okay,' he said and before I could move, before I realized what was happening, he'd cut my calf again with a crossways slash.

'Ow!' I yelled, launching myself from the steps at him.

It was not a wise action. I found myself rolling on the floor, my hand spurting blood, bruised and battered and shocked. Philip and Kenny had gone. They'd run off down the south corridor towards the lower school classrooms. I sprang to my feet, stumbling towards the stairs.

The san. Not for myself, although my socks and sleeve were now streaked with blood. I needed to find David before they did.

He wasn't there. But my mother was, calmly sorting the laundry. 'Lulu, good heavens, whatever's the matter?'

I'd thrust my hand into a fold of the dark blue robe and it fell below the level of my socks, so it must have been my face which gave it away.

'Where's David?' I blurted out. The san was empty, the beds neat, no signs of occupation at all.

My mother was frowning, looking at me. 'I haven't seen him all day. I missed him after breakfast, and I haven't been down since, there's all the trunks to pack—'

'Mum!' I shouted. 'Philip and Kenny are looking for him and Philip's got a knife—'

'A knife? What are you talking about?'

She wouldn't understand. We were children to her, teasing, sometimes wilful, often unwise, but not wicked. I could see only incomprehension on her face, and some concern for me.

'Oh, never mind.' David still had to be found and quickly. I was on my way to the door when I turned back to her. 'Mum, David's in trouble. Philip and Kenny have got it in for him, and I know you think it's just kids' games, but it's not, it's worse than that—'

'Lulu, honeybun, they're just playing.' She was almost laughing, although there was a flicker of doubt.

'Mum, please!'

'Don't worry, love, I'll keep an eye out for him. He'll be all right.'

I ran downstairs, throwing open classroom doors on the way, shouting his name everywhere. I didn't care if other teachers heard me, I wanted everyone alerted. I pictured David curled up in a corner somewhere, hiding behind a door, under a table, as in all the old childish games. The entrance hall was filled with rushing flakes of white. Someone had left the front door open and the wind had caught all the paper snowflakes. A whirlwind of white fragments span in the darkened air. I ran out through

201

the front door, perhaps he had gone that way, perhaps he was alone, out in the cold.

And cold white snow cascaded silently around me. Those heavy clouds had brought more than rain. It was too dark to see much. I shouted, 'David!' and the sound was muffled by snow, dispersed, diffused.

The front gates were locked and anyway, I knew he wouldn't be there. I turned back to the school.

White moths settled on its roof tiles, clogged round the window ledges. And I saw a tall figure in white, white-hooded, pass behind the windows of the long corridor. Philip Stroud, dressed as a shepherd, part of our own mystery play, our very own crucifixion scene.

Nativity. The one implied in the other, an understanding I did not welcome then. I ran round the front of the school to the side steps. Down to the outside door to the basement.

I met Joss and Owen coming out and careered into them.

'Where's David?' I panted. 'Is he there? Philip and Kenny are on the warpath—'

They exchanged glances. 'Forget them. We're off for a smoke, coming, Lou?'

I was babbling. 'But David, that man—'

'What man?' Owen looked over his shoulder. 'There's no one there, Louisa, believe me. Neither David nor Kenny nor Philip nor anyone else.'

I pushed past him. The basement was deserted. The one naked light bulb swayed a little in the wind from the door. It was cold. Had the heating been turned off already?

I knew David was there. A heavy weight of misery filled the dark, sour little room. He was there somewhere, crouched between the coats and the shoe bags and heavy, outdoor shoes.

'David—?' I breathed.

The door at the top of the stairs opened. The light bulb swung suddenly in the through draught and shattered, burst into a thousand vicious fragments. I saw a figure silhouetted against the light from the corridor, tall, thin, dressed in an off-white tunic.

'Philip!' I shouted. 'Philip?' more quietly. Was it him?

Whisks of white fluttering flakes twirled around him and all at once I thought I saw faces, other faces peering round the doorway. Crowds of people, cramming themselves into the narrow space between the stairs and the corridor. I didn't know who they were.

They were nothing to do with me.

I took a step backwards. Somewhere to my right I heard a movement. Frantically, I glanced towards the shadows but it was too dark, too cold and the coats hanging on the pegs rustled and lifted in the wind.

Another step backwards. The tall figure at the top of the stairs was crouching, his arm extended, his eyes squinting along the length of it . . .

Shadows fell over his face from his hood and for a moment I doubted that this was Philip. He was pointing slightly to my left. Only then did I realize that David was there, huddled behind the racks of shoes, crouched against the cold wall. I rushed over to him. 'Come with me!' I yanked at his arm.

His eyes were blank and unseeing. He wouldn't look at me.

'Come on!' With both hands, I tried to pull him out.

He didn't resist. Awkwardly, he unfolded from his cramped position and struggled to his feet.

'Come on, this way.' I tugged at his hand, trying to haul him to the open door. He wouldn't move. Snow was blowing around us and the mob at the top of the stairs seemed to be overspilling, hand over hand down the sides of the stairs, until there was a crowd on our level and I thought I saw faces I knew, Kenny, among others. They were so quiet! I didn't understand their silence, but I knew it was menacing. Still the tall figure at the top kept his arm outstretched, pointing it only at David.

Who took another step forward. I clutched him. 'David! Wake up, come on, let's get out of this!' His left arm suddenly shot out and knocked me aside.

Or was it David? The milling, silent crowd were now between me and him, and it could have been any one of them.

I fell against a bench, painfully knocking open the cut in my hand. A gusting flurry of snow hid from me what was happening by the stairs. I scrabbled to my feet and somehow found myself outside the door.

'Joss!' I screamed. 'Owen, where are you?' It hadn't been long, surely they could not have gone far.

A small orange glow over by the bikesheds. Owen and Joss, coming towards me, through the swirling snow.

'David's in there! He won't come out and there's all those people and Philip and Kenny—'

'Calm down, he'll be all right.' Joss, kindly, maddeningly calm.

'No, he's not all right! We have to get him out, they're dangerous, he's going to get hurt—' I pulled away from Joss and somehow he stumbled, fell awkwardly against the stone wall and I saw it, I saw his ankle fold sidewards beneath him and I swear I heard the crack, the crack of bone breaking. Joss gave a noise that was half scream, half moan. I crouched down beside him and didn't see Owen go into the basement.

'Christ! Jesus Christ!' Joss was bent over his ankle, his hands fluttering uselessly round the laces of his boots. I saw the basement door shut. And Joss caught my arm. 'Go and get someone,' he gasped. 'It's broken—'

'Yes, I know, but David—'

'Owen's there, forget David, he's all right!'

'There're all those people there—'

'Lou, I don't care.' His face was white, his lips drawn back in the effort of not howling.

'I can't—' I glanced back at the shut door and thought, we need help, we need an adult to stop this, to sort us out, this is

too much, too hard . . . 'I'll find Mum,' I said and made for the front door, slipping and sliding on the fresh snow.

The front door was still open. Snow was blowing into the porch, and the paper snowflakes were damp and soggy, clinging to the parquet floor. As I skidded across the floor, the door from the hall opened. Ben came out, still dressed in his angelic costume, great wings of paper fluttering in the draught. 'Louisa, they're all looking for you. And where's Owen got to?'

I clutched his arm. 'Joss has broken his ankle, but please, please, go and help David . . . He's in the basement, Owen's there too and Kenny and Philip, there's something awful happening—'

'How did Joss break his ankle?'

It was as if he hadn't heard more than a few words.

'He fell,' I gabbled. 'But it's David who's urgent, he needs help.'

'Okay, keep your hair on. I'll go and find David.'

'He's in the basement—'

'I know, I know.' He ambled slowly off down the long corridor, his great wings trailing damply over the floor. I flung myself up the stairs to the san.

Mum was still there, sewing on buttons. I told her about Joss and she was immediately on her feet, grabbing a bag, telling me to ring for Doctor Willis, the school's GP.

She clattered off down the stairs and I followed after her, making, as instructed, for the office where the telephone was. She was going to cut through the basement, I realized with appallingly mixed, chaotic feelings. But before I could stop her, or warn her, Mr Redmond emerged from his office and I had to explain about Joss all over again.

He swept out of the room, pausing at the hall to give Mrs Redmond instructions to phone the doctor, before following my mother down the long corridor.

I trailed after him, suddenly so weary that I could hardly move. The door to the basement stood open. Kenny and Philip came out. They walked in silence past me, their faces set rigid.

But as Kenny's shoulder brushed mine, he said, 'He's dead.'

Chapter Twenty-Two

I knew instantly who he meant. I stood there in the long corridor, my hands raised helplessly to my face, my mouth open in a sound-less wail. I could think of nothing, hear nothing. Somewhere the choir might have been singing carols, somewhere people went about their Christmas shopping, but thought, for me, had stopped.

The door to the basement, opening again. My mother came out, her arms round two boys. Owen and Ben. I hardly recognized them. They did not look at me. My mother's face was almost unrecognizable too, her voice stranger yet.

'Go and get changed, Louisa. Go home.'

'What happened?' At last I'd found words. 'What happened?'

'There's been an accident,' said my mother.

'David? Is David—?' I couldn't say it. 'What about Joss? Where's Joss?'

My mother's face blanched. She turned Ben and Owen towards her. 'Boys, go to your dorm now. I'll be up to see you soon. Get ready for bed.'

'But they haven't had supper!' I cried, as if this was the worst thing of all.

'I'll bring you up a tray,' said my mother to Owen and Ben. 'Wait there. Do not leave your dormitory until I arrive. Louisa, go back to the flat. Go now!'

I stared at her. I had never heard her shout like that at me before. Ben and Owen seemed dazed. Like mechanical dolls they moved along the corridor to the stairway, neither talking nor looking at each other.

'Mum—' I put out a hand to touch her and she dashed it away.

'Did you hear me? Go home, Louisa, now!'

I turned away from her and ran, ran past my two silent friends, along the corridor, through the entrance hall to the stairs. I kept running until I reached the unlit sitting room of our flat. I stood over by the window, looking down over the front driveway. I saw two ambulances draw up. I saw two stretchers carried over to the open doors, and Joss's face, closed eyes, tight mouth, bizarrely caught in the light from the front door.

The figure in the second stretcher had its face covered.

My mother got in the ambulance with Joss: I could not see her face and she did not look up at me. I saw the ambulances drive off through the thickly falling snow and still wondered, still fretted, about those other people, the mob who had filled the basement with their accusatory fingers, their incomprehensible cries, their malevolence and hatred. I stood there against the cold window for hours. I heard the bells go in the school below, heard the shouts and patter of feet as people went from supper to prep to cocoa to bed, and still my mother did not come back.

I wanted to go to Bishop dormitory and find Ben and Owen but I didn't dare. My mother had told me to stay at home and I held fast to that one clear instruction. I would wait there for her all night if necessary. She'd told me to change. Dutifully, I took off the blue robe and found my Clydella nightie. I stared at the cuts on my leg for a while, trying to remember how they had happened. It didn't matter. Then I washed my hands and face and brushed my teeth and went back to stand by the window again. I saw Redmond's Rover leave the school some time later. Later still, after the last bell had gone, the headmaster returned, bringing with him my mother.

Where was Joss? I fretted. People with broken limbs always returned to school from hospital within a few hours. But Mum would tell me what was happening, of course, as soon as she'd checked on Owen and Ben. She'd come and find me then.

I moved away from the window and went to the door of our

flat. I sat on the top step, looking down the stairwell. I saw my mother accompany Mr Redmond into his study. They were there for ages. I could hear nothing from my eyrie, but at last the door opened and my mother came out and there were both anger and fear in her voice as she said, 'I really cannot do as you suggest! The authorities must—'

A softer murmur from Redmond, words I could not make out.

My mother again, strongly. 'I'll wait till morning, if you insist. But—'

More soft words and she halted at the bottom of the stairs. She turned and went back to the headmaster's study.

I crept a few stairs down, hugging the banisters. The school was silent now. I thought of Ben and Owen, alone in their dormitory, still waiting for supper. Or perhaps someone had remembered them, perhaps Mrs Redmond had organized a tray for them. But I knew everything had changed. That all the old securities, all the unquestioning sense of order which had run through my life, was over. I knew that there was nothing safe, reason and good sense would not prevail. Because David was dead (I did not for one minute doubt Kenny's words), I knew I would never feel safe again. I knew that safety was not an option for anyone, anywhere, ever.

But what of Philip and Kenny? Would the police be called in, would they be arrested?

I knew they were responsible for David's death. I half expected to hear sirens, to see uniformed officers storming into the dormitories and dragging off the murderers.

I also knew it wouldn't really happen like that. Social workers would step in, it wouldn't be dramatic at all. But at least everyone would know, would understand how horrible children can be.

'Louisa, go to bed.' Mum was on her way upstairs, looking more weary than I'd ever seen before.

'Mummy, I don't – what about David? What happened to David?' I stood up as she approached and held out my arms.

'Oh, you're so cold, honeybun!' She swept me up and held me tight, and I could feel how tense she was. 'Have you been waiting here all this time?'

'You told me to get ready for bed, but you didn't come! No one came, and I've had no supper and what happened?'

She carried me through to the sitting room and turned on the gas fire and knelt down to chafe my frozen feet between her hands. 'It was an accident, sweetie,' she said softly, not looking at my face. 'A dreadful, sad and terrible accident—'

'No, it wasn't!' I shouted.

She sat back and stared at me. 'You weren't there, Lulu,' she reminded me.

'They said they were going to kill him. Philip and Kenny, they both said it and they had a knife—'

'Davey broke his neck. He fell down the stairs. There was nothing about a knife.'

'They pushed him, then! It's their fault!'

'Darling, it wasn't, you know. They were very upset too, we all are—'

'Did you see it? Were you there?'

'I arrived later. But it's clear what happened, and Owen and Ben were there, of course.'

'Owen and Ben?' I subsided back into the chair. I could not assimilate this. 'They saw it happen?'

'They – no, I don't think they actually saw anything. They had some ridiculous story about crowds of people—'

'It's true! There were all these people and—'

'Sweetie, you're over-tired, you're overwrought and you've been reading too many ghost stories. Let me make you a boiled egg and soldiers and some hot milk and I'll bring it to you in bed. How does that sound?'

'Mummy, there were people there, raggedy people—'

'You've been dreaming, Lulu. Both Mr Redmond and I were there only moments after Davey fell and we saw no one. There

210

was no one there at all apart from Owen and Ben, Philip and Kenny.'

'It's not true!' I was beginning to cry. 'I wasn't dreaming, the others will tell you, they killed David!'

'Come on, Louisa, enough of this. Pop into bed and I'll bring you a hot-water bottle and you'll feel much better in the morning. Poor little scrap, how can you be expected to think straight after waiting alone in the cold with no supper for all this time?'

'Mum—'

'Enough. Bed.'

I couldn't argue with her. Not when she looked so tired and when I was so confused, so upset. So I went to bed, and cuddled up with the hot-water bottle and fell dreamlessly asleep.

In the morning, Philip Stroud and Kenneth Pyper were sent home. We were told that they had caught the flu. Joss returned from hospital, looking interestingly pale, and hopped around on crutches, swinging his heavily plastered ankle in front. And Owen and Ben said that they'd seen nothing, that they'd been hiding behind the coats smoking when David fell. They said there had been nothing suspicious about David's death. They denied that there had been anyone else there apart from Kenny and Philip.

I said they were blind and deaf morons. They walked away and avoided me for the rest of the term.

And no one believed me. After all, I wasn't even there.

Chapter Twenty-Three

There were footsteps behind her. Louisa's pace increased. The steps speeded up and then she heard Owen's voice.

'Louisa, wait for me.' She didn't want to talk to him. She'd had more than enough. All she wanted now was her bed, her quiet, lonely bed, where she could begin to mourn her mother.

Under the trees of Lord Mayor's Walk, she halted, watching his approach. 'Owen, I know we have to talk again, but I can't do it now. You were right. I need to go home.'

'Louisa, I just wanted to say ... I'm sorry if I sounded angry. It's the last thing you need right now.'

'Too right.' But she couldn't just turn away. Under her feet the pavement was steady. No sign of threat, nothing to frighten or remind. She saw concern in his face, nothing but concern and affection. 'Come with me, Owen,' she said on impulse. 'I could do with some company.'

'Really?' He put his arm round her waist. 'That's more than I deserve.'

They started walking together towards Gillygate and she said, 'What's made you change your mind? How have I suddenly moved from distraught madwoman to old friend?'

He didn't say anything at first. Then, 'It was thinking about Leo again. How I would feel if it was Sophy. I don't think we can risk anything, not with children's lives at stake.'

She squeezed his arm, and thought, he's going to tell me what happened. He's going to tell me now.

But when they reached the house, she was so tired that she sagged against the wall while he took the keys from her and opened the door. The house was like an ice-box. In the course of the day's confusion she had somehow left both the kitchen and bathroom windows open. The through-draught had filled the house with icy air. She sat on the stairs while Owen shut the windows and turned on the heating. Then she heard him moving around in the kitchen, the tap running, the kettle boiling. He returned to her after a while with a mug of tea and a hot-water bottle wedged under his arm. 'Upstairs,' he said briefly and she didn't argue.

He put the hot-water bottle into her bed and then helped her undress. He'd hung her nightie over a radiator, and held it out to her as if she were a child. Then, because she was still so cold, he kicked off his shoes and got into bed with her. He held her close until she stopped shivering. As her breathing became more regular he gently disentangled himself and she said softly, 'Don't go.'

'Are you sure?'

'I don't want to be lonely tonight.'

'Then I'll stay.'

They lay curled together in the narrow bed she'd slept in as a child, and it was as calm and easy as if they were still children.

In the morning, she woke before he did. She looked at the arm lying across her shoulders, the hand spread on the sheet in front of her face and wondered that it seemed so natural, so comfortable. His hand had not changed. The fingers too long, the back of it tanned, the fingernails bitten down to the quick. There was a faint pale band round the fourth finger, where his wedding ring had been. She felt tenderness, and sorrow for him, and then remembered.

'Sophy!' She sat bolt upright. 'What did you do with Sophy last night?'

He rolled on to his back, blinking in the morning light. 'I

left her with the Pattisons,' he said mildly. 'I thought we might be rather late for conventional babysitters.'

'Oh, I'm sorry, of course you made arrangements—'

'Of course,' he confirmed. 'It's not difficult, you know. Soph's got lots of friends.'

'Has she?' Louisa turned her pillow so that it wedged behind her neck. She leaned back, looking at her oldest friend. 'Tell me about Sophy,' she invited. 'I've hardly seen anything of her.'

'We'll have to change that. Come to supper tonight. Come and meet her.'

'What if the message gets lost?'

He said, 'It reminds me of that fax machine in Joss's office the other night – God, was it only yesterday? I was using a telephone and it let me down, like the fax machine.'

'I think it was Sheepshanks who took your message. I think it was Sheepshanks who set the fax going.'

'I don't – altogether – dismiss that.'

'He was there, Owen. In the basement that Christmas. Don't you remember?'

'Louisa.' He stood at the end of the bed, his clothes rumpled, his hair messed, his eyes acute and intelligent. 'You think I'm hiding something. That I'm wilfully suppressing what happened.'

'You were there.'

'I saw nothing.'

'I don't believe you. How could you not see anything? The basement is *tiny*!'

'I'll tell you. I'll tell you it all. After breakfast.'

'Now.'

He ran his hand through the spiky black hair and it stood out like an old-fashioned golliwog. 'Not fair, Louisa,' he said plaintively. 'I need coffee to order my thoughts.'

She scrambled her way out of the duvet and knelt on it.

'The sun shall be your shriver,' she said, indicating the lozenge of light on the wallpaper. 'Now, before daily life catches up with us. Remember what happened.'

He said, 'It was cold, actually freezing in the basement. The door to the yard was open and the wind blew in, and there was snow in it, tumbling falls of white snow that drifted all over the floor. And yes, the basement was full of people.'

'Yes! They're proof, aren't they? Proof that this is not natural, not ordinary!'

'Perhaps.' He still sounded guarded. 'Certainly, Ben and I couldn't tell who they were, they were dressed in strange clothes, like a shabby operetta chorus. Assorted peasants, you know. But they stank, and their skin looked grey with ingrained, deep-seated dirt. I could not see David at first. Nor anyone else I recognized. And then he shouted out, David saw us and shouted our names, Ben and Owen. David was at the top of the stairs. As soon as I saw him – I don't know if I can explain this – I realized that all the other people weren't *real*. They were flimsy, somehow, for all their filth and smell. Except Kenny and Philip. Philip was by the door at the top of the stairs, Kenny a little further down. David was caught between them.

'It was Philip . . . who was the strangest of them. It's funny, Lou, I haven't thought of this for years. He was still in his shepherd's costume, that dirty white tunic, but he looked different. Older, somehow. Something about his eyes, although I couldn't see him clearly, the way his hood was pulled down. But he did this thing, I can see him now – he stood on one leg, and – crouched. God, Lou, I've only just remembered this, how could I have forgotten? He pointed a hand at David and squinted along it as if it were a telescope. It sounds stupid, but it was indescribably sinister.' He looked suddenly and directly at Louisa. 'I didn't really think it was Philip. Someone else—'

'Who?'

He smiled at her and there was no humour whatever in it. 'You call him Sheepshanks, don't you? That's who I saw. I can see now, that was who it was . . .'

'What happened then?'

'That's it, really. I saw – Sheepshanks – do his stuff and then the people round us, all that press of peasants, got in the way and I didn't see anything else. I didn't see David fall.' He paused. 'Truly, Louisa. I heard it. That's all. I didn't see what happened.'

'Why didn't you say anything?'

'What could I say? I was trying to push through, I wasn't even looking up the stairs. And who would believe me? When I looked back, all those people had gone. There was no one there but me and Ben, Kenny and Philip. David was lying on the floor, not ten feet away, and his head was stuck on wrong. That was what it looked like.'

'What did Ben see?' Her mind was working furiously.

'You never give up, do you? Ben would never talk about it. He said that he wasn't looking, blowing his nose or something. He never admitted to the people, either. No one else has ever seen them.'

'But I have,' said Louisa softly.

'I know.' He sounded bleak. 'But you were – upset. Distraught, everyone said. Hysterical, even.'

'So you decided to ignore it.' She was bitter.

'It made no sense!' he said angrily. 'I thought it was madness, a kind of delusion—'

'But we both saw them!'

'We were children. Imaginative, impressionable—'

'We were thirteen. In other cultures, other times we could have been married, or working full-time. We had the capacity for adult understanding, even if it was sometimes a bit skewed.'

'It's worse than that. You were a girl. It didn't matter, what you saw—'

'You can't believe that!'

'Not now.'

'*And* you saw it too!'

'I know . . . But Louisa, it had the quality of a nightmare. I thought I was dreaming, I *had* to be dreaming . . . And we were crass, Louisa, us boys. We thought the world was going to belong to us, that we would reach the moon and scrape the stars and our girls would wait patiently at home and applaud and do nothing to challenge us. You were a girl, Louisa. I couldn't back a nightmare with a girl's support.'

'And so even though you'd seen those people too, you couldn't align yourself with me.'

'Not against everyone else. But I have to tell you that it never seemed fair, even then.' His expression was totally serious as he regarded her. 'I owe you the deepest apology of my life, Louisa. I'll do everything I can to help.'

She felt like hugging him, like laughing and crying all at once. 'We need to find Ben,' she said. 'I don't think Kenneth Pyper is likely to tell us anything new.'

'Poisonous as ever, our Kenny.' Owen sat down on the bed again. 'I didn't find out he was a governor until after we'd enrolled Sophy.'

'Would it have stopped you?'

He nodded, once, sharply. 'I never could stand him.'

'Why? What did he ever do to you?'

He looked as if he was about to say something, but his mouth was clamped tight shut. He turned his back to her, crossing the room to stand by the window. He said nothing, and in her mind, Louisa filled in the gaps.

Kenneth Pyper killed David. And David was Owen's closest friend. Ben's too. 'How can you bear it?' she said. 'Meeting Kenny over and over again?'

'We were children then. We're adults now, we have to try to live together and put the past behind us—'

'And pretend it didn't matter?' She got out of bed and went over to him. Her hand ran through his hair. 'My mother tried to pretend, you see. And she died screaming. There was no rest for her, there was no peace and she died screaming.'

His face was haggard. He scooped her into his arms. 'But now matters too, Louisa. We mustn't forget that: the sun on the window, the shadow on your hair—' His hand reached up and touched the hair falling across her cheek.

'Forgive me,' he said. 'But I have never seen it before.'

'Seen what?'

'That you are beautiful,' he said simply. 'I know this is the wrong time, the wrong place. Shall we go out for breakfast? What about Betty's?'

She considered him. There were faint lines on his forehead, and other lines leading from his eyes. In the early morning light, she imagined that she looked much the same. She thought, like me, he has not found everything to his taste; he has known disappointment and has some self-knowledge. Now he wants to live for the moment, taking what pleasure he can, because he knows pleasure is hard to find, and harder still to keep.

'Not Betty's,' she said. 'I've got so much to do.'

'Of course.' He was immediately contrite. 'Can I help with any of it?'

'Don't you have to go to work?'

He made a face. 'There is that. Will you be all right, Lou? I meant it about supper, too.'

'Thank you. I'd love to come. I'll be fine.' She put her arms round his neck. 'Thanks, Owen. Thanks for everything.'

He kissed her lightly. 'About seven tonight? Then you can have a decent go at Sophy too.'

218

She saw him to the door, and then shut it against the cold, damp wind.

He'd been honest. But it hadn't explained everything. She had no real proof of the manner of David's death.

Owen had seen nothing crucial either. It left Ben; Ben, Kenny and Philip.

Chapter Twenty-Four

Leo was on his way to French, his least favourite lesson. He was stupid at languages, he felt, but this time he'd worked hard at his homework and really thought that he understood what the difference was between *tu* and *vous*. So he went along the corridor, thinking only of the coming lesson and at first didn't register the sound of his whispered name. But somehow, one's own name impinges even if it is almost inaudible. The voice said, slightly louder, 'Leo!' and he swung round suddenly, and found no one there.

This was not the first time. He was beginning to wonder, quite seriously, if someone had hidden tape recorders in odd places throughout the school. Usually it happened when he was in a crowd, but not always. Sometimes his name pursued him from one end of the playground to the other. Sometimes it followed him upstairs, or out on to the games field, or even to the loo.

He was even beginning to hear it at home. He was filled with terror in case his mother heard it. He was not thinking logically here. Eight-year-old minds are often diverted, often amazed, always open to suggestion and influence. Strangely caught between real life and the imagination. He recognized the voices as malevolent, and while one part of him wanted his mother to expose the trick, the fraud, another wanted to protect her from it. They can't touch her, he thought, so long as she doesn't know about them. His father was out of the question too. Tired after work, preoccupied at home with mountains of paperwork, with the sheer physical difficulty of managing life on crutches in a tall town house.

There was no one he could tell. No friends at school, no relations at home. And now Mr Bowen had disappeared and he was not quite sure about Mr Allbright.

His house was safe, his lion-protected house. He knew that, and counted the minutes each day to going-home time. And for the few hours before bed, he watched television and played with his Lego and answered his mother's questions and that was all right, too. Bedtime was different. He didn't like sleeping these days because he so often experienced nightmares of mind-numbing terror. They always involved his father. They would be in a strange dark place with high walls, and there were crowds of people around them. His father would be pulling a long knife from his belt, and there would be tears running down his face. He was holding Leo tight, and the knife descended, as all around them crowds of people cried and screamed and the scent of blood was everywhere. And then there were the flames, the smell of burning.

So he tried not to sleep. He read under the bedclothes and listened to his Walkman, but after a while he would find his eyes growing heavy. So he took to getting up again, usually waiting until his parents were in bed. Sometimes he chanced it as soon as they had crept up to see that he was asleep. They never missed this, and it was easy enough to fool them. He lay under the covers, breathing heavily and considering what would happen if he sat up and held out his arms and said that he was frightened.

They would ask why. And then they would know about it too and whatever it was that was whispering his name and stealing his things and seeping into his nightmares would start to afflict them too. So he kept quiet, kept his head down, and when his bedroom door opened, waited until the footsteps had stopped and it was safe.

He didn't bother to dress properly. He merely put on

jumper and jeans over his pyjamas, trainers on his bare feet and struggled into his old winter coat, which was now too small for everyday use and hung in his wardrobe awaiting its transfer to a jumble sale.

He managed to remove the central bar easily nowadays. He also knew where the creaky places on the fire-escape were. He crept downstairs, keeping an eye out for the cat who sometimes accompanied his midnight ramblings.

She wasn't in her usual place beneath the stairs. He wondered if she'd found somewhere more secret to have her kittens. In his pocket he had a torch, a pad and pencil and an apple. He was still on the lookout for any details of interest, and his pad was full of strange inn signs, of gargoyles and door-knockers.

He came to King's Square, and was glad to see that the pavement artists had moved their pictures of pretty ladies with red hair and lilies. The pavements by the toy shop were glistening in recent rain, and any drawings directly on to the pavement would have been ruined. But most pavement artists in York made no attempt to draw straight on to the stone: they made their pictures at home and brought them out when the sun shone, taping them to the pavements so that credulous tourists might be deceived. It made sense, thought Leo. Why spend hours on pictures which might be washed away in two minutes' downpour?

But as he crossed the square he saw that some colours remained, glowing softly in the lamp-light. A splash of crimson from a cloak, a swathe of green and gold from autumn leaves. A running together of ideas, of shapes and forms, distorted by rain, by the momentary whim of the weather. There were faces there, grinning at him, but all the detail was lost. They slid across the pavement beneath his feet.

It wasn't yet late: a couple walked slowly down Petergate, their arms intertwined. Their murmured conversation sounded friendly and reassuring. Leo felt, not for the first time, that he was right to explore York like this. It was a place where people came to enjoy themselves, to have fun. There were restaurants, theatres, museums, jugglers, musicians . . . although at this time of night, after the pubs had closed, it was easy to forget the happy daytime crowds. The only crowds left were those at his feet, on the pavement.

The murmuring couple had passed on. He turned left at the lights, and then right again into Swinegate. There was a lovely shop there, with a window full of clowns and candlesticks and paper flowers. He rather hoped that his mother might one day buy the doorstop in the shape of an orange tree which stood by the entrance. He stood for a while with his nose pressed to the glass, trying to make out if the orange tree was still there.

He was holding his breath so that it wouldn't condense against the cold glass. He concentrated. The lights in the shop had been turned off, but the street lamp gave some illumination. He could make out the gilt on a mirror gleaming, the shine on a lustre teapot. But was that shape in darkness by the desk really the orange tree? Or something else? Had it been sold—?

'Jewboy. Is that you? You just wait!' A voice he dimly recognized made him jump. Mr Pyper, Samuel's father, that was who it was . . . He bolted. He knew he'd get into terrible trouble if Mr Pyper caught him, if he told his father. He was coming from Grape Lane, so Leo ran back the way he'd come, found an alley-way opening off to his left and dived down it.

And immediately knew his mistake . . . because the pavement tilted and his hands flew out sideways to break his fall but the wall was no longer there, and his feet were caught in paving stones which ruffled up like playing cards. He tumbled painfully on to his knees and his hands, stretched out in front of him, met moving, living stone. He was too breathless to scream. He tried to crawl forwards but the upright moving stones were higher than his head, an impenetrable barrier. No way back, either. He was surrounded by sentient stone slabs which fenced him in like a rat in a cage.

And then, like all his dreams, hands started to pull and tug at his garments. It was too dark to see what was happening, but he could feel the fingers and thumbs pinching at his clothes. They were catching at his flesh as well. He whimpered, trying to huddle himself into a smaller shape.

A yowling sound somewhere ahead of him. It cut through the deep grinding sound of the shifting stones and made him look up. Through his tears he made out a lithe, dark shape springing over the stones towards him. His cat, his lovely cat, coming to find him! Somehow he surged to his feet, and the cat jumped into his arms and he buried his face in its silky, warm fur.

And when he looked up the stones had calmed, had fallen back into their ancient patterns and he ran to the end of the alley, still clutching the cat.

It was purring like an engine, rubbing its head against his chin and he gradually realized that it was lighter than usual.

'Your kittens!' he exclaimed. 'You've had your kittens—'

The cat wriggled and jumped down from his arms, as if suddenly reminded of her duties. She frisked a little way ahead of him and then paused, turning her head to make sure he was following. He scampered after her, forgetting, for the while, about the nightmare in the alley.

He also forgot about the man who had threatened him, the man who sounded so much like Mr Pyper.

Chapter Twenty-Five

It was Louisa who found him, half an hour later, creeping back along St Anthony's Lane to his house. She said softly, 'Leo? What are you doing out at this time?'

He jumped guiltily. 'My cat's had kittens,' he said and he could not have chosen anything better to say.

'Really?' She came closer. 'You never told me you had a cat.'

'It – she's not mine. She's a stray, but she likes me and she showed me where she keeps her kittens. So I came out to see if they're all right—'

'Your parents can't know you're out at this time.'

He said nothing. She considered him for a moment and then said, 'I have a proposition for you, Leo. I won't tell. This can stay a secret, so long as you let me know next time you feel like a midnight walk. Don't risk the city on your own. Not after dark.' She scrabbled in her bag and pulled out a diary. She tore a page from it and scribbled some numbers on it. 'You can ring me any time. I live just at the end of Lord Mayor's Walk. Let me know whenever you feel like exploring.'

'It's alive,' he said suddenly. 'The stones move.'

She took a deep breath. 'I know. There's an alley between Swinegate and St Sampsons Square—'

'Three Cranes' Lane.' He nodded. 'I know. It goes on to Petergate.'

'Does it?' She crouched down and peered intently into his face. 'Leo, most people don't know about the moving stones. Most people don't realize how dangerous they are. And if you try to tell them, they make fun of you. But you know they're real and so do I and let's promise each other to keep well clear of them.'

He nodded fervently. She began to walk with him towards his house and resisted an impulse to take his hand. She was very unsure about the wisdom of her suggestion. Surely she should let Joss know what Leo was getting up to?

But she'd seen how stressed Joss was, and knew how unwilling he was to take on her theories. For the moment, for the time being, she would hope that Leo trusted her and that that would be enough.

She saw Leo to the back gate and as she watched him climb the fire-escape to his room, she found an impromptu prayer running through her mind. *May angels guard and keep you safe.* At the end of the back alley, a cat paced. It rubbed against her legs as she passed and she could hear it purring. She felt minutely, unreasonably, cheered.

She was walking the city in the small hours of the morning because she couldn't sleep. That day she had attended the cremation of her mother, and she had been amazed by the numbers of people who had attended the brief service. She'd expected some of the school's staff to come, but they had been lost in the crowds of people from her mother's various gardening clubs and art classes. It had been exhausting, a day of such strain that Louisa had doubted her own ability to get through it all.

The worst of it had come in the afternoon, when she had been to a reading of her mother's will with the solicitor. And it was the contents of the will which kept her out of bed, pacing the streets, her mind skittering round like a rat in a trap.

Her mother had left her over four hundred thousand pounds. It was a vast fortune, enormously greater than Louisa had foreseen. Her mother had lived comfortably, not luxuriously. The house was pretty but modest, part of an unremark-able late Victorian terrace.

The solicitor had explained it a little by saying that her mother had placed, long ago, a lump sum in the hands of a broker who had served her extraordinarily well. But where did the lump sum come from? Her mother's family was not wealthy, and as far as Louisa knew, she'd never taken any chances, never gambled a penny.

Fifty thousand pounds had been placed with Brookwell Atkinson in 1967.

The year David died. The coincidence would not let her go. Private health insurance, and a lump sum. Her mother had been party to a cover-up.

She had not cried since seeing the solicitor. There was a hard knot of fury where there should have been grief. She felt betrayed, unable to mourn. So she paced the streets of the city and hardly noticed the figures in the doorways, the watching gargoyles, the unstable stones and swinging inn signs. They were patient, waiting their turn. At home, she returned to the systematic turning out of drawers. She opened every chest, took down every book from the shelves. She was looking for clues, some answer, some explanation for what she was increasingly, sorrowfully, seeing as her mother's corruption.

But as the slow dawn blotted out stars, she sat back, knowing that it was no good. She had not realized that an ordinary house could possibly hold so many items. She had never thought about the debris accumulated over a life.

Her own life, her flat in Fulham, was pared down in com-parison. Some books, but not many; she'd delighted in regular donations to jumble sales. She'd wanted to feel free, able to move on at a moment's notice. She bought new clothes twice a year, a couple of outfits that followed, not slavishly, the current fashions. She threw out jumpers that were bobbly, tore old T-shirts into dusters. The only possessions she cared about were her kitchen implements, crockery and china. She could buy whatever she liked now. Go to one of those posh culinary shops and buy saucepans worth hundreds. Antique moulds, German knives, Chinese baskets, Minton china.

And sickness filled her mouth. The money was tainted. She could not use it, she should give it away to charity or to David's family . . . His family. Why had she not remembered them? That pale, elegant couple in their Daimler; the mother who had died. A bad death, Tish had said. The memory of their arrival at the school was still vivid in her mind. That first day, when she'd watched David from the upstairs window. His parents lived in the country . . . the moors, was it? the Howardian hills? How could she find out?

The school might have records. Owen might know. Simpler still, she picked up the telephone directory and there it was. Seifert, O., Middlecross, Terrington.

She glanced at her watch. Only seven a.m. She would have to wait a couple of hours. She curled up on the sofa and rested her head on a cushion.

She was woken by the midday Minster bells. For a moment she could remember nothing, couldn't think what she was doing curled up on the sofa in the living room. And then she remembered. The phone directory was on the floor by the sofa.

She stood up, stretching, and then picked it up. In the hallway, she dialled the number, expecting to wait for a while, or find herself connected to an ansaphone. But the call was answered almost immediately, and a man's voice crisply repeated the number back to her.

'Oh, hello, I wonder if I could speak to Mr Seifert?'

'Oliver Seifert speaking.'

Her heart suddenly started thumping in her breast, and she couldn't think what to say, why she was doing this . . .

'Seifert here,' repeated the voice impatiently.

'I'm sorry, Mr Seifert, my name is Louisa Jamieson ... I used to know your son.'

'Yes?' The voice gave nothing away.

'I – I was at school with him. He was my friend.'

'The only girl in the boys' school.' There was something stretched about his voice. The clipped tone was now full of tension, full of complications.

'My mother was the matron of St Anthony's. That's why I was there.'

'I cannot imagine that we have anything to say to each other.'

Absolute finality in his tone. Louisa waited for him to slam the phone down, but it didn't happen.

'Mr Seifert, my mother has just died—'

'I know. She was suffering, I understand.'

'How do you know this?'

'I have made it my business, over the years, to observe the activities of Mavis Jamieson. She was intimately involved in the death of my son.'

Louisa gasped. This was too strong, too sudden. To have her worst fears confirmed like this ... But she knew why he said it, felt her heart wrench with the pity of it. 'Mr Seifert, my mother died in agony. She was in an agony of guilt, and I think it was about David. I think – although she was my mother – that she did something terrible then. She assisted in a cover-up.'

There was a long silence at the end of the phone.

He said, 'It was a very long time ago, Miss Jamieson. Your mother is dead. Is there any point in resurrecting such an ancient story?'

'Mr Seifert, I imagine that you remember your son every day. As I do. And I think we should talk. Please.'

Another long silence. Then, 'Very well. My house is at the

end of Main Street. I – do not go out much. I shall be glad to see you for tea, this afternoon, at four o'clock.'

'Thank you. Mr Seifert, is there a bus—' But the line had gone dead and she sighed as she put the phone down. There would probably be a bus, or she could hire a car, or book a taxi—

She was a rich woman. She could buy a car, and drive herself, if she wanted to. But then she had another idea. She picked up the receiver again and phoned Owen.

'Lou, I just can't get away this afternoon. I'm really sorry.'

She sighed. She'd just spent five minutes being passed from secretary to assistant, before tracking him down. 'Are you so busy?'

''Fraid so. Can't you re-arrange this for the weekend? I'd really like to meet David's parents—'

'His mother is dead.'

'Poor woman.' His voice was bleak. 'I'm truly sorry, Louisa. I would have liked to come.'

'Never mind, Owen. I'll see you later. Still on for supper?'

'Of course. I'll look forward to hearing all about it. At whatever time you like.'

She put the phone down thoughtfully. And then tried again. This time, she got through to Joss's office direct.

He wasn't there.

'He's got an appointment at the hospital,' said a young man's voice. 'Martin Shaw here, his assistant. Can I help you?'

'I don't think so, thank you.' Louisa put the phone down and wondered what to do.

Half an hour later, she was in the outpatients' department at the District, waiting for Joss. She'd arrived just in time to see him crutch his way to one of the cubicles. After a prolonged pause, she saw him emerge and turn down the corridor marked

X-Rays. She caught up with him without difficulty and touched his arm.

'Joss, are you okay?' She was appalled to see that his face was greyish in tone, slightly sweaty.

'They think they may have to reset the ankle,' he said. 'It's got to be X-rayed again.'

'Reset it? What does that mean?'

'An operation. They break it again.'

'God, how ghastly.' No wonder he looked so dreadful. 'Is Lily here?'

He shook his head. 'She's rehearsing. There's a concert tonight. Don't worry, I'll get a taxi home.'

'Joss, listen. This afternoon I'm going to see David Seifert's father. I wondered if you'd like to come too.'

For a moment he stared at her. 'Are you mad, Louisa? Won't it be unbearably painful to ask him anything about it?'

'Joss, I – my mother's left me a huge sum of money. I think she helped the school whitewash what happened to David. I need to find out what Oliver Seifert knows.'

'What's the use, Louisa? What good is it to anyone?' He suddenly shouted, 'And don't give me any of that nonsense about Leo again, about Sheepshanks. I refuse to believe any of it. Leo's perfectly all right, perfectly happy at school—'

'Can you swear to that?'

'I don't have to—' He broke off as a nurse approached, looking at a clipboard.

'Mr Fletcher? Can you come this way, please? Shall I find you a wheelchair?'

'Thank you.' He leaned against the wall as the nurse whisked away down the corridor. 'Louisa, we have to stop this,' he said abruptly. 'I don't want to keep rowing with you. Have you got a car in York?'

'No. I was going to hire a car or something.'

'You can take mine.' He fished in his pocket for keys and

gave them to her. 'It's in the garage on the corner of St Anthony's.'

The nurse returned with a chair and Joss subsided gratefully into it. But before she wheeled him away, he said to Louisa, 'Tell David's father that I'm sorry. Please.'

'Of course.' She watched him wheeled out of sight, and went to borrow his car.

Chapter Twenty-Six

Leo was late for Art. He hurried along the corridor towards the hall, his books clutched nervously under one arm. There was no one else around. He'd lost his pencil case again and it had taken him ages to find it, where he had left it, in his blazer pocket. No tricks that time, just everyday carelessness.

He burst into the art room, to find Mr Allbright consulting his watch, his foot tapping sharply on the wooden floor. 'Ah, there you are, Master Fletcher. So glad you decided to honour us with your presence.'

'Sorry, sir,' he muttered. He could not look the man in the face. Neither did he want to observe his classmates' expressions. So he examined his shoes and shifted uneasily from foot to foot.

A firm hand suddenly beneath his chin. His head was forced upwards until he was staring directly into Mr Allbright's face. 'Now, Leo . . . Why were you late?'

'I lost my pencil case, sir,' he said.

'Did you, now? Well, I shall need to see you during break. We must see how we can cure you of this chronic absent-mindedness. Now, everyone return to your drawings.' He put his arm round Leo's shoulder, steering him over to his desk. 'Leo, as you will see, we are endeavouring to capture the essence of that bowl of fruit in pencil, and then in poster paint. Settle down, put on your overall and *get on with it!*'

Leo arranged his pencils on his desk and did his best with the uninspiring subject. He was not looking forward to break.

This was the third time Mr Allbright had told him to stay behind on his own. At first he had been rather flattered by the obvious interest Mr Allbright seemed to take in him. He'd been sympathetic and Leo had almost revealed to him that people in his class weren't friendly, that he kept losing things, wasn't happy, all the things that he hadn't told his parents.

But in the end he'd told Mr Allbright nothing. There was something avid about Mr Allbright's attention: he wanted to hear about Leo's difficulties, he wanted Leo's confidence. It would be a source of happiness for him to know about Leo's disappointments.

Mr Allbright stood too close. This was Leo's only conscious reason for holding back. Mr Allbright came too near, his hands too often lay on Leo's shoulder, on his knees, on the top of his head. Sometimes low down on his back, near his bottom. He didn't like that at all.

In the art room at break, Mr Allbright said, 'This is not the first time you've lost your pencil case, is it? Have other things been going missing?'

He nodded miserably.

'Do you think people are teasing you, Leo? Are they giving you a hard time?'

He swallowed. He couldn't say it. And Mr Allbright's too-friendly eyes were watching his face, so he looked the other way and Mr Allbright reached out and put him on his lap.

Leo was rigid with terror. More than anything he wanted to wriggle free and run from the room. But he didn't want to offend Mr Allbright, who was only being kind. He sat there, and Mr Allbright cuddled him close and Leo smelled the peppermint taste of Mr Allbright's breath as he whispered to him that he was really a lovely boy, a sweet and beautiful boy.

On the table in front of them, Leo saw that a fly had settled on the bowl of fruit. Sunlight from the window caught across its iridescent back as it jerkily explored the soft tissue of the pear.

Leo's cheeks flushed and his eyes filled with tears. He tried to wriggle free but Mr Allbright wouldn't let him go.

'Look, Leo,' he said, moving slightly so that Leo could see the bulge in his trousers. 'Feel this,' he said, placing Leo's hand on it.

He snatched it away. He didn't know why, but this was wrong, all wrong. 'I don't like this,' he said. 'I don't like this or you, I'm going to—'

'What, Leo? What are you going to do? Tell your Mummy?' Mr Allbright leaned forward. 'I wouldn't do that, Leo. Not a good idea at all.'

Leo shuddered.

'Put your hand there again,' said the deep voice in his ear. 'Put your hand there. And remember, if you ever tell anyone, anyone at all, I'll take a knife – see, a knife like this one—' he picked up a palette knife from the desk, '—and I'll cut your heart out and roast it on the fire. And then I'll slice it up and spread it on toast. Understand Leo? You must never, never tell.'

'No, you won't. You can't do that, my Mummy will stop you.'

'If you tell your Mummy about this, I'll take my knife and cut out her heart first. I know where you live, down the road, it would be easy. And then I'll bring the heart to you and make you eat it. Understand Leo? I'm perfectly serious about this.' With the palette knife he stabbed the pear in the bowl and held it right under Leo's nose. 'I'll slice it and lay it out on toast and make you eat it. If you tell.'

Leo nodded. His hand lay on the hardened flesh in Mr Allbright's trousers and it leapt, moved beneath his fingers. Slow tears began to run down his cheeks. And when at last Mr Allbright let him go, when at last he found himself stumbling towards the door on shaky legs, he whispered, 'I'm going to tell. I'm going to tell my Daddy, and he'll stop you, he'll stop you—'

Louisa hardly noticed the drive out of the Vale of York. The flat countryside seemed drab and damp, the light fading in the gathering rain clouds. Joss's Peugeot was easy enough to handle. She put on one of his tapes, fleetingly amused by the slick Cole Porter arrangements, by the smoothness of Ella Fitzgerald's voice. But most of the way, she paid no attention to the music. She was wondering what she was going to say. Whether she'd be able to express her nebulous sense of dread, this dread which encompassed so much. Her mother, Leo, the past. It was complicated by her sense of guilt. She had failed to save Oliver Seifert's son, although she had known of the danger. She was more than nervous.

Of course, Oliver Seifert's only interest would be in what had happened to his son. She would have to focus her conversation on the past. He probably wouldn't want to be bothered by Leo's predicament.

But somewhere else in her mind, beyond the problems of the past and the coming meeting with Oliver Seifert, there was the death of her mother, a hard, unexpressed knot of angry grief. It was focused on the person who had always been there, in all her memories of childhood, at the end of a phone when she was abroad, at Christmas and birthdays and whenever she was bored or lonely or upset. And she could not even cry, not now.

There was something else worrying her, too. Ben's disappearance. Ben was the last remaining witness, the only one whose story she had not heard, apart from Kenny and Philip. Owen and Ben had been there, they had been present at David's death, but Owen denied seeing anything. And Ben had disappeared. And her mother was dead and she could ask her nothing.

The road was beginning to climb, heavily forested on one side. She'd forgotten how beautiful this area was, how quickly the scenery changed from the gentle, fertile valley to the high moors. Terrington was precariously poised between the two, its prettiness offset by the bleak loneliness of the tops.

She found Oliver Seifert's house with no trouble. It stood at the end of a long drive lined with mature oaks. The house itself was uncompromising Georgian, perfectly proportioned. She parked Joss's car outside the front door, and fussed around for a while, gathering her bag, checking her hair in the mirror, generally delaying the moment.

When she at last looked at the house, the door was open. A man was standing there watching her. She had no way of knowing how long he'd been there. She got out of the car and marched quickly across the gravel towards him.

'Miss Jamieson.' It wasn't a question. The elderly man standing there turned away immediately, obviously expecting her to follow. Unhesitating, she ran up the steps to the door and followed him into the depths of the house.

Immediately, a dog jumped at her. A retriever puppy, all eager tongue and loose, floppy fur and ears. She had to fondle those ears, greet it, play with it and delight in its irresistible, overwhelming, friendliness . . .

And she knew he was still watching her. The old man had paused by a door further down the hall, and she at length pushed the puppy away and looked up into his eyes. It was another world. Something so far from her experience that she had no frame of reference, no way of understanding or communicating.

He made no comment. Nervously, she moved towards him, and he stood aside so that she could enter first.

It was a music room. A concert grand piano stood by the window, a bowl of sweetly scented narcissus on the closed lid. A violin case was open on the sofa; the walls were lined with bookshelves, carrying volume after volume of music, scores and instrumental parts. A sophisticated sound system in one corner was complete with racks of CDs. The only light came from a standard lamp in one corner and a fire burning brightly beneath a carved wooden mantelpiece. The room was full of darkness, of rich colours, and old, glowing wood.

'Please sit down, Miss Jamieson,' came the sharp, contained voice of Oliver Seifert. He was by the door, his hand resting lightly on a bell pull. 'Do you like Indian or China tea?'

He made her feel uncouth, noisy, indelicate. 'China, please,' she said. He smiled, very slightly, and spoke a few words to an unknown person out in the hall.

'Please sit down,' he repeated, coming further into the room. He sat in a leather winged armchair, opposite her. 'Did you know my son well?' he asked.

She swallowed. This was in at the deep end, and no mistake.

'Very well,' she said, 'although he was not at the school for long. My best friends were Joss, Ben, Owen and David. We were always together.' She leaned forwards, resting her elbows on her knees. 'I knew he was in danger,' she said. 'I tried to get help.'

'But you were too late.'

'Yes. And because I was rushing round, trying to get help, I didn't see what happened. I wasn't there.'

'Who was?'

'Owen and Ben. Philip and Kenny. And—'

'Yes?'

She stared at her hands. 'You won't believe this,' she said. 'No adult ever did. Even Owen and Ben – were not clear about it. But I saw them, and no one can make me believe that they didn't exist.'

'Who, Miss Jamieson?' He was patient.

She sighed. 'A mob. A crowd of about thirty people dressed in mediaeval clothes. I know what it sounds like. But I was

neither hallucinating nor dreaming nor out of my mind—'
At that moment the door opened again and an elderly woman
with iron-grey hair put a heavily laden tray down on a coffee
table. She began to pour out the tea.

'Thank you, Mrs Ackroyd, that will do.'

The woman put down the teapot and with a courteous nod
to Louisa left the room. Louisa heard voices in the hall.

'Do you live alone here?' Louisa asked.

'My wife died. Six years ago. Mrs Ackroyd comes in from
the village most days.' His voice absolutely forbad further
questioning.

Six years ago. Long after David died, and Louisa wondered
if there was a link between the two events. But Oliver Seifert
was giving nothing away, and he had also evaded her question.

'You say there were strangers there, on the school
premises—?' he prompted.

Her hands were weaving together again. She continued, 'I
have no explanation for this. I expect you think I'm mad.'

'Children sometimes have – insights denied to the rest of
us,' he said calmly. 'No doubt, to you, they appeared real at
the time.'

'Yes! And they were the ones who killed David. I know
Kenny and Philip were there, I know they probably pushed
him or something, but they were being used by these
others—' She stopped. His face was turned away from her,
but she could see the severe line of his mouth, and his hands
were motionless on his knees. 'I'm sorry,' she said and could
think of nothing else to say, nothing in the face of this monu-
mental stillness. She was being crass. She knew nothing of
what it was like to lose a child, to live with horror. He was
Jewish.

She knew nothing of that, either. She knew no other Jews,
at least not intimately. York was uniquely shunned by other
racial communities. The Indians and West Indians and

Pakistanis who lived in the other great Yorkshire cities – Leeds, Bradford – had never settled in York. Provincial, someone had called it once. Uniquely English, an anachronism, isolated in a past which never existed. York, with its chocolate factories and heritage industries and hotels. And she wondered. Was it because the Jews had never lived here? Without the example of Jewish settlement, had everyone else felt repulsed by York's self-contained Englishness?

He was looking at her. Lightless eyes regarded her coolly and she realized the impossibility of what she was saying.

The ghostly mob was the least of it. What she could not say to him was, your son was killed because of his Jewishness.

She had no right. The Holocaust, the pogroms, York's own appalling record left her dumb.

'I'm sorry,' she said, standing up. 'I shouldn't have come, I didn't think—'

'There is another child, I understand.'

His voice seemed to come from so far away.

She could not move. Not so easy, this. She could not walk away, out of shame, and get on with her life somewhere else. She could not leave Joss's child to face the same fate as David. She would have to explain to this man all about it, and try to break through the immense barriers of the past.

'He's called Leo,' she said at last. 'He's Joss Fletcher's son—' and then she realized that she had not mentioned Leo to him. She had not told him that another child was under threat. 'How did you know about Leo?' she said.

'You are not my first visitor this week. I have someone staying here, someone known to you. I shall ask him to join us in a little while. But first, I would like to hear from you about this boy Leo, Joss's son.'

She was wildly curious about who it could be. But his voice kept her steady, and she found herself explaining about the little boy she had found wandering the streets at night, the little boy whose face was strained and too old for his age. 'But I knew he was in danger long before I actually met him,' she concluded. 'You see, it returns to things I can't explain, to the mob, and its leader.'

'Go on.' He gave nothing away, not in his voice or his eyes or his hands. He sat in front of her like an icon, and she still felt like weeping. 'Sheepshanks,' she said. 'He leads the mob. He dresses in white, and he has a hood ... He does this—' She stood up, on one leg, her arm extended, pointing—

'Don't do that!' For the first time, for the only time, Oliver Seifert shouted at her. 'Don't ever do that!'

She stared at him, shocked. 'Why?'

'It's dangerous. It is the position adopted by witches, by shamen, by the Evil One, in order to curse. It is the focus of malevolence, the way evil spreads itself—'

'Oliver, are you all right—?' The door swung open and Ben stood there, his large, florid face taut with anxiety. 'I heard you shout—'

Oliver Seifert took a deep breath. 'Perfectly all right, I thank you. I believe you and Miss Jamieson know each other?'

Louisa crossed the room to him and somehow found herself enfolded in a bear-hug embrace. 'Oh, Ben, where have you been? We were all so worried—'

'Sorry. Thought it best to keep out of the way for a bit—'

'Are you all right?' She scanned his familiar, kind face. His pale eyes blinked behind the glasses. He nodded. 'Needed some time to think,' he said. 'And found myself with questions, unanswered questions. I came here, and Oliver kindly took me in.'

She saw an indecipherable glance pass between the two of them. Her mind was racing. How much did Ben know, had he been in touch with Seifert before?

They sat down together on the sofa by the fire, and Oliver Seifert sat opposite them in the wing chair.

'Ben, was it you who trashed the computers?'

He nodded. 'Not very mature, perhaps. There will be a criminal prosecution, I suppose, when I return.' He looked harassed, but she felt there was more to it. Something he was hiding . . . She found herself, saying, without consideration, that she would pay for replacements.

'Why should you? I meant to harm the school, I meant to damage its reputation, I want people to know what goes on there. I would like to cause a scandal, I would like its name in the papers and on the news.'

'He and I are at one in this,' said Oliver Seifert. 'Miss Jamieson, your arrival here is possibly most opportune. Ben here has told me about the corruption surrounding the examinations at the school. But there's more to it, isn't there? What do you know, Ben?'

He was asking the questions Louisa wanted to ask.

'It's a sick place. An arena for murder and corruption and evil, all hidden behind that façade of quiet privilege, of discreet good taste. And that's the centre of it. If you're not on the inside, you can't possibly understand how far the success of any private school depends on its public face. Forget education. We're talking money here. The schools are in competition against each other for the children of parents with money. And in this tail end of the recession, the middle classes are all feeling the pinch, money's in short supply. Private schools are about selling. You need to make the product appear perfect, attractive, seamless. You need to hint at a different world, one of privilege, class, excellence. It's got to appear better than the (free) alternative, or any of the other similarly expensive schools—'

'And how much of this is due to the fact that you've just been dismissed?' Seifert said quietly.

'Like what happened to David?' Louisa said gently.

He sighed, brushing a stray lock of hair back from his face.

'I'm sorry,' he said again. 'You have to understand the sense of strain inside a private school, this mania to present a perfect, public face. The worst thing that can happen to a private school is a scandal. And that's what happened to David. He died on school premises, a victim of bullying. No one had noticed, no one had done anything to inform the parents—'

'Bullying happens in all schools.' A conscientious comment from Louisa. 'Children don't often die, but there's cruelty everywhere.'

'Of course. But in private schools such a scandal could – and does – tend to alienate potential parents. Punters. The punters may swallow a certain amount of "ragging" or initiation rites, or whatever else they choose to call the vicious-ness of the developing human. But not death. For a school to survive, to keep the paying punters on board, such a death would have to be concealed.'

'A cover-up.' Oliver Seifert nodded. 'I knew it.'

'Murder.' It was Louisa who said it. 'My mother participated in the concealment of a murder.'

There was a silence. Louisa regarded her hands. She saw the fingers intertwining, and then the sight was blurred, unstable and glazed. Tears, not yet falling.

'But you know about the pressures in a school community.' Ben took her hand. 'Your mother, particularly, was vulnerable. She lived there, she had a child to educate, no husband—'

'It's no excuse.' Bleakly, Louisa.

'No. But it's an explanation. Where would she go, what could she do, without a good reference from St Anthony's? What choice did she really have, with a young child in tow?'

'You could say the same about concentration camp guards.'

'Yes. You could.'

'Do you believe it, then? To know all is to forgive all?' she flung at Ben.

'I do,' he said.

'What did you see, Ben? What happened?'

He stared at her. All at once, she saw the boy, the boy with the silvery, beautiful voice, a voice too fragile and perfect to endure. 'I saw nothing,' he said. 'I was halfway up the stairs. There were all these people in the way, I don't know who they were, I think I must have been dreaming ... But anyway, when I heard David scream, I couldn't get through, couldn't get past this man who was blocking the stairs—' He paused. 'I tried. And I failed, crucially I failed. But Owen must have seen it,' he said slowly. 'He was right there.'

Owen.

'He says he didn't see anything.'

'Then he didn't.' Ben sounded quite certain. 'We never talked about what happened in the basement. We remembered Davey, we talked about him all the time, and we avoided Kenny and Philip like the plague, but somehow there was this sense of inertia—'

A sense of inertia, of forgetting. It was how the cover-up worked, how the past was concealed. And Louisa, like everyone else, to all intents and purposes, had forgotten too. She had not thought of David for years.

She was aware of Oliver Seifert's eyes on her. She knew what he wanted. 'I forgot too,' she said. 'It seemed like a dream, almost as if it had happened to someone else.'

'And Kenneth Pyper and Philip Stroud. You think they forgot as well?' Seifert said.

Louisa nodded.

'The City of York is good at forgetting,' said Oliver Seifert slowly. 'For all that heritage nonsense, the museums, the tourist walks, the souvenirs ... They've forgotten the reality of the past. They even hold fireworks displays on November 5th at Clifford's Tower, where the Jews died—'

'Who is "they"? The Council? The Tourist Board? The good people of York? Ben's lived there for years and I grew up there. We never said anything. Who are we talking about? Who are we to talk at all?' Louisa's hands were still twining painfully together.

'What use is guilt?' Seifert's hand slammed down on the arm of his chair. 'Nothing can change the past. That past. Nothing can alter what happened. What I am talking about is *justice*.' He leaned forward towards them and looked more than ever bird-like, keen, poised to strike.

'My son was killed,' he said, 'and my wife committed suicide. I don't want revenge. That is for the simple-minded, for children and fools. It's also not enough. I want justice.'

Louisa met his eyes. For the first time that evening, she thought she understood him.

Louisa drove back to the chocolate box city to her dinner date with Owen and hardly noticed the passing miles. Ben said he'd seen nothing, and she had no reason not to believe him . . . But she'd read enough about popular psychology to know that people's memories were often inaccurate. We reconstruct our memories, the books say. We rewrite them, so that they fit the pattern required. We forget the worst horrors, if we're lucky, and we reinvent the sequence of other events to fit the stories we tell ourselves.

And Owen's memory told him that he'd seen nothing. Or was it a lie? Had he colluded in the cover-up too? Come to that, how accurate was Ben's memory?

She was too depressed to think positively. It seemed all too likely that her friends had seen *something* in that small room. How could she make any sense of it? Had she really learned anything of real value?

Yes, her mind replied. Her understanding of her mother's acts had broadened and deepened, through Ben's humane words. She could not, by any means, condone what her mother had done. But it was, perhaps, a little more comprehensible.

She had time to shower and change before going to Owen's, but instead she sat in her mother's – her own now – sitting room and stared blankly at the dark windows. She would have to challenge Owen's story. She'd have to tell him what Ben had said, and then wait for him to defend himself.

Not yet, she told herself. With Sophy there this evening, she could hardly probe deeper. (Sophy will go to bed, her mind told her. There's no reason to put it off.) She dragged a comb through her hair and sprayed on some scent and changed her jumper and then found herself sitting on the sofa again, crying again.

She completely forgot that Oliver Seifert had already known of her mother's death. She had not asked him how.

Chapter Twenty-Seven

There was a dinner party that night. Mark and Caroline Morrell had invited three couples to dinner some weeks ago and although Caroline was tight-lipped with tension and Mark Morrell had a raging headache, neither of them wanted to cancel.

Morrell needed allies. He was too new to the school to have built up a solid base of support, and there were mutterings amongst the governors. Rolls were down. Two children had been found with marijuana and some unidentified tablets on them and were swiftly expelled. The press had had a field day with that. Three others had failed to get into their preferred public schools and there had been no lucrative scholarships that year. He was finding it hard to sleep, difficult to remain patient enough to present the necessarily correct and immaculate public face.

Morrell needed to talk to Kenneth Pyper and Richard Adamson in particular. There were strategies to be decided, steps to be taken to minimize the impact of Bowen's actions on the school, and he hoped to rely on Pyper and Adamson, who were both on the Board. Morrell had already decided on various points, but he wanted to be sure of his allies.

His wife Caroline also wanted to talk to Kenneth Pyper, but her motives were a little different. There had been a series of afternoons in a hotel by the racecourse, a weekend in Bristol and one night when Mark had taken Emma down to London for the Royal Tournament. But Kenny was beginning to be difficult. He wanted Caroline to use her influence with Mark and she didn't like that. Kenny had made one or two veiled threats and she was beginning to realize that she had been extremely unwise to become involved with someone so ruthless. Kenneth Pyper was used to getting his own way.

She experienced, not for the first time, a feathery touch of fear. Her mouth pursed as she started cutting up carrots for the crudités. Perhaps it would be best if she avoided private moments alone with Kenneth Pyper. At least Richard Adamson was coming: there would be few chances to be alone with him. Possibly she could avoid it altogether.

Morrell noticed nothing. His thoughts were pursuing a deadly circle of roll numbers, fees, expenses, projections. He was preparing what he wanted to say that evening. His first instinct, to pretend nothing had happened, was not going to work, now that Bowen had trashed the computers. It was worse than he at first had estimated: the damage extended to the system used by the entire school and too many people knew about it. Too many people knew about the exam, too. It was only a matter of time before the press got involved and that would be the last straw. Morrell cut his finger on the metal foil as he opened one of the bottles and swore.

He glanced at his wife, who had not looked up. She was still arranging those damn crudités on a plate, frowning in the unpleasant way that puckered up her forehead. She'd get lines soon, he thought, if she didn't watch it. She was probably irritated because the radishes clashed with the carrots. It was the kind of thing that often seemed to bother her these days.

'We'll say he had a breakdown,' said Morrell suddenly.

'Hmmmm?'

'Bowen!' Morrell snapped. 'Sometimes I wonder if you pay any attention at all to the outside world! I'm considering whether to tell the governors that Bowen's had a breakdown—'

She stared at him. 'What about the police? Didn't you get them in when you thought it was vandals?'

'We could drop the charges. Make it look magnanimous.'

'Magnanimous to who?'

'Whom.' He'd told her a thousand times. 'The parents, of course. The press, the governors . . . everyone. It won't do to look vindictive.'

'But it was criminal damage. You don't want to appear soft.'

'I think those expulsions established that I am not soft.' He was severe.

'Kenneth Pyper would like to see Ben Bowen crucified,' she said.

'An unusually florid turn of phrase for you, one I'm not at all sure I like.'

'Have you ever listened to yourself, Mark? Did you know how very pompous you sound?'

'Comes with the job.' He smiled, but he was inwardly furious. How dare she criticize? 'I'm not in the least surprised that Kenneth wants Bowen's blood. It was Geoffrey Pyper whose exam was faked. Of course he's furious, it's a disgraceful affair.'

'So let the police go ahead.' Caroline started calmly chopping herbs.

'No, I really think it would be better for us to appear generous.' Morrell considered pouring her a glass of the white but decided against it. She had displeased him.

'Kenneth Pyper won't let it rest,' she said.

Why wouldn't *she* let it rest? What did it matter to her?

'Perhaps I should leave it to you to influence Kenneth Pyper . . .' he said on a hunch, and was gratified to see her fingers pause in their competent chopping motion. She leaned forward a little over the board, as if she were feeling sick.

At that interesting moment the phone rang. He went through to the living room to pick it up and raised his voice only a little, to reprimand Emma for leaving books on the floor.

It was Richard Adamson cancelling. His mother had been taken ill, he had to drive down to Oxford immediately, although his wife Pam would still like to come . . .

Morrell was annoyed. He replaced the receiver with less than his usual care and then noticed that Emma still hadn't picked up her things.

'We have guests tonight, Emma! This room is a tip, kindly pick those books up at once.'

'I'm doing my homework.'

'Take it upstairs, please. Now.'

'But I wondered if you would help me with this algebra—' A whining tone in her voice.

'Emma! Off to bed with you.'

'It's too early.'

'Don't argue with me! Do as I say!'

'What will you do if I don't?' She was watching him speculatively.

'You are to go upstairs immediately and put yourself to bed.' He spoke with exaggerated and artificial patience.

'It's not seven o'clock yet! It's not fair, I can't get to sleep now, and besides I've still got my homework—'

'You can do your homework in your room.'

'It's art as well as algebra! I need a big table—'

'Emma! For Christ's sake!' He heard, with dismay, the crack in his voice. Emma heard it too. He saw her eyes flicker, the small, half-hidden smile. He took a deep breath. 'Emma. There is no need to push everything.'

'Mummy, need I go to bed yet?' his daughter called out.

Caroline put her head round the door. 'It's only half past six—'

'Emma has not finished her homework, and this room is hardly in a suitable state to entertain guests.'

'They won't be here for an hour yet—'

'Caroline!'

His wife winked at Emma. He saw her do it.

She said, 'You'd better be off then, sweetie. A quick kiss for Mummy—'

Emma gave her mother a loving embrace and pointedly ignored her father.

He took a deep breath. 'Richard Adamson isn't coming,' Morrell told his wife coldly. 'Pam is, however, so the numbers are out.' His wife was smoothing back the hair from her forehead. He discovered in himself an urge to throw things. 'You'll have to reset the table.'

'Ask someone else,' she said.

'I can't at this late stage! It would look ridiculous!'

'Surely you must have some tame member of staff who could fill in the gap.' He followed her back into the kitchen.

Emma heard him pick up the phone. Alone once more in the drawing room, she opened her satchel and found there a tube of Rolos she'd taken that day from one of the First Years. She leaned back against the sofa and slowly and deliberately began to chew them, one by one, until the whole packet was finished. Fortified by this, she felt ready to put away her home-work books, as her father had instructed her. She discovered there a note, written in an unfamiliar hand.

'Dear Enema,' it read. 'I hope you like your new name. We all do. It suits you really well, everyone laughs all the time when we think of you. Luv from Leo.'

She stared at it for a moment and then screwed the note into a tight ball which she hurled across the room.

At that moment her father looked into the drawing room.

'Don't do that! You little vandal!' His face was livid with rage. 'Get up to your room NOW!' His fury made him appear stupid to her. She slowly dragged her feet all the way across the drawing room floor to the ball of paper. She picked it up and deliberately tore it, bit by bit, into shreds, which she let drop behind her all the way to the door.

Her father wasn't watching. So she kicked the door open, letting it bang back against the wall.

'Emma! Stop that at once!' her father shouted. 'How many times have I told you?'

But he didn't even comment on her trail of torn paper. Emma let the door slam shut behind her, knowing that it would enrage him. Almost anything enraged him these days, and she took some pleasure in the exercise of her power. She stood in the hall for a moment.

Fuck homework. It was Leo she wanted, Leo she'd get. She knew how, too. So she went up to her bedroom and put on two thick jumpers before placing her pillow sideways beneath the covers. She turned the lights off before creeping downstairs again, making sure that no one heard her. She left her coat on the hook. Her parents might notice if it was missing. Her Wellington boots would be useful but not essential, and besides they were in the cupboard under the stairs. She waited for her mother to go through into the dining room and then slipped through the kitchen to the back door, knowing that neither of her parents would check on her for some time. She had a key and could return whenever she wanted. But she knew that it wouldn't take long.

Cold, dark, wet and windy. A wild night and Emma felt released, almost exhilarated to escape the oppressive house. She skipped as she ran, thinking what she might do later.

On her way up Clifton she ran headlong into Mr Allbright, who was bearing flowers.

'Now, now,' he said softly. 'What have we here? Little Emma Morrell, no doubt out on an errand for her mother?'

'Yes! I mean, no, I'm going to see a friend of mine.'

'And who might that be?'

Emma's face took on a closed look. Her rather large eyes blinked once, slowly. 'Jemima,' she said without pause. 'Jemima Snowdon.'

Jemima lived down Sycamore Terrace and was in Emma's class and so in one way, this was a natural, even likely explanation. But Dominic Allbright was observant and knew full well that Emma had no friends among the girls in her own class, and merely terrorized the younger girls into an appearance of friendliness. He had also observed other factors within the social structure of the school. He had even learned of Emma's nickname and had hidden a smile; he had never liked her, recognizing in Emma Morrell the self-obsession of the true bully. One step removed from the psychopath, he thought to himself.

He had also noticed her animosity towards young Leo Fletcher. Indeed, he had even made use of it, offering comfort and consolation to the vulnerable boy. In some ways, Emma was an unwitting ally.

'Leo,' he said conversationally. 'It's Leo you're going to see, isn't it?'

Emma said nothing.

'He lives over there, doesn't he?' He pointed along the line of Clifton, up through Bootham Bar towards the Minster.

'Near the school,' she confirmed.

Dominic Allbright smiled happily. 'Give him my love,' he said softly. 'Tell him I'm looking forward to our meeting tomorrow. Tell him I'll have something special for him, a little treat to eat.'

'Why are you giving Leo treats?'

'None of your business, Emma Morrell. I shall see you later, Emma.'

'Why?' she said.

'I shall be having dinner with your parents tonight,' he said mildly.

'Mr Allbright . . .' She sidled up to him and most uncharacteristically took his hand. 'It's a secret I'm out tonight,' she said, with what she imagined to be a winning smile. Don't tell, she meant. Don't tell them I'm out on the town . . .

'Do you know any other secrets?' he asked on a hunch.

'Leo talks about you,' she said thoughtfully. 'You and he have private times together, don't you? Because he's so good at art. He says you're strange—'

'Strange? What does that mean? What else does he say?' All at once, Allbright's voice became quiet, almost a whisper. But his eyes were sharp as icicles, ready to snap, to hurt and stab. Then he nodded once, seriously and gave Emma a small, formal bow and then walked past her on the way to the Morrells' house. His long pale raincoat flapped in the wind.

Emma forgot about Dominic Allbright almost immediately. Adults rarely impinged on her consciousness for long. She walked along the line he had indicated towards the Bar, and it seemed as if the wind was behind her, pushing her along, the pavement rippling beneath her feet so that each step seemed to carry her yards.

The pub signs swung in the swiftening wind, and in moments she was crossing the traffic lights at the Bar. No cars blocked her path, no pedestrian questioned her presence, a little girl alone, out at night. The streets glinted glassily in the recent rain.

As she sped through the Bar, blackness closed behind her. A whisper rustled through the city, disturbing the smooth-lying pavements into unstable seas of darkness.

No one around: shops all closed, pubs full, restaurants filling, and there was no one out, no one to notice the swelling stone, the way the signs scraped and swung on their hinges, the liveliness of the painted pavements, where rabbits jumped and babies crawled and faces winked . . .

Emma saw none of it. She had only one aim, to get to Leo's

house, where the fire-escape led to his room, where there was a way in . . .

At the windy west end of the Minster, she met Samuel Pyper. His white hair shone in the dull street lighting.

'Emma.' He sounded not at all surprised. He turned and began to walk quickly towards St William's College. 'It's Leo's turn, don't you think?' It was as if he was continuing a conversation they had begun earlier.

As they had. At school that day.

'He's a little turd. He put a note in my bag, calling me that name.'

'Stupid as well.' But Samuel's eyes were hidden from her and she did not see the smile lurking there. He'd taken a chance that she would be too furious to recognize his writing. He liked to tease and make mischief.

'How did you know I'd be here?' Emma said.

'I didn't. But it's a great night to be out, isn't it?'

The wind ruffled through his hair and his eyes were glinting. Emma felt a wild impulse to laugh. 'Let's get him, then.' There was no need to mention Leo's name. 'Now!'

She reached out for his hand and they took off together, skimming over the heaving stones.

'What's the matter, Joss? Surely we should be celebrating?'

'Hmm?' He looked up from his newspaper. 'Celebrating? Why?'

'That your ankle is all right. That you don't have to go through an operation.'

'I don't feel much like it, to be honest, Lil.' Joss was sitting on the sofa, his ankle propped on a stool. He sighed. 'I wish we hadn't come here.'

'A stiff drink. That's what you need.'

'No. Thanks. Did Leo go off all right?'

She nodded. 'Tired out, poor lamb.'

'He's so pale these days. Is he sickening for something, do you think?'

'All children seem to have perpetual colds in York.' Lily glanced at her watch. 'I'll have to run, love. Are you sure you don't want to come to the concert?'

'Left it a bit late for that. We don't have a babysitter.'

'Not really your kind of thing, anyway, is it? All that Mozart and Cimarosa. A bit early for you.'

'Yes.' He wished she would just go. He was waiting for Louisa's call with some anxiety. Lily was dressed entirely in black, her concert kit, with the full skirt and bare arms, and he knew that she looked lovely. She *was* lovely, his Lily. And he didn't want to worry her, he didn't want her to know about the unfolding nightmare.

'Don't get cold in that church, will you? There's quite a wind tonight.' And indeed, they could both hear it whistling through the garden railings. There was a distant clatter from a falling dustbin lid further along the street.

Lily kissed him goodbye and left the house, her flute case tucked under her arm. He picked up the remote control and trawled through the channels. Early Saturday evening inanity or fatuous political discussion. There was the newspaper on the sofa beside him but he didn't want that either.

The phone was on the coffee table. He found his eyes returning to it, willing it to ring. Louisa said she'd ring, and he wanted to know about David's parents. Desperately, he wanted to know. And although the phone remained silent, and he'd turned off the television, the wind outside was too wild to allow him to hear the faint sound, high above, of a sash window being lifted.

Leo looked up from his train set. Surely that was the sound of a cat? He put the engine back down on the track and got to his feet. He drew back the curtains and peered through the bars. There was no moon, but as usual the city lights cast a pale glow in the sky. Below him the garden was lost in blackness. He could see no movement there. The cat cried again. It was his cat, he would swear to it. Without a second thought, he lifted the window and pulled the three central bars out of their sockets.

The wind whined through the fence. He hesitated for a moment. Was the noise really his cat, or merely the wind?

'Leo!' No doubt about that, he even recognized the voice. Emma Morrell, his sworn enemy. 'I've got your cat, Leo.' Her voice carried effortlessly on the back of the wind. 'Samuel's here, he's got the kittens. Why don't you come down and see what we're up to?'

He felt breathless with panic. Without care or consideration, he clattered down the fire-escape, not worrying if he was heard.

In the living room, Joss had turned up the CD player. Sibelius's *Tapiola*, one of his favourites. The wind howled through those bleak northern wastes of sound and drowned the tread of his son on the fire-escape.

At the bottom, Leo said, 'Let them go. Please.'

Emma shifted her grip on the cat and it snarled, its eyes flashing, claws extended. Leo was glad to see that there was a dark rip across the back of Emma's hand, but she merely tightened her grip. No frail flower, Emma Morrell. At her side, Samuel held up one of the kittens by its tiny tail. The faint mewling galvanized the mother cat to further struggles. Emma was finding her a real trial.

Samuel began to swing the kitten around. It was difficult for him to keep hold of the pathetic little tail, so he shifted his grip to the back legs.

'Put it down!' said Leo. 'They don't like that—' He stopped, his eyes wide with horror. Samuel had flung the kitten at the garden wall with great force. The mewling abruptly ceased. There was hardly any noise at all as the tiny creature slid to the ground. It lay there motionless, its spine strangely twisted.

Samuel bent down and picked up another kitten from the ground. Leo was appalled to see his cat's entire family squirming on a piece of old blanket at Samuel's feet.

'Don't!'

'Why shouldn't we?' Samuel grinned. He took hold of the kitten's two back legs and spread them wide. The mewling increased.

Leo did everything he could to dislodge Emma. But some part of him was transfixed by Samuel's actions. He couldn't look away. Samuel pulled his arms apart and with them the kitten in a moment of wrenching violence. Blood and rags of flesh hung from his fingers, and Leo felt the sickness rising, a rising tide of black nausea about to overwhelm his senses. He couldn't bear it, this was the worst thing in his whole life by a long way, the most terrible, evil thing he knew.

Samuel was reaching towards the nest on the ground.

Leo sprang at him. Samuel was expecting it, and anyway Emma was right by his side. Without trouble, they manhandled Leo to the ground, Samuel sitting on his chest, pinning both his hands down with his bloody left hand. Emma was solidly placed on his knees.

Slowly and thoughtfully, Samuel produced a large gobbet of spittle which he let fall on Leo's eyes. He was struggling all the time, but he was small for his age, and both Emma and Samuel were on the large side, as well as being older.

Emma had dropped the mother cat, who immediately started moving her kittens, one by one, out of the way. There were only three left. She had nosed round the remnants of the two dead kittens, her back arched, her whiskers sensitive. But now she was alert, her whiskers twitching, tail flicking from side to side as Samuel drew a pair of compasses from his pocket.

Leo stopped struggling. He watched the glinting metal in

Sam's moving hand hopelessly. And then he screamed, with stratospheric intensity. But the wind was howling, blowing Samuel's pale hair into wild streamers and his mouth was stretched out into a blazing mask of victory, and Leo knew that no one in the world would hear him, just as no one had heard the kittens cry.

Samuel raised his hand high above his head and Leo knew he was going to plunge the sharp points into his eyes. Leo's mouth was too dry now even to whimper and his mind was retreating into panic.

The arm fell, and the compass points stabbed into the soil at the side of his head. He moaned. The hand rose again, and he knew that this was a tease, a deadly teasing terror that could only have one outcome. Again the sparkling points plummeted towards his face.

Again they missed.

'Get on with it,' said Emma. She was beginning to get cold.

'Third time lucky,' he said softly, his eyes fixed on Leo's, drawing back his arm. And then the cat jumped. It sprang at Samuel's upraised arm as if it were a tree trunk, and its claws raked through the woollen jumper to score deep into the flesh. He screamed, threshing about, trying to shake it off, and let go of Leo's hands. At the same time, Emma dived forward to help and Leo found himself free.

He scrambled to his feet and ran. But Samuel and Emma were blocking the way to the fire-escape and he knew that his best bet would be out into the back lane.

He turned left, dodging the dustbins and hurtled towards the city wall.

It was gone seven. Louisa washed her face quickly before walking the short distance to Owen's house, carrying the book she'd bought earlier for Sophy.

'Come in, come in—' He smiled quickly as she walked into

the hall, and she thought, he's nervous. Owen Rattigan, he of the exotic French background, pride of the Latin class, demon on the rugby field, successful architect and father, is nervous. It was only when she saw the small figure waiting in the living room doorway that she realized why.

As she watched Sophy unwrap the book and give polite thanks for it, she was aware that he was observing them both. Seeing how we get on, weighing the chances of a possible future, perhaps ... she knew she'd do the same, if their positions were reversed. She sipped nicely chilled wine and wondered where to start.

Fortunately, Sophy's presence made it easy. Dinner was served almost immediately, because of her bedtime. They ate in the kitchen, at a glass-topped table decorated with a jug of crêpe-paper flowers, Sophy's work. They talked about how people ever discovered that artichokes were worth eating, about what it's like to be a goldfish and after a while fell into silence.

Like a practised hostess, Sophy took it upon herself to enquire after Louisa's day.

'I went for a drive out into the country,' she said. 'To a village on the edge of the moors.'

'We sometimes take a picnic to the moors,' said Sophy. 'Once I saw an adder there.'

'Did you, indeed? Were you frightened?'

Sophy shook her head. Black curls bounced on her shoulders. 'It was trying to get away from me. They're really rather nervous creatures.'

'Are you sure it was an adder, Soph?' Owen asked.

'It had a V on its head. V for viper. That's an adder, you know.'

'Are you particularly interested in reptiles, Sophy?' Louisa said to this curiously composed, confident child.

She shook her head. 'No.'

'Music is Sophy's passion,' said Owen. 'She's got Grade 5 piano already.'

'But what's going to happen?' Sophy suddenly pushed her plate away. 'Now that Mr Bowen's gone?'

'I saw him today,' said Louisa, without hesitation. 'He was staying at the village I told you about. I'm sure he'll come back to York to see you.'

'But not to St Anthony's,' mourned Sophy. 'They all hate him there.'

'Who's "they"?' said Owen. At last he was looking at Louisa, his eyebrow raised in enquiry.

'Well, everyone! Of course,' Sophy said to her father as if he were half-witted, 'he made the school look silly. He made us look as if we didn't matter—'

'Matter, Sophy? What do you mean, "matter"?' Owen said.

'Well, as if we were at an ordinary school! With people called Sharon and Tracey, and, people who didn't care about things, about doing things right, excellence, other people's property, people with no standards—'

'You think Ben Bowen has no standards?' This from Louisa.

'He's brilliant!' She spoke very fiercely and Louisa was glad. She couldn't bear for Ben to be maligned. His pure voice, so clear, so perfect . . . the clarity of it. She remembered it shining through her schooldays at St Anthony's. It seemed in some ways the only thing worth holding to, it seemed to cut through everything, all the crap, all the shit, all the difficulty. The memory of it endured, even now. It shone in his kind eyes, in his warm humanity.

Sophy was still talking. 'But he's different, not like the other teachers. He doesn't like Mr Morrell, you know.'

'Why do you think that?' said Owen.

She shrugged. 'Mr Bowen always smiles at us. But his mouth pulls down, like that—' she made a face, '—whenever Mr Morrell comes in.'

'Do you like Mr Morrell, Sophy?'

'I think he works very hard, and he never shouts at people. But I never see him laugh.'

'I don't think I've ever seen a headmaster laugh,' said Louisa thoughtfully. 'They're not a species much given to humour.'

'What was Ben Bowen doing at Terrington, Louisa? That is where you went, isn't it?'

'He was staying with Oliver Seifert. Did you know that they were friends?'

Owen shook his head.

He turned to his daughter. 'Have you any more homework tonight, scamp?'

She shook her head. 'Half an hour, and then it's bathtime,' she said, mimicking the cadences of Owen's speech with frightening accuracy. 'But Daddy, can't I watch Mummy's video? For a while?'

'Monkey. Marie recorded the Matthew Passion in St Mark's last year. Channel 4 did it live,' Owen explained to Louisa. 'It's one of Soph's favourites.'

Sophy cleared away her plate neatly and washed her hands under the kitchen tap. Then, composed as ever, she smiled at Louisa and left the kitchen.

'So, Louisa.' Owen leaned back in his chair. 'You went to Terrington to see David's father and met Ben Bowen. I assume you're about to tell me all about it.'

She felt cross. 'Actually, no.'

'Still saying actually, Lou? Does nothing ever change?' He was being at least as brittle and difficult as she was, and she was in no state to handle it. She was so tired. Perhaps she shouldn't have drunk so much of Owen's wine.

It had been a terrible few days. Devastatingly, the loss of her mother deprived her of words. She stared at the wine glass on the table in front of her, at the light from the candles flickering through the golden liquid, flickering across the glassy table.

'Lou—?'

'I'm a rich woman now. Did you know that, Owen?' she said. 'My mother's left me almost half a million. I need never work again.'

He said nothing, frowning as he looked at her.

'It's tainted money. Hush money. Given to Mum by the school to keep quiet, when David died. What did they give you to keep quiet?' It was reckless, offensive, unwise. Too much wine.

'What?' He still didn't understand.

'You saw what happened to David. Why didn't you say anything? Why didn't you tell the truth?'

'I told you I saw nothing.' He looked very angry.

'Ben said you were standing at the bottom of the stairs. He said you must have seen it.'

'Good God.' He stared at her. 'And you really think I've been lying? That I was bribed, or bullied or something, into saying nothing? Is that all, Louisa? Are you sure you don't want to accuse me of murder while you're about it?'

'No. Not that.' She had made a terrible mistake. Of course Owen hadn't lied, of course . . . She felt pushed this way and that, at the mercy of differing moods, extreme events. She wanted to stop it, to gather her forces and then to be free to look at Owen, her old friend, and draw these questions to an end. He was looking tired, worn out. For the first time she noticed the creeping grey at his temples, the deepening lines from nose to mouth. What had she done? Would he ever forgive her? 'Not *murder*! Of course, not murder.'

'I'm relieved to hear it.' He drained his glass. 'I was at the bottom of the stairs, it's true. And I saw David fall, but nothing else. I didn't see what made him fall, or what happened to him on the ground, because of all those weird people. I saw nothing relevant. I've told you this before and I must say, Louisa, I am not at all gratified to be the object of your continuing suspicions.'

'My mother kept quiet for years. For money. If she could do so, my mother, the person I love best in the world, why should you be incapable?'

He was silent for a while. Watching him, she could almost sense the anger dissipating. He said eventually, 'This must be so hard for you, Lou.'

'Yes. I don't really know how to handle it. I have to know what happened. It's why I went out to Terrington. I have to understand what happened to David. Who pushed him.'

'It was an accident.'

'You said yourself you couldn't see what happened. You remember those people, that crowd of dirty peasants . . . They were out to kill, weren't they? It was written all over their faces.'

'The mob.' He exhaled slowly. '*That's* the central part of this mystery, Lou. Don't you see? I'd even forgotten about them, and no one even asked at the time who they were.' He frowned, his eyes abstracted. 'And when I remember the aftermath . . . your mother opening the basement door and looking down at David, they'd gone, the mob wasn't even there then. They were there when David fell, but not afterwards. They're why I didn't see what happened, but where did they go? Who *were* they? What kind of dream of evil were they?'

'Sheepshanks' followers. His mob, his friends, his servants.'

'Yes! But that's not enough now, is it? Who *is* Sheepshanks?'

'Who do you think?' She held her breath.

'I think – he belongs to the past. Another time.' He wouldn't look at her.

'Do you mean he's a ghost?'

'I'm not sure I believe in ghosts. But I think there are –

264

imprints. Traces left in the atmosphere, bred in the bones of the city, in its horrible, shifting stones. You've seen them, you know what I mean. Something so strong that time – history – has no effect on it. Where does he come from? What time gave birth to our Sheepshanks and his mob?'

'Think of it the other way round. He was there when David died. He seems to be after Leo. There's something about children, Jewish children, that attracts him.'

'The massacre. The York massacre. Children died then, they were killed by their fathers in Clifford's Tower while the mob raged outside.' He stood up and went through to the living room. He returned a few moments later, a slim pamphlet in his hands. 'This is the Borthwick account. It's dry reading, but it's all there.' He broke off, staring at the pamphlet.

She knew at once what was wrong. 'Have you still got it?' she whispered. 'That thing we found in the library?'

He shook his head. He put the Borthwick pamphlet down on the table as if it didn't matter. Neither of them thought to read those few pages, not then.

'I don't know what happened to that original summoning. The end of that term was – somewhat traumatic, if you remember. But surely, surely, this can have nothing to do with that childish piece of arrogance!'

She could say nothing. She remembered David's reluctance to try Owen's experiment. She had found the summoning parchment, but it had been Owen who had made the conjuration. Owen's idea to use candles and go to the basement and say those things in Latin in the dark.

'And Kenny sneezed. And David laughed, and there was a fight, remember?' Owen's hands still rested close to the pamphlet on the table. They were very slightly unsteady.

'It was the first time we knew that Kenny hated David,' said Louisa slowly. 'Really hated him, not just a childish feud.'

'Yes. It all came from that.'

'You remember the old story about sneezing, don't you? That the devil enters in if the sneezer is not immediately blessed? Do you think it could have anything to do with that?' It seemed extraordinary that they should be discussing such an atavistic superstition.

'It's absurd. But undoubtedly, that was the moment when it all changed, when it became so serious. We were children playing dangerous and unpleasant games at my instigation, and there was something waiting to take advantage of it.'

'But it wasn't your fault! We were all in it, it was my idea, and besides it was Kenny who hated David, it was Kenny who—'

'Who killed him.'

'You did see what happened!'

He shook his head. 'Truly Louisa, I did not. But I have thought about this for years and I always wondered whether it had been Kenny, Kenny and Philip who pushed David.'

'What's he like now? Kenny, I mean. Has he changed much?'

'I hardly know.' Owen shrugged. 'Our worlds rarely coincide. He seems a fat-cat type. His children take after him in every way, being both objectionable and musical, a very unpleasant combination. Poor Ben has dealings with them. Had, I should say.' He looked at her. 'What was he doing with Oliver Seifert? And why, why on earth, did he trash the computers?'

'He didn't really say. He and Seifert are old friends, it seems. They play piano duets together . . .'

'Good heavens. I had no idea.'

'Have you been close to Ben? Living here in York all this time?'

'No. It somehow hasn't worked out like that. Marie knew him much better than I.'

'Did they play music together?'

'Yes. She sang, Ben accompanied her. Ben is a rather good

pianist, or so I'm informed. It's not as special as that wonderful high soprano of his, but Marie was glad to have someone so fluent and sensitive.'

'I thought her speciality was early music.'

'It was. Is. But she enjoys moonlighting. She flirted with lieder, melodie, even Berio . . .'

'You sound very knowledgeable.'

'I was married to her for almost ten years. You tend to pick up the jargon over that time.'

'When did you separate?'

'Two years ago. Sophy has adjusted amazingly well, or so we all like to say. She was used to her mother being away for long periods, of course. Marie was always on tour, or at rehearsals, in London, or singing with Ben—' He stopped. He was cynical, she realized. Deeply untrusting, suspicious. 'That sounds begrudging. I – was not perhaps as understanding as I might have been. But she—' Another pause. 'I've rather hijacked this conversation, haven't I?'

'Owen, I know I'm being obsessive. It's a relief to think about something else.' She smiled at him, thinking, it will be no good, nothing good can come of this without a break in these defences. 'I think your Sophy is enchanting. Frighteningly competent. Does she run rings round you?'

'How did you know?' He looked happily harassed. 'I'd back any eight-year-old girl against most middle-aged men any day. I, at least, have no defences at all.'

On cue, Sophy put her head round the door. 'Are there any of those pears left? Please?'

'Okay, honey. But then bed.' Owen dished out another pear stained with wine and cinnamon jelly.

'I'd like to go out for a walk first,' Sophy said.

'At this time of night? When we've got visitors?'

'I saw Leo go past just now. If he can go out for night-time walks, why can't I?'

'Are you sure it was Leo?' Louisa was already on her feet.

Sophy stared at her. 'Yes, of course. But—' She stopped. 'Oh, dear. I shouldn't have told you. Will he get into trouble?'

'I hope not.' Louisa was already at the door, shrugging on her coat.

'Wait a moment.'

Owen was right behind her. 'I'll get Sally from next door—'

'I can't wait—' Louisa turned to Sophy as Owen dived out of the door. 'Which way was Leo going, Sophy? Was he alone?'

'I didn't see anyone else. There were all these moths fluttering. Big white ones, you see. That's why I went to the window. I saw the moths, and there was Leo, going towards the moat.'

'Tell your Daddy. Stay here, sweetie.' Louisa bent down almost without thinking and gave Sophy a hurried kiss.

Then she left the house, running.

Chapter Twenty-Eight

She lost him. Owen had caught up with her by the time she reached the moat, but there was no sign of Leo.

She was breathless and panicky, her mind racing through the possibilities. 'You go through Monk Bar,' she pointed towards Gillygate, 'I'll go along the moat—'

'No, let's stay together.' He grasped her arm as she was about to set off. 'Come with me.'

'Leo comes first!'

'Of course. But Louisa, just think for a moment. Leo's probably gone through the Bar because that's the way home. Come on, this way.' They ran towards the gate in the walls, the gate where the figures at the top hold great stone balls, ready to hurl them down on passers-by.

And although they were moving so quickly, although her coat was good tweed and her gloves real leather, Louisa was shivering. What if they were too late? And why hadn't Leo contacted her, as he'd promised—? Of course, she'd been out all evening . . . He might have tried, and there would have been no answer.

They rounded the corner into St Anthony's Lane, and there was still no sign of him. The cold was vicious. Louisa could feel her face beginning to ache as they came to the Fletchers' front door. They rang the bell and hammered on the lion knocker and in seconds Joss was there, letting them in, allowing Owen to dash up the stairs to check Leo's room.

'He's not here!' Owen shouted from the top.

'He uses the fire-escape,' Louisa said.

Joss glared at her. 'How do you know?'

'I met him once late at night. I promised not to tell—'

'The bars at the window look like they've been tampered with,' said Owen, breaking in. 'We'll get after him right away, but you should wait here.'

Joss was white. 'Damn this ankle. Go on, go on, don't hang around!'

Louisa and Owen left the house together but it soon became obvious that they would need to separate if they were to have any hope of finding Leo in the city. Owen went towards the market, while Louisa went round by the Minster.

She was full of dread. It was still comparatively early in the evening, but the streets were deserted. The restaurants and concert halls and pubs were in full swing, and there was no performance in the Minster that night. An enormous edifice, it towered over the city, floodlit so that the stone carvings were cast into sharp, elaborate relief, jagged as frost. She glanced up as she hurried along the pavement. The flying buttresses rose into the deep shadows cast by the roof. She knew there were gargoyles up there, grinning faces far beyond the reach of centuries of vandals and wreckers. Closer to ground level there were empty plinths on every façade, where the statues had been torn down and broken.

But although there was no one around, and the Minster silent, she could hear something. It was quiet at first, almost no more than the scratching of leaves on the pavement, leaves skidding over the stone, rustling in the wind. It couldn't be leaves, she thought, for although the wind was growing, all the leaves had been swept away long ago. Was it litter, perhaps, the discarded waste from the city's tourists? (Or even small animals, rats, mice perhaps, running ahead of the bone-crushing cold?)

Her steps slowed. She was distraught that she had not told Joss and Lily about Leo's night-time excursions. This was all her fault. Oh, Leo, she thought, where are you? What is happening? The cold wind was wrapping itself around her, whipping her coat and skirt painfully against her legs. Her breath felt like it was being ripped from her lungs. But at her side, the Minster was enshrouded in a clinging, dense mist. Why was the wind not blowing away the fog? It was deeply frightening. You could see the Minster for miles and miles, and here she was, standing right next to it and it had, to all intents and purposes, vanished. For although the Minster was covered with stone imps and devils, she knew it was a place of protection and beauty and because she could no longer see it, York's central beating heart, she knew she was denied its sanctuary.

She desperately regretted parting from Owen.

And Leo, lost in this wicked cold. Somehow she had to force herself to keep moving. Again, that scratchy, skittering noise, and she saw rags of white paper blowing in the wind. She knew what they meant, what they presaged, and it was all she could do to keep moving. What if she met Sheepshanks again? What if the stones started their deadly destabilizing dance again? She was breathless with fear, but there was nowhere safe to go, and a child was lost, wandering the dangerous, scandalous streets. Ghost walks.

'Here Margaret Clitheroe was pressed to death—'

'Here the plague killed a family of eight—'

'Here the orphanage where children died—'

People paid to be frightened in the streets of York. There was even a museum devoted to instruments of torture and execution. Louisa would have given a fortune – almost half a million, to be precise – to be anywhere else in the world, so long as Leo came too, so long as Leo was safe.

She had to move on, although the Minster was only an absence to her right and the city a labyrinth of danger and deceit to her left. Clutching her collar close around her throat, she began to move towards Stonegate.

There was music coming from St Mike's, carelessly, gorgeously beautiful music, threading through the wind. Vaughan Williams, she thought. Heartbreakingly lovely, but no good to her now, that vision of deep peace and calm. And then something struck the side of her leg and she realized that she had stumbled into the billboard advertising the evening concert. Lily's orchestra was doing the *Fifth Symphony* and for a moment Louisa wondered whether to go and get Leo's mother to join in the search.

But then, some way ahead of her, the mist parted and she saw two small shapes. At first she thought it had to be Leo with a friend. Then she saw that the two children were both taller than Leo. They were hurrying along Petergate and she knew she had to follow them.

Her footsteps seemed to make no sound on the slippery streets. The two children were hand in hand and appeared to be skipping along. Then she saw they were not skipping, but being propelled along by the numbing wind, the wind that ran through the fog without dispersing the slightest part of it.

Louisa could feel it herself, like a hand in the small of her back. The overhanging buildings of Petergate were speeding past her, their brightly lit windows lost in a blur of dazzling colour.

The colours receded. The streets seemed much more narrow, and there was muck and rubbish underfoot. Smells she could not place choked around her.

And people. For the fog was pregnant with life and now it gave birth to legions, to masses. They grew out of folds of mist, emerged and became solid, living, breathing, flesh and blood. From the mind-chilling loneliness of a moment ago she was now surrounded by people, shoving, bustling, pushing, stinking, shouting and somewhere ahead of her the two strange children were swallowed up in the crowd and Louisa murmured, 'Leo—?' without hope or expectation that she would find him.

Joss stood at the window, looking out into the gathering fog. The forced inaction was a torture to him. He had already run through various scenarios, calling a taxi, wandering as far as he could on crutches, calling the Morrells, anyone, to help. He had actually rung the police, and they had been entirely unworried—

'And you say your friend saw him only half an hour ago? Off Lord Mayor's Walk? Now that's not far from you and I realize he's only eight, but still, sir, this sounds to me like a schoolboy prank, nothing more—'

'He's not like that,' Joss had protested. He could almost hear the man at the other end of the line shrug.

'Perhaps he was meeting a friend, led on by his mates. Now, don't you fret and when he comes back, as I'm sure he will, give us a ring. I'll send someone round if he hasn't appeared by – well, say, ten o'clock—'

'Listen, officer, Leo is not the child to play—'

'Try not to worry. You'll have him tucked up in bed where he belongs before you know it.'

Joss had slammed the phone down. He couldn't believe it. The fool sounded like some bit part from *The Bill*. He returned to the window, stared at the street, but its outlines were now blanketed in fog. For two pins he'd leave the house and start scouring the city himself – but what if Leo came home and found no one there? Damn it, why did Lily have to be out, tonight of all nights?

His breath had misted over the window pane. Impatiently, he rubbed the moisture away, but he could see nothing clearly. The fog outside was dense and impenetrable. He stood there for a long time, watching the fog.

*   *   *

Owen tore down Goodramgate and in his mind he sought not Leo, not his old friend's small son, but Sophy, wandering alone and friendless through the treacherous streets. Louisa had started it. She had said, how would you feel if it were Sophy at risk? If Sheepshanks were after your child? Sophy was safe in the hands of a long-trusted babysitter and was in no danger whatsoever. But in his heart he knew that there was no difference. His daughter, Joss's son, David Seifert, those lost children of the massacre ... How could anyone with justice separate one from the other? A world entire, the phrase on Schindler's ring. Each human life, infinitely precious, entirely extraordinary and unique. He remembered the memorial to the children of the Holocaust, those fading infinities of candles set against mirrors, light reverberating into eternity ...

Leo, he thought. Leo, not David, not Sophy, not any other child but Joss's particular little boy, a child Owen barely knew.

Why hadn't he paid more attention to Leo? Made more of an effort with Joss and Lily?

He'd been in deep freeze. He hadn't let himself be involved, hadn't let himself become involved.

It was Louisa. He'd been wrapped up in self-pity about Marie, he'd felt threatened and offended by Louisa's aggressively left-wing views and more than that—

She unavoidably reminded him of his lack of courage. She reminded him of the past, the past which was catching up with them now. Like Joss and Ben, she was involved in events which had shaped his adult character. She stirred him up, as ever. She pushed him further, asked more than he was prepared to give. And yet he *wanted* to give more. She was right. What was a half-life worth?

He'd reached the market, the lines of empty stalls looming out of the dark. The stones underfoot were slippery with damp, uneven and insecure. He skidded on some vegetable matter but somehow managed to keep his footing. It was necessary, important and crucial, that he should not fail Joss and his son. Neither should he fail Louisa.

He stood still for a moment, looking about him. The various exits from the market were barred from sight by the thick, cloying fog. It stank, this fog. It carried with it intimations of noxious life, a primeval soup, a swamp of genes and bacteria and cells waiting to coalesce. But he could see no one at all, no sign even of the familiar landmarks now, the Tudor bakery at the market's centre, the line of brick-built fish-stalls – and someone jostled him. Pushed at him, and he nearly overbalanced, except there was someone else blocking his way. All at once he was surrounded by people, a crowd of stinking, squabbling, noisy strangers. They'd emerged from the fog and Owen was not at all clear whether perhaps they'd been there all the time. Anger was running through the crowd. He saw faces straight out of Bosch, hooded and cloaked, with blackened teeth and pitted skins, but their fury was focused elsewhere. They were all moving in one direction, towards Parliament, and he found himself swept along. He went with the crowd because he knew what was going to happen. It had happened before and he'd been unable (unwilling?) to stop it. This time it would be different.

Chapter Twenty-Nine

At the Morrells', the Gerwürtztraminer had been followed by a good Rioja, the Rioja by Beames de Venise and then by port. But just as Mark Morrell was about to introduce the burning topic of the evening, the phone rang and the Gilligans' baby-sitter, sobbing audibly down the phone line, reported that little Russell had vomited up his dinner all over her A-level history notes ... Grumbling, the Gilligans left, together with Pam Adamson, who needed a lift, and everyone else transferred to the drawing room. Mark Morrell offered brandy and liqueurs with coffee, but his carefully constructed mood had evaporated.

'What about Bowen?' said Pyper aggressively. 'What are you going to do?'

'Play it down,' said Morrell. 'The less fuss we make the sooner the whole affair will be forgotten.'

'*Forgotten?*'

'He will be. He won't get a reference from us and no one will take him on.'

'It's not enough.' Pyper drained his glass in one. 'Nowhere near enough. He's responsible for thousands of pounds' worth of damage, and as a governor I have to deplore that. But if you consider that in addition he has ruined my son's chance of a scholarship—'

'Oh, I'm sure Geoffrey will get into Ampleforth—'

'Without a scholarship. Yes. Bowen's actions will cost me a great deal of money.'

'The school has lost far more than that. We should make an example of him.' Allbright's voice was silky-soft.

Morrell saw his eyes flickering from face to face, gauging the sympathy, the mood of his listeners. He's clever, thought Morrell. And I know what his agenda is, I know why he's so determined that Bowen should pay.

Bowen the scapegoat was a diversion that Allbright needed. There had always been whispers about Allbright's behaviour circulating, but of late these had been difficult to ignore. Leo Fletcher's name had been mentioned, for one. But Morrell was used to such rumours in the schools where he worked. They usually died down, given time and a little bit of luck.

'I think it really would be most unwise to make even more of a fuss about this,' he said to Allbright. Perhaps it was a mistake to have invited him this evening. 'Ah, Caroline, my dear, let me take that—' He took the coffee pot from his wife, wondering whether a little diversion might be in order. Pyper was clearly out for blood and Allbright wasn't helping. 'Tell me, Janice, how's the bridge going?'

'Not very successfully, at present. It's proving difficult to establish a regular four.' Her voice was cool.

'So Caroline tells me. I would have thought there must be many other parents who might be interested. Shall we put up a notice in the school? Or take a page in the *Anthonian*?'

'Actually, Janice has found another hobby at the moment,' said Kenneth.

'Tell me,' Morrell invited. 'What can have taken the place of bridge?'

But Janice Pyper was looking away. 'Oh, you wouldn't be interested,' she said vaguely.

True, he thought. 'Try me,' he said.

'Don't mock. The Tarot.'

'Janice! Really!' Caroline Morrell laughed gently. 'It'll be crystals or foot massage next.'

'It's quite remarkably accurate.' Her flat tones compelled attention.

'Fortune-telling takes advantage of the credulous. There's no scientific basis for it,' said Mark Morrell.

'People who have no knowledge often say that.' She sounded bored.

'I'm sorry, you caught me in my headmaster's role. Such matters occasionally arise at the school and it always causes trouble. The children start following horoscopes or reading each other's palms and become silly and giggly and we start getting complaints from the parents.'

'The Tarot is certainly not suitable for children,' Allbright put in. He sat forward, his hands clasped together. 'There is some very potent imagery in the faces of the Tarot. Some of the packs I've seen are extremely beautiful.'

Janice shrugged. 'It's not a toy, or an *objet d'art*. There's a high proportion of negative cards, and it can be frightening.'

'Not as frightening as Owen Rattigan's little book of horrors.' Kenneth Pyper held out his brandy glass to Morrell to be replenished.

'What are you talking about?' His wife looked animated for the first time that evening.

Kenny stared into the dark amber liquid. 'When we were children,' he said, 'at Anthony's, Owen Rattigan got hold of this old manuscript . . . it was jammed down the back of some shelves in the library and the Jamieson girl found it.'

'What date was it?' asked Allbright.

'How should I know? Mediaeval, Tudor, who knows?'

'I'm surprised a schoolboy could make sense of a mediaeval manuscript, if that was what it was.'

Kenneth thought for a moment. 'I didn't look at it in detail, but I don't think it was really old. The writing was difficult to read, but not impossible. Perhaps it had been copied out at some stage. I mean, the school isn't that old, is it? It must have been put there by someone at a later date.'

'What about it? What did it say?' Allbright's pale blue eyes watched Kenny fixedly.

'Owen said it was a grimoire. Something to call up . . . summon . . . I can't really remember. We sneaked out one night and gave it a go, all in the dark in the basement . . . Wonder if kids at Anthony's still get up to things like that? What do you think, Morrell?'

'Very few boarders these days, remember. And none of them could begin to make an attempt at a Latin manuscript.'

'Rattigan was always an oddball. Still is, I suppose.'

'So what happened?' Janice Pyper regarded her husband without blinking. It made her look reptilian.

Pyper shrugged. 'I can't really remember. We were just silly children mucking about.'

'Why do you call it a little book of horrors? If nothing happened?'

He was unconcerned. 'We got into trouble. There was a scrap, a bit of a fight. Jamie – Matron Jamieson – discovered us there. She made us darn socks and sew on buttons for weeks afterwards.'

'Good for her!' Mark Morrell looked surreptitiously at his watch. Almost midnight. They'd be going soon, and he still hadn't got Pyper's backing for his plan.

'Bowen was there too,' said Pyper suddenly. 'All of Bishop dormitory, and that damn girl, Jamie's daughter, what's-her-name, Louisa. We were all crammed into the basement.'

'What happened?'

'There was an accident. We were larking around. A boy called David Seifert got hurt. He's the one that fell downstairs and broke his neck at Christmas.'

'Was the grimoire involved in that too?' Janice Pyper asked. And everyone looked at her, because surely the death of a child warranted some acknowledgment, some form of words, even if it had happened twenty years ago.

'Can't remember,' said her husband flatly. 'I never saw it again after that first night in the basement. I expect Rattigan tried to sell it or something. Godfrey's or Spelman's might have been interested.' He was not lying. He had forgotten.

'I wonder if perhaps I've got it,' said Morrell. He got to his feet and went over to a glass-fronted bookcase at the side of the room. He opened one of the doors and drew from the shelves a thin, discoloured pamphlet.

'Was this it?' he said, holding it out to Kenneth Pyper.

'Good Lord. Wherever did you find that?' Pyper made no move to take it. He looked rather pale.

Morrell flicked through it. 'It was in a drawer in Masterton's desk when I took over. I was going to get Christie's to take a look at it one day.'

'May I see?' Allbright held out his hand. He opened it, frowning. Then, '*In nomine spiritui sancti—*' he read.

'What? What's that?' Kenneth Pyper's grip on his glass tightened . . .

'In the name of the Holy Spirit: Latin O-level has its uses, Kenneth. This is fairly conventional stuff,' said Allbright without looking up from the text. His lips were soundlessly spelling out the words.

Kenneth Pyper put the glass down and it rattled against the table top. His hands were shaking and even Morrell noticed it. He stood up hurriedly. 'Anyway, this is merely a curiosity.' Morrell took the pamphlet back from the art teacher, putting it down on the mantelpiece. 'I really think we should discuss what to do about Bowen.'

'I told you. Get the police in.' Kenneth had pulled himself together.

'We have to think about the implications for the school. Bowen has been on the staff for fifteen years. It will make us look like fools, bad managers, dupes.'

'Not our fault that he's had a breakdown.'

'Not his either, if it is a breakdown. Don't you see? Either he's ill, and we can't possibly prosecute, or he's bad, in which case we should have realized it years ago. We have to let this go. There's nothing we can do.'

Pyper was silent. As if from afar, Allbright was watching him. His eyes, cold and colourless, fastened on Pyper, obsessively, consumingly. 'Bowen should be pilloried,' he said. 'We can't afford to let it go.'

Pyper spoke at last, his voice was low and thick. 'I hate Ben Bowen. I loathe his guts. I hope he fries in hell and that soon.'

'Whatever did he do to you?' Caroline Morrell looked faintly shocked.

'He stopped my son getting a scholarship. He put into question the reputation of the school. He's a fucking homo.'

'We have no evidence of that.' Morrell was severe.

'Of course he is! It was clear even when we were children.'

'What happened then?' Allbright again, smooth as glass.

'It was a long time ago.' Pyper glanced across at the book on the mantelpiece. He turned back to Allbright and looked him up and down quite deliberately. 'Of course, such things are endemic in closed societies. You probably know all about it. But I'm glad Bowen's out of the school now. I hope he's suffering. I hope he—'

His wife stood up abruptly. 'Time we went, Kenneth. Double rates after midnight, you know.'

He swallowed, and somehow jerked himself to his feet and pulled himself together enough to say, 'A great evening, Mark, Caroline. Thank you.'

This was abrupt to the point of discourtesy. But Morrell was pleased to see them go: he'd failed to win over the Pypers, and there was no point in extending the event.

He accompanied them to the door and saw them off. Allbright was still in the hall, about to put on his mac.

'Dom,' he said. 'I'll come with you. Part of the way.'

Allbright raised an eyebrow. 'Fresh air. Now that's the thing.'

'I'm just popping out for a moment or two,' Morrell called back to his wife.

Outside the fog was anything but fresh. A thick, soupy atmosphere was cold and clammy around them. Morrell could hardly make out the trees on the other side of the railway. He pulled up the collar to his coat.

'Now,' he said, 'entirely off the record, Dom . . . I wondered if any rumours had reached you . . . There's a certain amount of talk in the school.'

'About Bowen?'

Morrell shook his head. 'A little closer to home, I'm afraid.'

'I'm not entirely sure what you're getting at, Mark.' Allbright spoke softly and Morrell wondered whether this was a mistake, whether he should perhaps not pursue this. These things usually blew over . . .

'There are rumours,' he began, 'the kind which so often circulate in small, closed societies. Usually without foundation, of course . . . but single men in contact with little children often find themselves the target of malice—'

'Who, exactly, are we talking about here?'

Allbright was being deliberately obtuse. Morrell's step quickened. 'I have to say that in my final interview with Benedict Bowen, the subject was raised of other staff members whose behaviour is less than immaculate. And I have to say that if we pursue Bowen through courts, or make any attempt to exact retribution, we may find more mud attaching to the school's name than any of us have ever envisaged.'

'What has he said? What are you talking about?'

He sounded very angry and Morrell knew that he had hit the truth.

'Leo Fletcher has apparently told Bowen that he is – uncomfortable in your presence. That you touch him – well, we

282

don't need to go into details, do we? I think you have been less than careful here, Allbright.'

'And had Bowen nothing to gain from this? He was blackmailing you, Morrell. Don't you see? If you prosecute him, he's going to bring the school down. It's a simple threat, without any foundation in truth.'

'Of course, I believe you.' Morrell fell silent after this, a deliberate ploy. In his experience, people often revealed too much after a long silence.

'And anyway Bowen smashed the computers. He's hardly a reputable source.' Allbright's voice remained undisturbed.

Morrell glanced quickly at him. 'Leo's word is another matter.'

Bowen had actually said nothing of the kind to Morrell in his final interview. But Morrell knew his staff. He knew men like Allbright, he'd worked with them before. It was a reasonable assumption that he would be unable to resist Leo's vulnerable innocence, and he knew that here he had made no mistake.

'Very well.' Allbright stopped and looked at Morrell face to face. 'I know what you want, and I'll go along with it. No prosecution of Ben Bowen, no hounding of the devil in our midst.' He turned abruptly and without another word walked off into the fog, his pale coat flapping.

Mark Morrell returned to his house and went straight into the drawing room, intending to have a closer look at Owen Rattigan's little book of horrors.

The mantelpiece was empty. Only the clock and the Limoges jug. The pamphlet was gone.

Chapter Thirty

'Louisa! What are you doing here?'

A voice so familiar that she stopped dead, unable to believe it. The crowd pushed against Louisa and it was only with difficulty that she stood her ground.

'Ben! Is that really you?' She peered through the throng. Mist swirled over the faces around her. And then she saw Ben's large, lumbering frame emerging from the masses. 'I thought you were staying out at Terrington.'

'Unfinished business.' He took her hand. They were pressed tight together by the people around them. 'You're cold,' he said. 'What's going on here? Why are you out?'

'It's Leo,' she said. 'He's gone missing, and in this crowd, this fog—'

'I don't like all these people,' he said. 'They're not the usual York mob. Is it one of those daft historical dos?'

He's wrong, she thought, chilled. They are indeed the usual York mob. She and Ben were moving more quickly towards Piccadilly, jostled all the time by the crowd. The stink of unwashed flesh, of fish and damp and sweat was overwhelming. 'These people – they were the ones in the basement at Anthony's, don't you remember?'

'Shut it!' A man with great gaping holes in his teeth pushed violently at her shoulder.

'Do you mind!' She swung round furiously. 'What do you think you're doing?'

'Get out of my way!' The man pushed her aside and for a moment the crowd parted and she saw briefly, off towards Coney Street, a trio of small figures, children . . .

'There!' she cried. 'They're over there—'

Ben was right behind her, but the crowd had closed in again and Louisa lost sight of the three children. Somewhere, over the heads of the mob, she saw a tall white-hooded figure and the sickness rose in the back of her throat. Sheepshanks, she thought. Sheepshanks has Leo. And the two other children, who are they? At risk, like Leo? Or were they with Sheepshanks, were they part of this nameless, eternal, malicious mob?

In front of her the crowd was densely packed together, filling the narrow street. No one would step aside, no one would make way. And even when Ben managed to push his way through to her side, there was nowhere else they could go. The crowd was moving slowly, pressed shoulder to shoulder, stinking and unkempt, and their voices were comprehensible only in patches to her. They were driven by anger, only that, and the language of it didn't matter. Resentment and fury ran through them, and it was all directed ahead of them.

Somewhere, far off, she was aware of a clock chiming, its sound almost but not quite muffled by the fog.

A man beside Louisa suddenly swung round to face her. A hot blast of sour sweat struck her in the face. He was massive, inadequately covered by swathes of damp newspaper, tied together with string. Greyly-white flesh bulged through the gaps. He was barring her way. 'Fuck off,' he said. 'We don't need your sort here.'

'Let me through!' Louisa was determined to get to Leo, but the man was having none of it. He bent towards her, and she saw the blackheads clustering round his nose.

'Get back where you came from!' he hissed at her. 'Vile, heathen woman, devil's spawn—' His hand moved to his belt and Louisa saw him draw a wickedly serrated knife from a sheath.

'Watch it!' Ben reached beyond her to seize the man's arm but his fingers closed together on empty air. The man was fading, all that vivid stink and dirt and scraps of white paper evaporating into nothing. Around them, colour seemed to be bleeding away. The mob was whitening, blanching, waning. Louisa saw Ben grow pale, his large, moon face frowning. 'What's happening? We seem to be losing them,' he said shakily. 'They're disappearing—'

And then Louisa saw it too, the way the mist was threading through the crowd, washing over their features and clothes so that they were out of focus. The noise and the smells were dissipating: memories of a dream.

'Oh, thank goodness! I think they're going!' Louisa sighed with relief. It didn't last long.

'No! No, Louisa, what if they've taken Leo, too?'

And then she saw what he meant. The crowd was moving far out of reach and she knew that they were content, purposeful, determined. They'd got what they wanted.

'No!' She started to run towards them but the street ahead was wavering in the wandering mist, out of focus, insubstantial. She rubbed her eyes, as if waking from a dream and when she looked again there was no one there, no sign that anyone ever had been there. The empty street glistened with recent rain, and there was no one there at all.

No sign of Leo. She would have run on, scouring the side streets, but Ben held her back. 'It's no good,' he said. 'We're too late.'

The buildings around them were solid, the pavements under their feet smooth and free from the noxious waste. Electric lights illuminated the fountain, glistened from the wet stones.

Louisa was frantic. 'He must be here somewhere! We have to find him!'

Ben kept hold of her arm. 'I don't think we'll be able to. They've taken him. The crowd has got him. Look, there's Owen—'

And Louisa saw him coming towards them, half running

over the shining stones, his black hair disorderly and wild.

'Any sign of Leo?' Owen said as soon as he was within hearing. He was panting, out of breath.

Louisa shook her head. She felt like crying, she felt like touching him, holding out a hand. And she knew that Ben was right, that Leo was far out of reach. 'The crowd took him,' she said. 'The mob.'

Owen exhaled. She knew, watching him, that he clearly understood what she meant. At once his arms came up and enfolded her. She clung to him. 'What shall we tell Joss?' he said.

'What does that matter? What about Leo?' She pulled away from him. 'We have to get him back! It mustn't happen again, not again!'

'Louisa.' He caught hold of both of her hands. 'Don't panic. There's a long way to go yet.'

'He may still be wandering the streets. He may be back home now, even while we speak.' Ben was prosaic, but Louisa knew he didn't believe it: this was false hope.

They started walking back towards Joss's house, and Owen's arm was round her waist and even in the anxiety of the moment she knew that that was where it ought to be.

The overhanging buildings of the Shambles crowded over them and a cold wind lifted the edges of their clothes. A couple of young men, well-dressed, laughing, came out of the Italian restaurant and set off towards Piccadilly, their arms round each other's shoulders. They were carelessly happy, pleased with themselves and each other.

Louisa shivered. Had they seen the fog, the crowd? How had it all appeared to everyone else? She experienced an impulse to stop them and ask, but they were gone, turning the corner.

'Did you see it?' she said to Owen. 'That creeping mist and the crowd that came with it?'

'Remnants,' he said. 'Suggestions, rags, murmurs, only that.

I kept half hearing words, but I didn't know the language. It was like looking through torn paper, there were gaps in the fabric, uneven glimpses. But it doesn't matter: the meaning was plain. They were vicious, those people. Just like before.'

'What can we trust?' Her hand was tight on his jacket sleeve. 'When reality fractures, when the past leaks through to the present? Where does it leave us? We think there's a logical sequence to events, but nothing seems – predictable. Orderly.'

'Order is an artificial construct,' said Owen bleakly. 'We like to look at things like that because it makes us feel we're in control. If cause and effect work logically, then we can handle it. Chaos is intolerable.'

'And who's to say this is chaos, anyway?' Ben said. 'We have to believe that there's a reason for this, that something happened to trigger this. And if that's so, then surely we can do something to stop it, to defuse the – the curse, or whatever it is.'

They could see Joss's house now. The door opened as they approached.

'You didn't find him?' Joss stood there on his crutches, white with anxiety.

Louisa shook her head. 'I'm sorry, Joss. The city was full of people and at one stage I thought I saw Leo in the distance, with two other children, but then they – disappeared—'

'They disappeared? What do you mean, "disappeared"? Why didn't you go after him?' He was shouting.

'Come on, Joss, let's get in.' Ben attempted to guide him back into the house.

'No! Where was he, which way did he go?' Joss shook off Ben's hand. He looked as if he was about to start off down the street.

'Joss, we have to think carefully.' Owen blocked his way. 'We have to tell you what happened, and you have to know what we're up against.'

288

'What do you mean? We can't afford to waste time!'

'I know, I know. But this is complicated and it depends on what happened when we were children,' said Louisa hesitantly.

'Oh Christ. That again.'

Somehow they'd managed to get him back into the house.

'Listen, Joss. What is happening now relates to David's death. To understand now, we need to be sure about what took place in the past—'

'But Leo! Where was he, what was he doing?'

'The crowd took him. The mob. You remember, when we were children—'

'I don't understand! This is nonsense!'

'No, Joss! Think! What do you remember?' Louisa knew of no better way. There was, as Joss said, no time for delicacy or subtlety.

He stared at her for a long moment. And then he crumpled, sagging forward so that they could no longer see his face. 'I remember everything!' His head was in his hands. He took a ragged breath. 'I was outside, crouched in the snow. You were there, you saw me, didn't you? Just by that little wall in the yard . . . The door to the basement was open, but my ankle was on fire, and I wasn't looking, wasn't thinking of anything much except when was help coming, when would you be back . . .' He put out a hand to Louisa and she took it. 'But then I heard a scream. And the air was filled with snow, or was it paper? And through all that snowy stuff, I could see that the basement was full of people.' He shook his head, as if even now he couldn't believe it. 'There were crowds crammed into the basement. All those people, but I was alone, out in the yard. It was so cold, so lonely. I thought you'd never come . . .' Joss still stared at her. 'And you think *they*'ve got Leo? That crowd, that mob—?' He took a deep breath, and when he spoke, it was calmly. 'We have to get Lily. She needs to be here, she needs to know. Will one of you go to St Mike's and get her out?'

Owen glanced at his watch. 'It's almost twelve now. Won't she be back soon anyway?'

'They'll have gone out for a drink. Back to the conductor's house or something. Please, one of you go and get her now?'

'Of course.' Ben got to his feet. 'I'll do it. Won't be long.' He shrugged on his coat and gave a half wave before disappearing out of the front door. A blast of cold air ran through the house as the door closed.

Owen sighed. 'Joss, do you want coffee or brandy or something? You look done in.'

'I don't want anything. I'm sorry, my wits are wandering. Help yourselves to anything you want.'

Owen disappeared into the kitchen.

Louisa put her arm round Joss's shoulder. 'We'll get Leo back. I know we will.'

'How can you know?'

'We very nearly saved David. We were so close—'

'We didn't save him.'

'I knew he was in danger. I did what I could to warn my mother, but I was just a pesky kid to her, she wouldn't listen. But now we're adults, we know what the risks are, we know what we can do, we have power—'

'Makes no difference, Lou. Sheepshanks and his bloody mob have got Leo and we have no way of finding him.'

'He works through human agents. Remember.' She looked up as Owen returned to the living room with a tray of hot drinks. 'Sheepshanks used Kenny and Philip before. Remember Philip dressed as a shepherd in that nativity play? I think Sheepshanks cannot act on his own, he needs allies.'

'He's got the mob. Who else does he need?'

'He needs someone *now*. Someone contemporary.'

'Who? Who hates Leo? He's just a little boy, how could he inspire such cruelty?' said Joss.

'Children are often cruel,' Owen said.

'So who are Leo's enemies now?' Louisa looked at Joss. 'Who has it in for him?'

Joss looked desperate. 'I don't know! He doesn't say anything, he never brings anyone home, and even if he did I was always out at work, preoccupied . . . we never noticed anything!'

'Children often hide the worst things.' Louisa was nervously cradling her mug of coffee. 'I never told my mum what really happened. Not that she would have listened.'

'I could ask Sophy,' said Owen slowly. 'She may have noticed something at school.'

'She's in a different class. They don't have much to do with each other.' Joss sounded completely hopeless.

'We should have thought of asking Ben before he left,' said Louisa. 'I think Sophy's our only chance now. And it's something to do.' She stood up. 'Don't you see? Our options are limited. We have to make use of whatever presents, we must take every slim, small chance—'

'How have you done it, Lou?' There was an expression on Owen's face she could not decipher.

'What do you mean?'

'How have you remained hopeful? Energetic? Your mother has just died, you're full of doubts and worries and yet you can look at this situation and find things to do. A possible way forward.'

'It's called clutching at straws.'

'Let's do it.' Joss hadn't been attending. He hauled himself to his feet. 'Would you mind if we woke Sophy up, Owen? Can we go now?'

'What about Lily and Ben?' Owen asked.

'We'll leave a note. They can join us at your house.'

He began to crutch his way out into the hall.

'Where's your car?' said Louisa. 'We'll drive you.'

Joss smiled at her. It was heart-breaking to see. 'Good old Lou,' he said vaguely. 'Sort us all out, won't you.'

She took the car keys from him and went out into the street.

'We could have given Ben a lift,' she said, as she unlocked the car.

'It's not far,' said Joss. 'There may be someone still at St Mike's. It's the church right next to the Minster. St Michael-le-Belfry.'

'Bats in the Belfry, you mean. Home for the evangelical nutters. Deluded idiots who believe in the Deity despite the overwhelming evidence to the contrary.'

Owen spoke fiercely and Louisa said, 'You really haven't changed at all, have you? You always loathed religion.'

'The greatest force for evil in the world, I think I said once.' He almost smiled. 'I believed it when we were kids and nothing has since changed my mind. I know there are other evils, of course and the greed for money and power turn humans into savage animals with monotonous regularity. But the pretence of religion, the sanctimonious nonsense of it all still sticks in my gullet.'

I first heard Owen talking about religion one afternoon after prep. We were in the dorm. I was with them, playing truant from ballet, which was really getting on my nerves. We were now required to attend rehearsals twice a week, with an extra class on Saturday mornings, and I really wasn't sure that this was a path I wanted to follow. Okay, I'd read Lorna Hill, I'd thrilled to Margot Fonteyn and Rudolf Nureyev in Romeo *and* Juliet *and I thought the best music in the world, bar none, not even the Beatles, was* Swan Lake.

But dancing hurt. And I was getting too heavy and too big. I was aware that although I could pirouette with the best of them,

I wasn't getting the parts I wanted in the end-of-term show, I wasn't getting the right marks in exams. I was never going to be waiting in the wings at The Wells *or the* Garden *however hard I worked, because I was the wrong shape, too tall, too ungainly.*

If cutting off toes would help, I would have done it.

So I decided, unilaterally, to give it up. I spent the bus fare on Maltesers and Polos, and brought them along to the dorm, to celebrate my freedom with bravado.

I tipped all the sweets out on to the rug between the beds.

'Very Christian,' said David with a giggle. In RE that day, we'd all been discussing the concept of charitable donations. David's parents allowed him to attend RE, although he was excused prayers, because they said that David should at least know the basics about the religion of his homeland.

'You can't argue with the beauty of the Christian message,' said Ben. He'd sung one of the soprano arias in the school's truncated version of the St John Passion *that Easter and this had much to do with his decision to get Confirmed. He'd always been daft about music, but we considered that this was ridiculous. 'And the music! It's so wonderful, so awe-inspiring, there has to be something in it,' he said.*

'Bach inspired Christianity!' Owen was derisory. 'Soft in the head. Feeble, confused and deluded. Spot the brain cell. It's all fairy-tales! Where's the actual evidence for any of it?'

'The Scriptures are well documented—'

'Wild fantasies by people out of their heads on sun and alcohol—'

'What?' I choked and spluttered Malteser everywhere. I'd been trying to eat three at once by sucking off the chocolate and leaving the malted centre.

'The Romans were drunk all the time because the water wasn't pure, everyone drank wine, you know that—' We had been told as much the day before in Latin. 'Well, all this Christian stuff

happened in the Roman Empire, didn't it? They were all pissed as newts—'

'Blasphemer!' shouted David, standing up, his finger pointing at Owen. 'You will fry in hell for this!'

He sounded so funny that we all collapsed, shrieking with laughter. It was dangerous, we knew, subversive to laugh like this, wicked: we loved it.

Ben wouldn't let it go. When we'd all calmed down, he started again. 'But you're wrong. Think of Gladys Aylwood, think of all the missionaries working for the good of people all over the world!'

'Bloody do-gooders riding rough-shod over other people's cultures.'

'But there is such power in the Christian message, such understanding—'

Owen exploded. 'To hell with the fucking Christian message! I know what you mean, all that stuff about loving your neighbour, turning the other cheek ... All very well if it worked, but it doesn't! It's useless! People aren't like that, you need to be much cleverer than that to get people to behave well. The so-called Christian era has been riddled with wars and violence and rebellion—'

'It might have been worse,' said Ben stolidly. 'I mean, Attila the Hun and Ghengis Khan weren't exactly cuddly teddy-bears, were they—'

'But Christians are so hypocritical! They pretend to believe one thing and then go right out and do the opposite! At least Attila didn't pretend that he loved his neighbour!'

'Just raped, pillaged and murdered him.'

'Like the Crusaders.' No one could argue with this. So Owen kept on, ignoring the fast-diminishing pile of sweets on the rug. He was really fired up by this, I could see, it really mattered to him.

'No, what religion is about is separation. All religion, not just

Christianity. It's about divisions, about us and them. We'll do good to you, show you the right paths, the right way to live, because we've been shown the light and you're still in the dark . . . It's the pack instinct, it's animal. That's why jerks like Pyper and Stroud are so into it. Think of it!' He was intense, even though we were fast losing interest. 'And it's all nonsense! Fantasy! Not an iota of proof, or truth or reality about any of it! People telling fairy-tales to themselves, so that they feel they belong to a group, a pack, so they can bolster up their stupid, inadequate little personalities!'

'Isn't it a comfort, though?' I asked. 'To know you'd be forgiven, that there would be heaven in the end—'

'That's exactly what's wrong!' he shouted. 'Look, I could – murder David, here, for example. This works in two ways, first because he's Jewish, an enemy of Christ, so not really human, not part of the group, the tribe . . . but secondly, because, if I was a Catholic, I could just go and confess, I could say a hundred Hail Marys or whatever, and do penance and know it was all going to be all right! I could do anything I liked, so long as I wasn't caught by the police, I need never feel guilty! It's brilliant, a brilliant con-trick!'

'There's a good Christian upbringing for you,' commented Ben sadly. 'I bet your mummy just loves to hear you talk like this.'

Owen just looked at him, and I wondered if they were going to have a fight. But they didn't. They were too good friends for that.

Chapter Thirty-One

That difficult French mother, that lonely childhood. Like Louisa, Ben found himself thinking about Owen on his way to St Mike's. All that passion, all that fiery conviction, all focused on destroying something other people found full of comfort, of beauty and solace . . . And now a failed marriage: Owen had lost out all round, thought Ben twenty-three years later, walking past the pretty shops in Petergate.

It was tragic really, that someone so gifted, so charismatic, should not recognize the gifts of God. Ben's attendance at the parish church near his Wolds cottage was more than convention. His early enthusiasm for church music had transformed over the years into something deep and enduring. But in essence, he had to recognize that neither he nor Owen had materially changed their adolescent views about religion.

Ben had reached St Mike's. There was no one outside and he realized that the concert had finished long ago. But the door was still open and inside a tall thin girl was wearily stacking sheet music into piles. A verger waited by the door, keys in hand. The girl told him that Lily had indeed gone to the party at the conductor's house. Further enquiries gave him the address: Bootham Terrace, leading down to the river.

He set off again down Petergate and through Bootham Bar.

No portcullis barred his way; no black holes of cloying horror clawed him back to the past. There were people queuing at the bus stops, youths in leather jackets, girls in short flimsy dresses, giggling, smoking. The city was the same place he had always known, its stones sat at ease beneath his feet, and the wind that lifted through his sparse hair was merely familiar.

The city lived with betrayal, as he did. He was used to it. He'd given his adult life, his career, to St Anthony's, in reparation for the past. He had decided long ago that if he worked in the school, lived daily with the ever-present reminders, he might be able to expiate his guilt. It was a penance, no more or less. He had made a mistake once, in the basement at St Anthony's, a fatal mistake, and David had died, and in a well-meant and doomed attempt to exonerate this failure, he had thrown in his lot with the people, the place where it had all happened. It would never happen again, if he could help it.

Across the road he saw the fountains in Exhibition Square frothing with foam. People were clustered round the burger van, derelicts shared bottles on the benches by the Art Gallery.

'Got any change?'

One of them, youngish, filthy, trailing behind him a worn sleeping bag like a tail, came up to him. 'Got any change, mate?'

Ben dragged a handful of coins from his pocket.

'It's a bad night,' said the man, in way of thanks. 'I wouldn't be out tonight, if I were you.' He half-laughed. 'Of course, I wouldn't be out at all, if I were you. I'd be quiet at home, feet up, telly on, six-pack at my side . . .'

'I'm looking for someone,' said Ben without thinking. 'A woman . . . she usually wears a short fur coat, she's got dark hair—' He stopped. This was foolish beyond belief. Why should this vagrant know who Lily was?

But the man merely nodded. 'I saw her a while ago.' He pointed towards Bootham. 'She was carrying a small case, like this—' He sketched the shape of a rectangle. Lily's flute case.

'Out of town?' Ben was puzzled. He believed the man, but why should Lily have gone that way, which was quite the wrong direction? He did not see that the stones of the city were radiating from this man's shabby boots. He did not notice the deep blackness in the man's eyes, the way they betrayed no suggestion of a soul, an internal world, a past history.

The blackness reached out and caught Ben. It washed over his thoughts and memories like oil, thick, dense and merciless. He found himself turning, walking like an automaton towards the crossroads.

With a deft motion the man rolled up the sleeping bag and tucked it into itself. He took a piece of string from his pocket and wound it round. Then, carrying the bag as if it were a rucksack, he followed Ben over the road.

'He's a bit lonely,' said Sophy. She had been fast asleep, but warm milk and chocolate biscuits had encouraged her into good temper. She was curled up on Owen's lap, snuggling in her rose-pink duvet. 'Leo doesn't play much with anyone else. At break, he usually has his pad and pencil out. He draws things. He's really good at it, he once did a picture of this cat and it looked properly alive, just like you could almost hear it purr . . .'

She stopped, looking at her father with some bewilderment. 'But I don't understand,' she said. 'Why isn't he in bed?'

'He went for a walk, honey,' said Owen. 'You saw him, remember? And he hasn't come home yet.'

'He'd better not go to Emma's!' She laughed as if it were a splendid joke.

'Why?' said her father gently. 'Why not Emma's?'

'He called her Enema! Everyone in the school knows! It's a thing you put up your bottom—' She stopped, suddenly aware that this might be out of order.

'Are you talking about Emma Morrell?' Owen asked. 'The headmaster's daughter?'

Sophy nodded. 'And Samuel. He's her best friend. They're always together and they don't like Leo, because Leo called Emma Enema. It's brilliant, she was so cross! But they really hate Leo now. Although, they don't actually like anyone much.'

'Samuel Pyper.' Owen sat back. 'It might be worth ringing the Pypers and Morrells to find out.'

'Well, Leo won't be there, will he?' Joss snapped. 'If they're enemies that's the last place he'd go. Anyway, you just spoke to Mark Morrell and he didn't say anything about Leo being there.'

'He might not know,' said Owen thoughtfully. 'Those are big houses, they could be hiding in the attics or basements or God knows where—'

So Owen put Sophy back to bed while Joss and Louisa started phoning again. All of them were unconsciously waiting for Ben to return with Lily. Outside, the city was briefly noisy as the pubs came out. Then it quietened once more as the night settled down, and the great beast stirred.

Its tusks were stained with ancient blood, its eyes glowed with slow-burning centuries of hate. Every time the city rearranged itself, rebuilding houses and shops and churches and offices, repaving roads and pavements, planting trees and gardens, the coarse, wiry fur ruffled and then lay flat again. It thrived in periods of distress: the Civil War, the Victorian slums, the Blitz, all of these times leant it strength, revitalized the slumbering monster that lurked beneath the city stones.

There is an evil heart to the centre of so many cities. When people live close together, when times are hard, scapegoats must be found. Those identified by colour, by race, religion, age, sex, poverty, almost any external characteristic, are at risk. And then the sleeping malice of the mob awakens, the monster stirs and carnage is unleashed.

In York at the late end of the twentieth century, the heart of the beast was beating strongly again, the blood pulsing down the veins and arteries. It moved with the times: at each turn of the screw it found new ways to manifest. Its lair, beneath the Minster itself, was open to tourists, a place for innocent curiosity, for mildly interesting ghost stories about Roman legionaries. Its dark corners hid shadows deeper than the tourists saw, black holes of sinking darkness, pathways through to the heart of evil.

The beast fed on fear and hatred. The city was running with violence again, and its snout scented blood, down by the river, in the covered pathways, the parks and churchyards. It heard the calling and obeyed the summoning.

'God, that was a bore!' Janice Pyper yawned. 'Why did we bother? That pompous fool and his idiot wife.'

'Nevertheless, he's the one who can make Bowen's life hell on earth. I intend to ensure he does just that.' The Pypers were walking quickly along Bootham, shoulders hunched against the biting cold.

'Why don't you try this?' She stopped beside him and caught hold of his arm. In her other hand she held the yellowing pamphlet.

'Jan! You didn't! This is all I need, a kleptomaniac wife!'

'Better than a failed son.' He glanced at her with approval. She reminded him so often of her brother Philip. Her behaviour no longer surprised him, nor did it make him uncomfortable. Contrary to appearances, she was not the boring, middle-class, aging housewife she presented to the world. Kenneth Pyper knew that his wife had all sorts of strange preoccupations that would make the average dinner party guest throw up into the tiramisu.

She dabbled in astrology and the Tarot, but he always knew that it went further than that. He'd chosen to ignore most of it, never asked where she went for her occasional nights out. After all, he had his own agenda for nights away . . . But once he'd found a strange young man in the kitchen, streaks of blood round his neck, as if he'd worn a collar of thorns. He was staring at his hands, as if they belonged to someone else. His eyes were dead. There had been a hunk of unidentifiable meat in the dustbin once, its surface scored with yellowing patterns, wound round with a twining plant. There was the locked drawer in her dressing table which he'd felt no inclination whatsoever to investigate.

'So, why don't you use this?' She was still offering the pamphlet to him.

He took it from her, handling it carefully. Philip had shown it to him once, but he'd never held it before. He'd left that side of it to Philip that Christmas, when Seifert had died.

They were nearly home. But at the gate she turned once more and said to him, 'You want Bowen destroyed, I know. Is there anything else?'

'What do you mean?' Sometimes she made him feel stupid.

'Anyone else, I mean, anyone to whom you wish harm? Any other grudges, curses, resentments you wish to vent?'

He smiled. 'Leave it to me, sweetheart.'

'My beloved husband.' There was only the faintest tinge of irony in her voice. When they entered the house, she went immediately to her study. Kenneth Pyper took himself off to the library and turned on the gas coal-effect fire.

He held the pamphlet in his hands. He considered the past, most particularly that cold December afternoon in the basement.

He missed Philip. That special bond between them so strengthened by that fateful weekend at Coverham, the secrets they had shared. But Philip was no longer with him, at the end of a phone or a short car journey. He had died years ago, the year after Samuel was born.

A strange thing, that. Up until the date of Philip's death, Sam had been of no interest to Kenny. A small baby is little more than an irritant to most men, he reckoned, leaking at

301

both ends and noisy with it. But on Sam's first birthday Philip – who was also Sam's godfather – died. And Sam's eyes had looked knowing from then on. His face took on an expression that never failed to remind Kenny of Philip, although it was quite distinctly Sam's own. And ever since then, Kenny could never quite get rid of the idea that Philip's spirit was somehow watching over Samuel, somehow involved in Sam's life.

His Samuel. His beloved, dearest younger son. Kenny's adoration of Samuel was the central passion in his life. He gloried in Sam's confidence, his instant dismissal of sentimentality, his lack of respect for anyone or anything. And if Sam teased other kids, fought them, played tricks, whatever, well, that was life wasn't it? Dog eat dog. And if Sam liked to kick cats, or pull wings off flies or chop worms up, well that was just natural wasn't it? All kids did it.

He was clever, too. There would be no problems with Sam getting a scholarship. Even if he should have the misfortune of a teacher like Ben Bowen, Samuel Pyper was going to get a scholarship whatever happened. He found all schoolwork easy, was in top sets for everything, would skim through any exam with contemptuous ease. Since Philip died, there was no one who meant so much to Kenneth Pyper.

He went over to the bookcase and squatted on his well-padded haunches. In one corner, low down, were the *Old Anthonians*. There was an obituary there, in the 1987 issue. He had often read it over the years, often wondered why it should have happened, that freak accident. He pulled out the relevant magazine, with its glossy self-congratulatory photos and text. But there it was, among the deaths of old boys who'd served in both World Wars, Philip Stroud, born 1960, died 1987, of a head injury brought about by a building accident. Vividly, the details returned to Kenneth Pyper.

Philip had not followed his father into the ministry. Instead he'd made his way in the property business, buying up old houses in up-and-coming areas and renovating them in flashy, cheap style. He'd made a fortune.

He'd also died. A barn conversion, something like that. The picture in Kenneth's mind was vivid and strong. A brick, falling from a height, crashing into Philip's head. He'd never have worn a hard hat of course. Philip Stroud was always careless of personal safety . . . He was reckless, passionate.

A knock on the door interrupted these reminiscences. Janice put her head round the door. 'I hope I'm not disturbing you, but there's something I feel impelled to show you.'

She held in her hand one of her Tarot cards. She showed it to him.

The Tower, falling. Bricks, tumbling all round a fallen man.

'Why? Why show me this?' He was staring at her like a fool, his mouth dropping.

'It's happened before. You and I know that.' She glanced at the obituary he was still holding. 'It happens all the time, in all ways. The proud are brought down and order is upset. All change, as the guard says. *The Book of Changes* knows it, and the cards show it, again and again. This evening I have done the same layout three times, with regard to past, present and future, and every time the Tower is there, crucially pointed, crucially placed. I've never seen or heard of such a thing before.'

'What do you make of it?'

She smiled. 'A time of significance. That's what this is. A time of potency, of change, of momentous acts. A good time to act, Ken, if you want to.'

He said nothing in reply. After she'd gone he picked up the pamphlet again. Benedict Bowen. That was who he wanted. His mind returned to that winter afternoon at the school and he remembered the words Philip had spoken. He relived the events that took place in the basement. They were vivid and strong in his memory, more vivid than anything else that had happened to him since. That strange confusion between Philip and the praying man, the way it had been so difficult to turn round, to look Philip right in the eye.

But now he had a moment of illumination: it didn't really matter who was who, who had actually made it happen.

'Why aren't you here now?' he said. 'Where have you been all these years?'

He lived in the past much of the time, but it was the present that occupied him now. He had one particular enemy, one vendetta he needed to resolve. He wanted Benedict Bowen's blood, and he held in his hands a pamphlet which promised retribution. The memory of his friendship with Ben was shameful, hateful. He'd been soft, pansy, hopeless then. He'd needed Philip to sort him out. Carefully, he began to read the difficult words, the ancient shapes of the curse. And every few moments he stopped, and said, 'Benedict Bowen,' and let the name linger in the air like the words did.

Ben walked swiftly down Bootham. Where could she be, why hadn't Lily gone home? He was distracted, worried, feeling guilty. He blundered through the chill night air, wondering what to tell Lily if and when he found her. He didn't want to worry her too much, but on the other hand . . .

But at the top of St Mary's he met Dominic Allbright. There were two men in shabby leathers just behind him.

'Well, well, well, Ben Bowen, the scourge of St Anthony's. I'm surprised you're prepared to show your face in this fair city.' Allbright smiled nastily.

It was offensive, but Ben was used to that from Allbright. 'I'm looking for Lily Fletcher. Have you seen her anywhere?'

'No. What's the urgency? You look all hot and bothered.'

'Leo Fletcher has gone missing. Have you any ideas?' he said coolly.

'Little Leo. Such a sweetie-pie. Probably playing with himself somewhere, safe and sound. You needn't worry about Leo, Benny-boy. He's not for you.' Allbright started to move off.

Ben reached out and took hold of his coat. 'Wait a minute—'

Immediately the two men took a step nearer. Ben could smell their sweat, cigarette smoke, alcohol.

'Take your hands off me,' said Allbright softly.

'Don't let this happen! Leo's father's frantic and it's essential to find his mother. I'm not playing games here, the boy's gone missing!'

Allbright shrugged. 'He'll have to trust to his luck then, won't he? I have no idea where he might be.'

'Leo's one of your pets. Who are his friends, where might he be?'

'No, Benny-boy, I think not. That little peach is not for your plucking.'

'What do you mean by that? Is Leo *your* peach? For you? Is that it?'

'What has he said? What do *you* mean?'

'I know you, I know what you're like.' Why hadn't he seen it before? He'd never liked Allbright, but he'd never thought he was a serious risk to the children. But there was something lascivious about the man, something sick and sour. Through a haze of fear and anger, he tried again. 'Leo is just a little boy, vulnerable and articulate—'

'So these rumours *do* originate from you.' Allbright spoke almost under his breath. He looked down at Ben's hand, still clutching his coat. 'Take your hands off me, Benedict Bowen.'

'Where is Leo? Have you got him?'

'No, I have not got Leo.'

It was no use talking to him. Allbright would never give himself away. The crucial thing was to find Leo and Lily. Ben turned on his heel, about to walk off.

'Bowen.' The soft voice brought him to a stop. He turned

round. Allbright was standing in front of a street lamp, and his pale clothes hung like a shroud about him. 'You're going the wrong way. Bootham Terrace would be quicker. Leo was down by the river,' he said gently. 'Walking towards Clifton.'

'By the river? When? How long ago?'

'Just a while ago. I've been at the Morrells', I saw him in the distance as we came out . . .'

Ben said nothing more. He began to lumber off along Bootham once more.

Dominic Allbright's eyes followed him. 'Now,' he said softly.

The two men shifted away from the street lamp, where they were joined by a third, a dark-haired man carrying a rolled-up sleeping bag. The three of them followed after Allbright.

In the distance, Ben could hear Allbright whistling.

He was walking quickly, filled with anxiety. He turned down Bootham Terrace and soon lost all impression of the main road. There were cars and houses on one side, big trees hiding the railway on the other. It was very dark, very quiet.

He didn't notice that Dominic Allbright and his three companions were standing at the top of the terrace, watching his progress. Behind them stood a large group of people. And when Allbright lifted his right arm and pointed to Bowen along the length of it, curiously crouched, so that his attention seemed keenly focused, they set off at a run down the leafy road.

Ben never even heard them coming.

Chapter Thirty-Two

Some elements were the same. The boy, lost. The cat. The city cold and windswept and filled with malice. Fragments of white falling through the air.

He tramped the streets too, those narrow windy streets where the gutters ran with rain and rubbish. Houses had burned down in the night, and his father's friend had died. The sharp smell of burning in the air, and people standing at street corners, muttering. But he'd lost his cat, and although it wasn't safe ('Don't go out today,' said his mother. 'Stay here. It's not safe'), he had to find her.

But he found instead the boar, the stinking beast the Christians loved, the pig-thing they ate. It rushed at him in the courtyard of their house where he'd gone to look for his cat. He thought he heard his cat there, that was why he crept inside their dark, cold house with its effigy of the tortured man everywhere you looked. Red paint splashed from the circle of thorns on his head, from the gash in his side, from the nails in his feet. His neck was awry, turned like a bird to look at the rafters.

He heard them coming and he'd hidden in a cupboard, but white moths flew at him from their dirty robes and the white monk laughed at him, before putting him out into the courtyard where the boar's eyes were red, its tusks dirty and blunt and powerful.

It rushed at him and he jumped and swerved and its tusk caught the fabric of his cloak. He was crying with terror, but the monks only laughed and the white monk pushed his hands off the wall where he was trying to haul himself out of the way. So he ran across their muddy garden to the street wall, and scrabbled and somehow managed to get over it. He ran home.

But there was no cat there either. Everyone was packing, his mother tight-lipped, his father shouting with something in his voice which made the boy shiver. No one noticed the rip in his cloak, or the tear-stains on his face.

Then they went to the wooden Tower which was the Castle keep, where the Sheriff's men said they'd be safe, and there were prayers, but still he hadn't found his cat and he didn't know why everyone was shouting and crying. He cuddled up to his mother and watched the crowds gathering on the muddy grass outside the Tower.

Behind him the foreign rabbi preached. The boy didn't understand what he was saying.

A learned man, his father said, a doctor in the true law. Sent by God to guide them, Rabbi Yomtob of Joigny would ensure that they would sit at last at the right hand of God, they would have eternal honour and glory and the angels would sing. This all sounded very fine, but the boy still didn't understand why everyone was crying and why there was so much shouting while the rabbi prayed.

And when the Christians started throwing rocks and the Sheriff's men left, and he saw soldiers at the bottom of the slope, he buried his head in his mother's skirts and tried not to hear, or see what was going on. But the rabbi's voice was louder than anything else. His words wrapped round the people in the keep and carried them away on visions of glory. But to the boy who had lost his cat, it seemed very remote.

He knew nothing of glory.

Later, he thought he heard his cat again. He was curled up next to his mother and she had fallen into an uneasy doze.

The cat called, a plaintive miaow, so he wriggled free from his mother's arm and went towards the wall.

The stones from the siege machines had stopped falling earlier that evening. The men were still praying, while the doctor chanted over them. The boy saw his cat balancing along the top of the wall. He glanced around. Most of the women and children were huddled together. The children were asleep, but he saw that some of the women were crying.

The men were somewhere else. Not far physically: indeed the Castle keep was rather cramped, but their minds and hearts were elsewhere. They paid him no attention. They were talking, chanting, breathing thoughts of God.

No one was watching him. So he tiptoed across the flat-packed mud floor, stepping over sleeping bodies and looked through one of the window spaces.

They were still all there, the Christians, standing in huddles round their fires. He could see the white monk there, talking to an enormous man who seemed to be covered in paper. He'd noticed him earlier, shouting noisily. There was the smell of pig, frying. They are doing that on purpose, he thought, they are doing it to torment us.

He didn't understand why, but he knew he and his family were hated. They said that the Jews had killed their god, that they had nailed him to the cross. But I didn't, he wanted to say. It wasn't me, I wasn't there, neither was my father nor any of my friends. It wasn't us . . .

But then his cat suddenly appeared in the gap in the wall, its tail whisking swiftly from side to side as if it were angry. The boy held out his arms to it and it jumped into them, but immediately wriggled free again. It yowled, as if in pain, although it did not attempt to run away. Its ears were flattened against its head but it waited there, looking up at him, crouched at the base of the wall. He saw then that the fur on the back of its legs was singed, that the bare flesh was red and raw.

They had done it. The Christians. He had seen it happen before. He remembered seeing the fat boy pulling another cat into bits. They had burned his own little cat, and he hated them!

In an unthinking fury, he pushed at one of the stones that had landed on the window gap. It wasn't a large rock, but too heavy for him to lift. But it was insecurely balanced and toppled easily over on to the grass. And from there it rolled and bounced and tumbled down the slope, gathering momentum and finally leaped into the air after a collision with another stone and came crashing down into the crowd.

He watched with satisfaction as they scattered. Like skittles, he thought.

Then he heard the scream. A man's scream, a terrible, agonized sound. And he saw them lift up a heap of rags, a heavy mess of grubby white material, but then he saw that it was the white-cloaked figure of a man, a tall thin man, the white monk.

He was unmoving, lying there as if carved from stone. Was he asleep? People were shouting and crying. Was he dead? Had the boy actually killed a Christian man?

Was that what happened?

The white monk and the red-eyed boar. Moths, fluttering through the air like flakes of snow or fragments of paper. The child and the cat and the cruelty of men and children and the patterns of the city, shifting under the weight of sin.

The only Christian casualty was the white monk, the Canon who had preached a mean local crusade. Don't leave your families behind for the Jew to prey on. Don't fight the Jew in the Holy Land, he is here at your gates. Which of you does not owe him money? He takes your money and steals your children. He takes the bread from your plate, the peace from your hearth. He murdered our Saviour, he is every enemy you ever feared, every nightmare you endured. He takes your money, remember that. Your money, your status, your worth. And he's here now, in the Castle keep, in the City of York and at our mercy.

The white monk died, but his essence lived on. What he did, what he preached, lived on, throughout the centuries, throughout all of Europe. But most particularly, what happened was that he took his revenge. A Jewish child had ended his earthly life, a Jewish child would pay, again and again and again.

And fragments of white, paper, moths, blossom, snowflakes, feathers fell through the air, through the centuries and the cat ran loose.

And the boy was lost.

'Leo!'

He ran and ran until his heart was thumping and his breath rasping. He'd left the city through Monk Gate and then turned left, making for Sophy's house. Or even Louisa's. Friends lived this side of the walls and Leo needed friends more than anything.

But when he reached St John's Street he couldn't remember the number of Sophy's house. He knew it was on the left side of the road, but all the houses looked the same and he was too panicky to think clearly. Why hadn't he taken the horrible Mr Allbright's advice and noticed more?

Leo rushed on down St John's Street and came to the warren of terraced houses known as the Groves and within minutes was entirely lost. There was a heavy fog hanging over the slanted roofs and he couldn't even see the Minster. The rows of houses had no forecourts, their front doors opened on to the street, and all their curtains were drawn and there was no sound, no sign that anyone lived in any of them.

He tripped on something, an uneven edge of paving stone.

Somehow he kept his balance, but his next step also faltered against a jagged edge. The stones beneath his feet shifted. They were moving! They were grinding against each other and he heard a deep rumbling noise. He looked round frantically. There was no one else out in the streets. Beneath his feet the paving was beginning to slide. He whimpered, trying to grasp something. The stones jerked and buckled, shuffling him away from anything he could hold. He lost his balance and found himself kneeling, but the cold paving fell apart beneath his fingers, and his arms were pulled wide so that he was spread-eagled. He tried to reach out for something steady and stable, but it was like floating on oil. And in the midst of the panic – was this an earthquake? a dream? he became aware that he was being carried back towards the city, and that he could do nothing to stop it.

He tried to work his way to one side, to grab at lamp-posts, garden walls, to bollards, to gates and doors and shops but the stones were a sea and he was caught on a running spring tide. And although he was rolling round, out of control and sobbing with terror, he could see the city walls coming closer and closer through the fog and knew there was no way out of this.

His home might be inside the city walls, but so were his enemies. He saw the moat and the second-hand shop on the corner approaching through the mist and the figures bearing the huge stone balls on top of the gate were also moving. Their hands were loosening, widening, letting go. And as he entered the heart of the city, he heard the enormous crash of stones falling behind him, blocking the way out.

'Leo!'

Perhaps he knew the voice, perhaps it was indeed Mr Allbright come to show him the way home. This was a horrify-ing prospect, but the shifting stones in the street were worse. He sat up reluctantly. The figure looming over him seemed taller than Mr Allbright, but he was dressed in the familiar white tunic.

Bony knees jutted at him as the man squatted down. His hood fell forward, masking much of his face. Only the beak of his nose, sharp and broken-backed, was visible beneath the shadowy hood.

Leo scrabbled to his feet. Mr Allbright was disturbing all right, but this man was worse. Or was it Mr Allbright? He really wasn't at all sure, but he knew he wanted to go home more than anything. He was on the verge of bolting when the man's hand shot out and grasped his shoulder. The man sighed. A deep, long sigh of relief. The touch on Leo's right shoulder was like acid burning through his clothes and he started to wriggle. But the grip was iron-strong and there was nothing he could do.

'What do you want?' he whispered.

The man said nothing. His other hand rose slowly and took hold of Leo's left shoulder. Gradually, the burning, iron fingers moved closer together until he felt them enclosing his neck.

Where was his cat? His mummy? Anyone to help?

'Hello, Leo.' With sick dread he saw over the man's head two familiar figures approaching through the mist. Emma and Samuel.

He whimpered.

The man threw back his hood. Brilliantly black eyes gleamed with satisfaction. He leaned forward till Leo could smell his sour breath.

'Jewboy,' he said. 'I've waited so long.'

Sam and Emma watched Mr Allbright with interest. They'd known for ages that Leo was something special to him, but this was something else.

He turned to face them, and Emma shivered.

Yes, it was cold and windy and she didn't have a coat

on. But still, something caused her deep unease, almost fear . . .

Emma was not used to feeling fear. She found her parents contemptible, her contemporaries negligible. Only her elders at the school had ever worried her, but in the end she had merely waited, observing their techniques and imitating those she found useful. But the look in Dominic Allbright's eyes went further than that.

'Hello, Emma Morrell,' he said suddenly, and his voice wasn't the same.

For a moment she stared at him in doubt.

'I know you,' said Mr Allbright. 'I know who you are and what you are.'

She didn't like this. So she grabbed hold of Sam's hand and tried to drag him away.

'Wait!'

Her feet froze to the stone pavement. Unwillingly, with sickness in her mouth, she found herself turning to face Mr Allbright.

Or was it him? The light was difficult and her hair kept whipping in front of her eyes. Impatiently, she brushed it aside. It made no difference, for the man holding on to Leo Fletcher's neck was standing in front of a street light, and all she could see was his silhouette.

'You belong to the city this night, Emma Morrell and Samuel Pyper. You will play appointed roles and there is nothing at all you can do to avoid it. And when it is over, when you are home, snug in your beds, carrying on your daily lives, you will never talk of this night, for it will be embedded in your souls, too deep for thought. You will return home and if anyone sees you, if anyone asks questions, you will say that you went for a walk down by the river and then you came home again because you were cold.

'But your souls will never forget.' The voice was nearer now,

314

echoing through her head. 'Do you understand, Emma and Samuel? If anyone ever asks, you were cold, so you went home.'

Well, I'm cold now, she thought, hurrying back along Bootham. Sam was at her side, silent, and she'd never known him be so quiet for so long. His skin looked almost green in the street lighting.

At the top of the road where Emma lived, Sam caught hold of her sleeve. 'What happened just now?' he said. He was watching her with intensity. 'That man. Who was he?'

'Don't you remember?' She was playing for time. She could hardly remember anything herself.

'Did we find Leo?'

She considered him for a moment. He puzzled her sometimes, Sam. Usually she saw things clearly, she knew what to do, how things should go. But Sam was sometimes outside her plans, beyond scheming. And now that her memory was unaccountably fogged, she didn't know quite how to answer him.

Leo? Did they find Leo? Sam was shrugging, turning away. He knew the answers, he knew what had happened—

'Sam!' She caught at his arm.

'Are you coming, Emma?' he said softly, sounding rather like Mr Allbright. 'Or do you want to go home and go to bed?'

She hesitated. Turned to look down the road towards her home. And when she turned back, ready to reply, she found that Sam had gone. Disappeared into the cold night, back into the city.

Fuck that. Why should he have all the fun?

She followed him, even though her mind was unclear and dreamy.

The city opened itself to her.

*   *   *

315

Leo tried to get away. He'd made several attempts to make a dash for it, but every time the tall man's arm had shot out and grabbed him. Now the man was speaking to someone else, a man who was carrying a sleeping bag, and his foot rested painfully on the back of Leo's hand. The soles of the leather boot were hard and inflexible. Leo knew that with only a slight increase of pressure the bones in the back of his hand would shatter.

He was crying. He'd given up trying to be brave. He didn't care whether Emma and Samuel were there or not. He just wanted to be home, with Mummy and Daddy, he just wanted his bed. Bizarrely, he gave a great yawn. He knew that if only his hand didn't hurt so much, he would curl up there in the mud and dirt and fall asleep.

And in such ways does the despairing mind protect itself. Sleep is an inadequate refuge at best, a temporary sanctuary, but even *in extremis*, it beckoned to Leo. He fell into dreaming, into the terrifying passivity of the dreamer, where there is no defence, no way out. The assault gathers: the spirit quails, and where is wakening, where daylight?

Down the crooked alleys they ran. The news of the Canon's death spread and the anger of the mob flared. A heavy grinding noise. Shouts and curses. The crowd moved apart and then closed in again as the siege engines rolled into place once more. From his peephole in the keep the boy saw the stones falling again through the sky like snow. Would they quench the words of death and glory from the rabbi, would they break down the barriers that kept his father over the other side of the keep, deep in a huddle with the other men? What was happening, what was this sound of knives sharpening?

He didn't want to turn round, even though his mother was there. He did not want to see the look in her eyes. His father. His father was hidden from him, far away behind the words of the rabbi, the rabbi who had taken all the men in the keep from their families.

He heard the arm stretch back, the wood creak. It groaned as the scoop was hauled back, weighted, loaded. It creaked like gateways to forgotten places, opening slowly against the weight of accumulated time, accumulated sin. It opened wide, yawning back so that all the horror and destruction of countless years might proliferate and win through.

Centuries. Generations. Histories, unfolding in ancient stones, conjured into unwilling life by the same motives, the same old cruelties, dreary, deadly resentments. The scapegoat identified, trapped, sacrificed at the will of the mob.

The opening of the years jarred. A shift of perspective caused the pavements to rock, the buildings to waver and blur for a moment. Across the wide horizon of time a cat ran, ran along the walls and through the snickleways, through doorways and yards and alleys. It knew the city in every possible way.

Without hesitation, it launched itself at the man whose foot rested so heavily on the child. Claws raked through flesh, cut through to blood and nerves.

The man swore, and the boot on Leo's hand shifted. Just a little, just enough for him to wriggle and roll and get out of the way.

'Leo!' Lily flung herself at Joss. 'How could you—?' She stopped. 'What have we done? You didn't want to move here, did you? You always hated it here—'

Over her head, Louisa caught Joss's eye. She said, 'We'll try the police again. They'll take it seriously now, of course they will.'

'Of course,' he said calmly. She knew he was only holding it together because of Lily.

'But they'll be able to do nothing, nothing proper until daylight!' Lily was frantic.

'He's out there somewhere,' said Louisa, reaching for her coat. 'We won't give up.'

'The police will be here soon,' said Joss. 'Lou, why don't you stay and talk to them?'

'No. You can handle that.' She began to rummage in her pockets until she found the cigarettes that she'd left there the other day. Her fingers were shaking. Smoking, after all this time. She'd bought the cigarettes almost without thinking a few days ago, in that dreadful daze just after her mother's death.

Why should she smoke now? She gave it up three – four years ago. Why let it go now? But the tension was too much, the awful entrapments of the mind, as she tried to think of things to do, to say, without being paralysed by her fear for Leo.

It caught them all. Lily and Joss most deeply, but she could see it in Owen's face too, the imagined scenarios of what might be happening to Leo, a small boy, a little child in their care, who was now lost.

Through a cloud of smoke, she looked at Owen. He nodded. She thought, yes, I can trust him, he's not going to let me down again, this time, he – Leo, or David – won't die, nothing dreadful will happen, we can make it work this time. 'We'll be back soon,' she said to Joss. 'With Leo.'

Joss and Lily watched them get ready to go in silence. 'Ring,' said Joss. 'Send messengers.'

'Have you got a mobile phone?' Owen asked.

Joss shook his head. 'I wish I could come with you.'

'You weren't there before, you were out in the snow,' said Louisa. 'There's probably nothing you can do.'

He was rightly infuriated. 'Leo's my son!' he shouted. 'What do you mean, nothing I can do?'

'Christ, Joss, I know what's happening. A bit of it. You were outside the basement throughout it all, you weren't involved, this is not to do with you.'

'Still locked in the past, Lou?' His anger had gone, but now he looked bitter. 'I could do nothing for David, but that doesn't mean that I can't help my own son. And what about you? You weren't there either.'

'Joss, there's nothing you can do with a broken ankle,' said Owen reasonably. 'I *was* there, and it's no qualification. This is now, about Leo, about us all.'

'Joss—' Lily took his hand. 'Stay here, stay now.' Louisa saw her guide Joss back to the sofa, saw her sit next to him and knew that this was the best they could do. She had no idea, of course, whether there was anything more that *she* could do. On past records, it seemed unlikely that there was anything.

'Leo will need you both, when he comes home,' she said, and once more left the house.

Outside, it was entirely natural to take Owen's hand. 'Where shall we start?'

'There are two places, it seems to me. Two places of significance. The basement, where David died—'

'Or the Tower, where the Jews died.'

'Do we split up? Or stay together?' He was leaving the choice to her, as always avoiding pressure.

'Together,' she said, as if it were no big deal. 'I'm not facing that bloody city alone.'

They passed the school soon after leaving the Fletchers' house. It was shut up, the windows black and empty; there was no sign of life.

'Would he be there? Hiding somewhere?' Louisa said. They paused at the gates. The high, intricately entwined wrought-iron was locked, closely barred, high and surmounted by barbed wire.

'Good heavens, look at all this. Do they expect to be burgled?' She had never noticed barbed wire before.

'It's since Ben trashed the computers. They're afraid he might try again, I suppose.'

'How ridiculous! How absurd! Ben may have flipped but it was shock, a temporary thing—'

- 'Absolutely. But what matters now is that Leo would find it almost impossible to get in.' Owen shook his head. 'And why should he? It's hardly a place of sanctuary for him. It's Emma's – and Sam's – home ground, Emma's father's place of work. If he got this far, he'd go home. Surely. My bet would be on Clifford's Tower.'

'What if they've taken him into the school? Forced him there?' Her mind was running down terrible scenarios of kidnap and coercion.

'I really don't think they'd be able to get in. The school is empty.'

She peered through the bars and shrugged. 'You can't see the basement from here.'

'Lou, there's no one there.' He sounded quite certain. 'I think we should try the Tower.'

She looked at him doubtfully. There was an authority about Owen tonight which rather surprised her. How did he know, how could he be so sure?

He said, as if he'd read her unspoken thoughts, 'You see, I don't understand why David's death wasn't enough. I can't stop thinking about it. Why didn't the curse stop there, if it is a curse? He died, for God's sake! Wasn't it enough? Or is it to do with place, as much as people?'

'You mean, the – curse – has to return to Clifford's Tower? It has to take place there?'

'I think so.'

'And that Leo's arrival in York has started it all again?'

'Yes. But there's something else. Some other trigger.' He shook his head. 'It'll come to me. I just hope it's not too late.'

'Okay,' she said, absolutely accepting it. 'Let's take a look

320

at the Tower.' They turned away from the school, and hurried along through the market.

Cold, again. That familiar clamminess on her skin, the drops of water on the lampposts, on the walls. She was so tired of tramping the alien streets that she knew so well. No contradiction there, this was the place where she'd grown up, where she'd met friends, shopped, played; she knew it better than any other city in the world. It was the chill that made it so forbidding, so inhospitable. But was this an altered state to the city, this deep sense of unease? Now that it had fallen into its ancient rôle, had anything much changed? The externals were in place, the overwhelming mass of the Minster, the narrow streets and familiar squares. But she found that there was a sharp edge to the stones that evening. Had she just never noticed it before? Her shoes kept catching against the uneven edges of the paving. And there was an unwarranted sourness to the wind that so often smelled of chocolate or sugar beet.

She found herself still clutching Owen's hand as they hurried on past the homeless who crouched in so many of the doorways. They had littered centuries she thought, had blurred the outline of the architecture for a millennium. They rolled over in the cold wind that flung itself round the Minster, and with dull eyes watched her pass. She was acutely aware of her warm coat, the money in her purse, and remembered times when she'd stopped to give some away. Had the homeless always pretended gratitude when those few coins came their way? Looking now at the incurious eyes, she thought that savagery and contempt were not far beneath the skin, not far away.

She remembered the man with the sleeping bag, the look in his eyes. This was an alien city, one that betrayed its pretty, attractive front with a dark, desperate past.

Oh Leo, she thought, where are you?

*   *   *

321

He was running, slipping through the crowds, dodging and ducking, doubling back and swerving, knowing full well that he was pursued and that to be caught would be fatal.

He had no plan now. No idea where to go, what to do. Like an animal, he was operating on an instinctual level. The choking folds of damp cloth and dirty wool which flapped around him hid the buildings and streets from him. There was stinking slush beneath his feet, cobblestones and mud. He had no idea where he was.

Sometimes he heard shouting, sometimes he thought he heard his name called, but he never recognized the voices, and he trusted no one.

And so it was that he came at last to the grassy hill, the great mound which reared up in front of him. The crowd pressed in on all sides, pushing him forwards, onwards and upwards.

He had to get away from them. They were evil, the man in white, the man with the tail and the newspaper man. They belonged to the crowd. He stumbled on the grass, nearly falling to his knees, but his outstretched hands kept him upright. It was further than he estimated, but the stone wall at the top was unbroken, just as he remembered from that night when Emma had led him to the Tower. There's a way in, he thought, just round a bit. If I can get there I shall be able to hide, I'll be out of it . . .

No one had followed him up the hill. They can't see me, he thought as he traced his way round the Tower. It's too dark.

He came to the gatehouse.

There was a man there, holding a torch. He was standing with his back to the open portcullis gate, fumbling through a large bunch of keys. Leo didn't hesitate. He dived down the short passageway to the interior, past the empty racks and postcard stands. He had the vague notion that not only was

322

the Tower a place where he could hide, but that it was also a place of sanctuary, somewhere he could remain in safety behind those vast stone walls.

Boxes. Crates, stacked high against the walls. In the darkness he could not see the warning signs, the marks of danger imprinted in garish colour on the splintery wood. He had no idea what they were.

The gate clanged shut and he heard the key turn in the lock.

Never mind, he told himself. I'm safe here.

Chapter Thirty-Three

Beyond the Tower, the city waited. Of course, some were in bed, sleeping and trying to sleep. The ordinary citizens of York turned, uncomfortable and restless, unaware, but not unaffected. Others stood at windows or by back doors. Perhaps they had placed empty milk bottles there, perhaps they were calling a cat or dog home. Perhaps they liked to watch the stars, or to scent the night. Most had no idea what was happening, most carried on their lives as if it did not matter, even though they shivered in the unaccustomed cold and felt obliged to check locks and windows before going to bed.

But the city was alive.

One: with a sleeping bag furled up, tucked beneath his arm. A member of the miscellaneous crowd, a part of it and yet separate from it. Sometimes they called him Dickie-boy, sometimes Beastie-boy, but his given name was Richard. The mob was up for grabs: they were an argument looking for a cause, unfocused and malicious, but he was different. He knew Allbright of old. He'd been to St Anthony's and Allbright had given him his first lessons in the abuse of power. An early involvement with drugs had left him on the streets, avid for money, by any means. If there was trouble, he'd be there, with his friends and his dog, on the off-chance that there might be something to plunder, something to take. There had already been trouble that night, and he'd been at the centre of it. But this was just the start, a tiny taster of mischief to come. He joined the others who were now waiting by the fountains.

'Ready?'

'Yeah. Can't wait.' His friend Marmeduke, who was

immense, wore a covering of old newspapers tied round with bits of string. It made him look harmless, but beneath the papers he was rock-hard, built like a sumo wrestler. He'd been training, he said once, and Richard knew the truth of that. For years, they'd been getting ready, years and years . . . There were knife-throwers in the mob, people with smashed bottles and jagged bits of tin, meths and matches, crowbars and ropes, all concealed in enveloping folds of cloth. A mob of mixed grudges and smouldering resentments, inflamed with alcohol, they set off together, to the Tower.

Two: the master. An old adversary, sometimes known as Sheepshanks, the White Canon. His eyes were burning with resentment, his long limbs enfolded in pale cloth. He was inspired by a particular hatred, an injury centuries old, but he barely acknowledged it. There was another injury now, newer, fresher, but no less deadly. Ancient murder was overlaid by a more recent loss of reputation. Dominic Allbright knew nothing of the White Canon, but his blood ran to the Canon's call, the paths of his brain slotted into primordial patterns of malice. He had no understanding that all his actions originated in events which took place long before he was born. All he knew was that he had no illusions about what would happen to his career if Leo talked. His life, fêted, admired, civilized within its small York circle, would be over because the boy had talked and was likely to talk again. He had to be stopped, like Ben Bowen had to be stopped. Present enemies, and archaic motivations. Allbright's acquaintance with that other death lay at a deeper, unconscious level and it was a potent, virulent source of energy.

He had dreams, that was all. A child had let the stone fall. A child had committed murder. And although he could remember no details, his fury was unassuaged and sharp. This child or another? What did it matter? The injury was one that reverberated down the centuries.

Three: thinking of an old dead friend. With regret, if not affection, because they had been allies, close, sharing everything. 'Philip, where are you now?' whispered Kenneth Pyper as he stood by his front door, watching the wind whipping through the bare branches in the trees overhanging the railway.

Unusually, he could not contemplate going to bed. There was something in the air tonight, something disturbing and unsettling. He wondered what the pamphlet had unleashed.

He thought, without reason or logic, that his old ally was near. All evening, Philip had been present in his mind. It's not people, collections of bone and flesh and blood that matter, he told himself. It's what they do that stays in the mind, that lingers, that leaves its imprints—

On the stones, on the air, in the fabric of the city.

He loved it. He loved the way the stones shifted, ran beneath his feet like rats, because he was used to it. He'd been most alive then. When Philip and he had become allies, shared blood – (a ceremony at dead of night on their return from Philip's home. Till the death, they'd said. Till the death, and beyond) – and shaped their own lives at St Anthony's. They'd been kings then. Invincible. No one had crossed them, no one dared to say, no, you can't do that. Only teachers, with their petty rules and silly preoccupations, and what did they matter? It had been him and Philip, against all comers . . . Nothing had touched the loyalty of it, the unbreakable, blood-stained bond. It was brotherhood, family, like father and son.

Something he and Samuel shared. He had recognized it in others, stories of men in previous generations who had fought in the war, Battle of Britain and all that. Their names were on walls at school, shiny gold lettering against dark panelling. Allegiances mattered, that was all. Who gave a fuck who the enemy was? Germans, Jews, women, blacks, whoever . . .

David Seifert.

That open, trusting face, looking for friendliness, asking for it from others. Kenneth found it contemptible, irritating, soft, deceitful. And the cleverness, the mimicry, the subtle under-cutting of established ways. David had never understood how things were done, he wasn't English enough to know. He'd asked for it, he'd asked for everything he got.

Like Bowen. That florid face, those loose jowls, that slack approach. He'd tried to teach Geoffrey and failed. What could you expect? Bowen didn't know how to behave either, he was a fucking homo. Kenneth considered that he had had a narrow escape, before Philip had shown him the light. What on earth had he ever seen in that feeble fairy? Bowen didn't know about discipline, he hadn't the faintest idea about the importance of authority. He was traitorous, he had set himself up against Kenneth Pyper and that was the problem. His son's cleverness and talent were now in doubt and this was bad enough. But more crucially, Benedict Bowen's actions had cost him thousands of pounds. And money was not easy to come by these days, his business was not doing well and the school fees for two children were difficult to find.

None of this was enough. A pretext, that was all. It went back to the basement, years ago, when he and Philip had stared down the stairs towards Ben and Owen.

Between them, halfway up the stairs, David. He was shouting, 'Why don't you leave me alone? I'm so sick of this!'

'Diddums,' Philip sneered.

'Do you think I'm frightened of you? You want a fight? Well here I am!'

'Oh goody,' said Kenny. This was turning out to be fun. Seifert didn't usually rise to the bait in this way. He saw with approval how white Seifert's face was.

His mouth was hanging open. Kenny knew he was full of cold, that David Seifert's breathing was noisy and inefficient, and it made him look stupid, he looked lost and stupid and ill. Seifert began to move up the stairs and at the same time the door to the yard was flung open by the wind and there was a flurry of snow blowing into the basement, enveloping them all in flakes of white. It was covering every surface, changing shape and outline of the familiar environment. Everyone was shivering, but no one thought to close the door.

Kenny blinked, and passed his hand over his eyes. Behind Ben and Owen crowds of people were gradually emerging from the blanket of white. Kenny didn't know who they were and recognized none of them, not even the huge man who seemed to be wearing a coat made of newspaper. But they were cramming their way in through the door, for the snow there was like a thick white blanket hung across the opening. It seemed that the flakes inside the door were clinging together in strange massy forms, hiding the figures of the people coming in from outside.

He did not doubt that these were townspeople. He did not pinpoint a moment when snow became flesh and bone and dirty, stinking wool or torn newsprint. He shut his mind to the crowd's presence, just as he shut his mind to the change in Philip.

He did not look at his friend.

Seifert was still shouting, 'Come on, let's settle this! Are you cowards?'

Ben was nearly at the top of the stairs too. 'Davey, leave them be. You don't need this—'

Seifert shook his hand off. 'I've had it up to here, trying to be nice!' he shouted at Ben. 'What good does it do? All that sanctimonious rubbish!'

'Fucking heathen!' said Kenny, and David put out both his hands and pushed at Kenny. He actually dared to push him! Kenny almost lost his balance, but not quite. He swung his fist and it connected satisfyingly with Seifert's nose. A flower of red bloomed in the centre of the Jew's face. At the same time Philip brought up his knee and got him in the balls. Seifert moaned

328

and crumpled up soundlessly on the narrow platform at the top of the stairs.

Ben was looking round for help, ineffectual as ever. Kenny took no notice of him. There was no need. Just as Owen was out of it, effectively barred from the stairs by the crowd of people, so Ben Bowen, soft as tissue paper, would never interfere. He was gaping foolishly, his eyes indistinct behind the steamy glasses, and Kenny smirked, clutching Philip's arm. It was almost amusing, that fat fool blinking at them, and David Seifert snuffling up the blood that ran from his nose.

Seifert was near the edge of the drop, rolling on the floor beneath the banister rail. It was easy, the work of a moment to give him a push. So that's what Kenny did. And he and Philip shrieked as Seifert over-balanced. It felt like Tom and Jerry, like the Flintstones, like fun! The Jew fell, but his fingers caught the edge of the platform. He was hanging there, his fingers white and scrabbling, trying to find some purchase.

And better than everything, better than he ever hoped, it was Ben's foot that trampled on the fingers that clutched at the edge of the drop.

Accidentally, of course. Kenny and Philip were stamping round in a kind of wild, celebratory dance and Ben was trying to stop them, to get them out of the way and Kenny hardly even heard David Seifert's cry as he fell. But he saw what happened, he saw what Benedict Bowen did.

They heard nothing of the impact, did not know – or care – whether he lived or died, for the crowd was surging forward, muttering and rumbling. The drop wasn't that far, David was probably all right—

But the crowd convulsed. A shudder ran through it as if it might collectively vomit.

And Philip was down there with them, although Kenny had not noticed him move. And it was then that Kenny heard the crack, the sharp, breaking sound of bone and the appallingly *curtailed half-groan that came, unmistakably, from David Seifert.*

Kenny could see nothing of what happened next, because Ben and Owen were trying to push through the crowd to get to David, shouting as if to wake the dead.

For he was dead, of course. Now. He was unwakable, unreachable, for ever and ever, and Kenny wanted to shout, to cheer and celebrate. The enemy was dead, and the pact sealed.

The crowd sprang back. Leaped away from the small hunched body as if it might sear them, leaving it displayed, the head bent appallingly to one side, one hand stretched out, the legs curving at the knee. It was as if a curtain had been drawn back, a veil over reality suddenly lifted. The mob dissipated into the dark, snow-filled air. Even the immense man faded, his newsprint coat dissolving into snowy fragments which concealed nothing at all.

Ben was on his knees by David, tears streaming down his face. And Owen staring, his eyes too big, from Kenny to Philip to David and Ben to the door.

At the top of the stairs the door to the corridor opened. And Jamie, Matron Jamieson, said, 'What—? What's happened?' before running down the stairs and pushing Ben out of the way.

Kenneth Pyper went back into his house and put on his coat. He took the pamphlet from the study and slipped it into a pocket. Then he left the house, without telling his wife, without checking that his two sons were sleeping.

He was abstracted, half caught in the past, and half in the present, a whole set of inter-related problems. Money, status, Seifert, his children, Bowen. At least Samuel was flourishing: he was the son Pyper had always wanted, bright, strong, good at sport, tough. He'll go far, that lad, Kenny thought to himself as he entered the city through Bootham Bar. I wish we'd called him Philip, but at the time it hadn't occurred to him. Sam had never given him a moment's worry, not like Geoffrey, who was altogether a more complicated proposition, more of a mummy's boy. In Samuel he saw himself, a winner all the way . . . No one put him down, no one got away with anything where Samuel, or his father, was concerned.

He was making for the Old Yorker, a bar where he sometimes met Dominic Allbright for a drink after hours. He wanted to see if their little strategy had borne fruit, whether Ben Bowen was now out of the reckoning, adequately punished for his treacherous behaviour. He'd never return to York, with any luck. He'd know that the city was set against him.

He was preoccupied as he passed through the gate, walking quickly, and didn't notice the swelling blackness behind him. At some subliminal level he must have heard something, however, because as he approached the Minster, he turned once to look back to Bootham Bar.

He frowned: was there a suggestion that something was blocking the gate? A grid of some kind? He took a half step towards it, but then someone called, 'Dad! What are you doing here?'

He turned immediately, all thoughts of the blocked gate vanishing, for Samuel was standing by the pavement paintings in front of the Minster.

'Sam! Whatever are you doing out at this time?' He was astounded. 'Come here at once! I'll take you home.'

'No! Listen, Dad, it's really interesting. Leo Fletcher has gone missing and everyone's out looking for him.'

'How do you know this?'

'I saw Mr Allbright just now. He was looking for him.'

Kenneth Pyper docketed this one away in his mind. If Dom Allbright was looking for Leo Fletcher it was with no altruistic motive. And the last thing the school needed was another scandal, another focus of unfavourable publicity. 'Are the police involved?' he said.

'I haven't seen anyone. But Sophy's father and that tall

woman were going towards the Tower. They were calling out his name, so I know they haven't found him yet. Shall we help look? I was just coming to get you, you see, to help . . .' His voice trailed off. Pyper wasn't listening. He was looking at the rain-washed remnants of the picture at their feet.

It showed a picture he didn't recognize, although he knew the theme. Abraham, about to draw the knife across his son Isaac's throat. The moment before the angel stopped it . . .

'Come with me,' he said abruptly. 'We'll go and see if there's anything we can do.'

Out at Terrington, Oliver Seifert was woken from difficult dreams by the telephone ringing. He rolled over and turned on the light. He picked up the phone.

'Seifert,' he said.

'It's Joss Fletcher here. I'm a parent at St Anthony's. I'm terribly sorry to disturb you at this time, but I'm trying to contact Ben Bowen. I believe he's been staying with you?'

'He's not here now.'

'Could you check? This is an emergency.'

'What sort of emergency?'

There was a pause. 'My son has gone missing,' said Joss. 'Ben was helping us look, but he's disappeared. I wondered if he'd returned to Terrington.'

'I'll look in his room. Hold on, please.'

Seifert knew, without doubt, that Ben was not in the house. The dog would have barked a greeting, he always heard when someone came in. But he was an honourable man, so he padded across the landing in bare feet and pushed open the door to the spare room. No one there, as he knew. But still he paused in the doorway, hesitating, before returning to the phone.

A child was missing. Joss's son. And although Oliver Seifert had not acknowledged that he knew Joss, he remembered the name perfectly well. This was one of his son David's friends. He was also the father of the boy who was at risk. The boy who was now lost.

He returned to his bedroom and picked up the receiver. 'No, he's not here. I have a mobile phone number—' he read it out. 'Would you be so kind as to give me a ring when Leo is found? I shall be on my way to York in five minutes.'

'Please do not disturb yourself—'

'I do not sleep well, Mr Fletcher, and the more people who search for a child, the sooner he will be found.' Oliver Seifert did not wait for Joss's reply. He put the phone down and then quickly dressed.

The roads were empty and the night sky clear. He reached York in less than half an hour and drove round the outskirts of the walls, along Lord Mayor's Walk and Gillygate and past the station until he crossed Skeldergate bridge.

Ahead of him the Tower was caught in the headlights.

Chapter Thirty-Four

'Leo!' Louisa called as they approached the Tower. 'Leo, are you there?'

There was no answer, so she took a few more steps towards the hill. At once her hand snagged on something and she stopped, sucking her finger. 'Damn! What's all this?' In the dark, the circles of barbed wire were barely visible. 'He can't be here, Owen. It's been fenced off.'

'I wonder why.' Owen sounded thoughtful. 'That usually only happens on Bonfire Night, when they've got all the fireworks in the Tower. Repairs, perhaps. Let's see if it goes all the way round.' They walked round the mound, calling Leo's name and found no way through, even at the stone steps which led to the Tower, where the wire was firmly nailed to a pair of wooden posts. There was no sign of earthworks or scaffolding either. The stone walls sat massively on top of the hill, uninterrupted, inviolate.

'I don't think he's here,' said Louisa. 'He would have heard us.' She found herself unwilling – more than that, utterly repulsed by the stone circle. The ranks of daffodils which covered the grass gave it only a specious prettiness, for the Tower was a place of horror, and, like the city, it seemed almost alive. There never used to be daffodils, she thought, the daffodils were planted to accord with York's tourist identity and they were *fleurs du mal*. Lilies would be more appropriate. This was a mausoleum, a living sarcophagus.

'I hate this place,' she said.

'It's not the original. That burned to the ground. This was built later.'

'Makes no difference. It happened here.' She knew that very little of York dated back to the twelfth century; but the city remembered, it knew only too well what had really happened. It needed no museums, no exhibitions or archeological trusts. The events of the past sink into the soil, she wanted to say. It runs like a river beneath the city and every time a building is erected, it soaks up the true heritage of York. This artificial celebration, these jolly japes were absolutely inappropriate.

And this place was the worst of all. It seemed right to Louisa that the Tower should be hidden behind jagged barriers of metal.

'It should be hung with black,' she said.

Owen glanced at her. 'I know what you mean. There are times when even a hardened sceptic like myself wants to cross fingers, touch wood, whatever. And I bloody resent it, don't you? To be reduced to such basic superstition?'

'It's not superstitious to acknowledge evil. There's no choice then, is there?'

'Not when a child's life is at stake.'

The coils of wire were over a metre high, a vicious crown of thorns round the mound. She was shivering now, and it wasn't purely because of the numbing cold.

'I don't understand why they're using barbed wire, it's no good for crowd control.' Somehow, without her noticing, Owen had taken hold of her hand. He was winding his handkerchief round the jagged tear in her thumb. His touch was very gentle, very sure. She realized that he was trying to soothe her, although he was clearly feeling it too. 'You can't have this kind of thing happening to kids, to innocent passers-by—'

'It's probably temporary. There's something in the Tower they want protected.' She paused. 'Who do you think "they" are? The Council? The Archeological Trust? It sounds rather paranoid.'

'Let's take a look.' Owen went to one of the two posts and

pushed at it. It remained solid. He had better luck with the other, which shifted minutely. Together they pushed and pulled at it, until it was possible to draw it from its hole.

'There!' Owen was triumphant. He twisted the post so that the coiling wire was lifted a good two feet above the ground. 'Under you go.'

She had to force herself to do it. Within its shadow, she thought, within its power. She ducked down and crawled through inelegantly before holding the post clear for him. Owen was considerably more graceful. Ahead of them the stone steps were narrow-treaded and uncomfortably steep. Another barrier, another chance to turn back, go away. But Owen had her by the hand, and she had only to remember Leo to know that going away just wasn't an option.

It was further than she thought and at every step it seemed that their feet were weighted, heavy with invisible chains. They were both out of breath by the time they reached the top. The portcullis gate there was locked and double-padlocked. It entirely filled the entrance to the Tower. They could see nothing through it.

She wanted to call his name, to say 'Leo' yet again, but the word stuck in her throat. 'Owen—? Christ, what's that?' For the darkness was sliced through with brilliance as if caught in car headlights.

'What do you think you're doing here?' The torch light was dazzling, the voice both cultured and sharp with annoyance.

They'd heard nothing. No approach, no other tread on those stone steps. Whoever it was at the top of the steps must have been there already.

Owen's hands were shading his eyes. 'Looking for a lost child,' he said calmly. 'Who are you?'

The torch beam dropped a little and over the brightness Louisa saw an unfamiliar face, sharp-featured, tight with annoyance. 'My name's Martin Shaw,' the man said. 'I'm here to make sure no one disturbs the fireworks for tomorrow's Festival. There's no one here, no sign of a kid.'

'Festival? What's this?' said Owen.

'It's a one-off. A one-day event to celebrate the Duke of York's visit. We're having a parade of local schools—'

'Whatever for?'

'Each school has taken a historical theme, some event from York's past . . . Past Present has arranged it—'

'Past Present? But that's where Joss works! It's Joss's son who's gone missing!' said Louisa. What did all this talk of festivals matter?

'I'm very sorry to hear that,' said Shaw and Louisa suddenly remembered that this was the man that Joss didn't trust, this was the man who tried to sabotage whatever he did. It was Martin Shaw who had organized the Festival Day, much against Joss's advice.

'How come you've got landed with guard duty?' she asked. 'Doesn't the fireworks company provide guards?'

'Usually. But they couldn't find anyone tonight, and seeing as I booked them—'

'You volunteered to be watchman,' said Owen. 'If you haven't seen Leo, then I suppose he can't be here. But do you mind if we take a quick look in the Tower?'

'I'm under instruction to let no one in. No matter what.'

'Don't be absurd.'

'The fireworks company insisted. It's all set up in there, ready to go.'

'All the more reason to check that Leo's not there,' said Owen.

'Of course he's not there!' Shaw sounded angry. 'I've been here all evening and I check inside every half hour and I know – *know* – there's no one in there!'

'Are you being deliberately obtuse?' Louisa had had enough of this. 'Have you had your eyes on the gate all evening? If you've been opening it regularly, how can you swear that no one slipped in? Did you never turn your back? Give me the keys!'

'For God's sake!' Shaw took keys from his pocket and opened the padlock. The torch beam swung swiftly over the crates and boxes, strange wire assemblies, scaffolding and ladders. He walked to the centre of the Tower.

'See?' he said. 'Nothing.'

Louisa pushed past him. 'Leo?' she called, 'Leo, are you there?' Her voice echoed strangely round the encircling walls but there was no reply. For a moment she stood there, listening. The Tower's silence hung heavily over the garishly painted boxes and nothing moved, nothing breathed any kind of life into the place.

Outside once more, they watched while Martin Shaw locked up.

'Just why do you think Leo Fletcher would have come here anyway?' Shaw spoke resentfully. 'And whatever is a child of that age doing out at this time of night?'

Louisa glanced at Owen. How could they possibly begin to explain? 'It's a long story,' she said lamely. 'He's – rather fascinated with what happened here.'

'Hardly a suitable subject for children, I would have thought.' Martin Shaw glanced at his watch. 'I wish you well in your search, but as you see, there are dangerous substances here. I can't possibly leave my post.'

'Of course not.' Owen was at the top of the stairs. 'He must be somewhere else. Come on, Louisa, let's try back at the school again.'

At the bottom of the steps, Louisa said to him, 'I can quite see why Joss dislikes that man so much. Jumped up little Hitler.'

'Poor Joss,' said Owen. 'I wonder how he's coping.'

*   *   *

Joss said, 'I can't stand this any more. I'm going to look for him.'

The police had just left. They'd taken descriptions and details, had asked appalling questions about birthmarks and other distinguishing characteristics, and had been vaguely reassuring.

It was not enough. Lily was sitting on the sofa, white-faced and dry-eyed, turning her rings over and over. 'Don't go!' Her eyes were enormous as she looked at him. 'Don't leave me here!'

'Come with me.'

'I can't. What if they phone? What if he comes back?'

'Do you want to go out and I'll stay here?'

She shuddered. 'No.' Her voice was very faint. 'I want to wait here until he comes. He's going to come back home, I know he will—'

Joss sighed with frustration. 'I'll just go as far as the school. The school and the office, he's quite likely to go there, isn't he?' Leo had visited him at work before, had enjoyed playing CD-ROM games. It was possible, at least.

She stared at him. A long shuddering sigh as she stood up. 'Louisa was right, wasn't she? This is all to do with what happened when you were children. You unleashed something then which is still around. What was it that started it off, what triggered it?'

'That bloody pamphlet, I suppose. And the extraordinary enmity of Philip Stroud and Kenneth Pyper towards David. There was something horrible about the way Philip dominated Kenny, the way they stuck together. It was as if their contempt for Davey was the glue that joined them together. That and Philip's horrible home. They kept going back there at every exeat, somewhere in the Dales. Coverham, it was.'

He stopped suddenly and looked at Lily.

She too had seen it. 'The skull,' she whispered. 'The skull

at your office. It was found at Coverham.' She pointed at one of the publicity handouts that lay on the sideboard.

'It can't have anything to do with it, I can't believe it. It's too simple, too – Indiana Jones or something.'

'You said the office was sick. That nothing works there.'

He nodded slowly. 'Okay. I'll take a look.' He remembered the fax machine's madness, the dying plants, the hysterical secretaries and obstructive Martin Shaw. She might even be right . . . He crutched his way across the floor and dropped a kiss on her forehead. 'I won't be long,' he said. 'And I'll ring—' he glanced at his watch, '—from the school and from the office, to see if he's come back home. Cheer up, my love. We're on top of it now, we have some clue why now. And Leo's not a baby—'

'Yes, he is!'

He shook his head. 'No fool, our Leo. He won't have gone far.'

But as he left the house, and the city closed its grip about him, he knew she was right. Their baby, their only child, the most beloved, the adored, lost in a city where dreadful things had a way of happening . . . The thud of his crutches seemed less significant than the beat of his heart.

The pavements were dark and shiny, glinting with moisture. A cat yowled from a high window-sill and he looked up to find a tiny stone face grinning down at him. Even the houses had gargoyles to support their gutters in York. Someone had chalked hopscotch figures on the pavement, a door knocker like a fish swam uneasily before his eyes. Shifting shapes, shifting colours, shifting times. The blank eyes of the skull drilled through his mind. He was more deeply frightened than he had ever been before in his life. His hands were sweating, too slippery to hold the crutches securely.

The school was in darkness, the gates firmly barred and padlocked. It looked like a prison.

There was no bell. He stood there for a moment or two, trying to remember where the living accommodation had been, wondering if anyone might hear him if he shouted. But of course no one lived there now, no boarders or staff. No one would be there to let him in even if he sounded the Last Trump. So he passed by St Anthony's and went on to the office, where the skull was.

He knew Leo wouldn't be there. The door would be locked too, Leo couldn't get in—

At his touch the door swung open. This was wrong, very wrong. At once he called out, 'Leo? Are you there?'

Utter silence. No breath of wind, no hum of electricity. There was no one there, there couldn't be. The open door had to be merely an accident, carelessness: Shaw had simply forgotten to lock up. That had to be it.

In his heart he knew differently. The skull in his mind was here in truth. And then, somewhere far above him, he heard the faintest of sounds, the minute click and swish of the fax machine receiving a message.

Not again. He briefly wondered whether to cut and run, go and get help, anything so that he wouldn't have to face it alone. But Leo might be up there, he would have to look first . . .

It took him too long to get up the stairs. In the end he tucked both crutches under one arm and hauled himself up by clinging on to the banisters. But this time he knew he was going to keep hold of his crutches. In the office, he went straight to the fax machine and turned it off. He wanted no repeat of the other night.

He glanced at the message. Something about the next day's Festival, arrangements Martin Shaw should have dealt with, just as he should have locked the door to the street. Nothing to worry him there.

No sign of Leo, either.

He called his son's name once or twice and then stumped round the various cubicles of the central area, checking again. He flicked on lights, looked behind doors and under desks and in cupboards. Nothing. But he came at last to the Norman skull, still positioned on its plinth.

At first it looked like someone had spilled paint over the cranium. It was the smell that alerted him. Metallic, almost sweet, unmistakably blood. Dark liquid ran down the side of the plinth, and it was coming from the skull.

The top of the cranium was shattered, smashed. Blood welled from it, blood ran from the eyes and mouth.

Joss stumbled backwards and collided with the door. His balance was insecure: the door swung against his back and he fell, the crutches jerked from his grip. His head struck the corner of a bookshelf and the blaze of pain tore across his mind.

From its place of isolation, he saw the skull watching what happened with bloody eyes. He was filled with revulsion. He dragged himself to his feet and found his crutches. He wanted to take the skull and destroy it.

Bury it, he told himself. That's what you do with human remains, you bury or incinerate them.

But it had been buried at Coverham for centuries. And its seeping evil had infected the people who lived there, had burrowed into the souls of Philip and Kenny and transformed childish resentment and jealousy into something infinitely more dangerous.

He could hardly bring himself to approach it. He was used to seeing the skull stained with red: the laser light scanning it had bathed it in roseate warmth. But this was different.

How had it happened? What had impelled someone to shatter the cranium and pour red paint – or whatever it was – over it? The office poltergeist, Martin Shaw, vandals from the street – there were any number of likely candidates, and did it matter? Joss had to get it out of here, take it away somewhere and destroy it . . .

A kind of frenzy gripped him. All thoughts of his missing son left him. He was obsessed with getting the skull out of the office and away from there. In the cleaning cupboard by the stairs he found an empty Sainsbury's carrier bag. With utmost reluctance, he reached out his hand and picked up the skull, closing his mind to the smell of the red liquid which covered it – *Does paint smell like that?* – and put it in the bag. Then he slowly crutched his way down the stairs and out into the street.

It was out. Living and breathing in the streets of York, and its heartbeat contained all times, all stories, all events. Invisible and immortal, this was no god of forgiveness. It paced the ancient streets, where it had all happened before. Its tread was silent, its mantle of darkness turned away regard. The unfortunate homeless, those with no axe to grind, stirred with instinctive rejection. They pulled their hats down further and turned up their collars. The others, the wild mob, became one with its body and its breath, its heart and soul and will.

Its two eyes were figures of darkness, one with the tail of a beast, the other covered in words written on cloth and paper and sheepskin. Its spirit was the White Canon, living and dead and beyond death. The beast turned its back on the Minster and took the stony path to the square over the cemetery of St Helen. Down the rabbit street, past the big Jewish houses with their burning timbers, while the smell of the fish market mixed in the air with charcoal, with sweat, with beer and vomit and fear and violence.

Kenneth and Samuel Pyper went with it. They did not notice the ancient clothes, made of coarse wool, tied with string and bits of leather. They did not notice that the crowd spoke in words from other times: it was a language they knew, it was a fellowship they had joined long ago. They were swept along from the top of Stonegate, with only a token question:

'What—? Where are you going?'

'Looking for the boy,' said the man dressed in newspaper. 'A boy like this one.' His hand reached out and stroked Samuel's face. 'Come with us,' he said pleasantly. 'We'll help you find your friend, don't you worry.'

'He's not my friend,' said Samuel.

Kenny was about to say something to pull Samuel away from this enormous, foul-breathed man, but the man had moved, so that he was standing between them.

'Sam?' he said, not yet seriously worried. But the crowd was beginning to jostle and push and he couldn't see his son.

The beast passed the bridge over the river and turned the corner, and saw for the first time that night the Tower. Its twin eyes of light flooded it with brilliance.

The beast was home.

Chapter Thirty-Five

They'd gone. Leo had heard voices calling but he only recognized one of them, that man he didn't like from his father's office. He'd shouted at him, told him to get away from the cameras, away from the skeleton head on the plinth. And his shouting hadn't been friendly or concerned, it had been panicky and angry and Leo had been disturbed by it, made uneasy.

So when he heard Martin Shaw's voice, he stayed there, crouching low beside the crates and waited until they were gone. He'd be safe there. No one would find him. But he was curious about his surroundings. In his pocket, Leo found matches. It was dark and cold and he wanted to see what it said on the crates and boxes around the walls. But the box was damp and the first few matches he tried failed to strike. So he tried a trick he'd seen in films and TV programmes, that of striking a match against the wall. Friction, he thought. It's friction which does it. But the stone too was running with damp and he broke several matches before trying one against the side of a box.

It caught immediately.

He saw the signs: DANGER; FIREWORKS; INFLAM-MABLE and the red crosses which shrieked at him. He stepped away from them hurriedly, still holding the lighted match. And stumbled against one of the signs that gave information about the Tower and fell backwards and the match fell from his fingers on to a framework of wire strung with catherine wheels.

Dazzling light flooded his sight.

*   *   *

Ben stirred. The pain in his gut convulsed him and he rolled over, vomiting. He felt cold and shivery, and every time he retched, a vile stab of agony caught in his chest. A rib, probably. He hung over the patch of vomit for too long, feeling like death.

He could remember few details, had no idea who had attacked him. Out of the bushes they'd run at him, and he'd seen none of their faces clearly, had no idea *why*. Warily, bracing himself, he sat back on his heels. With shaking hands, he felt in his jacket pocket. The touch made him shudder. But his wallet was still there, nothing had been taken.

Except his glasses. He couldn't see to look for them, although he thought they must have fallen close by. He didn't know where he was, he had no way of telling from the shadowy trees whether he was in the country or city. How long had he been unconscious? It was still dark, still night-time. The mess of undergrowth was deep in ivy and brambles and he knew his chances of finding his glasses were remote.

Why? Who were they, why had they attacked him with such concentrated ferocity?

He heard, somewhere to his left, the distant rumble of traffic. A car, crossing a bridge. And through the trees straight ahead of him, a small light glinted and bobbed. The river. He was lying in the shrubbery at the bottom of someone's garden, less than twenty yards from the river. He hadn't gone far at all.

He'd been walking down Bootham Terrace, looking for Leo—

Leo! Allbright had sent him down here, but there had been no sign of the boy and he remembered thinking that this was a wild-goose chase, that Allbright had deliberately misled him.

He needed to find out if Leo was safe yet. He had to get back to Joss's house.

346

He might as well have decided to climb the Matterhorn. He lurched to his feet and the movement made him gasp. One step, and he was down again in the undergrowth, thorns tearing his hands, weeping with pain. His right knee wouldn't work, could bear no weight. That one step had sent flares of sickening weakness up into his groin. The knee had buckled as if it were made of grass. Warily, he tried to sit up, to roll up his trouser leg and take a look, but the pain in his ribs made it impossible. With one hand he reached down and found that his knee was swollen out of shape, thick as a football.

Dear Lord, he prayed. Help me now, help me. *Miserere me.*

Close by, he heard rustling in the undergrowth. A large, long-haired dog emerged from the branches and immediately began to bark.

'Who's there? Is there anyone there?' A woman's voice, quite loudly, and a torch flickering through the leaves around him. Thank God, he thought.

'I'm here,' he said unnecessarily as the beam steadied on his face. His eyes were screwed up against the glare. 'Can you help me please? I've been mugged.'

Another crackling of dead wood as she came towards him. 'Here, let me take the weight. Just relax.'

Immensely competent and strong arms helped him upright.

'My knee doesn't work,' he explained.

'Lean on me,' she said calmly. 'I'm a nurse. Now tell me, just what are you doing at the bottom of Mrs Crossley's garden?'

He made no attempt to answer, concentrating instead on not crying out as she supported him out of the shadowy garden and along the riverside walk to another house, where French doors stood open.

Once in the light she examined his face with professional thoroughness before gently probing his ribs. 'Off to hospital with you,' she said. 'I'll drive you. And perhaps we'd better ring the police, too.'

'I have to make a phone call first,' he said and explained about Leo. With no fuss, no attempt to dissuade him, she brought him the phone and he dialled Joss's number.

At the second ring it was answered.

'Yes?' said Lily's voice, so tight with anxiety that he knew immediately that Leo had not been found.

'Ben here,' he said. 'Are you on your own, Lily?'

'Joss has gone out to look. You didn't find any sign? Nothing?'

'No. Lily, I'll be right over. You wait there, put the kettle on. I'll call a taxi.' He put the phone down.

'I'll drive you,' said the nurse. 'And while we're waiting for your friend's son to turn up, I'll see what I can do about those ribs.'

She was middle-aged and grey-haired and plump and he liked the way she'd made no attempt to change his mind. Her voice was intelligent and musical and he found himself wanting to trust her.

'I'm Benedict Bowen.' He held out his hand and she took it.

'Letitia Farmer. Otherwise known as Tish. I'll get you some aspirin, and then we'll be off.'

'There's something I need to do first,' he said suddenly. 'Before we go to Lily's. We have to go to Clifford's Tower.'

'*Why?*' She was astounded.

'I think he may be there,' he said. 'It's where it started.'

Oliver Seifert saw it in the headlights. The Tower, harshly white on its green and yellow mound. It was bathed in light, the floodlights that highlighted all of York's major sights. But there was something odd about it tonight, something that seemed to curdle the white of its stonework, so that the darkness of the surrounding night was pulled down to shroud it.

He could not look away. And felt his car hit something, a small thud to one side that made him stamp on the brakes.

There was no other traffic about. He reversed cautiously and saw the small huddled shape in the road. Not a dog, he thought to himself, too fluid, too subtle a shape. With misgiving he opened the car door and got out.

A cat, quite unmoving. Regretfully, he knelt down beside it. Its eyes were open, glassy in the Rover's headlights, dead. He picked it up gently and took it to the side of the road.

To his right, beyond the barbed wire, steps led to the Tower.

'Oliver!'

Ben's voice, but strangely uneven. Seifert turned towards the sound, and then bent hurriedly to lay the cat's corpse on the ground.

The figure coming towards him was supported by a woman, someone he found faintly familiar. Ben was limping painfully, his face pale and contorted.

'My God, Ben, what's happened?' He helped the woman guide him over to the steps. Together, they eased him into a sitting position.

For a moment Ben said nothing. His left eyelid was swollen, almost closed, his upper lip split.

'Let me ring for an ambulance. Or better still, I'll drive you to hospital—'

'Do you think I haven't tried?' The woman who had arrived with Ben sounded only mildly irritable and he realized who she was. The nurse on the Intensive Care ward.

'I suppose you're in good hands,' Seifert said. 'But who did this, Ben? We should contact the police.'

'Thugs,' Ben said wearily. His words were indistinct and clumsy. 'I didn't know them. Drop-outs, tramps. The mob.'

As he said it, his words were drowned in the noise of

fireworks. A fizzing, whooshing noise as a rocket was released at a low angle, crashing into the hotel wall opposite. A shower of sparks fell through the air all about them, an alarm bell went off with high-pitched intensity.

Golden rain. Fragments of fire, splitting the darkness, splitting sight and vision, the sound of explosions splitting moment from moment, time from time.

It came from the Tower, frothing over the edge of the walls, spilling in fountains of brightness on to the grass. And all at once, people were shouting, were pushing forward at them, and Oliver Seifert wondered for an instant if there was some event, some celebration of civic pride about which he knew nothing. He would not have been surprised: he paid little attention to what happened in York.

But *now*? After midnight, when the pubs were closed and the restaurants empty? And the mob, the crowd, who were they? Where had they come from?

'You can do nothing here,' he said to Ben. 'I'll find the boy. Go and get yourself sorted out.'

'He's up there,' said Ben, looking at the Tower. 'I don't think I can make it.'

'We'll go and find his mother,' said the nurse. 'You'll bring Leo back to us, won't you?'

'I'll do my very best,' said Oliver Seifert and turned back to the Tower.

The barbed wire was no longer there.

Louisa and Owen had only just reached the bottom of the hill when the first firework went off. They heard Martin Shaw shout, 'Fire Brigade! Quickly!' and Louisa looked over towards the Fire Station, so close—

And so far. Standing between them and the Fire Station was an immense crowd of people, a mob, seething, shouting. She had no time to wonder why the mob was out at that time of night because Owen was shouting, 'Fire! Get the Fire Brigade!'

He was staring up at the Tower. In the hectic glow from the phosphor-driven rain, his skin was bronzed, shining, unearthly. His wild hair was blown back from his face, his eyes black and sparkling.

She thought she had never seen anyone so alive, and at the same time feared for him and herself. It could go so wrong, she thought, we might fail again.

'It has to be Leo,' she said with certainty. 'Leo's in the Tower and somehow he's managed to set the fireworks off. We have to get him out!'

They could see nothing of Martin Shaw, but an exotic bonfire of exploding chemicals had been lit inside the Tower and golden froth tumbled over the walls, explosions and rockets detonated within the circle of stone.

'We have to get him out!' Louisa repeated, beginning to run up the hill.

Owen caught her arm. 'Louisa, no. Stay here. Promise me,' and before she could protest, he vanished back up the hill.

She wasn't taking that, even from Owen. She was about to follow him, but someone pulled her back.

'Louisa—? Isn't it? Louisa Jamieson?'

She found herself staring at a face she hadn't seen for over twenty years and one she certainly didn't want to see now. White hair fringed bulbous, sagging folds of skin. Pale eyes were sunk into pasty flesh, the lips were blubbery and moist. Kenneth Pyper was grasping her arm, his face uncomfortably close to her own. He was perspiring, running with sour sweat, and she felt revulsion and disgust.

'Kenneth Pyper. What are you doing here?' She was trying to pull her arm away, but he didn't let go.

'I've lost my son,' he said. 'My boy Sam. Have you seen him anywhere?'

'No. I'm looking for another child, Joss Fletcher's Leo. We think he might be up there—' She gestured towards the exploding Tower. 'Perhaps they might be together—?'

'No! Surely not!' But he'd let go of her arm, was struggling up the steep slope, slipping and sliding on the crushed daffodil leaves.

'Miss Jamieson!' Another familiar voice, older, kindly. She couldn't at first place it, but then his face emerged from the mob and she recognized Oliver Seifert.

He looked calm and unflustered, although he must have had a difficult time of it, getting through the mob. 'Louisa, have they found the boy? Joss's son?'

She shook her head. She had no idea how he'd got there, or even why he should be there.

'They're up there,' he said and it wasn't a question. 'Stay here,' he said to her. 'Don't attempt to follow me.'

She couldn't have followed him if she'd wanted to. The crowd had closed in after Seifert, and she was effectively barricaded away from the Tower.

Déjà vu. The moment when a memory feels so ancient, so well-established that it must have been a dream. She remembered running through the snow to find Joss crouched over his broken ankle, remembered not seeing, not knowing what was happening within the basement—

Joss. It came to her with astounding clarity. Joss needed her, she had to go and find him, Joss would have to be told what was happening. She would be of no use at the top of the Tower, she'd get in the way—

Around her the crowd drew back. She was dimly aware of a figure with what looked like a tail of cloth winding along the ground behind him. Someone else, a giant of a man, seemed to be dressed in newspaper, but he paid no attention to her.

352

She looked back once more to the Tower, which now ran with flame, and then pushed through the crowd on her way back into the city.

She hadn't even noticed that the barbed wire was gone.

Chapter Thirty-Six

Owen couldn't believe it. The gate was still locked. 'For fuck's sake! What are you playing at?'

Martin Shaw was wrestling feebly with keys, his face white and sweating. 'It's not going to be much use, I don't think we'll be able to put it out ourselves,' he said.

Owen pushed him out of the way, trying to see if there were any gaps round the gate. A cascade of burning sparks suddenly shot into the air over their heads.

'For God's sake, leave that! Go and get help. We need the Fire Brigade, this is dangerous!' Shaw was yelling now. 'There's nothing we can do here!'

'There's a child in there!'

'No! You're mad! We looked!'

'How else did this start? Spontaneous combustion? Lightning? Use your *brain*! Which key is it?' Owen had grabbed the keys from him.

'Here.' Shaw's fingers were slippery with sweat, fumbling through the bunch, maddeningly ineffective.

A series of rockets burst into the air over their heads, only just skimming the walls. And through the noise of the explosions, through the heat and the sparkling violence, Owen thought he heard something, the small sad sound of a child crying. The key turned, and he flung the door open.

Leo was standing in the middle of it, his face blank with shock, running with tears. His mouth was open in a soundless wail. He was flinching at every explosion as if he was being whipped. Around him the walls seemed to be moving, shattering, bursting and it was like some mediaeval version of hell, limned with red violence.

Owen did not think. He ran, and clutched the child up into his arms.

The stones seemed to explode. The golden rain had touched catherine wheels and rockets and fountains and the Tower was blooming in flowers of passion, with beautiful and blossoming rockets, fretted with fire and danger, a furious outpouring of sulphur and potassium nitrate.

Gunpowder.

Owen said, 'Okay, Leo? You're all right now.'

He lied. There was nothing all right, no safe way he could get Joss's son across the floor to the gate. Deadly sparks had reached the bank of crates against the wall by the gate and the whole lot was erupting in uneven plumes of fire, an infernal chaos of heat and choking smoke. It was impossible to guess what might happen next.

There were rockets going off everywhere, enormous pyro-technic monsters emerging from the fire, battering against the walls, some overshooting, some crashing like demented dragons at their feet.

Owen held Leo within his coat and, head down, made a run for one of the two spiral staircases which led on either side of the gate to the walkway round the top of the Tower.

Just a few steps up and they were out of it, crouched against the uneven stone in the dark, listening to the chaotic cacophony.

Outside the Tower, Martin Shaw hesitated, unable to see what was happening through the curtains of flame. He decided that there was nothing he could do without endangering his skin. The professionals could take charge. So he stumbled down the steps on the other side of the wall and did not see the other figure run forward into the Tower as if sucked in by a great whirlpool.

Kenneth Pyper was dazzled, blinded, made mad by the light. A Roman candle had burst into light-bulb ferocity within a few feet of him and its glare had stunned his sight and mind. Brightness was drowning his mind, his reason. He put his hands to his eyes, rubbing them.

When he looked up, he saw Dominic Allbright staring at him.

Or was it Allbright? The flowing pale coat was familiar, but the hood was up and Kenneth could not see the man's face in the flaring light.

'What are you doing here?' Allbright yelled. But now the confusion was complete, because Kenneth was suddenly reminded of Philip, the way Philip was dressed that Christmas over twenty years ago. 'Why aren't you in the Tower with the others?'

'Others? What others?' He spoke hesitantly. He really did not know what Philip was talking about.

'The Jews. The rest of the Jews. They're all in there, so what are you doing out here?' The man in white grabbed his arm.

'But I'm not Jewish!' he cried, hanging back.

'Your grandmother was Jewish. You told Benedict, remember? You're a lying stupid little Yid, and belong in there with the rest of the pack. Get along with you!'

He felt the man's hand at the base of his spine, propelling him towards the hill.

Still he resisted. The Tower was overspilling with flame.

'Your son is up there,' said the man in white. 'Go and find him.'

And so Kenneth ran to find his son, hardly noticing the grass or the degree of slope of the hill as the world exploded round him. He fell, and found his hands grazing against stone. A flight of stairs. He forced himself forward, and the shifting

356

stone steps to the Tower moved beneath his feet, easing his passage to the top. The barred gate swung open and swallowed him.

Into another time. His eyes had been screwed tight shut, but now he opened them, and found himself staring at a stranger. Or was it a stranger? The confusion in his mind settled, fell into place as other thoughts took over. The stranger was Rabbi Yomtob, and he was holding a child, by the throat. It was Samuel.

In his other hand he held a knife.

It caught in the flames which raged by the door to the Tower, glinting, burning bright and all the light which had swamped Pyper's reason came from this. It held madness in its clarity, in its fatal acuity. And it posed choice, an inescapable choice.

There was firelight playing across the rabbi's features, so that his skin looked golden, fearless as a lion. His dark eyes were wild and passionate, his hair was swept back from his face so that the austere bones showed sharp in the uneven light.

How could he not fear? Kenneth Pyper heard the mob outside howling, screaming for blood. They offered Christian baptism, but how could they be trusted? They would take his child and kill him. Samuel would be torn apart like a cat, torn limb from limb, because they were mad barbarians, who had no knowledge of God, no mercy, no sense of sin—

He was Jewish because his mother and grandmother were Jewish. He could not deny it, the line held true. And his heritage held horrors, there were precedents and heroic examples for this.

My child, my son, he thought in anguish. When first I held you, it was between my two palms. Small and perfect, you looked at me with wonderment at the strangeness of life, but now you look, now—

357

Now you are going to die at the hands of Gentiles, now you are going to suffer their brutality, their cruelty, horror upon horror, and I shall hear your screams, see you suffer. Is there anything worse? What hell could match this, what had he done to earn this terrible punishment?

'Save your child from horror,' said Rabbi Yomtob. His voice was stripped of passion, arid with the breath of holiness. 'He need not suffer the death you fear for him. With your child, you can sit on the right hand of God, you can follow in the footsteps of your Fathers. Abraham was prepared to sacrifice his son, and we should align ourselves with him. This is a time of testing. This is the will of God, God to whom we ought not to say, Why do you do this? He commands us to die for His law – and behold, our death is at the door, as you see; unless you think that the Holy Law should be deserted for the short span of this life ... do you wish to live as apostates, through the mercy of impious enemies? We should prefer glorious death to infamous life. Therefore, let us willingly and devoutly, with our own hands, render up to Him that life which the Creator gave us ... for this many of our people are known to have done laudably in diverse tribulations, setting us a precedent.'

He pushed the child towards Kenneth and held out the knife.

Kenneth was weeping. This was the worst.

The knife offered only that choice: death or apostasy.

Hiding in the stairway, Owen heard the fire raging and the words of the rabbi. Dream or truth? Memory or vision? In the exigencies of the moment he had no time to speculate. He held the boy in his arms, crouching down by the walls in the desperate hope that they might stay concealed from the mob outside. Instinct told him they'd be safer there than anywhere else. The boy was shuddering against his chest, so he stroked his hair, murmuring the meaningless words he used so often to comfort his own child, his little daughter Sophy.

But this boy, his friend's son Leo, was beyond comfort. 'I want Mummy, where's my Mummy and Daddy, Mummy, Mummy—' An eternal wail that absolutely required an answer.

'Hush, hush now,' he said. 'We must stay quiet here—'

'God will protect us—' came the rabbi's voice. 'Trust and believe it. God will protect us.'

How could he believe this? The man knew that God protected no one, least of all innocent children.

Through the narrow opening below him, he could hear the rabbi's words, he could hear the wailing of women, the anger and despair in the voices of the men.

Oh God, he thought. They're going to do it. They're really going to do it, because there have been precedents, times when in desperation we have killed our best-beloved . . .

He cradled the boy against his chest and rocked him back and forth and listened to the rabbi preaching. Keeping Leo's face turned into his coat, he edged forward to the slit in the stone and looked down.

Samuel felt the grip on his neck loosen. He stumbled a little, away from the rabbi. He could not bear to look at his father: there was something terrible in his face and it held Samuel back from running to him. His father's hands were fluttering helplessly at his side, as if they could not bear their own action. His mother was in the corner, clinging to her sister; Mistress Hanna was cuddling the new baby; Becca and Rachel were taking their doll to show old man Ephraim.

Stupid, he thought. Why should Ephraim be interested in girls' toys? But Ephraim took the dolls, silly little rag things, and threw them on to the fire he was tending.

It was shocking, ridiculous! But then all the others started throwing their possessions on to the fire, building it up to an enormous conflagration. They were smashing up furniture, breaking open their boxes of belongings, tearing up their clothes, the fringed shawls, everything was going on to the fire in the centre of the Tower. Even the books, the holy books, were being hurled on to the flames.

He didn't understand. 'Father!' he cried. 'Father, why are they burning the books? Why? What's happening—'

His father looked at him with a stranger's eyes. He was over with the other men now. Some of them were holding knives, big, heavy knives like the one used at the butcher's.

His father was crying. His father, strong, unflustered and calm, was crying. The boy saw tears in his father's eyes and it seemed to him that there were tears everywhere. The faces around him were caught in flame, washed with tears, removed from any experience he knew.

His stomach churned. And it was cold, too. Although there were flames around the Tower, flames within the Tower, the cold was seeping into his bones, making him shudder, making him tremble.

Knives. Why was his father there, holding a knife in front of him as if it terrified him?

'Come here, Samuel,' he said. 'Say your prayers, and come here.'

A confusion of noise and dirt. The fire consumed the darkness, but nothing was clear. The air was full of smoke and tears. He hesitated, rubbing his eyes.

The rabbi's face was transfigured. He was ecstatic.

'In the name of God,' said the rabbi in the true tongue.

The knife was waiting. The father took hold of his son and bared his neck.

The firelight caught on his tears.

Chapter Thirty-Seven

Lily waited.

She could feel lines of stress deepening in her face. She made herself coffee, but could not drink it. She poured gin, and watched the ice melt. At midnight, she started to prowl the house, opening cupboards, kneeling to search under beds and tables. Leo used to wander at night, she told herself; what if he had just tucked himself away somewhere and fallen asleep?

So she searched and called and her voice sounded sad as gulls, lost in a distant wind.

She was waiting for Leo to come home, but also for Joss to ring, for Ben to arrive, for the police to call.

In her wanderings through the house she had seen from the stair window that the Tower was alight, but it meant little to her. She paused to watch the sparks fly and the rockets shoot into the sky: some city celebration, she supposed. She was too anxious to speculate. But out of the front bedroom window, she saw something else.

Her view was indistinct. There was a low mist hanging over the damp pavements, and she could not be sure exactly what was happening. At first she thought they were drunk. Two men were stumbling about in the street just below one of the lamps, shouting words she did not understand. There was a dog snapping at their ankles. Tramps or vagrants, she assumed, in some kind of alcoholic brawl, and was about to turn away when her attention was caught.

One of the men had a tail.

It trailed over the damp pavement, winding around the legs

and feet of the other man. He was enormous. He seemed to be dressed in paper, old newspapers caught into place with string. They were wrestling with each other, tangled up together like snakes and the dog was snarling at both of them and for a moment Lily received an impression of utmost violence, of teeth clenched and eyes wild with hatred.

It couldn't really be a tail, of course it wasn't. But it threaded around them as if it had a will of its own and at the same time she realized that it was merely the mist swirling, running through their clothes and limbs and pulling them apart.

She could not move away. She saw the dog run away down the street. And then it began to happen, and she saw the start of dissolution, saw them stretched, attenuated by the mist and the colour of their drab clothes became as grey as the mist itself. The newspaper fluttered, tore into scraps and some of it flew up towards the window where Lily stood.

It fastened itself to the window in front of her and by the time it fell away, only a few seconds later, the street outside was empty.

And although she was still frantic about Leo, still overwrought with worry, she breathed a little easier. They've gone, she thought. They were evil, but they've gone.

She walked downstairs and the memory of what she had seen faded as she heard the car draw up outside.

Ben saw Lily standing at the open door, her face thin and pinched with strain. She came over to the car before he had a chance even to open the door. 'Have you found him? Any news?'

He shook his head. 'I hoped you'd heard something. Where's Joss gone?'

'To check the school. Then the office – Ben, he thinks it's the skull, it's the skull at the Centre that's started this all off again! And I can't stand this, not doing anything—'

He didn't know what she was talking about, but her distress was clear. 'Come with us. We'll go and get Joss.'

'But what if Leo comes home? If the police ring?'

'I'll stay here.' Letitia Farmer got out of the driver's door and held out her hand to Lily. 'I'm a nurse,' she said. 'A friend of Louisa and Ben. You can take my mobile phone and I'll ring you if there's any news.'

She was holding out the phone to Lily. Her competence was completely credible and Lily had no problems in trusting her. She took the phone from Letitia Farmer with relief. She got into the car and turned it there and then in the narrow, one way street.

The gate to the Tower itself was standing open, and light fell from it, shone round Oliver Seifert, bathed him in the appalling clarity of the past and carried him through the stone walls, so that he stood there amongst his kind and saw his friends, his people, holding knives.

The women were crying. Not all of them, some were stone-faced, enduring, dead to feeling. They were stunned, driven into wordless panic by the noise, the violence of the mob outside, the wild fire inside the Tower, the chanted words of Rabbi Yomtob and the looks in the eyes of their men. Others stood outside their lives and allowed the words of the rabbi to fill their minds and hearts, were transfigured by glory as he was, by dreadful words of redemption and heroic glory.

The children were blank-faced with incomprehension, terror and acccptance.

Oliver Seifert saw one of them, a man he knew as Kenneth, reaching towards his son Samuel. There were tears on his cheeks, his mouth was working. This man is in hell, he thought. He is suffering the torments of the damned, as are they all.

The knife was so close. It glinted in the firelight and in an instant it became clear. Seifert knew this man, he knew the particular hell he faced: the loss of a son. His own life ran on that one thread only: the death of David informed every day, every hour of Seifert's life. It was the only vivid thing he knew, the only thing that made him touch reality, that showed the world in deep, passionate, darkened colours.

Nothing else mattered.

He saw the man Kenneth raise the knife and knew him as a murderer, past and present. He had murdered once and now he was about to murder his own child. This man was guilty in every possible way. And although he was guilty and a murderer too, Seifert could not let it happen.

'Stop!' he cried. 'It must not happen! Nothing is worth this, no revenge, no ideal, no fear!'

The knife falls.

The child died, they all died. No one survived the massacre in Clifford's Tower, even those who did not accept the rabbi's dream of glory. The dissenters, those who hid in the small passages, those who refused the knife, those who hoped to go unobserved, were indeed offered baptism by the besiegers. They emerged into the hands of their enemies, into the blood lust of the mob.

The mob, led by Richard Malebisse, Marmeduke Darrell and the White Canon.

Those wishing for baptism emerged into the hands of these men and were killed. One hundred and fifty died.

But there was also forgiveness. The stay of the hand, the climb down, the restraint, the rare, precious moments of grace. Not then, not eight hundred years ago. But later, when another rabbi came and blessed the Castle on the mound.

Oliver Seifert stayed the hand of his enemy.

Kenneth Pyper saw his son wriggle free, saw the cascading

firelight around him, and heard the alarms and the shouting and the fire-engines draw up, and dropped the knife. He wondered what strange dream had gripped him, why his cheeks were wet, why his hands were shaking.

The explosions in the Tower were ebbing, but it still felt unsafe. Not all the boxes had gone up, but those near the gate lay broken as firewood, and the dark tunnel to the outside was clear. From a hole in the wall to one side of the gate, Owen Rattigan appeared, cradling another small child.

'Let's get out of here,' he said. His eyes avoided Kenneth's, but this was not unusual, they had never liked each other—

What was Owen doing here? What nightmare was this? It was a deep mystery Kenneth did not understand, the whole night was a mystery without answer. But Samuel was clutching his hand, demanding attention, and he crouched down beside him.

The boy's face was shocked, his eyes dark with terror. 'Dad, Dad, I dreamed, I think it was a dream—'

'A nightmare,' Pyper confirmed. 'You were sleepwalking,' he said. And thought, I have been sleepwalking too. I faced the death of my son, and remembered that other death, that murder when we were children. He looked up into Oliver Seifert's eyes.

'Who—?' He was stupid with bewilderment.

'I am David's father,' said Oliver Seifert. 'I am the father of the boy you killed.'

Kenneth Pyper began to cry again. His son pulled his hand away. He was looking at him with hatred and contempt.

Some hells endure for ever.

Chapter Thirty-Eight

Louisa waited at the bottom of the hill. And as fire-engines squealed to a halt and men in uniform dashed up the hill with their enormous hoses, she saw a number of figures coming down.

Owen was carrying Leo, and behind them came Oliver Seifert. Leo's not moving, she thought in panic. He's not moving—

'He's all right,' said Owen, as soon as they were within earshot. Shuddering relief made her knees unsteady. She took Leo from him, hugging him tightly. He was white-faced, dry-eyed, rigid and unresponsive with shock. He needs his parents, she thought, we must go and find Joss and Lily immediately, this has all been too much for him. She looked up and saw that Oliver was watching them.

'Leo,' he said gently. 'Let me take you home.' There was something cool and ordered in his voice. Wondering, she put Leo down and saw him walk forward and tuck his hand into the bigger hand of Oliver Seifert. Beside her, she felt Owen's bewilderment.

'Owen, this is David's father,' she said quickly, 'Oliver Seifert, Owen Rattigan.'

She saw a glance pass between them, an acknowledgment of recognition and understanding. What had happened in the Tower? What did it mean?

Seifert held out his hand to Owen. 'I'm very glad to meet you at last. David was very fond of you.' He took Owen's hand in both of his and for a moment it looked as if they might embrace.

'We have to return this little one to his parents,' she said and Seifert looked at her, as if suddenly recalled to the present.

'I've got a car,' he said. 'Show me where Joss lives.' He gestured to the Rover by the side of the road and Louisa abruptly realized that yet another change had taken place. Although the Tower still frothed with fire and gaudy extravagance, she could breathe freely. The mob had gone.

She turned to smile at Owen, but her eye caught on a huddled shape on the kerb. 'Oh, look, a cat!' she said, and her words must have reached Leo, who was about to get into Oliver Seifert's car.

He turned round and ran to the kerb. His hands hovered around the cat, his face anguished. And then he crumpled, his face, his hands and his body, folding into a paroxysm of grief, and when Louisa bent to hold him, he clung to her, sobbing as if his heart was breaking.

'She's dead, isn't she?'

'It does look like it, Leo. We'll have to find her kittens—'

'They're dead too!'

'Dead? Really?'

Leo whisked away from her. 'They're dead,' he said, 'and Samuel killed them!'

He was pointing beyond Owen.

Kenneth and Samuel Pyper stood there. They were near the foot of the steps to the Tower, and there was a small and significant distance between them, as if they could not bear to touch. Samuel said, 'They're not all dead.'

He took a step towards Leo. 'I didn't kill the others, they're still there—'

'Where was this, Leo?' said Louisa.

'At his house,' said Samuel sullenly. 'In the garden.'

Everything pointed in the same direction. 'Come on,' said

Oliver Seifert. 'Jump in. Let's go and see where the kittens are and restore Leo to his parents.'

So Owen, Louisa and Leo got into the car with him, and Kenneth and Samuel watched them go.

'You were going to kill me,' said Samuel to his father. 'You had a knife.'

'It was a dream, a nightmare. I would never harm you.'

They both knew he lied. They walked home, and the distance between them widened.

It took them only a few minutes to get to the school. As Seifert's car rounded the corner just before the gates, the headlights met another car coming towards them. It drew up in front of the school just as they did.

Lily opened the door at the same time as Louisa did and Leo tumbled out, running towards his mother with his arms flung wide.

'Oh, thank God, thank God!' Her voice was muffled in his hair. 'Oh, Leo, Leo, my love, where have you been? Are you all right?'

For a while, they clung together in silence, rocking backwards and forwards. And then Leo withdrew a little.

'Mummy, are there kittens in our garden?' He seemed anxious, but not unduly so. Louisa thought that he sounded calm for the first time that night.

Lily took his hand. There were tears of relief on her face. 'Shall we go and see? Ben, Louisa, Owen, can one of you go and find Joss? He's probably here somewhere. There's something about the skull in the office, too . . . He may be there. Please—?'

'Leave it to us,' said Louisa. She looked at the school. The gates were now open, the padlock and chain trailing on the damp pavements. A single light shone from one of the rooms on the ground floor.

The lower corridor, she thought with misgiving.

At her side, Owen drew in his breath, sharply. 'It's the basement,' he said.

Oliver Seifert drove Lily and Leo back to their house to await Joss and look for kittens. Louisa, Owen and Ben crossed the playground to the front door of St Anthony's and it was like going home, to a home where nothing was safe, nothing loving or delightful: everything was merely, terrifyingly, familiar.

The front door was open. No other light on, just a faint glow from further along the corridor. It was enough to point out the gold lettering of the names on the wall, enough to highlight the small eyes of the pig on the ceiling, St Anthony's swine, looking down at them with focused, malign intelligence.

The smell of daffodils; of disinfectant and polish; of tears.

And there was a sound. An uneven tread, a stumble, as if some wounded thing was clawing its way towards them. The light flicked on.

Dominic Allbright standing there, leaning against the door to the art room. Only Louisa did not recognize him.

Allbright spoke first. 'And just what brings you back here, Bowen? Should I call the head or perhaps the police? What are you going to destroy this time?'

'Out of the way, Allbright.' Ben pushed past him. With some hesitation, Owen and Louisa followed.

Halfway along the corridor to the basement, Louisa looked round.

The man in the long white mac was no longer there. And then she heard Ben's shout from the basement door and started running.

It was Joss. Standing there below them, precariously balanced on his crutches, his face was hidden by the shadows which hung round him like a cloak. He was by the external door to the yard, and there was hung over his arm, incongruously, a carrier bag.

Sainsbury's, Louisa read, blue and orange writing on cream plastic. And a small stain of deep colour, something dripping from a tear in the base of the bag.

Dark red, it formed a puddle round his feet. She didn't want to think what it was, but somehow it held her silent. She didn't know what to say, she didn't want to say anything.

She wanted to turn and run and leave the school behind her for ever.

She said instead, 'Joss, we've found Leo! He's home with Lily, safe and well—'

Joss looked at her as if she were a stranger. There was a streak of blood running down the side of his face and his mouth loosened, about to say something. He crutched his way forward step by step, until he was right at the bottom of the stairs.

'I brought the skull,' he said. 'I thought, it should be incinerated. And I wondered if the boiler still worked—'

'Skull, Joss? What skull?' Owen said.

'The one from the office. You know, the mediaeval skull we found in the Dales. In Philip Stroud's back garden. It's – it's bleeding. It won't stop.'

In the carrier bag, Louisa thought, with mounting revulsion. It's bleeding in the bag and dripping on the floor.

'Let me take it from you,' said Owen, moving down the steps a little. 'I shall be only too delighted to put it in the boiler.'

Meekly, Joss held it out to him. Dark liquid splattered on the stairs and on the landing where they stood.

And then the man in the long mac pushed his way through, and Louisa stumbled against Owen before catching her balance against the railing at the top of the stairs.

Dominic Allbright leaned against the banister and said, 'If

that skull is of any antiquity it should be preserved for a museum. If not, it should be buried with full Christian rites.'

'Not this one,' said Owen grimly. 'Let me pass, Allbright.'

'Joss!' she said. 'We can leave Owen to do this, we can go home, it's okay, Leo's fine!' It seemed to her suddenly urgent that they leave the basement immediately.

No mob. There was no one else there but the five of them, and no possible reason to stay there. 'Let's go home,' she repeated, and it looked for a moment as if they might all do just that.

'Leo's gone home?'

A voice from the door to the yard. Louisa saw a small figure there, a child she didn't know, someone quite irrelevant, quite unknown in the St Anthony's she remembered. The girl followed Joss into the basement and stood at the bottom of the stairs.

'Emma, whatever are you doing out at this time of night?' Ben slipped back into schoolmaster mode without difficulty.

'If Leo's gone home, it's not fair!' said the child with her harsh, unattractive voice. 'He wrote me a note—'

'Did he?' Allbright looked over the rail to the child below. 'Do you know what it said?'

'What will you give me if I tell you?'

'Emma Morrell, you should be more worried about what I'll give you if you don't tell me—'

'Be careful, Allbright.' Ben was standing next to him at the top of the stairs.

And the blood on the floor at Owen's feet continued to drip from the carrier bag, to run, spreading in a wide circle around their feet.

'You see, I don't *understand*!' said Joss and his voice sounded odd, higher than usual. High with stress, Louisa told herself. That's what they say.

'I don't understand why the people were here!' Joss went

on, as if it made sense. 'I was out in the yard, but I could see through the door! And I saw *you*—!' he pointed to Owen, 'and you Ben, on the stairs and then there were all these people in the way, that man with the tail, the Beast man and at the top of the stairs there was—'

He stopped suddenly, and Louisa saw his already pale face drain of the last vestiges of colour.

'There was *you!*' he said, and it was no more than a whisper.

Dominic Allbright, in his long pale mac, his nose beaky and sharp, his hands knobbly and cruel.

'I haven't the faintest idea what you're talking about.' But Allbright's eyes were abstracted, as if listening to some far distant voice. He turned slightly, so that he was facing Ben. 'I suggest you get out of here pretty quickly, and take your lame friend with you. You both look in need of medical treatment. And you, Owen Rattigan, should return that object of antiquity to the proper authorities. In fact, you'd better give it to me. I'll look after it.'

'Let it rest, Allbright.' But still Owen made no effort to leave the basement.

'And what are you doing here, anyway?' Ben sounded cold. 'At this time of night?'

'I might ask the same of you.'

'We came to find Joss. To tell him that Leo is safe and well.'

'Leo's note to me said—' Everyone was distracted by the small, whining voice.

'Shut up, Emma,' Allbright said.

They saw the girl in the doorway pause; saw her consider; smile. Evil, thought Louisa, chilled. That child is evil.

Emma said, 'Leo doesn't like you, Mr Allbright. Shall I tell you what he says you do to him—?'

The rage on Allbright's face was all-consuming. He took a step towards Emma and then flung himself round, ripping the carrier bag out of Owen's hand. But the speed of his action threw him off balance and his foot skidded in the running blood. White-coated, it seemed that he was going to fall, to fly, to swoop like a bird of prey on her. And when his foot slipped, he fell towards Ben and his hands were reaching out to grab him—

Ben stepped aside so that Allbright fell further, flailing and tumbling like a great bird, headlong down the stairs and straight into the insecurely balanced figure of Joss, propped on crutches.

A crack, a cry, a mess of limbs and tangled clothes. Joss pulled himself to his feet, slowly. There was blood all over his hands, all over his clothes.

On the floor, the white-coated man lay spread-eagled in death, the top of his head crushed and dribbling with blood. And next to his head, mimicking the blank-eyed, open-mouthed horror, was that other ancient skull, and the blood that flowed bound them both together, mixed past and present fatally and finally.

The girl turned on her heel and ran. She ran through the streets as if the wind owned her, ran back across the city to her home and crept in through the kitchen door and found her way to her bedroom.

Her shoes were slippery with blood, but she didn't care. Shivering under the blankets, she replayed in her head what had happened. And thought that perhaps she should feel glad, that Mr Allbright was now out of the way for ever, but instead the memory of that ancient skull peered through her thoughts, and she knew that its bloody print would stay with her through every uneasy hour at night, when sweet sleep was far away.

Owen said, 'You stepped aside before. Ben? Didn't you? Ben, was that it?'

Ben stared at the broken body on the floor, stared at the face of his friend and raised his hand to his mouth. 'No. Not that. Worse than that. I trod on his hand.'

'Because David didn't want you? Was that it?' Owen's voice was compassionate.

'I didn't mean him to die!' Ben sounded anguished. 'It was an accident!'

'Oh, Ben, of course it was! Is that what you've been hiding all these years?'

'I – I—' The words were ceasing, grinding to an inarticulate halt. His face was covered with sweat, running with moisture. He took a handkerchief out of his pocket and began to wipe his face so that they could no longer see it.

Louisa put her hand on his arm. 'Ben, it was long ago.'

'But what if time doesn't matter?' Owen said slowly. 'Isn't that what we should learn from this evening? The past is all around us, all over us, it lives in us, it makes us act—'

'Owen, what *happened* in the Tower?' Louisa had to ask.

'Shades of the massacre, Louisa. That's what I saw. Shades of horror and death and grief. Despair, the worst kind of despair. I'll tell you, some day . . . But at the very least, what happened in the Tower confirms what I said, that putting the past behind us is almost impossible—'

Joss said bleakly, 'There's no hope, that way.'

'And there was grace, too.' Owen looked puzzled. 'Grace and forgiveness.'

But Ben looked as if he didn't understand the words.

'Come on, Ben, come home.' Louisa tried to guide him to the door, but he was immovable.

'None of you understood,' he whispered. 'None of you knew what it is to love and love and love until it hurts and then be – ignored. To know it doesn't matter. To know there is no significance in it, no matter how true your love, no matter how it hurts—'

'Oh Ben!' Louisa found tears in her eyes. 'Come with us now, let's all go home and get warm—'

'I want to see Leo,' said Joss. 'Now.' He took a few steps towards Ben. 'Come home with us, Ben. Come and have a whisky, and we'll ring the police and get this over with.'

'I'll wait here,' he said tiredly. 'You go on. I'd better explain to the police what happened.'

'At least there are enough witnesses this time,' said Louisa. 'No doubts now about what happened.' Ben was shaking, she saw. 'I'll stay here with you. We'll wait together.'

'Are you sure you don't mind, Louisa?' Joss was courteous as ever. She shook her head, and he turned to Owen with some relief. 'Let's get out of here,' he said. 'Will you drive me?'

'Of course. But there's something I have to do first, don't you agree?' Owen looked at Joss.

Joss nodded. So Owen went down the stairs and, having wrapped his hand round with a handkerchief, picked up the skull and put it back in the carrier bag.

The blank eyes of Dominic Allbright seemed to follow him as he climbed the stairs and left the basement.

They waited in silence. After only a short time, Owen returned, his hands empty. He put his arm round Louisa briefly. 'It's done. I'll take Joss home and be back as soon as I can. I'd go and sit in the head's office, if I were you.'

For the smell of blood was overwhelming, and the basement was full of horrors.

Chapter Thirty-Nine

Louisa turned the lights on and drew the curtains. Ben looked awful, pale and sweaty, and there was still blood at the corner of his mouth. His left eye was completely closed. She helped him to a chair and looked around. 'It's a beastly place, isn't it?' she said. 'Why do headmasters always have such awful pictures on the wall?'

A view of Clifford's Tower in pastels, and an undistinguished landscape of Swaledale. Photographs of rugby teams.

'You have to please the parents,' said Ben tiredly. 'It's better to be safe than sorry.'

'You don't really believe that, do you?'

He shook his head, but the movement clearly hurt him. Strong drink, Louisa thought. That's what he needs. 'Isn't there a drinks cabinet somewhere here? Purely to entertain the parents, of course.'

Ben almost smiled. 'My room's down the other corridor,' he said slowly. 'There's some whisky in one of the violin cases on the piano.'

She gave him a small wave. 'Won't be long,' she said.

As soon as he heard the door to his study open, he got to his feet. Walked quickly across the room, across the hall to the stairs, and hauled himself up to the top corridor. Every step hurt. His old flat lay at the end of the top corridor, and he still had a key.

No one had thought to change the locks, no one had bothered to move out his things. It was cold there, but just as he had left it.

In his bathroom the unopened packet of razors still lay on the shelf over the sink. He poured himself a glass of whisky from the kitchen while waiting for the bath to run.

He didn't look at the pale crucifix over the bed, he said no prayers. He had no regrets, except that he stood on David's hand once and watched him die.

He put a CD of the *Missa Solemnis* on and took off his clothes.

In the bath, he opened veins in both wrists and watched while the water stained pink.

Louisa found the whisky and had poured two glasses when the police arrived. So she went with them to the basement and gave a bald account of what had happened, wondering all the time where Ben was.

Perhaps the wound to his head was more serious than they had thought? Had he collapsed somewhere?

'Look, we'd better go and look for him,' she said to the young officer who had escorted her back to the head's office.

'This friend of yours . . . He's the one who knows the dead man?'

She nodded.

'You stay here, madam, and I'll have a quick look round. Head wounds can be nasty.'

She subsided on to the chair in the study and stared at the two glasses of whisky, considering whether to drink at least one of them. She was filled with dread. It's all right, she told herself, Leo's safe, Ben's got all of us, we won't let him down and Owen will soon be back. The chair was soft and comfortable. She eased herself back against the cushions and let her head drop to one side. For a time she must have fallen into an uneasy doze, for the next thing she heard was the sound of the policeman walking across the hall towards her.

'Ben—?' she said, hauling herself to her feet. 'Is he all right?'

The policeman shook his head. 'A large man, did you say? With wispy hair, a bruised face—?'

She nodded dumbly.

'I'm afraid . . . No, he's not all right.'

Eventually Owen came to get her. He'd come in Lily's car, in case she didn't feel like walking the short distance to Joss's house, and she huddled against him on the brief drive. Outside the Fletchers' he asked her if she wouldn't prefer to go straight home.

She was dazed with tiredness and grief and could barely frame words together to answer him.

'Home, I think,' he said, assessing the situation. 'It's – what, getting on for five o'clock now. It's been enough, tonight. A lot more than enough.'

He drove on through Monk Bar and along Lord Mayor's Walk. 'Do you want me to stay with you?' he asked as he pulled up outside her mother's – her – house.

She shook her head. 'I just need to sleep, it's all right, I'll be all right.'

She wanted to be alone; in silence and alone.

Her sleep was dreamless and untroubled.

She was woken at lunchtime by the phone ringing. It was Owen.

'Lou, are you okay? Did I wake you?'

'Yes, to both questions. Except – oh Owen, it's so awful about Ben!'

'I know. But it's difficult to know what we could have done to stop him.'

'I shouldn't have left him alone. I knew he wasn't well—'

'Lou, he was severely depressed. If he hadn't tried last night, it would have happened some other time—'

'That's no comfort.'

'I know.'

'And Mum, too!' She was beginning to cry again.

'Listen, Lou. Hang in there and I'll be over later. There's something I've got to do first.'

She put the phone down and it was then that rage seized her. A welcome change from all the tears. She banged round the kitchen and broke a teapot and scowled at the bright sunlight shining on the golden forsythia outside the kitchen window.

Why did Ben have to die?

Why had her mother died in agony?

There were so many reasons. Guilt and loneliness seemed to her the worst, both of them trapped in guilt since David's death, both with no one to tell. It's no good living alone, she thought. We're social animals, we need each other, and then the past is not so overwhelming. Other perspectives become possible. She crucially wanted to talk to Owen, to be with him and experience his touch.

She tried to pass the time by ringing the Fletchers' to make sure that Leo had suffered no ill effects.

'He's just fine,' said Lily. 'The resilience of children never fails to amaze me. In fact, he's got a little present for you. Will you be in for the next hour or so?'

Louisa put the phone down, wondering what the mystery could be.

The house was a tip. She'd made no attempt to put away her mother's papers and the living room was in chaos. So when Lily and Leo arrived a short time later, she took them straight through to the kitchen and Leo, still a little pale, put on the table there the covered basket they'd brought with them.

The faint mewing sound gave it away. Louisa lifted the cover and found there one very new kitten, its eyes closed, squeaking pathetically.

'The vet says they'll need hand-feeding for a while,' said Lily. 'I hope it's not going to be too much trouble for you.'

There was a glint in the back of her eyes and Louisa groaned. 'Don't tell me,' she said. 'Feeds every four hours round the clock—'

'Something like that.'

'If it's too much for you, we'll take him back,' said Leo politely. 'We've brought you a dropper and a bottle, so you don't have to get anything special. But I thought you might like him because his hair is the same colour as yours.'

It was, too. 'How can I resist?' she said. The little creature's heart was beating so strongly that its entire frame throbbed with it. She crouched down on the floor and held out her arms to Leo. 'Thanks, Leo. He's a little treasure. You'll have to come and visit him often, won't you, to see how he is?'

'Does that mean that you'll be staying in York?'

'For a while,' she said, looking up at Lily, who grinned at her.

'Oh goody. More girly lunches!'

They went soon afterwards, and Louisa put the kitten on a cushion on the sofa and sat down next to it, prepared to watch some mindless television. It was more than she could stand, so she went to the kitchen and poured herself a glass of wine. Then she tried to feed the kitten a little milk and was absurdly gratified that it took some. Tidying the room came next, but she could sustain no interest in that at all. She got as far as picking everything up off the floor and putting it on to the chairs. Deciding where it all should go was another matter. It would take for ever, anyway. She couldn't settle to anything.

The door bell rang at last.

Owen stood there, and he wasn't alone. Letitia Farmer, the nurse from Intensive Care, was standing on the step next to him.

Louisa stared blankly.

'Might we come in?' asked Owen politely. 'Tish here has something to tell you.'

She led them into the living room without remembering the mess and then had to sweep things on to the floor again so that they could sit down.

Letitia Farmer immediately picked up the little kitten and cuddled it to her plump breast. She refused the offer of wine. 'I haven't got long, Louisa, I'm afraid—'

'Next shift coming up?' Beneath the sensible tweed coat, Louisa could see the uniform.

'Yes. Now, I know that you were not with your mother before she died. I felt I had to tell you this, and was going to make contact . . . Last night's events showed how urgent it was. Louisa, your mother didn't die in despair.' Letitia Farmer spoke coolly, but her eyes were warm. 'I was there. Mr Seifert came to see your mother just before she died. He put her mind at rest. I was going to tell you, as soon as I could. I don't know what he said, but after he'd gone she was at peace. She asked me to tell you that she loved you and that it was all right. That the past was all right. There is forgiveness, she said.'

Louisa took a deep breath.

She looked at Owen wordlessly. He'd bothered to go and get Letitia Farmer, he knew what it meant to her. Tears again, tears of thankfulness.

The nurse had put the kitten back on the chair. She was standing up, patting her hair into order, although it was entirely neat and tidy. 'I'll be off now,' she said composedly. 'If there's anything else, Owen here has got my address and number.'

'Thank you, thank you so very much. This means so much—' She was inarticulate with emotion.

Letitia Farmer saw herself out and Louisa found herself crying again. It seemed that she'd never be able to stop crying, but then Owen was still there and his arms were warm around her, and his breath on her cheek was sweet and kind.

'Come home with me,' he said. 'Sophy will be there. You'd better bring that—' he pointed to the kitten on the cushion. 'We've got one too. Leo's been busy. They'll be company for each other.'

They walked together back to his house and the sky was still light.

'That was the longest night of my life,' she said.

'A turning point, I think,' said Owen. 'It's made me reconsider so much. The school was hell, you know. Still is. I suppose you had your mother on hand, so perhaps it wasn't so bad for you, but I made a mess of it. Thought that loving closeness was out of bounds, because my parents hadn't wanted me to live with them. It's barbaric, isn't it?'

'I always thought so. And so did my mother, although she never admitted it. She saw all those children crying. She told me that children need the context of home and family, they need secure individual and personal love from their parents and siblings.'

'Quite right. I shall not be sending Sophy to Cheethams or any of those other prestigious music colleges. She can take her chance with the day schools.'

'What, one of the York comprehensives?'

He smiled at her. 'Now that might be a little hard to take – but, yes, why not? It seems to me that I need to make a new start. Perhaps even go somewhere else, leave this place behind.'

'But it is beautiful,' she said. Clear light had touched the ornate tracery of the Minster tower. Early blossom clouded the flowering trees in the Deanery gardens.

'Other things are more beautiful,' he said, looking at her.

She loved the warmth in his eyes. 'What have you called your kitten?'

'Monty. Short for Monteverdi. Sophy insisted, I'm afraid.'

'Shall we let her choose for this one too?' she asked.

'It'll have to be Dowland or Couperin. Something daft like that.'

'Orlando,' she said. 'The marmalade cat. And Orlando Gibbons, of course.'

'Perfect.' He tucked her arm into his.

There was a flowering tree in Owen's road. As they passed it, a wind caught in its branches and a scattering of petals drifted over them.

Around them the city was quiet.

NOTE

The commemorative tablet unveiled in 1978 by the Chief Rabbi and the Archbishop of York says:

On the night of Friday 16 March 1190 some 150 Jews and Jewesses of York having sought protection in the Royal Castle on this site from a mob incited by Richard Malebisse and others chose to die at each other's hands rather than renounce their faith.

According to historical sources, after the massacre of March 1190, Richard Malebisse, the baron who owed money to Jews, led the mob to the Minster, where they burned the Jewish bonds deposited there. Then he disappeared.

He was said, in legend, to have a tail. The beast who gave his name to Acaster Malbis, just outside the city, who paid no price at all for leading the mob, founded a Premonstratensian Abbey in Lincolnshire. There was also an Abbey of the Order at Coverham.

The white hermit, the hooded Canon who was the only Christian casualty, belonged to the Premonstratensian Order.